The Lovely Ship

Storm Jameson

A BERKLEY MEDALLION BOOK
published by
BERKLEY PUBLISHING CORPORATION

FOR
G U Y

SBN 425-02776-7

BERKLEY MEDALLION BOOKS are published by
Berkley Publishing Corporation
200 Madison Avenue
New York, N.Y. 10016

BERKLEY MEDALLION BOOKS ® TM 757,375

Printed in the United States of America

Berkley Medallion Edition, MARCH, 1975

In this book none of the characters represent real persons, living or dead. They are wholly imaginary. The geography of the book is not without imaginary elements, and the shipbuilding history incidentally related is true in essentials but makes no attempt at being true of any one shipbuilding town or river.

Book One

HANSYKE TO ROXBY

Chapter One

1

MARY HANSYKE was born when her mother was travelling from Liverpool to her home on the southern edge of the Cleveland Hills. She had stayed in Liverpool longer than she meant and she was afraid that her first child would be born away from her home, and resolute that it should not be. The railway, with its known discomforts and unknown dangers, terrified her. For let us realise at once that, without being aware of it, Charlotte Hansyke was living in the dark ages. There were less than a thousand miles of inefficient railway in the whole country, and the coaches that carried passengers from one end of the land to the other were admitted, by all sound persons, to be infinitely safer and more comfortable than any clumsy cindery train could ever be. Not that Charlotte Hansyke had any intention of trusting herself to the coach, more especially as she had with her three trunks of new dresses from Paris, where Madame de Pompadour was that year considered the model, at least of fashion. She insisted that her husband should hire a carriage to make the journey across England, from Liverpool almost to the Yorkshire coast. He urged her to stay where she was. The country was in a very disturbed state, alarmed by rick-burning and rioting Chartists, and startled by the extraordinary emergence into the light of day—thanks to the rash tongues of certain so-called reformers—of gangs of young women who were normally kept in proper obscurity in the mines, where they hauled tubs of coal all day, an occupation that necessitated their being naked to the waist, with canvas trousers below that, and an iron chain attached to a leather belt running between their legs. Their untoward appearance, like Devils from a trap in an old miracle play, had lent quite a sinister air to the rumour of subterranean trouble. There was much talk, in the landowning and political circles where the Hansykes were staying, of revolution and bloodshed, and all things considered, a journey across England in the winter of 1841 presented itself as no fit proceeding for a gentlewoman in delicate health. But Hansyke's protests were silenced by the obstinacy of the childbearing woman. Charlotte rejected the first carriage he procured and at last set out in what was practically a closed barouche, very roomy inside but with no provision for carrying luggage. Her woman, attended by her husband's stable-bred servant, followed in another carriage with the luggage.

In Manchester the driver fell ill and giving himself up for lost began to testify loudly to the state of his soul. Richard Hansyke, descending to the stable yard at the earnest entreaty of the innkeeper, tried to reason with him, and thereupon he began to testify even more poignantly to the state of his stomach. Hansyke was compelled to leave him and hire another coachman of the innkeeper's acquaintance. This was a sergeant, an excellent fellow who had been in the French wars, had lost a leg and kept his appetite for hollands. Hansyke watched him closely, but on the evening of the third day of their journey he thought that the man might be tipsy. They had entered Yorkshire and were following up one of the narrow valleys cut between the West Riding hills. It was like any other of the valleys they had traversed since leaving the plain of East Lancashire asleep under a blaze of heat. Grassy foothills, sparsely wooded, rose in a series of slopes to the moors and the higher, bleaker hills of the Pennines. A small stream ran down the valley through what was once a cluster of cottages folded in fields of pasture-land, and now was a small and starkly hideous village huddled around the mill. A spatter of mean houses spread up either slope from the banks of the defiled stream. They halted, tailing off in straggling lines along the hillside, well short of the grounds of the great house, built of stone and opulently parked, where lived the millowner and his family. Down in the town itself a few houses, more solid but no more gracious than the rest, stood up among the rabble, their upper windows drawing the last glances of the dying sun. These were the homes of his doctor, his manager, his banker. Above them all, weavers' hovels, houses and mansion, the moor mingled its pure breezes with the vapours rising from the murdered valley.

The barouche, its brakes dragging, started down the steep cobbled road that led to the centre of the town. The coachman started to sing in the same instant. He stood up on his box and swayed as the carriage rocked down the hill.

> "O Polly love, O Polly, the rout has now begun,
> And we must be a-marching at the beating of the drum;
> Go dress yourself in all your best and come along with me,
> I'll take you to the cruel wars in High Ger-ma-ny."

Richard Hansyke, his head and half his body out of the carriage window, ordered him to stop. He was angry, and alarmed for his wife, but neither to excess. The road poured down into the pool of the town, the man sang, the carriage lights danced, Charlotte whimpered, the night rushed up from the valley to receive them.

The coachman threw him a surprised glance. "Song o the army," he explained, and prepared to begin another verse. They were passing a low building with dusty windows offering torches to the gloom. The doors stood open and a crowd of children rushed out. They straddled across the road, as befits men and women of five and six and seven who have been at work for ten hours. One waved a skinny arm at the carriage, another, emerging from under its wheels, lifted incurious eyes and pale lips to the windows; all were wrapped in jackets and mufflers, shivering in the hot summer air after hours spent in a tropical steam. The coachman pulled up to avoid an inevitable catastrophe. Leaning down, he addressed them in a familiar manner.

"Miserable droppings," said he. "Deformities. Run away home, pretty loves. Loves. Doves." He broke into song again.

> "O Harry love, O Harry, do hearken what I say;
> My feet are all too tender, I cannot march away."

Charlotte Hansyke looked fearfully out of the barouche.

"Who are they all?" she asked.

"Children from the factory," her husband said briefly, his eye on the horses. The coachman spoke confidentially about marriage and family life.

"But—unhappy," Charlotte murmured, suppressing a violent shudder.

Charlotte Hansyke was a wilful, pleasure-loving woman with no apparent depths in her nature, but she suffered a severe revulsion of feeling at the thought that the child in her womb might have been destined to join that doomed company. A tremor that seemed to start in the recesses of her body ran through her limbs, loosening her joints and disordering her brain. At the same moment certain uneasy sensations that she had been enduring in silence for the past mile of the journey, drew themselves into one definite and rending pain. She looked at her husband with a blind, stricken gaze.

"What is it, Charlotte?" he asked sharply.

"It's come," said she. "We must stay here."

He sprang up and directed the man to drive to the millowner's big house that faced them from the other side of the valley, but his wife shook her head.

"It will have to be the nearest house," she told him. "This place here," and the barouche, with the driver's voice cracking on: "O cursed are the cruel wars that ever they should rise," was stopped in front of a weaver's cottage. It had two rooms and two storeys, and the lower room was, by Richard Hansyke's peremptory orders, cleared of five children who lay alseep where they had dropped in their factory clothes, and were pushed and carried up the stairs. Charlotte lay on cushions dragged from the barouche, staring at the horrors of the ceiling, less than six feet above her head, while another order, less peremptory but as urgent, was sent to the big house for linen and coverings, and a woman holding a shawl round her meagre body scurried for the doctor.

Charlotte's child, a girl, was born about midnight, and its loud wails failed to wake the children sleeping upstairs. In the early morning, when Charlotte was lying exhausted and appeased, conscious of an intolerable ordeal tolerably endured, her eyes, fixed on the shadowy stairs leading to the upper room, became aware that the shadows were moving. Without a sound, like small mutilated ghosts, the children were going out to their work.

She closed her eyes so that the woman attending on her might suppose she was asleep and had not seen. After breakfast at the big house, her husband came down to her. His courteous inquiries concealed all the annoyance he felt at her preposterous choice of a birthplace for their child. He explained formally and in minute detail what arrangements he was making to move her.

"To-morrow," said Charlotte, and shut her eyes.

"I beg that you will let it be to-day."

His wife moved her head in dissent. She opened her eyes suddenly and surprised him looking down at her in polite despair.

"Look at your daughter," she said, and lifted the child's coverings.

He regarded his first child with no show of interest. He was indeed lost in a curious memory of his own boyhood. He saw himself standing, a very small boy, for his head did not reach the top of the table, between his father and another tall gentleman in a plum-coloured coat. Outside the windows of the library the sun shone down on the soft, vivid green of the lawn dappled with the shadows of the trees. He fixed his eyes on the bare brown patch under one tree, the ancient of the garden, as old as the house, incalculably old and secure. Behind it he could see the brown and ruffled silver waters of the lake. He was listening but not intently to plum-coloured's questions and at last heard a vibrant voice say: "The boy's a fool: he never heard of Xerxes." Then he was outside with a smarting ear, and a groom was showing him a small, wriggling body all tail and sharp wicked teeth. He was in the field behind the big barn, ferreting with the young groom. A warm musty scent pervaded the dry ditch into which he pressed his small body. The field was flooded with sun, and the burning whiteness of the marguerites scorched his eyes. He crept closer to the groom, whose hot bright eyes shone like the eyes of the ferret, sheltering himself under the lad's crouching body, growing drowsy with the heat and the mingled smell of ferret and warm velveteen, until he fell asleep, dimly conscious of white teeth in a thin brown face, and not sure whether it was the groom's face or the ferret's so close to his own.

He came out ot his dream to realisation of his wife's voice. He had not the least idea what she was saying, but he answered her soothingly and agreed to leave her in the weaver's wretched cottage for another day. He bent another look on his child, wishing that Charlotte had seen fit to give him a son, and then excused himself. The ladies of the house were, he said, on their way down to visit her. Charlotte became very anxious about her looks and he reassured her politely before going away to pursue inquiries about the other carriage, which with luggage and servants, had apparently dropped out of the world some time during the previous day. . . .

Charlotte drowsed through the long hours in the bed brought down from the big house. The room was very close, but her bedroom, if she had been in her own house, would have been kept just as warm and stifling at this time. She endured it silently, but she was grateful when dusk, insinuating itself into the room, brought with it a breath of cool air. She was alone, and, as the room grew darker, she fell into a half sleep that passed by imperceptible stages into a nightmare. She seemed to be lying in pitch dark while the strength ebbed from her body, leaving it empty, light and remote—so that there was nothing left of her but a spark in the enveloping darkness. She knew that she was dying, and when an ancient hag crept up to the bed she did not know whether it was the woman of the house or an emissary of death. She tried to cry out, but her tongue and all her limbs were paralysed. Horror, vague and stifling, muffled her up to the throat.

A slight sound roused her. Hardly believing in her escape, she woke from the nightmare to a room not yet quite dark. There was no old woman, but as she looked round nervously for that dreadful personage of her dream, she saw another apparition. This was almost as terrifying as the other, and she gave a little cry of fear. Whereupon the apparition came forward and placed a candle it carried on the table by Charlotte's bed. It stood there, uttering sounds of which she could make nothing. She eyed it fearfully. Its eyes were almost on a level with her own. Its head, sunk between its shoulders, was too large for the tiny body that did not so much support as endure it. Cheeks and lips, both bloodless, were distorted into an expression of what Charlotte first thought to be hate, and then saw, by some miracle of perception, to be a timid and ingratiating smile. It stood with one hand extended towards the bed and Charlotte saw with horror that this hand had lost three of its fingers.

She found her tongue.

"What do you want?"

At that the apparition advanced another step, and whispered almost in her ear. Still she did not understand what it said, though she seemed to herself to be listening with her whole body.

"What have you come here for?"

"To see the babby."

Ready to faint with relief at having understood, Charlotte drew back the clothes round the sleeping child and took heart from her visitor's mouthing admiration of the *babby* to question him. When she had made out that he was six years old, she thought that she had never until then known what grief was. The memory of the birth pangs she had endured, her first experience of pain, receded before a confused vision of the sum of human misery. She might have been giving birth to a soul. She asked the child his name. He produced it with a frown and a struggle with his tongue. "Robert Estill."

Charlotte closed her eyes, and when she opened them again he had gone, and for a while she lay turning over in her mind the idea that he, like the hag, was a creation of her tired brain. But he had brought her back to life, and confusedly, recalling his name with an effort, she thought that her husband must find him, do something for him. . . .

2

Mary Hansyke at eight was a small, stolid child, pursuing a life of her own in a household that was not so much a household as a civil liability. Her father, holding stiffly to his conception of the good life which—in the middle of the nineteenth century—wavered hardly a pin-point from the mixture of ruffianage and politeness that composed an eighteenth century Hansyke's code, held as stiffly to the last inches of the land that an abbot of Whitby had allotted, for services rendered, to the first Hansyke, thus emerging into history like a dog with a bone between his teeth. It was, as land, not much good, being half peaty moor and ling and half impoverished grass-land. Roxborough is a moorland parish running down to a valley, on the far side of which rise ridged hills called Riggs, dotted with agile black-faced sheep. It is wild and poor, and Hansyke Manor, a Gothic barn of a house, very cold and inconvenient. What money remained of Hansyke accumulations had been dissipated by Mary's father when he met Charlotte Garton and fell impetuously in love with her. He married her before discovering that he could have had her on less exigent terms. She was tall and shapely, with a warm, flushed, dusky beauty, too early ripe. She came of solid bourgeois stock, heavy purse-proud people. Her brother was a shipbuilder of Danesacre, and Charlotte brought her husband more money than he knew she had.

She brought—what he had not bargained for—wits to spend it, and in a very short time the mortgages on house and land were renewed and Charlotte Hansyke was selling out her interest in the Garton shipping firm. She had in her nature a strain of the wildness that crops out in the stolidest of Yorkshire stock, and Hansyke Manor—between her friends and her husband's—was a queer place for their child. The fifties of the nineteenth century were wildish, with an odd lingering echo of an earlier century's licence, rather cracked and uncertain, a little disconcerted by the piety that was creeping over England from Windsor and Balmoral, and separated by turbulent years from the splendid extravagance of a later era. Gentlemen still drank themselves under the table as a seigniorial gesture, but gallants were out of fashion, and the number of Charlotte Hansyke's masculine friends shocked the gentry of the district and angered her husband past contempt.

One day, in her eighth year, Mary Hansyke stood on the steps below the main door, coolly watching her father laying his crop about the long legs of a strange young man, whom he held bent double under one arm. There was something very raffish and delightful about those long checked legs. They were tremendously active and contorted. Mary Hansyke laughed and clapped her hands. Whereupon her father threw the young gentleman away, and, brushing his hands, came to pick her up and carry her off to the stables. He put her on a new and bad-tempered mare and she fell off, hurting her head. In the library her father gave her a biscuit soaked in sherry because she had contrived not to cry. After that he offered to carry her out of reach of her Scots governess, but Mary Hansyke had a profound sense of duty and took herself back to the schoolroom, where Miss Flora Cunningham waited for her, primed with caraway tea and the names of the Jewish kings. Mary disliked the smell of caraway and the genteel belchings it produced in its dealings with Miss Flora's digestion, but she stuck stolidly to the Jewish kings, having bargained with herself to add them that week to a hoard of particular information gathered from Miss Flora. She was the seventh pupil to whom Miss Flora had taught the names of the Jewish kings, the use of oil, leeches, sage, aniseeds and cardamom, together with the nature and composition of Noyau, Hippocras, Capillaire, Ratafia, and Hollands or Geneva, and the history of silk manufacture. Curious creature, who existed solely to be picked over, like a rag-bag, by inquiring youth.

In the afternoon, Mark Henry Garton, her mother's brother, rode over from Danesacre. He was many years older than his sister, a man of fifty odd, with the face of a Flemish devil, and a habit of speech so full of the furies and fancies of his mind that few of his sentences reached an appointed end. He stuck his fingers into the pockets of his coat and strode up and down the dining-room while his sister rated him for cheating her over the sale of her shares. Mary, withdrawn into the farthest corner of the window-seat, listened attentively.

"Eh," said Mark Henry, addressing his sister. "Eh, you beauty. Cheated you, did I? You roll of Spanish cloth, you. You're devilish suspicious. Do you know I've robbed my own pocket to pay you out at a good price? And what shall I get from you when I'm cleaned out? Not a penny: women are always bad parters. Do you know what's happening in London? I'll be bound you don't. You know nothing but shamelessness and junketing. You needn't think you're not the talk of Danesacre. You are. Why, there was a verse cut last night on the gates of my own house about you that would make you blush, if you could blush."

"And what," Charlotte asked sullenly, "have happenings in London to do with my money?" She pulled at the tassels of the curtain.

The negligent curve of her tall body in its crimson silk drew her daughter's eyes. Mary thought her mother the most beautiful of creatures.

"London is ruining me," cried Mark Henry. He grasped the folds of an ample belly. "I'm living on my own fat. I'm crushed. I'm done for. Did you ever hear of the Navigation Code? Did you ever hear it was to be repealed? Did you ever hear that British bottoms were to be crowded off the seas by all the dirty scows that any frog-eating, tobacco-chewing scoundrel likes to send us? I'll be bound you did not. Mark my words. In five years' time there'll not be a British-built ship afloat. Have I cheated you? Have I pauperised myself for your sake? Tell me that. Be a sensible girl now, and I'll buy you something good next time I go to London. Something that'll pawn for a couple of hundred when you need it, as you soon will do if you go on living in this menagerie. Why, the place smells like the monkey house at Brighton. I met a young gazebo in the hall just now who asked me for advice about some shares he was thinking of buying. 'Don't touch 'em,' I said. 'You go away and spend your bit of money on some nice little woman who'll be good to you and as kind as kisses while the money lasts. You'll make her happy and yourself happy, and that's better than making some greasy-faced promoter happy, which is all you'll do if you go trying to make money out of shares.' If you can't be clever be comfortable, that's what I say."

The man was half buffoon and half blackguard, and his sister knew that she was helpless in his hands, since Richard Hansyke could no more easily stoop to question his brother-in-law about money than make a penny himself. So she shrugged her fine shoulders and asked Mark Henry to stay to dinner.

He agreed to stay, and advancing on Mary picked her up in one hand, opened the lid of the window-seat with the other, and dropped her in. Then he shut the lid, leaving a crack to which he set his small twinkling eyes, while Mary shrieked with terror, and her mother ordered him to let the child out at once. Released, Mary took the opportunity of her mother's caresses to ask if she might come down to the drawing-room after dinner.

"Children and little pigs go to bed at seven," Mark Henry said, and chanted: "Little pigs lie with their tails curled up."

"You can come if you like," Charlotte said carelessly, and at ten o'clock Mary presented herself in the drawing-room. It was empty. She thereupon made her way to the dining-room, taking a circuitous route through the window and across the lawn, to escape Miss Flora, waiting mournfully on the stairs, ready to pounce on her charge when she crossed the hall. Miss Flora suffered agonies of fear for Mary's soul in this house of wickedness, and prayed over the little girl for hours, kneeling stiffly by Mary's side in the schoolroom. Mary was impressed by the prayers. She found it hard not to promise to keep out of the Devil's way. That she did not promise was due partly to an obstinacy that rejected Miss Flora's tears and partly to curiosity.

Entering by the dining-room window, she slipped unobserved into a corner of the room, avoiding the window-seats. Her father, supporting his thin, fastidious face on his hands, was talking to Mark Henry Garton. A decanter stood between them, and when it emptied, another appeared like a conjuring trick, while Mary was not looking. The other gentlemen at the table were also much occupied with decanters and bottles, but whereas her father's face was pale, theirs were all in varying shades of crimson deepening to the colour of lustrous blue plums. There were gaps in the company at the table, and a few of the guests stood grouped round Mary's mother, on the stone flags of the empty fireplace. Charlotte was in white, gleaming and sparkling, and leaning towards a tall gentleman with a fine, reddish beard. Mary studied his legs, frowning. They were not checked, though they were well-shaped and very long. Could this be the same gentleman? Mary had seen only legs in the morning's war, but those at an intimate moment. She thought she would have known them again in their checks. It was puzzling. She sighed, and gave the problem up when a burst of song at the far end of the table distracted her from it.

The gentleman who was singing had a loud rich voice that gave Mary an inexplicable pleasure. Thrills ran up and down her small body, and she balanced herself on one foot, with her head thrown back in unconscious imitation of the singer.

"We'll sport and be free with Moll, Betty and Dolly,
Have oysters and lobsters to cure melancholy:
Fish dinners will make a man spring like a flea,
      Dame Venus, Love's lady,
      Was born of the sea."

Mary forgot her caution and moved into the light, stamping her feet
and shouting. A moment later, without knowing how, she found herself
on her father's knee. He dipped small pieces of bread in his glass and
gave them to her. The drops of wine ran down his fingers and on to the
shining damask. Absently he went on feeding her with sops, while
Mary leaned back in his arms, conscious of a warmth that spread
through her limbs, making her feel at once light and swollen. Her
uncle's face advanced and receded, like a comic fire-balloon. The
voice of the singer rolled over her in waves of sound. "Will be
damnably mouldy a hundred years hence," he roared. Mary wept, and
opened her mouth for another sop.

A long time after that she was conscious of her uncle's face very
close to hers. He seemed to be expostulating with her father, who stood
up and laid Mary in Mark Henry's arms, where she tried to struggle, but
found herself unexpectedly lax. Then she was near her mother, to
whom her father was speaking with such gravity and politeness that
Mary was surprised to see her mother's face turn scarlet. After that she
was in the cool well of the stairs, still in her uncle's arms, with her
mother swaying in front, like a pillar of smoke, gleaming warmly in the
candle-glow at the head of the stairs. Her mother was laughing, Miss
Flora was sniffing urgently, and Mark Henry's voice rumbled over all
of them in an incomprehensible threnody of his own. She was alone
with Miss Flora, whose sniff had become a continuous whistling like
the sound of the wind in the granary, trying to tell the governess that her
mother was Dame Venus, Love's lady. Miss Flora would not listen. . . .

Much later that night—Mary always insisted that it was the same
night, but it was probably the next—Mary roused to find her room filled
with receding circles of light, in the centre of which stood her mother,
wrapped in a dark coat. The light came from the candle in her mother's

hand. Seeing Mary awake, Charlotte Hansyke put the candle down and took the little girl in her arms.

"I'm going away," she whispered, "but I'll come back. You'll be good, and mind the sanctified Miss Flora, and don't forget me while I'm gone."

Mary understood nothing except that misfortune had overtaken her.

"Don't go. Why are you going?"

Charlotte Hansyke left hold of the child to fling her arms wide open.

"I'm dull," she said. "I'm dull. The tedious house. The useless, sneering man he is. I'm going to London, to friends. Listen, Mary, don't cry, and I'll come back for you. You shall sit in a box and hear the most divine music in the world. Mario, Mario in *Meyerbeer*. Oh, marvellous! The streets are lighted up at night as if the town were going to a dance. Think of it, Mary. That's life. There's nothing here."

"Take me now."

Charlotte stood up, disentangling her coat from the hands that clutched it. "You're too little. I'll come back for you." Stooping again, she caught Mary into a warm smothering embrace against her breast, and laying her quickly down, went away. "Good-bye," she called softly from the door. "Good-bye. I'll come back. Good-bye."

Mary lay silent in her bed, crushed by this stroke. . . .

In the morning she awoke to a heavy sense of desolation and remembered that her mother was gone. A faint hope that the thing was a dream sent her, half-dressed and trembling, to her mother's door. The disorder there and the maid's face as she bent over half-emptied drawers and boxes told her the truth before the girl spoke. Her mother had left her.

A week later, she accompanied Miss Flora to Danesacre and her uncle's house, and life began again.

3

Mark Henry Garton's house was built just above his own shipyard. A gate in the wall of his garden gave on to a path that led directly across a short grassy slope into the shipyard itself. All day long the sounds of the yard came up to the house, and from the rounded windows of the big sitting-room Mary could watch the progress of the boat on the stocks and the traffic of the upper harbour. The little town of Danesacre is built in a cleft of the cliffs, where the brown narrow Danesbeck, running down the valley from the moors, widens as it reaches the sea into a natural harbour with a muddy shelving floor. Garton's Yard was on the east side of the town, in a basin of the upper harbour. Beyond it, up the valley, the hillside was wooded. Towards the sea, the narrow cobbled streets of cliff-fast houses stretched away from the Yard, and above them, a landmark for eight centuries of sailors, the church gripped the windy cliff-top. The stones outside its walls were grey and wrinkled like the sea itself and bore old names, and names of men who were lost at sea or, stricken in strange lands, saw with dying eyes the little town in the fold of the hills and the shore at home. Mary Hansyke was moor-bred, and yet to the end of her days it seemed to her that this was her home. Its little houses were thoughts that she had had, and its cobbled streets, steep steps and narrow ghauts were the tender gestures of a mother.

She came to Danesacre in February and the harbour was filled with the masts of sailing ships that had been laid up for the winter and were now preparing for sea. The graving-docks on both sides of the river were full, and when Mary Hansyke walked with Miss Flora along Harbour Street towards the new bridge that crossed to the west and fashionable side of the town, she passed under bowsprits and jib-booms stretching right across the street from vessels moored in the east-side docks. All day long from six o'clock to six o'clock work went on in the ships, and the Town Hall bell rang when it began and again when it left off. Sails were bent. Watertanks filled. Old cattle, driven in from the surrounding villages, were killed, salted, and stored away. Crowds of sailor lads in blue jerseys and billowing trousers, and fair-haired apprentices, who all winter had been living and studying in attics and kitchens of masters' houses, thronged the streets, and from Garton's Yard, as she listened, fragments of song came floating up to her enchanted ears, with the sound of calking hammers and the shouts of the lightermen loading ballast on to the ships going out light to their loading ports.

"Red-nosed men frequent the ale-'ouse
    Oh, ho, yes,—oho.
Sandy-'aired men are always jealous
    A hundred years ago."

Mark Henry Garton had ten frigate-built vessels that traded to India and China. These were licensed India-men carrying guns to use against the pirates in the China seas, strong roomy boats, taking passengers as well as cargo. Their departure roused Mary to a pitch of excitement that excluded every other thought. She abandoned her studies, heard Miss Flora's exhortations, threats and groans with indifference. The most truthful of children, she promised Mark Henry to work for two hours, and slipped away as soon as his back was turned. Perched on a shelving grassy ledge below the garden wall, she watched the men running round the capstan to bring up the anchor of a ship lying out in the harbour. The wind blew cold across the steely ripples of the water and brought with it the intoxicating music of men's voices. She could not hear all the words, though she listened with her thin little body braced forward and her hands clasped in a rigor of attention.

"The ship went sailing out over the bar,
    O Rio! O Rio! . . .
Turn away, love, away,
    Away down the Rio. . . .
Then fare you well, my bonny young gel,
    We're bound for the Rio Grande."

A single voice, like bells ringing on a sunny morning, came to her on the wind. She sat stiffly, a stolid little girl in a short jacket, with unbound hair. Only her eyes betrayed her. "Were you ever in Rio Grande?" Back came the swelling chorus. "Away you Rio." Mary Hansyke from a worshipper became a child, and whooped with delight. Her ankle was grasped from below, and, looking down, she saw the grinning faces of her two boy cousins. She wrenched and kicked herself free, and rather than endure their jeers, ran back to the house, scarlet with mortification and disappointed rage.

The two young Lings were not, speaking by the table, her real cousins. They were the sons of John Ling, who was only the stepbrother of Charlotte and Mark Henry Garton. Their parents were dead, drowned at sea, and George and Rupert Ling, aged twelve and ten, lived with their half-uncle and were expected to succeed him at the Yard. Mark Henry had never married and had no other heir, though sporadic reproductions of his peculiar cast of face appeared in houses up and down Harbour Street. The Ling boys were at school, when they were not at home teasing Mary. She hated them. They were big clumsy lads, and Mary was small for her age, quick-tongued, light on her feet, but they neutralised these advantages by every form of ingenious torture they could without actual cruelty apply to her. They crept up silently and jumped out upon her. They untied her sash and her ribbons. George held her fast while Rupert brought his red freckled face close to hers, in a series of horrible grimaces. Mary loathed the nearness of his face, the smell of his hair thickened with bear's grease, and the damp warmth of his breath on her cheek. They arranged the loose seat of her chair so that she fell through in humiliating postures.

Oddly, though together they were devils, apart they were human. Once Rupert, when George was for some crime confined to bed, took Mary fishing. He baited her hook for her and told her his secrets. He had a small peculiar stone he had found on the beach: he thought it might be a pearl. He was in love with the wife of Soal the baker. She had a broad round bosom that smelled of musk.

"How do you know that?" Mary asked curiously.

"Because she once let me feel it," Rupert said solemnly. "She was wearing that glossy red bodice," he added, "and I scratched my finger on one of the brooches. Look, that finger. Just there. There was a mark, but it went away in a day."

When they returned home, they were both soaked to the skin and smelling overpoweringly of fish. Rupert escaped to the kitchen, but Mary, being waylaid by Miss Flora, was soundly thrashed after Miss Flora had offered up a prayer that the chastisement she was about to inflict on His child would be blessed by the Lord.

The following day George and Rupert shut a large dog in the cupboard where Mary kept her school books, but it was Miss Flora who opened the door and received the horrid impact of its released body on hers. She went into a series of fits and rigors, and emerging from them, had the boys banished for the duration of their holiday. They avenged themselves on Mary before they went by various torments of an ingenuity that surpassed any previous efforts, and brought Mary, for the first time, to shamefaced tears. . . .

One day, before this exile relieved her, Mary was running away from the Lings and found herself in a large shed at the farthest end of the Yard. One end was open to the harbour and a flight of wooden steps led to an upper room. Climbing them, Mary discovered the sail loft. Mark Henry's manager of the Yard was there, directing the workers in the preparing of sails for a new brig. Mary slipped her hand into his, and stood silently listening. The low raftered room smelt pleasantly of canvas and tar. Through its dirty window she could see the *John Garton* moving down the harbour. Mary knew her by heart. She had been built in 1841, the year of Mary's own birth, of American rock-elm. The top sides were of greenheart and the beams of oak. The decks were of yellow pine. A glint of brass from her mast entered Mary's eye like a splinter. She blinked and shut both eyes, opening them when she felt, by the change of light on her lids, that the *John Garton* was past the window and out of sight.

She fell to studying her uncle's manager. John Sacheverell Mempes was a satisfactory figure. He wore his white top-hat, a foppish and youthful affectation, tilted over one eyebrow. His boots were long and pointed, and the hand to which Mary clung wore an immense ring, an onyx set in filigree gold, carved with a unicorn. He took Mary down into the Yard and talked to her with a polite and rather puzzled consideration. He hardly knew what to make of her innocent dignity, but the softness of her skin ravished him and so did her eyes, which had normally a depth of blueness that ordinary blue eyes achieve in anger or under a stormy sky.

Mary observed him while he listened to a shipwright's excuse for coming late. A lean and melancholy man, he explained that his wife had fallen on her back and he had stayed to fetch the doctor.

"Surely," Mempes said smoothly, "you could have attended to her yourself," and had moved on before the shaft pierced the other's hide.

The brief incident was characteristic of Mempes. He expended on the men in his charge an irony that they resented without understanding it, and he suffered because they disliked him. Yet he had a knack of handling them. Garton's Yard remained free of trouble when other yards and other ports were in violent disorder. He had an intuitive sense of coming trouble, and provided he could refrain from laughing at the wrong moment, more often than not he contrived to avert it.

On their way to the ropemaker's, they met a buxom young woman who blushed and paled at the sight of Mempes. Mary admired the elegance of his greeting. She said so, and he flashed her a humorous glance.

"Do you think she liked it?"

"I am sure she did," Mary answered gravely. "I expect she loves you. Miss Flora had a brother who drowned himself for love."

The young man groaned gently. "Ere I would say I would drown myself for the love of a guinea-hen, I would change my humanity into a baboon," he said.

Mary did not understand the quotation and left him, a little offended. Mempes looked wistfully after her short, retreating back. He was sorry that the child did not like him. . . .

Except for her self-ordained holidays, Mary's life in Mark Henry Garton's house was sufficiently industrious. She rose at six and studied divinity for an hour with Miss Flora. After breakfast, and for the rest of her day until tea-time, she worked with the tutor whom Mark Henry had engaged for the Lings, and from absence of mind never discarded. For this young man, a Dutchman of the name of Wagener, she had a real affection. He neither thrashed her nor scolded her, and in the intervals of giving her a very solid grounding in Latin and arithmetic, he talked to her about his life.

"At fourteen I was the most pious of boys. I was everything a mother would like her son to be, and my father hated me. Then I went to the University and learned to play the flute and read all the books in the world. I wanted to see the world, so I ran away with a man and his wife who owned a travelling booth. I couldn't act—in Compiègne I was hissed off the stage in *Hamlet* for my accent, which was that of a Dutch boor. So I faked up plays for them out of my reading. I had successes, Mary, that are pleasant to remember. It was a jolly life on the whole, going from fair to fair in France, drinking the wine of the country after the performances with men and women streaked with paint and warm with exertion and excitement, ripe for anything. Those were days—and nights. Jolly people. No unnatural ideas about washing their bodies, so that they retained all their natural odours and added to them the smells and sweats and cheap scents of the audience in the booth. When you kissed the little soubrette you kissed every fair ground in France, and the smell of trampled grass, and dust and spilled wine and the scent of hedges and fields and women's warm hair and the exhalations of wet earth and the breath of cheering crowds—oh, life, life, Mary. I dare say I should have been there still but for an unfortunate incident in which I admit I was to blame—but youth, extreme youth, is thoughtless and rash. I was nineteen then, and I am twenty-six now, and I am prepared to admit that I made a fool of myself. However—those days unfitted me for a serious life.''

''You ought to be serious,'' Mary said earnestly. ''A painted wooden tablet hangs on the wall above our pew. It's very faded, and I can only just read it by staring at it till my eyes smart. *Be ye doers of the word and not hearers onely, deceiving your own selvs.* It means that we should all work hard to fit ourselves to lead a good life.''

Wagener looked at her comically. ''Then why did you run away before breakfast yesterday morning to see the *Mary Gray* launched?''

''I don't know,'' Mary confessed. ''I couldn't eat with the thought of her taking the water and me not there. It was splendid. There were flags, and people cheered, and old Mr. Smithson fell in the harbour, and when they dragged him out he said he was eating his way through the mud to the pier. The band played and the sun shone on the water. And the *Mary Gray* stood out to sea like an angel. When she was out of the harbour I went up to the cliff top to watch her out of sight. The wind was right for her and she lay over to the waves like the lady she is. When she's fullrigged she'll carry thirty-four sails, counting three skysails, moonsails, and sky-stunsails. I was talking to her mate in the Yard the other day. He said stunsails were almost no use, and the Old Man liked crowding on everything he had until the whole lot was fit to tear itself to *ribbins* in the forties. What do you think of that? She's off to London and then to Australia. My uncle says they're scooping gold out of the country with a knife. I don't know whether to believe him or not. Everyone's going. I thought of going myself. My uncle has three ships building in Nova Scotia for the Australian trade, and he's going to take three frigates off the Indian for it. . . .When I came home yesterday morning he thrashed me. So did Miss Flora. She hurt the worse, and prayed too. Ah well, it was worth it.''

"Why did you tell them where you'd been? They would have thought you were studying with me, like a good girl.''

"They asked me.''

"You never tell lies, do you?'' Wagener said. "I wonder why. I tell them by the hundred. It's a social duty. People can't stand the truth. No one ought to go round being so truthful as you are. It's indecent. Why, Mary, you might as well go round naked.''

Mary frowned, and Wagener, feeling reproved, bought his way back to favour with his flute. He played the *Wanderers Nachtlied* to her, and for that air, than which no air more poignant or more lovely was ever made, Mary forgave him everything, even his want of earnestness.

She thought of her mother and tears filled her eyes. . . .

After dinner she sat with Mark Henry Garton in the dining-room. He was sunk in gloom, and told Mary that he was done for.

"Imagination has been my ruin,'' he said earnestly. "Don't have anything to do with imagination, Mary. Stick to probabilities, and if you must punt do it on the ready in a small way. Look at me. I can't be content with Garton's Yard, but I must go and start a blast furnace at Middlesbrough. Why? You ask me why? Of course you do, and I answer that it's because I am a fool. I go over there—for nothing—just to pass the time of day with an old friend, heaven rot him, and place an order for engines for that steamboat we're going to build. Think of that, Mary. The first steamship in Danesacre and I'm building it. That's one for old Smithson, and his miserable Spital Yard. Spittoon Yard, I call it. Why, a hearty smoker could fill one of those dry docks of his in an afternoon.''

Mark Henry bounced on the sofa. It was of new, shiny horsehair, and he was only saved from sliding off by clutching at the window ledge behind. A plant pot crashed down and Mark Henry surveyed the fragments and scattered earth with rising fury. "Plants,'' he said.

"Plants! Rot all plants. The place for plants is the garden, and not too much of that, and I won't have my house turned into a shrubbery for all the horse-faced dragoons who ever masqueraded as the gentle sex. I could tell you things about women, Mary—well, throw the damned things out of the window. Go on, all of them."

He came to her help, and with a fearful delight Mary saw Miss Flora's pots of musk and trailing greenery hurled down the slope of the garden to crash against the Yard wall. Mark Henry enjoyed the sabotage. He said something about Attila, and when Mary asked a question, told her that Attila knew how to deal with women.

"Rapine," said Mark Henry darkly. "A firm hand. I've known women rapine was too good for. Gr-r-r! Woman, woman, lovely woman, give her a pot of musk and she thinks it's the Garden of Eden." He slammed the window down and surveyed his work with a satisfaction that turned rapidly to gloom when Mary reminded him about the blast furnace.

"Going to Middlesbrough to buy a boiler or two, and buying a whole damned furnace. What d'you think of that? I bought everything. I bought a complete iron mill, with blast furnaces, and a small separate works alongside, where they're making boilers and marine engines. It was all the fault of that fellow in Vyner's. Says: 'You can't have your boilers in March. We're working for the Government.' 'Government be damned,' I said. 'I'll show you whether I'm to be hindered by a lot of nincompoops in office,' and I went down into the town and there I met young Gossop. He was pea-green, and they said he'd been losing heavily in the Funds. I said: 'D'you want to sell your works?' and be damned he did. And I went over to the bank and arranged it there and then. And there we are. Gossop's—*no*—Garton's Iron Works. And I can have all the boilers I want, and when I want 'em. Oh, I'll be buried in a boiler. I'll shut myself in one and roll down the cliff. Soon as I get home I'm told that the new brig was run down off Hartlepool last night by a damned great schooner. On her first voyage, and all hands lost. Carrying coal, she was, and I hope they're using it to roast 'em where they've gone. Dark night. I'd give 'em dark night if I could get at 'em. They'll be refusing to sail at night next. What with their tea and their sugar and benefit clubs and higher wages, we'll soon be sending every

man on board with a nurse. Mary, whatever you do, never give in to
these Unions. They're ruining us. They'd like to see me cutting capers
for ha'pennies on the Scotch Head. In every port, from Peterhead to
London. Putting ideas in the men's thick heads. Devils. Mind what I
say. Don't you ever give in to them, Mary. Promise.''

Mary promised.

Her uncle was pleased with her. He said that she was a sensible,
obedient girl, and asked her how old she was. Hearing that she was
thirteen now, he sighed.

"I wish you'd been a boy, Mary. I'd have adopted you. You've got
hands like a boy. You're sure you're not a boy? Under those petticoats.
Well, I couldn't tell, could I? That woman's capable of anything to
spite me. You be off to her before she comes to fetch you. Be off.''

Mary understood that he was talking of Miss Flora, for whom he had
an irrational hatred. He considered that her sniffs were directed at him,
and once at breakfast he burst into indignant speech.

"Blow your nose, woman,'' he shouted. "Don't go on trifling with
nature like that. Blow it and have done. Here, I'll show you.''

He produced a red bandana, and trumpeted into it with the blast of a
fog-horn. Miss Flora rushed from the table. He stared gloomily after
her.

"There she goes,'' he said to Mary. "Rushing about like Jonah, but
no whale could stomach that. Did you ever see the jawbone of a whale,
Mary? That's one over the gate into the orchard. Drive a coach and four
through it. Don't you ever take to sniffing. I'll wring your nose.''

Lingering in the doorway after saying good night, Mary observed
that she would like to build ships. Mark Henry was amused.

"You can't build ships in petticoats,'' he said. "Trip up and show
your drawers. I'd look rare and queer running round the Yard in
drawers, wouldn't I?''

Mary stood her ground.

"You don't build the boats yourself,'' she said urgently. "*I*
wouldn't, either. I'd tell them what to do. I know a few things about it
already, Mr Mempes says steam is bound to cut out everything else.
He showed me a plan of an engine, and explained the pressure and the
cylinders to me. I asked him would it be a good thing if he could think of

a way to squeeze more pressure out of less coal so as to leave more room for the cargo, and—"

"It would be a damned good thing," said Mark Henry boisterously, "and, by George, if you're still having ideas in five years' time I'll take you into the firm, I will. We'll set 'em all by the ears. Never did like those Lings. Rotten stock, eh Mary? Here, be off, be off. I'll not have that fog-faced woman in here. Shake her up and away you go. Step handy, my girl."

Mary conceived the idea that he was a little nervous about the plant-wrecking. She withdrew, and went to bed, solemnly happy in the thought that her future was now settled. . . .

Her mother came next day.

Charlotte Hansyke had in four years changed not a little. She had broadened, and she was helping out the freshness of her complexion by various adjuncts that her brother referred to flatly as harlotries.

"You ought not to do it, Lottie," he grumbled. "You don't do it properly. You could put it on badly to show what a great lady you were, or thoroughly, to show you were t'other sort. But you do it to deceive. It don't deceive a cat, and you're getting a bad name in the town. Decent women don't rouge themselves up to the eyes, and go round with the plackets of their skirts torn. It's a bad sign. You wash your face, my girl, and get Horse-whiskers to sew you up."

Something in Charlotte's expression must have struck him, for he rested his hand on her shoulder in awkward kindness.

"We all got to come to it. Your varnish is blistered, your waist running a neck to neck with your dressmaker, and you don't feel a day older than you did twenty years ago, eh Lottie?"

Charlotte stared at him and went away without a word. She mended her skirt, but gave up none of the tricks that displeased him. She used all her blandishments to attach John Mempes to her side. The young man paid court to her with a melancholy grace that infuriated Mark Henry, and for some reason she could not explain to herself, distressed Mary so much that she avoided both Mempes and her mother. She disliked the sight of her mother leaning on the manager's arm. She disliked Mempes' habit of whispering stories in her mother's ear, which made Charlotte laugh loudly, and were always broken off when Mary came into the room, to be resumed, Mary knew, when she left. She felt awkward in her mother's presence, and the tender longing with which she used to dwell on Charlotte's memory, lying awake to imagine the door opening and her mother there, candle in hand, come back for her little girl, passed imperceptibly into disapproval and distrust. Charlotte did not seem to notice it, but the more sensitive Mempes did. He made an effort to win the little girl back to friendship, but her blunt refusal of his advances baffled him. Too indolent to persist, he allowed Mary to rebuff him, and devoted himself to her easier mother.

Charlotte had come up to negotiate the sale of her few remaining shares in Garton's Yard. The allowance Richard Hansyke made her was enough to have kept her in narrow comfort in London, but Charlotte could not have lived narrowly anywhere. She did not spend money on rent. She had lived ever since she ran away to town with a friend who had a small house in Islington. But she had to have clothes and amusements, and Charlotte was not calculating enough to make the men for whom she dressed pay for either. She was in debt to dressmakers and milliners, and even, Mary gathered, listening to Charlotte's long wandering monologues, to the friend she lived with. Charlotte talked to Mary as if the little girl were her own age. She did not seem to notice that Mary was unresponsive, and when Mempes made his appearance and she pulled herself together to be bewitching and witty, she did not observe Mary slipping from the room, with a funny mixture of scorn and bewilderment on her round face.

Mark Henry would not buy Charlotte's shares, except at two-thirds of the market rate, and even at that price he insisted on half the money being put back into the firm in Mary's name. Charlotte raged. He was stubborn.

"Sell 'em yourself," he said. "Sell 'em in the open market if you don't like my price. But why sell 'em? You can stay on here, you and Mary, and I'll treat Mary as if she were my own girl. I'll do nothing to help you rake about London like an old ship painted up to do duty as a river inn, open to all comers."

Charlotte was helpless. She had no idea how to get rid of her shares except by selling them to her brother, and in the end she sold them to him on his own terms. Then, furious, she announced her intention of going back to London and taking Mary with her.

"You can't do that," Mark Henry said flatly. "Hansyke hasn't given you leave to take the child away, nor likely to. He's a cold-hearted brute, but he's not a scoundrel. Now, I am, but then I'm warm-hearted, and you can't have everything."

So it happened that Mary was wakened once again by her mother's appearance in her bedroom in the middle of the night. This time, Charlotte got the little girl up, and admonished her to dress herself quickly, while Charlotte packed some of her clothes into a bundle.

"Are we going away?" Mary asked sleepily.

"Hush," Charlotte said. "Don't talk. If your uncle hears us, he won't let you go. I promised to take you to London and I will. Be quick. Never mind all the buttons. You can fasten them afterwards."

But Mary insisted on fastening the ultimate button and tying the last tape before she would come away. Charlotte fretted with impatience while the little girl continued her methodical preparations, but she waited, defeated by Mary's stolid perseverance. At last she was ready, and Charlotte caught her up to carry her down the stairs.

"You'd better let me walk," Mary observed. "You'll tread lighter yourself if you're not carrying me, and I can slide down the banisters."

This she did and slid into the arms of John Mempes, waiting there to give his arm to Charlotte and escort them both to the carriage standing in Harbour Street. Charlotte leaned out of the window and kissed him on the mouth as the carriage moved off. "Bless you and thank you," she whispered. "You've been an angel, helping me."

"I feel more like a less reputable person in fiction. The wicked uncle, Cressida's uncle, in fact. Who knows what I'm helping you to? Send for me, if you want help."

He spoke to Charlotte, but he looked at Mary as he uttered the last words. She shrank back into the carriage, resolute not to show him any favour. Too young to put her thoughts clearly to herself, she yet had an instinctive sense that he was helping on this romantic flight less out of kindness than from an indifference that was ready to yield to any woman's entreaties. Perhaps even, Mary thought darkly, he was glad to be rid of her mother. Miss Flora said that John Mempes was a flirt and a breaker of hearts, who led women on and wearied of them as soon as he

had got them into a state when they were ready to do everything for
him. Perhaps he was tired of Charlotte. She looked at the tall grave
young man standing at the side of the road, hat in hand, his face pale
and remote in the cold half-light of dawn. The idea that he had led her
mother on must be dismissed as an inadequate comment on a situation
that puzzled Mary not a little. Charlotte had surely come more than
half-way. Mary sighed. She felt that she was becoming wise and
worldly very quickly. The carriage rounded the bend of the hill and the
romantic figure of Mempes vanished out of sight with the house, the
masts in the harbour and the erection of poles and scaffolding round the
ship on the stocks in Garton's Yard.

By the time they were on the open moor, the sky in the east was warm
and flushed with day. They stopped at the highest point, to breathe the
horses, and Mary craned out of the window to look back over the way
they had come. Danesacre was a whisper of houses in the mouth of the
valley. The harbour was invisible, and a haze of smoke hid all but the
topmost roofs below the church. The floor of the sea was splashed with
silver in pools and rings of light, shifting and flashing in the early sun.
Mary jumped out of the carriage and stood a moment on the fine short
turf at the roadside. The moor wind was cold on her cheeks. It looked
warmer down in the valley. Her intent gaze followed it until its green
slopes and dark patches of wood were lost in the shadows of the hills.
Charlotte called her sharply to get in, and reluctantly, filled with a
childish sense of irrevocable loss, she climbed back into the carriage.
They set off again on the twenty-mile drive to the town where they
intended to take train for London.

Charlotte talked in a sleepy fashion as the carriage crossed the moors
and came down into the Vale of Pickering. She gave Mary fragments of
her life, beginning with Mary's own birth.

"You were all but born in a carriage, Mary. We were driving home
and we had to stop at a cottage. Cottage it was called, but it was more
like a hovel. You can't imagine how squalid it was. Your father was
vexed at it happening like that, as if I should have chosen to lie up in
such a place. But he was inconsiderate even in those days, and he got
worse as you got older. Until I couldn't bear it any longer, and I went

away to London. I hated leaving you, Mary. You were such a round soft little thing then. You've got positively bony. I can't think what that woman has been feeding you on. I used to cry sometimes when I thought of you. Particularly at night. If I was alone." She broke off, and Mary, suddenly ashamed because she had been thinking that it was just like Charlotte to have her baby in the most inconvenient and untidy manner possible, got on to Charlotte's knee and kissed her like the loving little girl she was when she was not a disillusioned and experienced woman. The experienced woman vanished completely in the little girl. Mary lay in Charlotte's arms while Charlotte petted her and stroked her, and mother and daughter clung together, closer in mind and body than they had been since Charlotte's return. When they reached the town, Mary stood guard over Charlotte's box and her own bundle while Charlotte got the tickets and asked agitated questions of all the officials in sight, and of one gentleman who was not an official, but who kindly answered Charlotte's questions and helped her and Mary into the train, handing up Mary's bundle with a polite smile. Mary eyed the bundle distrustfully. It was very small, and Mary considered that either her mother had not packed her new frock or it was being lamentably crushed. Both prospects were sufficiently gloomy, but she forgot, in the excitement of sitting in a train for the first time in her life, to question Charlotte about it.

When they reached London she was very tired, and dozed all the way in the cab that took them to Islington and Miss Short's house. She was dimly conscious that the cab was climbing what seemed an endless hill, after hours of which the cab stopped and she was lifted down and carried into a small warm room, very full of furniture, by a lady who afterwards ran round the room, clucking and upsetting things as she went. She was given a bowl of bread and milk, and in spite of every effort to keep awake, fell forward into it and was removed, to the accompaniment of a frenzied clucking, into a candle-lit bedroom, where she was undressed, and it was discovered that Charlotte had forgotten to pack any of her nightclothes. There was a good deal of laughter over this, which Mary thought ill-occasioned, and she was rolled in a garment belonging to Miss Short, and put to bed with an admonition to keep over against the wall. She fell asleep at once, with one despairing glance at a mass of crumpled silk, lying under a chair where it had fallen, that she thought must be her best frock.

When she woke up the sun was shining and Charlotte was standing in front of the glass coiling her hair. Mary gazed sleepily for some moments at her mother's big white arms and smooth shoulders. Then, remembering her frock, she sat up in bed and looked round for it. There it was, still lying on the floor. But it was not her best frock. It was an old one, hopelessly too small and old-fashioned for her to wear. Charlotte laughed, but seeing how chagrined the little girl was, she came and sat down on the bed beside her, and promised her any number of new frocks.

"London frocks, Mary. Real frocks. I'll take you out after breakfast to the shops. Thank heaven I've got some money now and needn't go to Madame Rose, with her sickening Requests for Immediate Payment and tossing her head and her airs. As if I hadn't bought more frocks from her in a month than most of her customers do in a year."

It occurred to Mary that it might be the very number of the frocks bought that caused Madame Rose to toss her head, and she hoped the lady would now be paid off and not have to go on indulging in such a tiresome exercise. She said as much, and Charlotte laughed and told her not to talk like Mark Henry. "What's the sense in paying old bills when you've got ready money to spend?" she asked. "Most of the things are worn out, and you'd be no better off when you had paid for them."

Hopelessly confused in her mind by this aspect of finance, Mary followed her mother downstairs to the little sitting-room, which in the daylight seemed even fuller of furniture than the night before. Moving about in it was a tortuous edgewise process, in which at one point Mary was wedged between two pieces that overhung her like the Symplegades. The room looked out on to a garden and a cherry-tree covered with immature cherries.

"You're looking at my tree," Miss Short said in her ear. "It's a lovely tree. I brought the slip from my dear father's place in Kent, when he died, and it was found that the house and the grounds and all his money had to be given to a lot of men who came down from London and made themselves a great nuisance, going round poking the chairs and even lifting the covers, my dear, to look underneath. Most indelicate, I thought, and goodness knows what they expected to find there but Legs. I became quite nervous about my own, if you understand me. They were going to take everything. However, it seemed there was something they couldn't touch, which annoyed them all very much, though how they could reconcile it with their Christian principles to want to rob a poor unmarried lady of her money, I don't know. I spoke to one of them about it and he said: 'Principles! If I'd even had the interest I wouldn't feel so bad about it, never mind the principle!' Well, I don't understand it, my dear. It was my father's money, and it seems to me unjust that it should be taken from me to give to a lot of men I'd never seen before. That is, all of it but a little in the Funds, as they say, which is paid me twice a year by a Person with very gentlemanly whiskers, and it's not that I grudge your mother any of it, but I can't help wishing she would show a little consideration for me and not speak so brusquely when I ask her about getting some of it back. She ought to remember I'm alone in the world except for Paul, and he's more of a companion than a help, as you might say. But it's got nothing to do with you, my dear, and I'm sure I'm very glad to have you. One mouth doesn't make much difference, does it? Have you a very large appetite, I wonder? Some children have, of course. But there, never mind, let's talk about my nice tree instead. I took the slip myself and hid it under my cloak, because there's no knowing what these men would have done if they'd seen me making off with a piece of what they said was their property. I felt almost as if I were stealing, but you couldn't call it stealing, to take a bit of our own trees, could you?''

Mary said she was sure it was not stealing, and, reassured, Miss Short allowed herself to display a little triumph at the thought of how cleverly she had outwitted the men, getting away with a slip of a valuable tree, and not letting go of it until she had planted it in the garden there, which she did before as much as looking round the house to see whether the sitting-room was big enough to hold her chiffonier and the mahogany pedestal table Mary could examine after breakfast when the cloth was off.

Charlotte came in at that moment and they sat down to breakfast, Miss Short looking at Mary with an odd air of guilt and appeal, to

which Mary responded with a friendly smile. Mary felt a certain
delicacy about eating, and in spite of being hungry ate as sparingly as
possible. She was wondering whether she could speak to her mother
about paying Miss Short some of the money she owed her. In the
meantime she resolved to eat only just enough to keep alive. Charlotte
noticed nothing, but talked to Mary with vivacious delight, of London
and shopping and fireworks and riding in the Park.

Left alone while Charlotte went up to dress, Mary tried to arrange her
ideas about London, but got them hopelessly mixed and gave up the
attempt. She examined the pedestal of the table and found it wreathed
with an engaging series of imps and devils, boldly carved and lustrous
with much polishing. She speculated on the amount of labour it must
take to get the dust out of all those dimpled cheeks and creased limbs.
After that she set out to explore the house, and discovered that Paul was
a large cat, with the most monumentally contemptuous face cat ever
had. Mary tried to stroke him but he turned his back on the little girl and
disappeared down the basement stairs. She was looking after him rather
forlornly when Charlotte came down, dressed for the street, and
they went out. Just as they emerged from the narrow street, Mary
spelling out the name, Lincthorn Road, as they went along, Miss Short
came running after them. She was out of breath and her head streamed
with agitated wisps of hair. She carried a little bag of asafoetida, which
she insisted on hanging round Mary's neck as a protection against
cholera. "The milkman says there are two cases in City Road," she
panted. "All black and bursting. It's against nature. You must wear
this day and night, my dear. Never mind what anyone says."

Holding tightly to her mother's hand, Mary set off down the stepped
terrace that stretched from the Angel as far as she could see. When they
had gone fifty yards, she looked back. Miss Short was still standing at
the corner of Lincthorn Road, and she began to make violent gestures
with her arms, indicative apparently of a cholera patient in the throes.
Abashed, Mary looked hastily away again, hoping that no one had
observed her connection with this pantomime.

They came back to Lincthorn Road in the late afternoon, with two
new dresses for Mary, and various purchases of her mother's following
by messenger. Miss Short was presented with an inlaid work-box. She
seemed about to say something, but changed her mind, thanked

Charlotte, and put the box away, clucking softly like a meditative hen.

Mary was tired, and dazed with impressions of streets, hurrying crowds, and traffic. She had enjoyed the Park, envying the young ladies on horseback, in bewitching toppers and voluminous skirts. A gentleman had greeted Charlotte, who smiled at him in the ingratiating way Mary had hated when Mark Henry's manager was the object of her mother's wiles. She found that she hated it as much now, and drew back when the gentleman put a finger under her chin. As he was going he said: "Who likes sugar-plums?" and balanced a coin on his finger.

"I don't know," Mary said coldly. "*I* don't."

He was a little taken aback, and Charlotte scolded her for her want of manners. "They've let you grow into a complete bumpkin," she lamented. Mary felt a sudden twinge of longing for Mark Henry's solid presence. She would not entertain it, and hardened her heart against her mother.

It seemed that Mary was not going to bed. She was going to dress herself in one of the new frocks and accompany her mother and Miss Short to a fancy-dress ball at Cremorne. Mary hoped it was not somewhere out of England and was relieved to find they were going in a cab. Miss Short did not want to go. She came downstairs dressed in a pink silk frock, in which she looked more distracted than ever, and remonstrated with Charlotte all the way to Chelsea.

"You don't want me to come with you, Lottie. You only want someone to hold you down when you begin to go off, like a balloon, in one of your wild fits; you know you do."

"Hold your tongue, you silly old grasshopper," Charlotte said. She was excited, and laughed so loudly that the driver begged her not to do it again. He said his horse had been at the battle of Waterloo and had nervous fits when anything reminded him of it.

"You know you're going to enjoy yourself," Charlotte told her. "And so is Mary, aren't you, darling?"

Mary said: "I hope so," but she was yawning and Charlotte cried: "What a pair of owls! I wish I'd left you both at home."

The fireworks in the gardens took Mary's breath away. She stood gaping at them until the last splendid conflagration had died to a sizzling star, and turned to find the tall gentleman of Rotten Row at their elbow.

"Here's the little lady with the salted tongue," he said to Mary. "I suppose you're all prepared to dance. Come along now, and I'll find you seats before I borrow your mother for a waltz or two."

Mary frowned, and tugged so hard on Miss Short's hand that the bewildered lady excused herself from accompanying Charlotte and Charlotte's friend to the ballroom. She said she would follow later with Mary, but when she did, they were stopped at the door by a man who announced that the tickets were ten shillings, five shillings to those in fancy-dress.

"Five shillings for the little girl," he said, "although she's not dressed. Ten to you, madam."

Miss Short gasped, and rose to the situation like a game-cock.

"But I am in fancy-dress," she declared, feverishly unbuttoning her coat. "I'm a Pink." She wrote her name with trembling fingers, paid over half a sovereign, and the door curtain was lifted for her to pass through.

"Miss Short. A Pink," the doorkeeper bawled, and with Mary at her heels, Miss Short sailed through. The dozen people nearest the door began to laugh, and Miss Short dragged Mary round the walls of the room until they found a comparatively secluded corner at the entrance to a plant house, which was very dark. Miss Short refused to explore it, on the ground that her father's only brother had been found dead in a similar place, with his feet sticking up through an ornamental shrub and his watch-chain hanging on one of the branches. "Like a Christmas tree, my dear. Apoplexy following on Defalcation, they said."

Miss Short sat down on the edge of a chair and looked nervously round, as if she expected to see the corpse of a defaulting gentleman behind her now.

"I don't see Charlotte anywhere," she complained to Mary. "You know, my dear, Charlotte's my oldest friend, but I don't feel that I'm being well treated. It's a very pretty box, I know, but fifty pounds is fifty pounds, and I would like just a little of it. Do you think you could see about my getting part? I might do such a lot of things with it. I might go to Paris for a holiday to stay in my old school. Do you believe, my dear, that in our hearts we have an awareness of God at all times and in all situations? That is what the sisters taught us but I had a dreadful experience on the French train the last time I went to see them and when

I tried to pray it was as if devils were laughing in my head and the power and the glory belong to the Evil One. There was a most inconvenient sort of lavatory at the end of the train and I went there, just as we seemed to be coming into Paris, to tidy myself. The door stuck and I couldn't get out. I was paralysed. It seemed indelicate to knock, and someone began to bang on the door from the outside, most impatient, and shouting in French. I didn't answer him, of course, and he went on until the train stopped and I saw we'd reached Paris. I didn't know what to do then. I knocked, and no one heard me through the noise they were making getting off the train. There was only one little window in the place, high up on the wall on the side away from the platform. I was trying to crane my neck out of this when a pair of legs came down the side of the train from the roof, and I thought: An angel sent. I grabbed at them. There was a yell and the man slid down and bumped on the ground. Not an angel after all. He got up and put his face to the window, and when he saw me he behaved like a maniac. You would have thought I'd bitten his legs, instead of only giving them a little tug. I said: 'I can't get out.' I couldn't make him understand, but after a while he went away and brought some sort of officials and they broke in the door. My dear, you can imagine what I felt like. However, I straightened my hat in front of them all and walked out saying: 'I'm English. I wanted to wash my hands. I'm English.' My brother was there to meet me and he went off in fits of laughter. I saw nothing very funny in it. Do you think it was funny?''

''I think it was perfectly dreadful,'' Mary assured her, shocked by the recital. She caught sight of Charlotte, on the arm of the tall gentleman. They seemed to be making their way towards Mary and Miss Short, but they vanished, and though Mary looked all round, she could not see them. She was very tired, and her head was nodding forward when she heard Charlotte's voice, coming apparently out of the wall at their back. She turned round in a fright. Miss Short seized her arm.

''They're in there, my dear,'' she whispered, jerking her head towards the plant house. ''What do you think we'd better do?''

Mary stared helplessly at Miss Short's twitching face. Really, she thought fretfully, the way Miss Short put everything on her was too bad. She did not know what to do, and sat still. Charlotte's voice sounded strange.

"You didn't say that a year ago," she said.

The tall gentleman laughed, and at the sound Mary conceived a hatred of him of which her earlier dislike was but the mildest of precursors.

"A year ago! My dear Lottie. Do show some sensibility. A year ago is not now."

"A year ago you wanted something from me. Now you don't. That's all."

"Listen, Lottie, I don't want to quarrel with you. I'm quite prepared to be your friend. If there's anything I can do—I'm not a rich man, but if fifty pounds. . . ."

"Just the amount she owes me," breathed little Miss Short. "How odd. Perhaps it will remind her."

It seemed that Charlotte was not reminded of anything but her incomprehensible grief. She began to scold the tall gentleman in a furious whisper that presently became a pleading murmur.

"I've never asked you for anything," she said. "I don't want anything. Except not to be left like this. Don't leave me. Don't, don't leave me. I'll always love you. See, oh see, I love you now. Have I grown less beautiful to you? Tell me why you don't want me any more? When I want you so much."

There was a short silence, and then Mary heard the gentleman say: "Good-bye, Lottie," followed by the sound of his retreating footsteps and a wail from her mother. Then Charlotte began to cry. Mary rushed into the plant house. It was quite dark, and she knocked over plants and grazed her forehead on some tall yielding stem, that rose up out of the darkness to bar her headlong way. She flung herself on Charlotte and hugged her close.

"Come along," she said. "Let's go home. Come on. Come with me."

"What are you doing here?" Charlotte said roughly. She hurried out of the plant house, dragging Mary after her, and confronted Miss Short with a face contorted between tears and rage. "How dare you come spying on me?" she demanded, and rushed out of the ballroom, pushing through the dancers, with Mary clinging to her arm and Miss Short clucking at her heels.

"Get me a cab," Charlotte ordered the doorkeeper. He got it, insolently enough, and she bundled Mary and the poor drooping Pink into it. All the way to Lincthorn Road she said nothing and took no notice of Miss Short's ejaculations. But once indoors Miss Short assumed a certain dignity.

"You had no right to speak to me like that, Charlotte. I'm not a spy. I never had the figure for it, for one thing, and I didn't expect you of all people to rush at me like a cataract and drag me through a roomful of half-dressed savages. Fancy-dress! Why shouldn't I be a Pink? Well, never mind that, I've put up with your wild ways all this time, thinking you were good at heart, just as I used to think of you at school when you got into such trouble, but this is too much. I've been spoken to to-night as if I were a Turk and compelled to trample on people I don't know and don't approve of. And all I've got is a little inlaid box. It's a very nice box, and I dare say will come in useful for something, but I'd rather you took it back and gave me a little of the money you borrowed from me."

Charlotte stood up and said bitterly:

"I'll give you your money. And I'll go away from this house now. Come, Mary, we'll go and pack." She swept Mary upstairs and stood there in the middle of the room while the little girl, with weary neatness, packed and folded and sought for Charlotte's scattered possessions in all the drawers and corners of the room. Charlotte's fine eyes were lustrous with emotion, and her hair lay in heavy coils about her shoulders. Her bosom swelled and lifted as she talked, moving out of Mary's way, sometimes offering dispassionate advice.

"I've been a fool," she said quietly. "Don't you ever make a fool of yourself like that, Mary. Let men beg and beg and threaten to blow their brains out, but don't give way to them. They won't blow out their brains. That's just bird-lime. I've been well caught, haven't I? Never give anything for nothing. The more you give the more you may, and a man doesn't value anything he hasn't had to pay for. But what could I do? I'm not young. I'm thirty-nine. I've lost some of my looks, Mary. If I'd been too stiff with him, as likely as not he'd have gone off—to find someone easier, or someone who dared to put a higher value on

herself than I did. I didn't dare, Mary. I loved him so." Charlotte
paused and went on in the same tone of voice: "Don't crush that
bodice, girl. Fold it the other way. He's fooled me. Well, I'll show him
I don't care. Hurry, Mary. Hurry! We'll go away. We'll leave my box
and send for it. We'll go and enjoy ourselves. I'll show you everything
in London. We'll laugh and be happy and pretend there aren't any men
in the world. Shall we? If your father had been different . . . There's
only one man you've the right to expect anything from and that's the
man you've married. The others are all—incidents. They don't owe
you anything and they remember that when they feel like getting
away."

"Where are we going?" Mary asked.

"I don't know. Far enough from here. We'll find somewhere.
Quick!"

At last they had finished. Mary straightened her back and began to
tidy her hair. A fury of impatience seized Charlotte.

"Come," she said. "It's getting light. It must be four o'clock."

"What about Miss Short's money?" Mary asked.

"Oh," her mother said doubtfully, "do you think I ought to give it to
her?"

Mary said she did think so. She waited while her mother extracted
some notes from an envelope in her bag, and, taking them from her,
went downstairs in search of Miss Short. She found the poor woman
asleep on the couch in the sitting-room. Her lips were pursed and open,
as if sleep had overtaken her in the middle of a cluck. When Mary spoke
to her, she bounced off the couch into a posture of agitated self-
justification and appeal.

"You're not really going, Mary? You can't go now. It's the middle
of the night. No one will take you in. You'll be murdered. I'm sure I'm
very sorry if I spoke hastily to your mother, but I was upset, and I'm
impetuous. My poor father always said it would be my ruin and now
you'll be brought back swollen corpses to my feet and I really don't
know what I shall do. What can you do with a corpse?"

"Here's your money." Mary said, thrusting the notes towards her.

Miss Short took them with a hand that trembled between relief and eagerness and a sort of shame. She looked from them to the pale little girl and murmured:

"You really mustn't go like this. I appeal to you, my dear. I don't know however I'm going to explain it to the neighbors. Besides, I'm fond of Charlotte, and I don't like living alone." Miss Short began to weep.

Mary looked at her with the indifference of fatigue. "You shouldn't have spoken to her as you did," she said. "You might have seen she was upset. Do you know what I think? I think you ought to get someone to come and live with you who'd look after you, and not want to go out to the fireworks. There's a good deal to be done in this house for anyone who likes that sort of thing. That pedestal, for instance. But don't try to live with anyone like my mother. You're not—not quick enough."

Charlotte's rapid footsteps sounded on the staircase.

Mary turned to go. She held out her hand. "Good-bye. I ate as little as possible. I hope you'll enjoy yourself in France, and not have any accidents."

Charlotte took no notice of the poor quivering weeping figure in the doorway. She stalked down the narrow gravelled path to the garden gate, carrying Mary's bundle, without a glance at her friend. Never was a Pink more draggled and broken by a night of storm. Mary felt sorry for her, but a touch of contempt for Miss Short's incapacity to deal with a situation she herself had created mingled with her pity. She waved her hand and stumbled down Lincthorn Road in Charlotte's wake.

Charlotte strode down the hill towards the town at such speed that Mary's short legs were taking two steps to her mother's one, and she was out of breath and gasping. They passed the reservoir, a sinister-looking place at this hour in the morning, when a light that was almost tangible, so grey and opaque was it, enclosed Mary and her mother, Pentonville Hill and all London in a quivering translucent globe, like a bowl of goldfish. They reached the bottom of the hill and there Charlotte hesitated. Mary looked round her at the deserted street. It was offensively dirty, and again she thought longingly of Garton's Yard and

Harbour Street, that even in its narrowest part was not sordid, like this, and as it climbed the hill out of the town became the cleanest windiest road in Danesacre. She drove the thought away. Here she was, and here in these squalid streets she was apparently to remain, and she would not allow herself to dwell on thoughts of Danesacre. She looked at her mother and for the first time realised what Charlotte meant when she talked of her age. The early light was cruel to Charlotte's face. There were lines down each side of her mouth, and the flesh under her eyes was stained and puffy. Mary came closer to her mother, moved to comfort. In the same moment she divined that Charlotte was feeling bewildered and helpless in the black tunnel of the street and a tremor of fear invaded Mary's own solid little body.

A cab crawling down the road from the city galvanised Charlotte into action. She hailed it, waving Mary's bundle. The man drew up and regarded the two of them in a stupefaction that presently issued in material form. He spat vehemently. Then he fell to studying them again.

"I want you to drive us," Charlotte began imperiously and paused—"across the river," she concluded. The cabman found his voice.

"Well," he said mournfully, "I don't know what you've been up to. How'd I know you an't the one as is wanted for doing in her husband last Friday night in the City Road, slitting him up from top to bottom like a herring, the saucy piece."

"You can see for yourself I'm not," Charlotte said. "Come. Are you going to drive us over the river, or aren't you?"

The man said nothing to that, but pointed with his whip to the door of the cab, which Charlotte took to mean consent. She lifted Mary in, and followed her, sinking on to the cushions with a sigh of relief. The cab proceeded slowly southwards. Once the driver stopped and, getting down from his seat, came to peer in at the window. He had a melancholy face, lined and grimy, and marked now with profound suspicion and disapproval.

"Get on," Charlotte ordered. "Why are you stopping?"

"Don't you go slitting nothing in there," he warned her, and clambered back into his seat.

They crossed the bridge and were crawling down a road bordered by gardens when two belated revellers, sprung apparently from one of the groves, ran out into the road and held up the cab. They were, Mary perceived, gentlemen, and looked as any of the guests at Hansyke Manor might look after dining with her father. They were very merry. One cried, "What have we here?" and opened the door of the cab. The driver sat unmoved on his box. He did not even look round to observe the fate of his passengers. His back expressed dejected resignation.

With the handsome merry face of the young man so close to her own, Mary abruptly lost her sense of him as a familiar object in her world. She remembered Miss Short's prediction. Her stoicism and her worldliness dropped from her in the same moment, and a frightened little girl of thirteen buried her face in Charlotte's dress and sobbed. Charlotte was superb. She said: "Well, gentlemen, are you sufficiently amused, to have frightened a child and insulted a lady? May we go on?"

The young man stepped back and flourished an arm. "Our mistake," he murmured. "The wrong bed again. Proceed, cabby. Proceed, Phaeton, your father's horses smoke upon the air."

"He's not wore out," the driver said. "He an't really smoking. He's a good horse."

He curled his whip lovingly round the animal's ear, and drove for another hundred yards before he pulled up, and getting down from the box, inquired just where Charlotte wished to be taken.

Charlotte did not know. To gain time, she began to accuse the man of cowardice in the recent encounter. He rolled a flaccid eye.

"Nothing to do with me," he said stolidly. "Strange females as drive about town in the early hours takes their lives in their hand. I an't going to get myself slit for no one. Where d'you want to go now? He's a good horse and he an't my dad's. He's mine. But he's been driven enough for one night. Where are you going?"

Charlotte confessed that she did not know, and the man looked at her with a return of all his old suspicions. "You can't stop here," he said. "This is a cab, not an inn. If you done it, you'd better give yourself up. I'm sorry for you. I dare say you been hasty."

Charlotte sagged against the back of the cab, and Mary realised that her mother was resourceless. She felt an access of confidence and courage. Stepping out of the cab and sticking her thumbs in the pockets of her coat in imitation of Mark Henry, she looked round. They were in Kennington Road. From either side, streets of smaller shabbier houses emptied themselves into the thoroughfare. Mary picked out one at random. "Drive slowly down Endymion Road," she ordered, "and stop at the first likely house for lodgings that you see."

The cab, lurching a short distance, stopped in front of a dingy little house, with a fly-blown card, inscribed BEDS, propped up in the window. There were signs of awakening life in the street. Mary descended and hammered on the door. There was a long wait. She hammered again, and the door was flung open with a suddenness that made Mary suppose the owner to have been lurking behind it, waiting for the hammering to begin again. The thinnest woman Mary had ever seen stood blinking in the dark entry of the house. She was so thin that her ribs and the whalebone of her bodice competed for notice. She was as melancholy as the cabman, and Mary had the fantastic idea that he had vanished and appeared again behind the door as his own sister. She glanced over her shoulder. He was still on his box, sunk in gloomy thought, and Charlotte was descending heavily from the cab.

Panic seized Mary, but she stood still. "You let rooms?" she asked.

The thin woman looked doubtful. "I don't know," she murmured.

"If you don't," Mary said severely, "you oughtn't to have that card in your window."

The thin woman glanced at it defensively. "It says BEDS," she pointed out.

"Beds must be in rooms," Mary argued. "Unless you keep them folded up in the attic, in which case I don't see what use they are."

Charlotte came and stood at Mary's side.

"We only want a bedroom," she murmured. "We can pay for it. We're quiet people, and my little girl is very tired."

The thin woman looked from Charlotte's ravaged face to the motionless driver, and back to Mary. The little girl smiled, and abruptly the thin woman stepped back.

"I've got one room," she said grudgingly. "You can come and look at it."

Charlotte followed her daughter into the dark little passage.

The room was at the end of the passage. It was small, indescribably frowsty, with a carpet the colour of dried blood. Charlotte shuddered, and looked shrinkingly at the brown expanse of bed.

"I don't like this, Mary," she breathed.

"Where can we go then?" Mary whispered back.

Charlotte said fretfully aloud: "I feel ill. I—I'm tired, Mary."

Mary turned to the woman. "How much is this room?" she asked, and when the woman told her she engaged it for a week. "We'll pay in advance," she promised, and taking Charlotte's bag from the hand that nervelessly relinquished it, went out to pay the cabby and rescue her bundle from the seat where Charlotte had abandoned it. She paid the man what he asked and then said boldly: "If you like to go to 26 Lincthorn Road and fetch a box we left there, I'll give you double." The man said he would fetch it when his horse had had a rest. He whipped up and drove away. Mary looked after his retreating back with a forlorn sense of having lost a friend. "Not," she said to herself, "that he was much good in a crisis, but I was getting used to him." The thought that she could feel regret at the departure of a gloomy and apathetic cab-driver brought home to her, more sharply than anything else, the desolation of this adventure. She hurried back into the house, and paying the thin woman a week's rent, shut the door of the bedroom on herself and Charlotte. She would have locked it, but she saw, with faint dismay, that it had neither lock nor bolt. She turned her attention to Charlotte, who was lying face downwards on the bed, abandoned to misery.

Charlotte lay there most of the day, exploring who shall say what by-ways of humiliation and despair, while Mary slept in a black shiny arm-chair, moving restlessly every time her face came into contact with a patch of uncovered hair. Towards evening, Charlotte woke her up. "I'm going out," she said. "I didn't want you to wake up and find me gone. You'll be all right here. I'll ask the woman to give you some food. Then you must go to bed and wait until I come."

Mary jumped up. "Where are you going?" she demanded. "I don't want to stay here alone. Take me with you."

Charlotte shook her head.

"I won't be late. At least"—a brief gleam came into her eye—"I don't think I shall. You must be a brave girl and stay here."

Left alone, Mary examined the room with a growing apprehension. She extracted a comb from the bundle and began to tidy her hair. There was a knock at the door. The comb clattered to the floor. The door opened and the thin woman's face appeared, attached to its edge.

"Supper's in the kitchen," she said, and withdrew.

The kitchen of 19 Endymion Road was a livelier place than Mary's bedroom. It was, to her first glance, overstocked with life. There was the thin woman, her name discovered to be Mrs Maggs, bent double over a frying-pan from which rose fumes of smoke and a smell of burnt fat, a small boy, so skinny and sad of face as to be patently her son, a man with reddish hair, and a man with warts. The last two presently took their departure: Mrs Maggs, Mary, and the little boy were left alone. They had barely started supper when the melancholy cabman brought Charlotte's box. Mary had to borrow the money to pay him from Mrs Maggs, who invited him to stop to supper. He accepted, with the first sign of alacrity Mary had ever seen in him, and joined the group round the table, where he displayed toothless and anticipatory jaws.

"They got her," he observed suddenly to Mary.

"Got what?" Mary asked.

"Her as did the slitting," he said. "The saucy piece."

Mrs Maggs looked up dreamily. "It's a pity they don't hang them open nowadays. It was an example like. I seen a hanging just before Henry there was born. They was selling the story of it in the street, and the murderer asked if he could have one to look over. He didn't seem satisfied with it, by his looks. Maybe they left something out or maybe he was just thinking of his end. Afterwards, we went to see a play they was giving, with dolls on wires. Like a Punch and Judy, but the dolls was nearly lifesize, and they acted the murder. It was a sight. You saw him come into the room and put his hands under the clothes. Some jump-up Janes laughed at that and my husband spoke very sharply to them, being not a man to put up with lightness. And then you saw him do her in, and the blood running over the floor. Out of a Bladder, they say. Very full it must have been. After that we went home and had a supper of stewed eels my husband bought off a stall near the hanging.

xcessively fond of stewed eels, my husband was. I've sometimes ought that's why Henry here turned out so thin.''

"Husband alive?" the cabman asked.

"Dead," said Mrs Maggs. "He was a sporting gentleman. He aught cold in the rain shuffling the cards for gentlemen to pick the Queen at Kempton. His feet soaked up the wet and it got into his tomach and he went off like a roast chestnut, breathing hot and izzling.''

"Oh," said Mary, "I thought that was your husband with the red air." She felt a delicacy about associating Mrs Maggs with warts.

"Brothers," Mrs Maggs said. "They have their own ways of pending the evening. How old are you, my dear?''

Mary told her. "Short for your age," was Mrs Maggs's comment.

"What d'you expect," said the cabman. "Rushing about the streets ll night.''

Mary felt that her dignity and her mother's dignity was assailed. She got up from the table and said politely: "Thank you for my supper. It tasted nicer than it looked. I'm afraid I must be going now. Good night, Mrs Maggs.''

"No offence meant," the cabman said earnestly. "Fair's fair and you an't one to bear malice. I had a sister once of the name of Mary. Kind she was, too kind, you might say. She done herself in by kindness and wanting every one to enjoy themselves. Leads to multiplication and gossip.''

"You'd better stay here," Mrs Maggs urged her. "Henry's going out for a walk, aren't you, Henry? There won't be anyone here but me.''

The cabman, taking the remark as a hint, rose to go. He shook Mary's hand with something as near fervour as his temperament permitted. "Everything forgotten and forgiven?" he asked urgently. Mary assured him that she would remember him kindly, but she felt less friendless now in the company of Mrs. Maggs and saw him depart without regret. The thin little boy made himself ready to go out and Mary looked wistfully at Mrs Maggs. Presently he asked her to come with him. She accepted joyfully, and they set off down Kennington Road, the thin little boy sniffing like Miss Flora, and with the air of a

person regretting a generous impulse. At the end of the road they
overtook the cabman, sitting in a silent fit on his box. He offered to
drive them anywhere in reason, and the thin boy said he wanted to go to
London Bridge. The cabman made no bones about that: he opened the
door, and the children climbed inside.

"Give my compliments to your mother," he admonished Henry, as
he was helping them out again. "I an't a marrying man, but if I was she
would have first pick. I never tasted better fish."

Standing on London Bridge Mary suffered the worst homesickness
she had known. The Pool was crowded with sailing ships, moored
almost stem to stern in two lines of two or three ships abreast. A channel
kept open in mid-river was alive wth paddle-steamers, and between the
sailing ships and the banks of the river skiffs and wherries splashed and
darted between barges that lay like shadows on the tainted water. Henry
gazed on the scene with glistening eyes and a cataract of sniffs.

"How you can do that, I don't know," Mary observed. "The smell
is awful."

In the warm evening air, the river, being little better than an open
sewer, gave off a symphony of smells.

"I'm going to be a shipmaker," Henry said obliviously.

"I don't suppose," Mary murmured, "that you ever heard of
cylinders and pressure in your life."

Farther down the river and below the bridge scattered lights came
out, and in the Pool itself the water broke them into a myriad pieces
before flinging them back against the flanks of the ships. As far as
Mary's eye could see, masts pierced the yellow dusk, as if the whole
world had poured its ships into the Thames, a lavish mother shaking
gifts and more gifts into a lap already full. Mary clasped her hands and
looked kindly at Henry. He was a vulgar little boy, but linked with her
in a community of desire. For some reason, she did not feel inclined to
tell him so. They made their way home through a black and odorous
labyrinth. It was nearly midnight when they reached Endymion Road,
and Mary's mother was not there. Mrs Maggs's brothers were at
home, and Mrs Maggs gave Mary a mug of ale, which she found
slightly acrid but comforting. The room was warm and the face of the
red-haired man changed places with that of his warty brother until Mary

supposed they were dolls in a puppet-show. After that she was not surprised at the abrupt appearance of a minute creature called Sylvia Maud, in a soiled ballet skirt, with the body of a child of eight and a mouth full of quips and fancies at which Mary laughed uproariously, slapping her thighs like Mark Henry. Sylvia Maud danced. Her shoulders were white china eggs: she stood on the toes of one foot, with the other leg stretched straight out from her body: she bent leg and head until the back of one met the back of the other. She began to turn so quickly that she became an incandescent globe, spinning on a quivering jet of light. The lamplit room was a background against which, for a fraction of time, essential grace postured and poised. After that Mary gave an imitation of Miss Flora and another of her father and the checked legs. These were received with generous applause, and the red-haired man invited Mary to sit on his knee. She was profoundly offended and her voice struck chill to his expansive heart: he sat down and looked apologetically into an empty glass. He did not know what he had done that called for apology but he felt uncomfortable.

After thus quelling Mrs Maggs's brother, Mary withdrew to her room and began to long for Charlotte to come home. When Charlotte did come she had fallen asleep. Rousing as her mother moved about the room, she sat up. Charlotte, dishevelled and colourless, made no comment when Mary, who trusted Mrs Maggs but not Mrs Maggs's brother, slipped out of bed and dragged the box across the door. Charlotte blew out the candle and got into bed. Coming close to her, Mary hugged her cold inert body, and fell asleep before Charlotte had given a sign that she felt the little girl's anxious caresses. . . .

4

The next day began a fevered week. Charlotte took Mary all over London. They visited gardens, churchyards, theatres, shops, statues, churches, canals, railway stations, arcades and fortune-tellers. They did not return to Endymion Road before midnight. Mary had taken charge of the envelope full of notes, but Charlotte's demands on it were so frequent, for hats, gowns, trinkets and sibyls, that it shrank with alarming rapidity.

Often Charlotte forgot meal-times, and Mary was hungry as well as tired. She became so tired that she cried, and having started to cry could not stop. She cried in shops, in omnibuses and as they walked through the streets. Charlotte remonstrated with her, and Mary made efforts to control the tears that poured from her eyes and splashed on the white collar of her jacket. She was so engaged one afternoon in the Green Park, when a familiar voice spoke in her ear and she looked up, her tears suddenly arrested, into a face she knew as well as her father's.

It was Archie Roxby's face, and more like a hake than his kindly nature warranted. He had been Richard Hansyke's friend at Oxford, and remained his friend, in spite of his disapproval of Hansyke as an inveterate rake. His land touched Hansyke's and was richer, of far greater extent, and more neglected, since there were five Roxby brothers, and all but the youngest of them lived on some part of it, and all detested agriculture. They claimed Hanoverian descent. Possibly they flattered themselves grossly, but Archie Roxby's face was actually that of an attenuated and degutted George I. He stooped over Charlotte's hand and asked how he could serve her. Charlotte poured out a Stygian flood of trouble, which he breasted gravely, glancing aside where, under the drooping brim of Mary's hat, he could see a firm white chin and a trembling mouth. He was cautious and polite. He advised Charlotte to go back to Danesacre at once, offering to provide money for the journey.

"I go north," he said, "myself. To-morrow, and I should be happy to accompany you."

Charlotte's voice shook. She wore an air of defeat. "I have written to my brother, Mark Henry Garton, for money. If it does not come to-morrow, we will join you."

He left her, and Mary began a fervent silent prayer that Mark Henry would behave according to his nature. He did. The morning brought nothing, and Mary packed her own and Charlotte's clothes with a joy she tried to conceal.

For Charlotte this return was a sort of death. On the journey north her spirits sank while Mary's mounted higher. As the train drew between the hills, crossing and re-crossing the brown-flashing Danesbeck, the light died behind them like the slow shutting of a door. Even so, thought Charlotte, light and youth had withdrawn from her life, and the ng journey she had made, marked by so many stages, of which one nd a strange one was a weaver's cottage, had entered on its last stretch.

At Danesacre, in Harbour Street, outside the walls of Mark Henry's arden, Richard Hansyke had a carriage ready, with Miss Flora already iside. He took Mary from Charlotte's arms, that clung to the little girl s if she had never before known what it was to lose her, and carried er, weeping and calling for her mother, to Hansyke Manor, without etting her set foot in her uncle's house, and without speaking to her xcept to tell her to obey Miss Flora and keep out of his way as much as ossible.

"You're not a little girl now," he said. "You're a young lady." He rowned, not unkindly, at the dejected girl. "You'll be fourteen in two days. You need different clothes. My good woman, get the girl decently clad, and have her hair dressed. A savage. . . ." He paused, and spoke reassuringly. "You'll forget your unfortunate adventure, Mary. You don't want to tell me anything about it? No?" He sighed with relief. "I was afraid you might want to confess you'd been ruined or found your soul. Either would be tedious. It isn't that I'm not temperately fond of you, Mary. I notice a good many signs of parental self-indulgence nowadays. I myself went to Eton in petticoats. I hardly knew my parents and they certainly did not trouble me with affection. I believe that's the right method and ought to be extended to daughters. England will go to the devil if this softness spreads. . . ."

5

London remained with Mary as the memory of a sprawling confusion that was at first totally unrelated to the life of decent people. Endymion Road was a nightmare. She tried to forget it, but it returned to her again and again until the windy spaces of Roxborough moor were filled with a fermenting life that mocked her loneliness. Mary had changed. She fretted for her mother, but Charlotte could not have satisfied her daughter's new impatience. The vision of the Pool, as she had seen it, cradling the trade of the world, worked like a fever on her brain. Her childish wish to build ships became something real, something almost grim, beating on her mind like a hammer, like the carpenters' hammers that sent a shiver and a murmur through the whole still body of the ship.

A shiver and a murmur ran through Mary's body when she thought of the Pool.

She was changing. She was growing up. In a vague fashion, she knew it and resented it. Her world, her simple easily-compassed world, had been invaded by Mrs Maggs, by Mrs Maggs's brother and the afflicted Henry, by Endymion Road, by the monstrous heaving swarming life of London. Living would never be a simple and easy process again. She made spasmodic fierce attempts to pretend that it was.

One morning, obeying an impulse compounded of longing for Charlotte, dislike of growing up and fear of the future, Mary took off her new frock, and dragged the clothes she had worn in London from the camphor chest where Miss Flora had hidden them. Then, making an asthmatic noise that she fondly thought was whistling, she set off for the moor. For a time she followed a narrow stony road, cooled by the trickle of a stream, and murmurous with bees. On either side the ditches frothed with meadow-sweet. She was wearing a flounced skirt that reached just below her knees, white stockings and a short jacket with a flat boyish collar. The soft skin of her cheeks was sun-warmed and lustrous with youth, and her lips were stained purple from the brambles she picked as she walked and ate off the palm of her hand. A thick plait of hair fell over her shoulder. She tossed her head to jerk it back, and the gesture was for the solitary watcher an act of grace. He had been lying on the short turf at the side of the road, trying to memorise the beauty of the place, the feel of the sun between his shoulder-blades and the smell of the moor. It was all so lovely, to a boy of sixteen, that he was aware of it as of an almost painful pressure on his mind, and he could have cried because the world was exquisite, and he alone. He longed, the vague tumultuous longing of youth, for some one with whom to share himself. The girl walking up the steep road walked straight into the heart of that longing.

Mary saw him five minutes later than he had seen her, and halted to look at him, her hand full of the ripe berries, half-way to her mouth. She saw a boy in shabby summer clothes, grey eyes under arched brows, grave shapely face, short lips parted in a faint smile. Shy, struck so with new shyness that she lost the power of motion, she looked at him in silence, while the miracle of transubstantiation was completed, from the raising of the Host to the blessing of the worshippers, and the boy-girl, short for her fourteen years, not even dressed as befitted them, became young Mary Hansyke looking at her first lover.

She murmured some commonplace about the morning and glanced at the dripping purple fruit in the palm of her hand. A thick drop oozed between her fingers. She said: "Oh, bother," and let the crushed berries fall to the ground. The boy would have liked to kiss the stained palm. He would have liked to say: "You're lovely, I love you." Instead of that, he told her his name, Gerry Hardman, that he was going up to Oxford next year, that he was walking for amusement and had come to Roxborough by a most fortunate accident.

"Fortunate because I met you," he said. Mary accepted this declaration with a crow of mirth, which made him blush.

"Because you never saw me until this moment," she explained, pleading with him to see that it was comic. "Forgive me." The curves of her mouth drew him to irresistible imitation, and they both laughed. After that, they strolled up the road, filled with a tranquil happiness, and emerging on the open moor, sat down there, with backs turned to Roxborough. Mary took off her wide drooping hat to fan her cheeks. She told him about Danesacre and Charlotte and Miss Flora, and discovered that she had lived her life only in order to tell him about it. He frowned over the story of Mrs Maggs's brother and she stopped on a pang of dismay.

"You don't like that?" she asked him, anxiously, waiting for him to speak and dreading what he would say.

He was silent for a moment, with dark brows drawn together in sensitive displeasure. Then, turning his head, he smiled at her very sweetly.

"Everything you do is right," he said. "Promise always to tell me about it."

Mary promised with relief, and repeated Mrs Maggs's story of the hanging. Gerry shouted with mirth, nursing his head in his hands. "You dear," he said. "You dear sweet girl. To know how comic that is. Weren't you frightened? Weren't you frightened in that dreadful bedroom?"

"I was afraid of Mrs Maggs's brother. Not much. Just a little." She recalled the childish fear of another girl with wonder.

"Poor baby," he said, and touched her hand. The touch sent a delicious unexpected shudder through him, and through her. Mary's bramble-stained mouth, warm, and ripened in an hour of sun, quivered between laughter and constraint. Gerry trembled and swung towards her, but not to touch her again, only to know that she trembled too and to savour exquisite joy in his knowledge. Not in his life again would he know so bright a joy, unmixed with any of the fears, greeds and remembered hurts that mar all moments except this one of first enchantment. It was for him one of those moments of exaltation when body and mind know a delight born of neither, pure delight, the merging of the senses in an emotion transcending sense. The balance of his soul was suspended between grief and ecstasy: a word would plunge him into either.

"I must go," Mary said, suddenly afraid of interruption.

"Oh, don't go. Suppose I lose you, after finding you like this."

"I must. I must." She stood up and unconsciously they drew closer. Neither of them realised that they had been making love to each other with the headlong inconsequent quality of a dream, but both were dismayed at the prospect of parting.

"Listen," Gerry murmured, "I must be in Danesacre to-day to meet my father. We stay the night there. I'll come back to-night."

"You can't," Mary faltered. "It's nearly twenty miles as the crow flies."

"I'll ride. I'll be here as soon after eleven as I can. You'll see me? Say you will."

Mary's eyes met his with steadfast candour. "I'll come to the lane below the house. Look, I'll show you. That is our house. Below it, where the hill road turns off to the village, the lane begins. There's a gate. I'll come."

"Then, good-bye."

"Good-bye."

"Good-bye. Dear."

Mary turned to speed straight across the moor. Her heart pulsed to a word. Her tongue trembled to repeat it. The startled moor-hens, rising from the reeds as she took her wild flight along the edge of the stream, said, "Dear. Dear. Dear." The solitary poplar dropped it in her ear as she fled past it over the lawn, and pausing in the cool stone-flagged hall only long enough to make sure of Miss Flora's distant presence in the house, ran up the stairs and shut the door of her room on everything but a word. She pressed her face against the sheets of her bed. The quiet room sheltered the new-born quivering creature until she was composed again, and could go downstairs to wait for night. . . .

Night came, after a day of eternity, but Gerry did not come. She waited for him until the first signs of dawn sent her back to the house, fluttering listlessly through the heavy grass. For a day or two she expected him, but he did not come, and after that she tried not to think of him. Weeks passed, and she learned to take a particular path to the moor without an alarming leap of the heart. She wore her new clothes and tried sometimes to behave like a young lady, and more often than not succeeded only in behaving like a boy in petticoats. She asked for Wagener to come and give her help with her studies, and Wagener came, but they did not study very seriously. They went out into moor or meadow with a book, and Mary sat on it while the young Dutchman talked. He talked more than she did, for she had nothing to talk about but herself and she was never, after that meeting on the moor, very communicative about herself.

Whether Wagener had a sentimental feeling for Mary Hansyke, it would be difficult to say, but he returned her frank liking in full measure, talking to her as he might to a young brother. She had a bluff good nature that was an echo of Mark Henry's and invited candour. She could laugh at herself, and Wagener found her intelligent. He was alarmed to find her also obstinate, and once at least he found her stupid and hard, when the occasion was that poor Miss Flora, whose hoard of knowledge her pupil had long since ransacked and would not now pretend to respect. Miss Flora tried threats, at which Mary laughed, and tears, from which she walked away. She knew that the trembling creature would not complain to Richard Hansyke, lest he should see merely her incompetence, and turn her off, to find an eighth pupil, and a ninth and a tenth in a series that stretched away into the bleak wastes of Miss Flora's future, to that dreadful day when she would be too old to impart to little girls the story of the Scriptures and the habits of the

silkworm and would creep into some hole to wait obscurely for her
soul's ultimate holiday. She had been so long with the Hansyke family
that she had almost come to believe that she belonged to it and to
encourage a little warm feeling of pleasure in belonging to something.
Mary's rebellion finished that. Miss Flora went about with scarified
eyelids and a sniff that threatened to become continuous, like the
trembling of her hand and the tear that formed in one eye, and fell, and
formed again. She even gave up speaking to Mary about her
deportment, and in her triumph Mary swaggered about the house more
in the manner of a young blood than a young lady. She took a malicious
pleasure in humiliating the poor woman by rough speech and boisterous
laughter in her hearing.

"Might as well go," she replied to Wagener's protests. "She's no
use." Wagener regarded her comically and she became so resentful of
his tolerations that he bowed to the storm and abandoned Miss Flora. "I
don't like pitying people," said Mary. "If I'm as useless as Miss Flora
I'll not ask for pity." Then she considered the matter calmly and told
Wagener that she had been wrong. "I'll keep her for the rest of my life.
I've been making a fool of myself, Wagener. Why did you not tell me
sooner?"

"What I like about you," the tutor said meditatively, "is that you'll
learn. Are you never afraid of failing to do what you want to do,
Mary?"

"No."

He talked to her about love, lying on his back with his flute sticking
out through a hole in his pocket.

"I would fall in love with you myself if I were not a tutor and you
Mary Hansyke. If I were not so confoundedly lazy, I mean. Your hair,
now that you've taken to brushing it, is a trap for fools. You are a little
too short, but unless you grow fat that will not matter. Your eyes would
make a plain woman charming. In your face, with its delicious air of
surprise, they'll drown men. Allow me to instruct you. You won't heed
it, but you like listening to talk about yourself. Love is an affection. Of
the senses, if you are lucky, since they cure themselves. Of the soul, if
you are unlucky. There is no cure for that and you go marked to your
grave. There is also the love which is an affection of the heart, or

whatever organ may be supposed the spring of tenderness. This too, once contracted, is likely to trouble you for life."

"I am going to build ships," Mary said.

"Paper boats, Mary."

"Mark Henry Garton promised me I should."

Wagener rolled over on the grass, waving his flute. "My poor dear," he murmured, "and I thought you had already learned something. Promised you! You have everything to discover. I shall now play you a little air I composed, illustrating the vanity of human wishes. . . ."

A few days after her fifteenth birthday, Mary set off to ride to Danesacre. She told herself that she wanted to see her mother, and discuss her future with Mark Henry. She was in reality driven by one of the restless impulses that had lately grown more frequent. The lazy life she led at Hansyke Manor had become intolerable. She had been endowed with an extra allowance of vital spirits and they raged in her these days like seven devils. She got up at four o'clock and rode down the Danesacre road through a river of mist. She rode astride in a short skirt, boots and thick stockings. She could not see the mare's legs or her own feet. Airy hob-goblins of mist clung to the trees and floated off down the road in front of her. Invisible peewits wailed in a milky twilight.

The wind on the high moor was cold and when Mary came upon a fire lit in a small hollow she got down off her horse and approached it. One of the figures crouching over the blaze turned round.

"Sylvia Maud," cried Mary. She hobbled her horse to a furze bush and descended into the hollow. From this point she could see the side of a caravan looming through the mist.

"My, if it isn't the Queen," said Sylvia Maud. She presented Mary to her companions. "The Queen, Queenie if you like. Mr Bob Smykes. Bertha, his old woman. Fearful cough Bertha has. Once or twice last night I thought I'd gone to bed with one of the fierce old sheep of this neighbourhood. Albert Smykes, arlequin and odd man. Hurry up with that frying-pan, Albert. Could you do with a hot potato, Queen?"

The mist exuded a lean youth with grotesquely developed thighs into the circle of the fire. He was certainly very odd. Mary averted her eyes from him and accepted a hot potato thankfully.

She asked after Mrs Maggs.

"She married the cabman, and it broke up the home. Both her brothers were taken off the same week. The old army game, my love. Science, not art. Turned the ace once too often. Maggs asked me to stay but I couldn't stand the widow's dream of love. Besides, he wasn't exactly amusing, was he? So little Sylvia Maud took to the road again."

Mary looked astonished. "He said he wasn't a marrying man."

"He ain't," Sylvia Maud said darkly. "She'll rue it. What are you doing here, Queen? Go on, you don't live here. Nothing lives here but parsons and devils. Last place we stopped at they put Albert and me in the pound, him for his tights and me for a joke I made. Both was a bit far gone, but not past decency." Sylvia Maud shivered and laughed and her teeth chattered lamentably.

Mr Bob Smykes cleared his throat. "We're outlaws," he said pleasantly. "No social order is complete without its outlaws. We supply the eternal need of society for something to persecute. We are the goats, the crucified."

Sylvia Maud made a joke that covered Mary with blushes. To conceal them, she stood up and said she must be getting on her way. The dancer said good-bye and begged her to drop in again later in the week if she happened to be passing.

"But where are you going?" Mary asked.

"The cruel three," began Mr Bob Smykes, when his wife was taken with a fit of coughing, at the climax of which Sylvia Maud explained that their horse had fallen the day before and breaking his collar-bone and two legs, had been shot. "We got to earn a sovereign and buy some farmer's worst nag before we can move on. And from what I seen of this countryside," she concluded, "I'd sooner try to buy a drink in hell than a horse off one of these——"

"I'll give you mine," Mary said hastily. "She's strong. She's not really a riding horse. Her mother's still ploughing. She'll do everything you're likely to want."

Sylvia Maud eyed her curiously. "You must be rich," she said.
"What were you at in Endymion Road? And who is likely to believe
you gave us your horse?"

Mary blushed for her stupidity. "That's right," she murmured.
"I'm sorry. I'll give you a letter about it. Have you a sheet of paper?"

Sylvia Maud darted at Mr Bob Smykes and began beating him about
the body with her minute hands. He remonstrated. "Paper," she said
feverishly. "Give me a piece of paper. I've found a fool. What have
you got in your pockets? I can feel everything but paper."

"You can't feel a shirt," he observed pleasantly. "Here you are."

Mary began to write. Struck by a sudden thought, she altered her first
intention and wrote out a receipt for the sale of her horse for ten pounds.
"That sounds better," she said, handing it to Sylvia Maud. "My, you
are smart," the little creature agreed. Mr Bob Smykes delivered
himself of an eloquent speech which made Mary very uncomfortable
until she realised that she represented in his eyes a large and
appreciative audience. Albert accentuated the peculiar conformation of
his body by a pantomime of delight that embarrassed her beyond
words, and only Bertha, speaking for the first time, asked what the
young lady was going to do without her horse. An expression of alarm
and dismay crossed Sylvia Maud's face. Mary hastened to reassure her.

"I shall be all right," she said. "I'm halfway on my journey. I can
walk the rest of the way." An unexpected thrill of pleasure ran through
her at the thought that she would be walking over the same road as
Gerry Hardman. She disregarded it instantly and hurried away, not
even stopping to say good-bye to the mare. A hundred yards down the
road she looked back. The mist had swallowed up horse, caravan and
hollow. Mary strode on.

She had covered about three miles and was walking through the
fields of a dale that bisected the moor, when she began to feel hungry.
There was an inn not far off along the road and she decided to go there
and ask for breakfast. Feeling for her purse in the pocket of her coat, she
found it gone, the whole pocket cut clean away. At the same moment
she recalled the glint of a knife seen in Sylvia Maud's hand. A hot wave
of indignation swallowed up her first dismay. She swung round to go

back and then halted, irresolute. "I must think this out," she said
aloud. She sat down on the wet grass and rested her elbows on her knee.
"It's no use going back," she thought. "They'll be far enough now.
With my horse. The ungrateful wretches. Mary Hansyke, you're a fool.
You've been feeling so pleased with yourself for playing the great lady
and you've been tricked and robbed and laughed at. Serve you right.
You didn't give them your horse out of kindness but just to show off.
They treated you exactly as you deserved to be treated. Well, I hope
they don't show the purse in Roxborough. It would be recognised and
they'd get into pretty serious trouble. I'd warn you if I could, Sylvia
Maud, but after all, you are a thief, and you'll have to take your
chance." Getting up from her chilly seat, Mary trudged on, with a grim
expression of her soft mouth, and a stomach so empty that she thought
she felt it sag.

Another mile and she was on the high moor again. The mist had
cleared and the hot sun sucked up a pungent scent from wet ling and
heather. Mary was very warm now and growing weary. An empty farm
cart overtook her and she hailed it. The driver's face puckered when he
spoke into a saddened multitude of wrinkles like a tragic mask, and
from his mouth issued a thin melancholy note, the sound of a bird
crying in the reeds. He might have been the first Tragedian in his rude
cart-booth. He was going into Danesacre, and once convinced that
Mary was Mark Henry Garton's niece, he agreed to drive her to the
Yard. Mary sank thankfully on to the floor of the cart. It was springless
and the jolts rattled her like a sack. After a while the man offered her his
coat to lie on. Mary demurred at taking it.

"You maun do as you like," the tragedy said indifferently. "I'm all
of a muck o' sweat."

Mary took it and lay a little softer. The man said nothing more until
they were nearly in Danesacre. Then he observed: "You'll be Charlotte
Hansyke's lass?"

Mary admitted it. "She's off to London again," the man wailed.
Mary restrained a cry with a violent effort. Humiliated by the thought
that the man might have noticed the effect of his words, she grunted and
sat up with a yawn. She would not show any interest or ask a question,
and they made their slow progress to Garton's Yard in silence, Mary

avoiding the significant glances of the passers-by. Her cheeks were burning and she could hardly stand when she climbed out of the cart. She felt bruised from head to foot.

Meeting John Mempes in the garden, on his way from house to yard, she asked him peremptorily to pay the man. "Where is my uncle?"

"Sleeping his dinner off," Mempes said. "What are you doing here, Mary?"

She brushed past him without answering and, bursting in on Mark Henry Garton where he lay asleep with a red and yellow bandana handkerchief over his face, woke him without ceremony.

"Where is my mother?"

Mark Henry glared at the heated girl. He was furious at being wakened, and cursed her without repetitions for five minutes. Mary waited until he was out of breath, and repeated her question.

"Gone back to the straw," Mark Henry said. "I wish she'd taken you with her, you shameless young piece. I've a good mind to take a rope's end to you."

"You can't," Mary said sweetly. "I'm a young lady now."

"You don't look it," her uncle commented. "Get out of my sight before I examine you to make sure. Be off, be off!"

He covered his face with his bandana and his indignation blew it off again.

Mary withdrew in haste and spent the afternoon in the Yard with John Mempes. He told her that Charlotte had gone back to London a week earlier after a violent quarrel with her brother.

"Couldn't you have kept her?" Mary asked.

Mempes looked at her sharply. Mary was kicking at a stone and he saw only her averted cheek. "I did my best," he said smoothly. "My attractions—palled."

"You mean that you did not take the trouble to exert them," the girl said bluntly. "Poor mamma. I hope she has gone back to Miss Short. She couldn't possibly manage Endymion Road by herself." Even to John Mempes she would not show her grief at Charlotte's going.

They discussed the Yard, and the new iron steamer now building. Mary told the manager that she had come to ask Mark Henry Garton to

take her on and train her in his office. Mempes showed no surprise. He
was as polite as always and a little formal. Mary noticed the formality
and set herself to get round it. She succeeded so far that Mempes
confided to her his thoughts of leaving Garton's Yard for a bigger firm
on the Clyde. Mary was alarmed.

"Oh, don't leave us," she begged.

"Would you miss me?" Mempes asked gloomily. "I can't imagine
why any one should. I seem to myself to be the world's worst failure. I
waste my wit on louts who would prefer a kick up the backside. I can
never make up my mind just what to drink with black coffee: I'm
inclined to stick to a sweet *Château,* but I'm conscious it's not the right
thing. I fall in love in order to fall out again. Last week a woman with
magenta hair and white boots called here and had herself announced as
my wife."

"Was she?" Mary interrupted, a little shocked.

"I think I must have seen her before," Mempes said vaguely. "But
she wasn't my wife. I never had a wife. It's a long ceremony and I'm
too easily distracted. Mary, if you take my advice you'll settle yourself
in life as soon as possible. Leave it too long, and you'll lose the knack.
You've probably had too many adventures already to be as stupid as
you ought to be. As for me, I'm thirty-two and when I left Oxford I
thought I was going to raise the level of humanity by building ships. I
raise nothing but your uncle's profits and upon my soul I am an ass to do
it. You haven't any rose-leaves about you, have you, Mary? . . . ."

Mark Henry Garton had recovered his temper before evening and
Mary spoke to him confidently about joining the firm.

"What's this, what's this!" he exclaimed. "You're not going to join
the firm. Girls can't build ships. What d'I tell you about your—well,
never mind, you're a young lady now. You're not a little girl any
longer. Don't be silly, don't be silly."

Mary's house of life came down about her ears. She stared at Mark
Henry. "You promised," she said breathlessly.

Mark Henry disposed of all his promises, past, present and to come,
in one comprehensive ordinance. Mary recognised the uselessness of
argument. She swallowed down a flood of speech, and slipped off into
the silent yard. There, sitting on the grassy ledge where she had often

stayed to watch the ships leaving harbour, she abandoned herself to a desolate fit of weeping. That over, she tried to reconstruct her future. "You can't go on living at Hansyke Manor," she told herself. She played with the idea of finding Sylvia Maud and throwing in her lot with the dancer and her friends, but the memory of Albert's grotesque figure decided her against it—that and a shamefaced reluctance to appear as beggar among people on whom she had lavished riches. "You're fairly caught, my girl. You're defeated. No, bless me if you are. There's a way out of this, if you can only think of it. At least you've learned not to rely on promises you can't enforce."

With a last yearning glance at the lights on the upper harbour she returned to the house and to bed. In the morning she waited tranquilly for Richard Hansyke's arrival. He came about noon and took her back to Roxborough the same day.

6

A week later he offered her Archie Roxby as a husband. Mary greeted the suggestion with a gurgle of laughter, thinking of Archie Roxby's hake-like face and solemn gait.

"You needn't marry him if you don't want to," her father said patiently. "But I'd advise you to think before you refuse him. Your mother—or shall we say I by marrying her?—has rather spoiled your chances among our pious neighbours. Piety has become the fashion since I was young. Your escapades haven't helped you. You're going to be good-looking too, which makes things worse, since I can't afford to show you. Archie Roxby is of your own class, not your mother's. He has a certain amount of money, though God knows how much. His own bailiff doesn't. He's my age, and brandy is his only vice. He'll die of it before you're old enough to be irked by him. Think it over, Mary."

The conversation took place in Mary's bedroom, and she sat silent for a long time. Glancing round her room, she wondered whether it remembered a word once repeated to it so many times that its walls might retain some faint echo. The involuntary image made her wince. She spoke hurriedly.

"What shall I do if I stay here?"

Richard Hansyke shrugged his shoulders. "Who knows? Marry elsewhere. Grow into an old maid and bring up thirty cats, like your Aunt Sophy, on the strictest principles of morality. Take to religion. I don't know. What could you do, Mary?"

Mary sat with a still face, thinking over her chances of escape. They seemed poor. "What exactly is marriage:" she asked next.

Her father looked at her curiously. "Ask Miss Flora. I can't tell you. Marriage is the most intimate of all relationships."

"Should I like being intimate with Archie Roxby?"

"I don't suppose so. But do you know any one with whom you would?"

"No," Mary said loudly.

"Very well. And since all intimacy, however pleasurable at first, in the end becomes wearisome, you might as well start with disillusionment. It will save you a later shock."

A powerful instinct assured her that he was wrong. She knew, in her own active pulsing young body, that there was an answer to Richard Hansyke but she did not know what it was. Again, a memory alarmed her by its power to stab. She thought: "This won't do. You're not going to miss a chance by being faint-hearted. You must get out."

"I'll take him," she said.

Richard Hansyke complimented her dryly and left her to her thoughts.

Archie Roxby paid his respects the following day. Mary stifled an impulse to laughter that seized her when she saw him coming, his long body cased in black and his face composed to an expression of ardour. It vanished as he straightened himself after bending over her hand. He smothered a groan. To Mary's polite inquiry he answered: "My kidneys are out of order. I have a pain in my back."

"I am sorry," Mary said.

Archie sat down carefully. "I suffer a good deal," he said complacently. "I have an excess of bile which affects the liver and that in turn puts a strain on the kidneys. My stomach is slightly inflamed too, and I have a crackling of the joints. I sometimes wake up at night thinking I hear shots, but it is only my own knees. You will soon grow used to it. My back is, however, very painful. If you will excuse me I will go home and my sister-in-law will iron it. I ought not to be out at all, but I naturally wished to see you and express my satisfaction in your goodness."

"Oh, don't go yet," Mary cried. "I haven't asked you any of my questions."

Archie sat down again with reluctant courtesy.

"In the first place," Mary said, "are your eldest brother and his wife going to go on living with you when I marry you?"

Archie looked surprised. "Certainly," he said. "Unless you feel strongly that they should not. I am sure you would find my sister-in-law a true friend and adviser. She prefers moral worth and intelligence to worldly considerations in the connections she forms. This is a rare opportunity for you."

"Oh, very well," Mary said. "I dare say she will be useful, if your back needs ironing very often."

"But my wife will naturally do that," Archie protested. "And now if you will forgive me——"

Mary was a little daunted by her future responsibilities, but she summoned up spirit to ask if she would be allowed opportunity to carry on her studies. The idea had filled her mind lately that she might become a great scholar instead of a ship builder. To be sure, she had little inclination for study of an abstract sort, but she thought she might acquire it. She proposed to Archie Roxby that Wagener should live with them too.

"Certainly," said Archie. "Is he any good with monkeys?"

"I don't think so," Mary answered, surprised in her turn.

"A pity. My sister-in-law has six, and they are often ailing. I believe she coddles them too much. But it's impossible to argue with her. She can't keep to one subject long enough. I must go now. Forgive an inadequate bow. My kidneys. I am very sensible of your goodness. I firmly believe you to be one of the very best of women and eminently deserving of the highest respect and affection. Good-bye."

He took his leave, with a succession of loud cracks, and Mary rushed to fling herself into Wagener's arms, in a paroxysm of mirth, of which, remembering Archie's concluding phrase, she was a little ashamed. Wagener scolded her. "You are nothing but a great boy," he said. "And you're to be married in a month."

Mary looked at him soberly, and was quieter at once.

7

Her marriage night filled in the gaps in her father's explanation and almost stunned her with shame and mortification. Archie Roxby proved himself a clumsy and inconsiderate lover, and Mary lay awake the whole night, bruised in mind and wretched in body. Daylight had slipped like an ailing ghost into the shuttered room before she was calm enough to sleep. "You certainly are not a little girl now," she said fiercely. "You're fifteen years old, and a woman of experience. You haven't got much left to learn. You're a little dazed, I think. Come now, Mary Roxby isn't going to cry because she knows more of life and men than Mary Hansyke did. At any rate you know the worst, and you must just stiffen your back and get what you can out of this marriage you've let yourself in for. I wish I could run away." She crept out of bed and opened first a shutter and then a window. The clean cool air comforted her burning head, and after a while she fell asleep, her cheek pressed against the oak window seat.

She discovered later that she had not known the worst, for on the next night Archie drank himself into semi-consciousness to get rid of an inexplicable sense of shame. Mary was too frightened by his appearance when he entered her room to realise that his state was her best protection. She got away from him as soon as she could, leaving him sound asleep, and ran to Wagener's room. The tutor was sitting on the edge of his bed, examining the stops of his flute. He held the distracted girl in his arms while she poured out her story, shivering with cold and terror, and sobbing in a very desolate fashion. When she had talked herself silent, he wrapped her up in his quilt and stood over her grimly.

"This won't do, Mary," he said. "You can do better than this. What do you want me to do for you? Run away with you? A nice pair we should make, shouldn't we? Do you see yourself living in an attic in Endymion Road with the poor tutor? You don't. You shouldn't have come to me. There are some things no one can protect you from, or help you through. About those things you mustn't talk. Do you understand? You must never never give yourself away like this to any one again. It's not—dignified, and it weakens you. Do you see? Drink this and get back to your room."

He gave her a drink of brandy and held the door open for her to go. She paused in the doorway to kiss him on his mouth. His lips were cold and did not return the pressure of hers.

"You are my friend, aren't you?" she asked piteously.

"Till death, Mary."

On her way back to her room she met one of her sister-in-law's monkeys. The poor beast was very cold and ran beside her with chattering teeth to the door of her bedroom. She buttoned it into one of her jackets and shut it out. It scratched on the panels of the door and whimpered at the keyhole. "Not like a lost soul," Mary thought, "because it hasn't one. Perhaps it's crying for one." She worried about it until she fell asleep. When she woke up the room was full of sunshine, and her spirits revived because she was so young that they could not remain in the depths for long. She recalled Wagener's words and thought: "I've learned another lesson. Apparently there's always something left to learn."

Archie Roxby was full of compunction. Taking himself in hand he gave up the rôle of husband altogether, and treating Mary as if she were an undisciplined daughter, set himself to teach her what he considered a more correct attitude to life. Grateful for kindness, she tried to compose her speech and gestures to his ideal of breeding and succeeded so far that she developed an impulsive grace of movement.

She was too young not to take her revenge by laughing at him. She mimicked him to Wagener with a broad humour that made him laugh until they fell into each other's arms in uncontrollable mirth.

A month after their marriage Archie took her to London, and she discovered another side of the odd creature she had married.

- William Palmer was being tried at the Old Bailey for poisoning. Archie attended the trial from the first day, leaving Mary alone in their hotel, and when he came back at night he described the day's proceedings with the gestures of an inspired puppet. "I don't want you to miss it all," he said generously. He reclined on their bed and imitated the victim snapping at a spoonful of toast and water to wash down the pills. He snapped, jerking his head and neck forward like a chicken, at the glass that held a "certain dark liquid." Dark liquid, Mary. Mark that." After that, he sat up suddenly, screaming "Murder, murder!" and beat the bed with his hands, his eyes starting out of his head. On the second day, the surgeon said that the body of the murdered man was twisted back like a bow, and Archie writhed on the bed in the contortions of death. On the third day he came home full of the post-mortem and the opening of the stomach by a medical student with much horse-play and suspicious circumstance. The fourth day produced the analogous case of Mrs Serjeantson Smith who died of strychnia, screaming, with her feet turned inwards. This evoked a dumb show from Archie that made Mary scream herself, with fright, but Archie was too preoccupied to feel pity for her. Later he paused in his impersonation of a man dangling from a noose. Mary had fainted. He picked her up and laid her on the bed. When she came round, he was looking at her so reproachfully that she was moved to apologise for herself.

"Never mind, never mind," he said petulantly, "You've spoiled the whole thing. No, I couldn't finish it now. I've lost the spirit." He sat down dejectedly to file his nails, a practice to which he devoted much time, sometimes filing Mary's for her, or operating on the paws of his sister-in-law's monkeys.

At the end of another month Mary wanted to go back to Roxborough. London was hot and she felt curiously languid, a strange condition, unknown in her experience. Archie refused to leave London. He said he needed new clothes and took Mary with him to Mr Moses in New Oxford Street where he had himself measured for a dozen suits. He was fastidious about cut, and the fittings occupied several mornings. When at last all were finished he prepared to celebrate his triumph by putting on one of the new suits and taking Mary to Surrey Gardens. Mary was tired and watched without interest Archie becoming more and more stately as the long evening passed into night. It was only when he made dignified advances to a marble goddess on a pedestal that she realised he was completely drunk. Frightened and angry, she tried to persuade him to come back to the hotel. A crowd gathered and Mary heard several unfavourable comments on her conduct. One woman said she had driven the poor gentleman mad by her cruelty: another suggested a ducking. Looking round in despair, she caught sight of a familiar face. At the same moment she felt a faintness seizing on her limbs. She staggered a few steps from love's frenzied slave and fell at Mrs

Maggs's feet. Her last conscious thought was that her hoop had swung over her head, leaving her underneath, like a dead rat in a barrel.

When she came to herself she had a momentary bewildered sense of waking from a dream. She was in Mrs Maggs's kitchen and the thin woman was bending over the fire. Of course, she had come in to have supper with Mrs Maggs because Charlotte was out. She was only a little girl waiting for her mother. She uttered a cry of relief. Mrs Maggs looked round, and simultaneously Mary knew that she had not been dreaming. Tears of disappointment oozed under her lids and Mrs Maggs wiped them away with the oven cloth.

"Poor worm," said Mrs Maggs. "It's a shame to treat you so, and you in the way of a family. I hope he's married you lawfully. Men are the meanest creatures God made and will slip out of everything you haven't got them tied hand and foot to."

"I suppose you're not Mrs Maggs now," Mary murmured. Some tremendous fact had just been thrust at her mind, which refused to accept it. She tried to think what it could be.

"In a manner of speaking," the thin woman acknowledged, "not. But you don't change your nature with your name. Maggs I was for twenty years and Maggs I am—to my friends. Which I hope I may count you as a link, my dear."

"Mrs Maggs." Mary sat bolt upright on the narrow couch. "Did you say I was going to have a baby?"

"Bless me, didn't you know it?" Mrs Maggs said comfortably. "Well, the ways of the Lord are indeed unscrutinised."

Mary sank back. "That's finished you," she said to herself. "I shall never get away from Archie." A grim satisfaction in the completeness with which she had been caught in the machinery of life, followed her first dismay.

"I'm not done for yet," she informed Mrs Maggs.

"Of course not," the thin woman comforted her. "And no reason why you should be. All these things are sent to try us. Your poor mother went through it, after all."

"I've lost my mother," Mary said. A desire to cry over her lonely state seized her. She felt that it was ridiculous and lay staring at a print of The Young Queen until its placid virginity restored her to calm. She

had walked confidently out to Lincthorn Road during Archie's first day
at the Old Bailey, only to be told that Charlotte had never been near her
old friend. A round of the shops she had visited with her mother was no
more fruitful, except to the shopkeepers, who produced old bills which
Mary paid. It was the only use to which she put the money Archie had
given her, feeling a sort of delicacy about spending it on herself.

Mrs Maggs was sorry for her. She gave her friendly advice and
Mary accepted it gratefully. Mrs. Maggs's records overflowed with the
catastrophes of friends who had neglected her warnings and died in
agony thinking the nurse the Devil, and growing restive at the
wholesale massacre, Mary said she must go back to her hotel. "George
shall drive you there in his cab," Mrs Maggs cried. She disappeared,
and a moment or two later produced George and his cab with the
pleased air of a conjuror. The cab lurched off and Mary had a panic-
stricken moment during which she felt that she was losing her only
friend. The cabman was even more melancholy than when he drove her
and Charlotte from Islington. When they reached Mary's hotel he
leaned on the door of his cab and said mysteriously: "I don't bear you
any grudge. No. But what I say is there's companionships that's worse
than loneliness, and if ever I take into my hand the wherewithal to end
my forsworn days, and my hand—as it naturally might at such a
dreadful moment—slips, it will be due to that trunk of yours and the
fish I was beguiled by. I dare say we got to come to it, but why? Why?"

Mary thanked him and left him still musing on the inexplicable
problem of existence. She went up to her room and spent a long time
praying. "It may not do any good," she thought, "but I need all the
help I can get." In the morning she felt an extraordinary assurance of
being strong enough to deal with anything. She took this as a proof of
the validity of religion, and Miss Flora's teachings acquired in her
pupil's mind a sacramental value they never wholly lost. About noon
Archie returned, and she greeted him cheerfully.

"You've ruined your new suit," she observed. "Did you sleep
under some one's bed? It looks like it."

Archie's face puckered childishly, and to comfort him Mary brushed
and sponged him into a presentable state and took him out for a walk.
She behaved like a tomboy and climbed to the top of a bus by the iron

ladder. Her crinoline swayed out with such disgraceful effect that a lady inside the bus fainted in self-protection and Archie became crimson with mortification. Mary took no notice of him. She lolled back in the seat with her feet against the parapet of the bus and laughed loudly at everything that amused her.

"You'd better lower me over the side by ropes, if you feel like that about it," she said callously. Archie suffered agonies of shame on the descent and once back in the hotel he announced his intention of returning to Roxborough the next day. Mary concealed her pleasure. She wanted Archie to think that he was punishing her for her good. A dim resentment against his power over her stirred in her mind, and she wondered if it would ever be possible for a man and a woman to live together in a state of friendly respect. It was a useless train of thought and she abandoned it.

The thought struck her that if she had married the boy whose form and features were growing day by day more indistinct in her memory, she would not have cared whether she was his equal or not. They would neither of them have thought about it at all. . . .

CHAPTER TWO

1

ROXBY HOUSE was large enough to have housed all four Roxby brothers, with their wives and dependents. Archie lived in a wing of fifteen rooms divided from the rest of the house by a gallery and a hall. In the other larger part lived the eldest brother and his wife, his second wife. George Roxby was very fat and had to be braced with a kind of steel framework into which his man inserted him every day. His groans during this operation echoed through the house. He became very fond of Mary and his wrinkled jovial face shone like a turnip lantern when she came to visit him.

"You and I ought to understand each other, Mary," he said. "You married a monkey and I married half a dozen of them. Lord, what a marriage night I spent, surrounded by gibbering homunculi. Monkeys are queer beasts, they push a man to the very bitter end of imagination. It was difficult to be decently affectionate under the circumstances. Sarah and I quarrelled about it for years, that is to say, I quarrelled and Sarah wept, until I gave it up and troubled her no more. It's queer that I'm only now beginning to understand her after being married to her for twenty-five years. I used to think she was wrong and I a righteous man plagued to death, and I've only just realised that since I never had any decent liking for her the whole fault was mine from the beginning. I wanted her, and disliked her for it, and can you blame the poor wretch for taking refuge behind her hairy little friends? I don't. They might have been worse—parsons or talking women or radicals. . . . I'll tell you what it is, Mary, we're far too ready to change the people we live with. Actually, it can't be done: only misery comes of trying. You couldn't change Archie, though you've more brains in your little finger than he has in his whole body, and Sarah has as much right to her monkeys as I to this ridiculous belly. Don't you go about trying to alter people. It's a fool's game. Life is so full of better and more amusing games that a man of taste has all he can do to try his hand at the finest of them. I wish I were not so fat, Mary. It generates thought, which is a bad thing at my age.''

Sarah drifted in and out of these monologues as she drifted through her days. She was a gentle soul, and so long as she was not worried by unkind attempts to pin her down, a happy placid one. She had the simplicity of thought and manner that comes from long communion with animals. She explained to Mary that if she had had any children she would never have felt they belonged to her as the creatures did. ''They would have gone off and laughed at me when I tried to stop them, Mary. Naughty little girls and fat impudent little boys.'' Sarah sighed. ''My cats know when it's time for morning prayer and they sit as still as china beasts until I've finished. As for the others''—she came close to Mary and whispered in her ear—''you may think me very foolish, but I baptise them all with Jordan water to make them acceptable to heaven.''

Mary discovered in herself a new gentleness. A year ago she would have told Wagener about Sarah and laughed with him at her simplicity. Now she felt that Sarah was groping towards some truth from which Mary herself was still a very long way. She found Sarah soothing, and on the night dreadful to Mary when her son was born, the older woman displayed a strange firmness and serenity. It was Sarah who wiped Mary's forehead and knotted a towel to the bed-head for the young girl to grip in her agony. Sarah received Mary's son and bathed it, and only when all was over did she lapse so far as to be discovered trying to stuff the child into a hat-box. Dissuaded, she wandered away, but Mary was asleep and did not miss her. . . .

It seemed to Mary—looking back—that during the next few months she was truly happy and peaceful. When spring came, with its thin intoxicating scents, she passed whole days in the grounds of Roxby House, playing with her son. Richard was a very attractive baby, with Mary's eyes and a fat friendly smile. Mary loved him with a tenderness into which she poured all her longing for Charlotte, her frustrate worship of ships, her homesickness for Danesacre, and, though she would not have acknowledged it, the memory of Gerry. She thought of him a little now, since it was all so far off that it was part of another life or a dream. But chiefly she thought of Richard, and planned for him, and kissed his wet slippery little body in the bath, and behaved with the immemorial folly of mothers with first-born sons. She had some follies that were in advance of her time. She bathed Richard all over twice every day and kept the windows open in his rooms on the coldest night. Where she got these notions from she did not know, but she clung to them in spite of Sarah's laments and Archie's fretful orders. Wagener upheld her and her native obstinacy did the rest.

She was very thin now, and in the tight-fitting bodice of her long frock she looked more than ever like a little girl in borrowed clothes. She wore her hair in heavy bands round her head and over her ears. It weighed her down, and she was never sorry when it tumbled over her shoulders as she romped on the grass with the other child. Then she plaited it and let it hang. So happy was she in her recovered health and the abounding energy of her body that when Wagener told her Archie was looking ill, she dismissed the news with impatience.

But Archie was ill. He grew more and more like a hake every day. He ceased even to complain, but drifted about the house talking to any one who would listen of his royal blood. He was dreadfully distressed by the admittance of Jews into Parliament and said that it almost justified him in listening to certain proposals that had been made to him from a loyal quarter. He even evoked, out of some dim boyish romance, the memory of a mysterious message about the Succession and a messenger, and when he did die it was from a chill caught waiting for the messenger through the whole of one cold night, standing mute and obstinate on the terrace below the west front of the house, coughing, shivering, peering into the hollow night, while another Messenger than the one he expected came nearer and nearer.

He died very quietly and Mary hardly had time to realise that she was, at seventeen, a widow, when the house was turned upside down by the arrival of the other two Roxby brothers, with—as in an old play—their trains. They filled the house, trod on Sarah's cats, screamed at the monkeys, and treated Mary herself with a mixture of scorn and deference. The scorn was for her years, and the deference for her position as mother of her son. He was, after George Roxby's one son by his first wife, the heir. And as George Roxby the younger was a childless hypochondriac of forty-five, the rest of the family were inclined to pay the infant Richard too much respect. The youngest Roxby brother of all, John Roxby, had three children, but he had long since cut himself off from the family by going into trade. Early in the forties he had married the only daughter of a tea and coffee importer and gone into the business. When his father-in-law died he inherited. He lived in London, and though informed of his brother's death, did not come to the funeral. No one thought of his children, the children of a Roxby turned tea merchant, as possible heirs, and Mary had to stand guard between her baby and the overwhelming attentions of his relatives. She soothed Sarah, helped her to nurse one monkey who had been foully assailed with a razor by James Roxby when he discovered it in his wardrobe, supervised the baking of huge glazed pies and roasting of sides of beef and killing of young ducklings, and found time to grieve a little for Archie.

"He was kind to me," she said to Wagener, "as kind as he knew how to be. It was as hard on him to be married to an ill-behaved girl of fifteen as for me to be married to him. He must have been bitterly disappointed. I wish I hadn't made fun of him, and I'm sorry he's dead. I was getting used to him. The question is what am I going to do now? I don't seem able to settle anywhere. Every friend I make is torn from me. Poor poor Archie."

"Heaven preserve me and all decent men from the insolence of your pity when you've got rid of us," Wagener observed. "I don't know what you can do. I'll think about it."

Mary was walking away. She turned and flung herself impulsively into the tutor's arms. "You're all I have. Don't you go away, too. Promise."

Wagener promised. . . .

The day of the funeral was very hot. Before entering the darkened room where the Roxbys were waiting to walk to the chapel in a procession which even the ladies of the family were required to attend,

Mary glanced in on the dining-room with its loaded tables. There were rounds of cold beef, ten hams that had been liberally soaked with sherry, huge raised pies with the Roxby arms in pastry relief and thick jelly between crust and meat, young geese and ducklings with green goose sauce made of sorrel juice, sherry and gooseberries, roast duck with port wine sauce, almond flummery, mince pies, jellies, cold soufflées, pickled walnuts, orange wine as potent as old brandy, shrub, white rum cellared in 1780, and on a side table a noble company of clarets and burgundies, with a few Rhine wines in thin bottles, like maiden ladies in a gathering of jovial citizens. Mary knew that every one for miles round, bidden and unbidden, would attend the feast after the burying, and she hoped fervently that she and Sarah would not be disgraced by a famine.

She reached the tiny private chapel fretted by Sarah's complaints. At the last minute Sarah had announced her intention of taking two of her oldest animals to the service, and all Mary's wits were called on in order to avoid an unseemly quarrel. Torn from her monkeys, Sarah wept bitterly. Mrs. James Roxby, who was not Mrs. James really but had to be accepted as such with as much civility as there was any need to show, was purple with emotion, and Charles Roxby was giggling. "Archie *shall* have a decent funeral," Mary said. She spoke crossly to Sarah and quelled Charles with brutal zest.

The chapel was almost warm, and bees droned in and out of the open door. A sense of abundant life outside mocked the handful of mourners within. Mary tried to listen to the service and to think of Archie, but her thoughts were beguiled by drifting summer scents and distracted by her own perplexities. "Hath but a short time to live and is full of misery." Archie was full of misery. Mary wondered what ambitions had died in him, what dreams he had drowned in an excess of spleen, and brandy. "He fleeth as it were a shadow, and never continueth in one stay." "That's me," Mary thought. "I never continue anywhere. I wish I did. I'd give anything to have my feet on something solid. Archie had much more stability in his life than I have. . . ."

Late in the day James Roxby came to her and began a long discussion about the unlegalised Mrs. James, whose name was Susan Putt.

"I have made the acquaintance of a lady of thirty-five, a person of great excellence, combining strength with sweetness. Every one speaks in favour of her *active piety and kindness*. She is very well off in the world, and is prepared to behave to me—if she becomes my wife—with great generosity and affection. Don't mention this matter to any of my brothers at present, Mary, but give me your opinion, as Archie's widow, on my prospect."

"What about Susan?" Mary began bluntly.

James's face expressed deep concern. "Susan has lived with me for twenty-five years," he said. "She has never had any other association, and she has gradually, with my help and example, refined herself to such a degree that I have repeatedly raised her allowance. My affection for her is unchanged, but I cannot help thinking that it is my duty to sacrifice both of us to a reputable marriage."

"If respectability is what you want, why not marry Susan?" Mary suggested.

"Sin can never be made respectable," James pointed out. "After all, Susan and I have sinned, though on my part, at any rate, with the most delicate and disinterested sentiments. You can't put that right, after the lapse of so many years. Besides, I am in the greatest need of money. Do you think that George will raise our allowances now that Archie is dead? After all, you and a young child cannot possibly require so much money as Archie did."

Mary left him to his speculations. He revolted her, but she preferred him to Charles, the youngest but one, who was a fool and tried to make love to her. He sidled up to her in the garden after her interview with James and excused himself from kissing her hands.

"So much too hot for fleshy contacts," he minced. "How young you are, and fresh and exquisite. It seems almost foolish to have made anything so charming for the very short space of time in which you will be permitted to retain your charm."

He gave her one of the embroidered cloths that he spent his time making, showing the utmost ingenuity in designing patterns and blending silks. "To remember me." His long pink face, a milder version of Archie's, the Hanoverian profile gone soft, peered into hers.

"I'd rather not remember you," Mary said tartly. "I wish you and James and all your women would go away. The house is like a bedlam and the servants can never get anything done because James is being scolded by Susan in one room and you are pilfering brandied cherries in another. I can't hear myself think for you all. . . .''

Her thoughts, when at last they did go, led her to no solution of her problem. She wanted to know how much money she and Richard had, but George Roxby either would not or could not tell her. He suggested instead that she should strengthen her position by marrying his son, and in spite of Mary's protest that she did not want to spend the rest of her life in marrying Roxbys, he sent for the second George, a retired major-general of Hussars. He arrived at Roxby House with an ugly mistress of forty whom he insisted on retaining, although he said he was very willing to marry Mary, peering at her in her flowing hoopless black with real kindness in his myopic little eyes.

"You would be reasonable about Catherine, wouldn't you?'' he asked her anxiously. ''I can't afford to pay her off, and she's used to my system. She would be of service to you. You see my point?''

Thinking pitifully of Susan Putt Mary said she did, but she refused to marry him. He stayed on in the house inventing household economies and seeing to it that they were practised by administering calomel and jalap ruthlessly and impartially for thieving, breakages, immorality and waste.

His son's intolerable dullness exasperated the elder George Roxby to such a pitch that he had a long-threatened stroke and lay helpless for a week. Mary nursed him. During this week a comet that had been filling the heavens with fire and the faithful and unfaithful alike with horrid expectations of a Last Judgment, reached its menacing height. Every night, when the old man slept fitfully, Mary stood at his window to watch it flung like a sword across the sky. Silent, blazing, sinister, it gave her an exultant sense of danger. George Roxby's stertorous breathing echoed in the dark room behind her, the comet flared, Sarah's animals chattered and wailed in a fever of excitement, and Mary's mind was filled with the thought of approaching change. George Roxby died and George Roxby succeeded, and Sarah woke Mary up a week later in the cold darkness of early morning to tell her that her husband had appeared to her and prophesied the death of his son. Mary sat bolt upright, shivering, among a sea of bedclothes like receding waves of

sleep. Her scepticism received a shock when a few months afterwards
George broke his long neck in the hunting field and was brought home
to the house that had seen three dead Roxbys in the last year.

"But he rode so badly that any one could have prophesied he'd be
killed," Mary protested, trying to explain away her own superstitious
awe.

Sarah pointed out triumphantly that only George, speaking through
herself, had done so. James and Charles returned nervously for another
funeral and there began an examination of the Roxby estate. It was
found to be in the most frightful confusion. Mortgages were falling due
and there was no money to meet them. Rents were in arrears and in the
middle of it all George's bailiff disappeared for America taking with
him all the money he had in hand, together with various deeds and
documents. James and Charles quarrelled and argued day and night in a
disorder of guttering candles and empty decanters. Charles was for
leaving things as they were, renewing the mortgages and applying to
the Jews.

"We're all done for," he said. "The old gay England is doomed.
The machines have dug its grave and our oh so liberal politicians and
our swollen traders are its undertakers. We shall never be gay again.
We shall only be noisy. Let us sell what we can and live like gentlemen
to the last."

James snorted, and Mary caught at a sensible word. She tried to think
how Mark Henry would act. She was fighting for her son, and she had
no intention of letting these older Roxbys cheat him of his inheritance.
Early in the new year Wagener fell ill and Mary was impatient because
he was failing her when she needed his advice. He knew it, and roused
himself to wrestle with her over papers and figures until even Mary
could see that he was too ill to go on. Then she was seized with panic
and sent for a doctor, two doctors. "You're not really ill," she told
him.

The dying man laughed at her. "I'm too lazy to work," he said. "I
should have sponged on you, buying my bread with advice you
wouldn't follow, until I was old enough to be shovelled decently aside,
like Miss Flora, and forgotten. I'd rather die at this melancholy and
romantic moment. I'll give you a last piece of advice. I wouldn't give it

to you if I weren't sure, moderately sure, that you have too much
character to make a feminine success of your life. Go back to Danesacre
and try your luck again with Mark Henry Garton. I've a queer feeling
that this is your moment. Try it."

"I was thinking of doing that myself," Mary said, surprised.

Wagener nodded. "Go back as soon as you can. And Mary, one
thing more. Don't expect too much of people. You'll be horribly
disappointed. Try to believe in advance that your best friends will play
you the worst tricks, and you'll save yourself a deal of pain.
Remember."

"You shan't die," Mary said fiercely. But he did die, and she,
absorbed in her struggle with James and Charles, hardly noticed his
going.

She had come to the conclusion that it would be better to sell
two-thirds of the estate and keep an unencumbered third for Richard.
The two Roxbys joined forces to defeat her. They pointed out that the
part she wanted to sell included their houses and their land. Mary found
herself arguing with these two middle-aged aristocrats as if they were
tiresome and unreasonable children. "It isn't your land," she said.
"It's entailed on the eldest surviving line. It's Richard's. You can all
come and live in this house—it's large enough to hold both of you and
Sarah—and look after the place for Richard. I have a feeling that this is
the third we ought to keep. Besides, it will fetch less than any other part
and we need all the money we can raise."

"So soft and young and so mercenary," Charles murmured.

"It's the Garton stock," James said.

Mary bit back her impatient anger and began again. In the end,
because her will and her desires were fiercer and even less scrupulous
than theirs, she got her way. She knew that she was behaving as no
Roxby or Hansyke would have behaved, and the thought pleased her.
"I'll be all Garton," she said to herself. "I'll fight over a ha'penny if
it's mine." Mild Sarah turned against her and her reproaches hurt
Mary. "I'm not heartless," she said. "I forgave Archie long ago for
what he did to me, and I loved George. It's strange how every person
I've accepted as part of my life has been taken from me in a few months,
just as though I were meant to start now afresh, without help or

hindrance. I dare say it's a good thing they went before I'd grown to depend on them." She remembered Wagener and tears filled her eyes because he had died alone in the middle of the night and because she could no longer go to him with her wild chatter and be comforted and helped by his whimsical melancholy wit. She tried to appease George's wife, but gathering her bereaved animals round her, the poor lady withdrew, deeply offended, to a cottage in a distant corner of the estate. Mary let her go. She saw the settlement to its lingering conclusion and then took the two-year-old Richard and went to Danesacre, driving there in the Roxby barouche, all her possessions and his in one small box of red leather studded with nails.

2

As she entered the house above the Yard, looking very small, very thin and young, with Richard walking manfully beside her in his short petticoats, she thought: "I'm coming home." Mark Henry's house, as large as any ship-owner's house in Danesacre, was yet less than a quarter the size of Roxby. It was grey and square, and it had seen so many fine ships sail away from under its very walls that something of the dignity and mystery of the sea invested it. The life of the harbour came up to its windows. Every room had its models of full-rigged sailing ships, eternally gliding over a green plaster sea. The walls of Mark Henry's own office, between the dining-room and the front door, were covered with prints, plans, specifications and a huge painting of the Garton Iron Works, which the artist had seen fantastically dark and solid under a menacing sky. A boy ran continually between this room and the offices of the Garton Line on the pier. He was running out as Mary approached, and held the door open for her.

Mark Henry, looking up to curse the boy for loitering, was pleased to see her. He reduced Richard to tears of mirth by antics that wrought havoc among the papers on the table, and asked Mary if she had come to stay, and hoped she had. Mary picked Richard up and seated him firmly in a chair.

"I've come to stay if you'll let me work for you," she said bluntly. "I asked you that before and you laughed at me. I'm eighteen now, but that's not too old to begin. I'm your nearest living relative except my mother, and if I'd been a boy you wouldn't have hesitated. I'm as strong as any boy. I'm quick at learning—I got that from you—and I'll work like a slave.'' Mary broke off and crossed the room quickly to lean on Mark Henry's breast and put her arms round his neck with unconscious coquetry. ''Please, please listen to me. Try me for a year and if I'm no good turn me out. No, don't say no. I swear I'll not make a fool of myself. You don't care what people think. Please have me.''

She kissed him eagerly, pressing her smooth young mouth against his cheeks. ''You will.''

Mark Henry gave a grunt of laughter.

''Damned if I won't,'' he said. ''I'll show those Lings. Had the impudence to tell me I'm not the man I was. As near as be damned said I was a fool to talk of building iron wool ships. To tell me I don't know what I'm talking about! I'll tell you, Mary, it's iron or nothing nowadays. Wood's doomed. We've built our last wooden boat. We've almost built our last sailing ship, whatever that doddering old fool Smithson likes to do. Ay, it's a pity. There's nowt so bonny as the *Mary Gray* will ever go out from here again, Mary. She's badly strained this trip and her repair bill goes up and up. I know what I'm talking about, and I never did a better day's work than when I bought young Gossop's engine works, poor green fool. We'll show 'em, Mary, eh? I always disliked those Lings. You behave yourself and we'll play such a trick on them.''

There was a knock on the door and Rupert Ling stood on the threshold. He had become a dark handsome youngster: his eyes examined Mary with amusement and a glint of mockery.

''Here's your Cousin Mary come to work in the firm with you,'' Mark Henry said gleefully. ''Don't you come bothering me this morning. She's starting at once and I'm training her.''

Richard set up a resentful yell.

''Is the brat coming in, too?'' Rupert asked ironically, and Mary swept up the crying child and carried him away. She handed him to a girl to look after, and his protesting wails followed her until she shut the door of Mark Henry's room on them. When, at the end of her first day's work, she went to put him to bed, he suffered her in a reproachful silence. . . .

3

The story of the next ten years of Mary Roxby's life is amazingly difficult to tell. It was not only troubled in itself but set in years so heavy with change and presage that inevitably Mary's decade of struggle becomes at times nothing but a shadow of greater events, the faint echo of a thunder that was rolling across the world. When it begins, the country is alternately thrilling and shivering at the prospect of the third Napoleon's landing. Mark Henry Garton, buttoned into a tunic that horribly constrains him, is marching his Volunteers out of the town to manoeuvres on the moor. The Secretary for War is a school comrade of Mark Henry's and he comes down to speak to the raw bands and to sit up until breakfast time discussing Mark Henry's French brandy and the immediacy of the French invasion, on which he pledges his head. In the same year, a scientist entirely unknown to Mark Henry and Mary deals such a blow at the old tree of the Established Church that every hollowness and rottenness in it is gradually exposed, and the trunk begins the imperceptible crumbling that Mary sees accomplished. The Americans quarrel murderously and one of Mark Henry's last acts is to seize himself a fat profit out of their brotherly hate. The Prince Consort dies, thus putting off the Teutonising of England for nearly another half century. So does the last of the great Englishmen, since whom the rest are all Jews or Scotsmen. The first Atlantic cable is laid, and the year of its laying is celebrated by mob riots in Hyde Park. Mary was curiously blind to the social signs. She never saw anything in the workers' uprisings but a shameful manifestation of human wickedness. During her third year at Danesacre, bands of haggard men, tramping over the country from Lancashire, came round the town, singing for money to send to their starving families. They sang a song of which the words, so profoundly sad and hopeless, were yet more ominous than any of the hundred clamorous cries of those fermenting years. They were the stones speaking, the walls of weavers' hovels lent tongues, the in-articulate mutter of a misery older than the splendid industrial century, older than the old old merry England. They were the most significant sounds Mary ever heard and she was so absorbed in helping Mark Henry Garton to evade England's official neutrality in the Civil War that she could not be said to have heard them at all. The gaunt shivering

band sang in Garton's Yard and the men took up a subscription in thei
caps. Mempes added a guinea and Mark Henry nothing. He cursed th
starving men vehemently and shut his window against their voices
Late the same night,. when the harbour was silvered over with a
borrowed radiance and the lights that the little town had hung round he
dark shoulders were reflected in the waters at her feet, Mary stood in the
empty Yard and heard the singing. The words went to a poignant mino
air, sweet and indescribably mournful:

> "Oh, hard times, come again no more.
> Many days have ye lingered
> Around my cottage door.
> Oh, hard times, come again no more."

The thin sound was carried off by a wandering wind and Mary crept
down to look at the frigate building for the Confederate Government. . . .

She worked during this time as she never worked again, in all her
long life. She knew that Mark Henry Garton would turn her ruthlessly
out of the firm if she proved useless. She had against her an incalculable
hostility made up of the Lings' jealousy, the shipwrights' distrust of a
woman, and the depths of her own ignorance, which everything and
every one combined to expose, leaving her to fight with naked hands
and wits in a world that conceded nothing to a woman except her right
to be protected from it. And the law of protection for women ran only
within the narrowest limits. Not that Mary worried about the state and
status of other women. She was never moved by any talk of women's
rights, having a queer rooted conviction that all rights were only powers
called by another name. Mark Henry's rebuff of fifteen-year-old Mary
Hansyke had bitten in. . . .

She brought to her struggle a curiously mixed equipment, a certain
fastidious arrogance that belonged to another class, almost to another
century, than the one with which she had thrown in her lot, and a stolid
proud conviction of her value that was pure Garton. In Mark Henry she
had a notable trainer and guide. He had a coarse erratic genius that flung
him into grandiloquent schemes of expansion, in which only a mixture

of luck and hard work saved him from disaster. He would sit up at night with her, talking and talking, flinging off suggestions, leaping in one sentence from inspired sense to the sheerest fantasy. Much of what he said, and many of the abandoned ideas he scattered so richly, dropped into Mary's mind to bear fruit in their time. At one time he had an idea of buying a vast oil concession from the American Government, then sorely in need of money. It was a fantastic scheme as Mark Henry outlined it, and went no farther than a sheet scrawled with figures and a sketch of the monstrous fine house he would build on the yield of his first well. . . .

Another time, he conceived a sort of floating pontoon. A fleet of these was to be moored at Dover and used to bridge the Channel in the event of another French War. He went up to London in great state to lay this before the Government and came back furious at his reception.

"A young ——," he told Mary, "sat up on his beam and asked me how I was going to preserve them from rotting in the water. I said they wouldn't be put out until they were wanted, and if his department wasn't more than a year later getting the troops on the move, my pontoons would be all right. He said that while the ships were towing the bridge into position they'd be attacked by the French and the men might just as well be landed in the usual way. I said: 'Oh, all right, have it your own way, invade her by sea, and land your seasick men, not that *you*'ll go anywhere near the sea, and if you did you've got no guts to fetch up.' And then I came away. I tell you what, Mary, this country is going to the devil faster than decent folk like you and me can hinder it, and it may go for me. I'm through. . . ."

His iron works at Middlesborough were of enormous profit to him. A share of the rich deposit of ironstone in the Cleveland hills had been Gossop's and was his, and the pig-iron production of the Garton Iron Works went up by leaps. Curiously enough, Mark Henry took little interest in the Works. He left them in charge of a young Cornish manager called Thomas Prendergast, with George Ling under him, and only at long intervals paid them a visit that was like the descent of Lucifer on his subordinate devils. The setting was hellish enough in all conscience. . . .

At the time when Mary joined the firm, it was swinging over from

wood to iron with all the impetuousness of Mark Henry's decisions. In
1858 Garton's Yard turned out an iron sailing ship with a registered
tonnage of 691 tons. She was built for the tea trade and she beat two of
the fastest American clippers of twice her tonnage in the race for
delivery of the season's teas in London. Right down through the fifties
and sixties Mark Henry's ships played an important part in the struggle
with the Americans, but almost as soon as the Civil War had delivered
the enemy into his hands Mark Henry began to lose interest and faith in
sailing ships and to turn his whole attention to steam. During the fifties
he built four steamships and engined ten more. The year after Mary
joined the firm, the Yard built two iron screw-steamers with geared
double engines, that he swore were more compact than anything being
turned out between Danesacre and the Tyne. One was on his own
account. Two years later they launched the *Mary Roxby,* built for a
London firm, in which for the first time surface condensers were used
with the compound marine engine. The boilers were made to Thomas
Prendergast's own design, of the water-tube type, remarkably efficient. Unfortunately the boiler-tubes quickly developed small erosions
due to a certain chemical action of steam and soot, and Thomas
Prendergast, after enduring much official criticism and an outburst
from Mark Henry of unparalleled violence, set grimly to work on the
necessary improvements.

During all this time Mary was absorbed in her effort, first to learn
enough to oust the Lings and after that to hold what she had got. Picture
her on a high stool in front of the shabby desk that had belonged to Mark
Henry's father. The monstrous folds of her skirt fall all round the stool.
Her hair is brushed straight back from her grave young face, and the
white collar she washes every night and sews in every morning is very
worn and shabby. She is frowning over cargo lists and looking timidly
towards Mark Henry to discover whether this is a morning on which he
will put everything aside to help her or one when he will roar at her for a
ninny and a fool. In the end she does not trouble him but glides silently
away in search of the necessary information. Perhaps she meets
Richard on the stairs and there is a brief, a very brief, interlude of
whispers and hugs before the small boy goes on to his private enterprise
and she to her endless toil.

She had a talk with John Mempes during her first months in the firm that remained with her for a long time, though afterwards she thought she had missed its significance. He had stayed late in Mark Henry's own office to explain to her the specifications of the new steamship, and at midnight, when he rose to go, he opened the wide curving window and stood there with her, looking out over the harbour. The town, save for a few nodding lights along the pier, was asleep. They heard the watchman in the Yard moving about his brazier, and a faint smell of tar and new hemp drifted up to them.

"I'm glad you didn't leave us," Mary said softly.

Mempes looked down at her with ironical pleasure.

"I don't know why I stay. Probably because I'm not sufficiently interested in anything to make a move. I don't fit in anywhere here. I believe I could talk more easily to my grandfather—he and I would at least agree on our notions of a gentleman—than I can to my contemporaries in this place. Or to my grandson—if I had any I could name. I have a fancy that all this wealth we're piling up—we're going, you know, to see an expansion of trade and money and possessions wilder than Mark Henry's wildest dreams—and the smug pleasure with which you people who are piling it for yourselves survey the process, will turn to a dust of death in my grandson's mouth. I've an idea he'll be as bored as I am, and as uninterested and as unmoved by your complacent dreams. You're a little complacent yourself. When I look at the vision of hell Mark Henry and his friends have erected on the banks of the Tees, when I see him building his ships and scrapping them and building bigger and planning to build bigger still, with never a thought for the ultimate effects of his blind greeds, I grow first hot and then bored. Let them pile it up, and let it topple over and crush their grandsons."

"Not Richard," Mary said.

Mempes smiled.

"We'll spare Richard. But what about Richard's son?" His voice changed abruptly. "And since we'll sooner or later move to the Tees you'd better help me persuade Mark Henry to take up an option on more ground between the railway and the river. Queer he can't see he'll need it. He seems to think he can go on building ships at Danesacre for ever."

Mary resented the swift change from personal to impersonal. She

tried to bring him back to a flattering intimacy, but Mempes eluded her,
as Mary was abruptly conscious he must often elude the women who
tried to pin down his graceful flutterings. She felt humiliated and said
good night with a stiff dignity. He took her hand and kissed it and
retained it in his own, looking at it absently, as if he had something
more to tell her. Mary's pulse quickened under his fingers, because
she was shy and because Mempes was a romanticf and attractive
creature.

They were interrupted by a frightful uproar, and running out into the
hall, saw Mark Henry on the landing above, in a nightshirt from which
his hairy legs protruded in a very graceless and shocking jig. Miss Flora
was half-way down the stairs, clutching at her thin bosom and dumb
with fear. The scene, fantastic in the quiet night, was illumined by the
candle in Mark Henry's hand and more sombrely by his flood of
comments. He had a magpie trick of hiding his possessions all over the
house and it appeared that, having hidden a box of pills under the
mattress in an unused bedroom, he had risen in the night and issued
forth to look for it, unaware that Miss Flora had that day moved herself
to the bedroom in question.

"Go away," he roared. "Go away and tell the town you've been
ravished. Ravished. Murdered. Scalped. Hamstrung. Filleted. Salted.
Smoked. Of all the plagues on an honest man to have his house filled
with females who lie in wait in beds to scream rape and murder at him in
the middle of the night. Come back. I'll ravish you. I will. It'll come
hard, but I will. G-r-r. I'd ravish you to perdition if I could."

Mary ran to soothe the terrified old lady and lead her back to her own
bed, while Mempes comforted Mark Henry with hot lemon and brandy
and finally tucked him up, still rumbling like an incipient earthquake,
near dawn.

4

Mary expected suspicion from the Ling boys. They must know her
presence was a menace to their own position. She congratulated herself
that George was safely in Middlesborough and that only Rupert
remained to be comforted. But Rupert surprised her. Two years her

senior, he had shot up into that beauty which some very young men have, a beauty so evanescent, compounded of youth and reckless spendthrift grace and scorn of careful living, that it is as pathetic as entrancing. His red-brown hair fell in an incorrigible curve over one eyebrow, his eyes under their dark lashes looked at Mary with impudent tenderness and his long mouth smiled more kindly than cousinly. Undoubtedly he suspected her. He made things hard for her, and he did it with such a sublime assurance that she would understand and forgive him that Mary was baffled.

One evening in Mark Henry's office, she found him folding up a sheet of notes that she had made.

"What are you doing with those?" she demanded and put out her hand.

He withheld the papers.

"They amuse me."

"I'm glad you find me amusing," she said demurely.

Rupert's smile broadened.

"No, you're not. You hate it. You hate me. Do you remember how George and I used to tease you when you were a little girl? Little and quaint and fierce. We were beasts to you. Boys are usually beasts."

"You were," Mary said fervently.

"If we'd known," Rupert mused, "that you were going to come here and try to do us out of our rights, we might have dropped you over the cliff and said it was an accident."

"I've as much right here as you," Mary retorted. "You're only half-nephews and I'm a whole niece."

"Bah, you're a girl. You're a sweet girl. You're my darling little cousin Mary and I love you but I shan't let you ruin me."

Mary went away and left him with her papers. She walked up the steep road from the Yard and took the narrow lane that ran inland along the side of the hill, dipping to the valley some two miles farther up. From a bend in the lane she could look back at the upper harbour and the sea. She turned aside here and sat down in a small beech wood. Below her the steep slope was masked with trees that hid the river from her sight. The air was warm, and Mary tired, but an old restlessness kept her alert.

It was one of those evenings, clear and golden, when familiar things are seen in a new light. The blue rim of the sea, the church on the cliff-top, spoke to each other like old friends, and the sense of their peaceful communion entered Mary's thoughts, but not to bring her peace. Instead, it filled her with a sharpened sense of loneliness. In the whole world she had only Richard, and though she poured out on him the treasures of her tenderness, he did not satisfy her longing for another mind, another voice in her ear, another hand to touch hers. She did not understand what was missing. She only knew that she kept turning to speak to someone who was never there, whose voice mocked her in Mark Henry's clowning inspiration and Mempes's courtesy.

She did not understand why sometimes at night this restlessness drove her from her bed to lean on the windowsill and look out across the harbour at the lights of houses in the streets of the town or the lonely lights of farms along the distant moor road. Sometimes she wept, without knowing why, and stretched her hands out and shivering went back to bed.

A step on the dead leaves of the wood roused her and she looked up to see Rupert Ling. He was holding the ravished papers in his hand and he offered them to her with solemn civility. Then he seated himself uninvited at her side and began to talk to her with his disconcerting friendliness.

"Since I saved your life, Mary, by not pushing you over the cliff, why are you not more civil? Do take your notes back. I cut your throat or you cut mine in this fantastic house of Mark Henry, and let's do it as gentlemen should."

"If I could only trust you," Mary sighed.

"Oh, don't do that, my dear. I can't endure being trusted. Never trust anyone, least of all your cousin Ling. No one trusts a Ling in Danesacre. They know us too well. Mary, are you happy here? They say your husband was a solemn old mule. If that's so, who was Richard's father? Did Jove descend on you? Lord, what a fool I am. Do you really dislike me so much, Mary?"

He was so close to her that she saw the dancing Maries in his eyes. She noticed, blinking her own, how thick his lashes were, and the smoothness of his skin. He was closer now and without warning, her blood betrayed her into a humiliating folly.

The thought coming into her head that she had never been so near a young smiling mouth, she swayed by a natural logic nearer. Rupert was looking down at her with a queer expression of insolence and excitement, and when he took hold of her thin shoulders she lay for a moment unresisting in his arms. Almost in the moment of surrender she knew that she had made a fool of herself. She glanced at him and read in his face, as clearly as if he had told her, that Rupert did not care for small thin girls with sleek hair. He liked tall, amply-curving creatures with bosoms that cradled his head. He was making fun of his little cousin. Mary's childish hatred of him rushed over her afresh and she jerked herself free with a force that sent him staggering back among the leaves. Now he was laughing outright and chanting in his young soft voice: ''Mary loves me. She loves me, she loves me not.''

Mary snatched her papers out of his hand and went trembling away. . . .

She suffered torments of self-abasement after this. Rupert did not kiss her again, but he made things harder for her than before. He spread about the Yard a belief that her presence in the office was one of Mark Henry's crazy whims, an unpractical practical joke. A woman in office! He spread a more sinister slander, that ran through Yard and town in an undercurrent of fleering looks and jests. It concerned Mary and John Mempes, and Mary remained ignorant of it for years. . . .

Rupert Ling was not the only complication in Mary's life during this time. She had been at Danesacre seven months when Miss Short wrote to say that Charlotte Hansyke had called on her to borrow money. ''She looked so old and distraught,'' wrote Charlotte's friend in her lovely etiolated handwriting, ''that I did not like to refuse her and I said I would send some if she would leave me her address. But, my dear, I am not a rich woman and I find it very hard with the Funds behaving in so odd and apparently *uncontrollable* a way owing, they say, to the be-haviour of Lord P——, to satisfy even my own poor simple needs. How can I send Charlotte twenty pounds or even ten, or five? And you were such a kind practical little girl as I remember you, and I appeal to you to reason with dear Charlotte and tell her that she must not come browbeating me in my own house."

She enclosed an address in Tottenham Court Road, and thither Mary hurried to find Charlotte living with an unpleasant little man of indeterminate profession and a habit of tweaking Charlotte's ears when things were going badly. Charlotte, looking old and ill, embraced Mary passionately and as passionately refused to leave her protector. He for his part was very willing to give her up for money down, and when this became clear to her, Charlotte flew into a violent rage. She accused Mary of being the ruin of her life from the time when she so inconsiderately forced her way into the world, of being in league with Mark Henry to ruin her, and in a fantastic climax, of intriguing to steal Charlotte's own lover. And all the time the unpleasant little man stood smirking by, fingering his notes, and delighted to be the cause of so much emotion.

As long as she lived Mary never forgot the sight of stricken Charlotte gathering up her few possessions in a silence heavier than tears. It came to stand in Mary's mind for the useless lives of all the wilful extravagant helpless women created by a masculine world and broken in it. She took her mother back to Danesacre and watched her, with an emotion between laughter and tears, translating herself from passionate Charlotte Hansyke into Richard's grandmother. Charlotte became, by the most natural transition, the boy's slave. She inquired from Mary all the details of his Roxby inheritance and expressed surprise and dismay that Mary had left it so long in the hands of James and Charles Roxby. She insisted on going to stay with Richard at Roxby House, and there she gave herself such airs as the grandmother of the reigning infant that the brothers combined to snub her. She came back to Danesacre and wept in Mary's arms.

"They said Richard was unfortunate in his vulgar connection," she said, "and they hoped he would lose the Danesacre accent in time. They made a fool of me by talking to me about people they knew I'd never heard of. Who was the Duke of Devonshire's crazy ward and whom did the third Earl marry? How should I know?" Tears of mortification shone in Charlotte's eyes, still dark and lustrous in her addled face. "I'm nothing now. I'm nothing, nothing. No one respects me. You don't respect me, Mary. You never tell me anything you're doing. Soon even Richard will learn to despise me."

Mary soothed the passionate creature and at twenty wondered if at fifty she would have half that fire, but she did not attempt to take her mother into her confidence about her ambitions and her dreams, She was very kind and considerate, but she kept her out. . . .

Her son was a problem of another kind. She adored him and he her. She collected his sayings and wrote them down in a book that she kept in her desk. One rainy morning she went to call him and found him lying with obstinately closed eyes. "Wake up, little son. Wake up," she said softly. He chuckled but would not give up his pretence of sleep. She bent over him, searching his features for signs of Archie. She could find none. He was like herself, and she thought that God had given him to her to make up for Archie. His long dark lashes lay on cheeks radiant with health, and his crimson mouth, compressed in an attempt at gravity, invited the kisses she presently gave him, covering his face with kisses, tickling him with her eyelashes, making him quiver with laughter and delight and happiness. At last he sat up and observed that he was like a flower because he always felt inclined to curl up and go to sleep when it rained. The corner of a note-book was visible under his pillow, and after a struggle Mary possessed herself of it. "That's my memory book," he said gravely.

Turning over the leaves, scrawled in pencil with indecipherable "memories," Mary came upon two that she could read.

"Whipped just for being sick."

."Banged for talking too much."

"Oh, Richard," she said reproachfully, "I've never whipped you for being sick."

"No," he said, "but you looked as if you would like to, and you did bang my head for singing after you put me to bed."

Mary fell on him and produced a tolerable imitation of a Cruel Mother Eating Her Child, at which he laughed madly and they rolled on the bed in a crisis of mirth and affection.

The memory book remained in Mary's thoughts for a long time. She wondered whether it was not unnatural for a very small boy to be confiding his thoughts to a book. A queer feeling that she was not

giving her little son anything like enough haunted her at odd moments
through all these striving years. . . .

She tried later to appease it by descending with ruthless vigour on
James and Charles Roxby and demanding in Richard's name an
account of their stewardship. Finding that they had done nothing to
maintain the value of the property and were selling the paintings in the
gallery, a Rembrandt, a Van Dyck, and five Gainsboroughs, for their
immediate needs, she put them on a fixed allowance to be paid twice a
year, and began to look round for a bailiff to act for Richard. . . .

5

The recurring note of these early years is Mary's extreme poverty.
She was wretchedly poor. Mark Henry paid her, grumbling at his own
ruinous good nature, an apprentice's wage. Out of that she had to clothe
herself and Richard and buy everything, but food, that they both
needed. What she got in a year would have kept them for a month. So
the meagre allowance was spent on her son, and for herself Mary
darned and patched and contrived until her growing beauty could no
longer carry off her shabby clothes. It was during this time that she
began to collect, with the infrequent tips that Mark Henry threw her
when he was pleased, very delicate, extravagant and useless under-
garments. She never wore any of them. She put them, bought one by
one over barren months, into a small drawer with bags of orris-root and
lavender, and sometimes spread them out to gloat. They were all
acquired, in obedience to some obscure impulse in the young girl's
mind, for an undefined occasion when she would take them out and
clothe herself in unabashed softness. Only the occasion never came. . .

For nearly four years she worked as an underpaid slave in Mark
Henry Garton's office. Mark Henry kept her in what he was pleased to
call the construction department, which was his own office in the house
above the Yard, and taught her details of the making of ships. That is to
say, he expounded his theories of shipbuilding and left her to get the
roots of the matter from the ship's architect, who had his office in
Harbour Street, on a floor of the Yard Superintendent's house. Then
suddenly Mark Henry flung her into the Line office, into the outward

freight department, and left her to find her feet among bills of lading, ships' manifests, schedules of sailings, agents' reports, details of docking facilities, and all the imagined and unimagined network of human effort following a ship from home port to home port—to see it safe and to make it pay. . . . She went about with a thin line between her eyes and an air of unyouthful anxiety that vanished only when she was free to go to Richard's nursery. Then she was a young girl again and her hair fell down and her cheeks were flushed and rounded with laughter. . . .

She had an uneasy ride of it. It was not courage, but a kind of blind hunger, an obstinate clinging of her hands to life and the things she wanted, that kept her in her seat. Humiliated and beaten off in one place, she seized hold in another. She was so much less agile-minded than Rupert Ling that he found it easy to make a fool of her. Bit by bit, like a beggar with one foot in a door, she insinuated herself inside, until captains coming into the office after a voyage to make their report, found their way to her desk because she could be trusted not to waste their time or to have forgotten their names. These were days when captains picked up their own cargoes for the return voyage, making friends with shippers in the ports where they unloaded, planning, keeping their accounts with scrupulous care in small note-books, as anxious to make a little extra money for the owner by clever calculation of freights, as the owner himself. Mary began to know which captains were popular with shippers, and which showed, in Galveston, an intuitive skill in balancing a cargo of cotton and cane to get the last penny of profit out of it. She knew which was inclined to overdrive his ship and which shortened sail on the least provocation. She learned their idiosyncrasies and became, partly out of real interest and partly because she was over-anxious to justify her presence, very skilful in the right word of greeting. She was learning how to handle men. . . . Captains began to bring her gifts, flowered silk and brown gleaming gods from China, little lacquer boxes from Sasebo, fans, trays, miniature pagodas, strings of amber and ivory. Some of the things went to Richard, some she put in her secret drawer. She began to feel a little confidence in the place she was making for herself. . . .

John Mempes puzzled her. When she came, she had taken it for granted that he was her friend and would help her. Gradually, after rebuffs so delicate that their significance only unfolded itself in chill humiliating thoughts of the night hours, she realised that Mempes was not going to do anything of the kind. He would not hinder. He would give her any explanations for which she asked, but of himself, nothing. He was neutral. Elegant, irresponsive, faintly smiling, he watched her puzzled progress from ignorance to dawning confidence, he watched her pick herself up after successive tumbles, and did not move to help, unless a desperate cry, forced from her by some unbearable urgency, brought him to her side.

It was characteristic of Mary that she did not resent him. It never occurred to her that Mempes ought to help, just as in all her life she never expected help, and never resented enmity or injury on the person of her injurer. I believe she was incapable of a personal grudge. It looked like weakness, but I do not think it was.

During her third winter something happened that did more to strengthen her position in Danesacre than all her hard work. One Friday evening she walked down Harbour Street to the east pier and found herself forced to cower in the lee of the lighthouse from a wind that cut the breath out of her body. It increased during the night and in the morning was blowing a north-easter of frightful velocity. As Mary sat at breakfast the first ship of the fleet of sailing vessels on the coast came ashore near the west pier. A coble manned by seven men took off the crew. Before noon, a Newcastle schooner, a Prussian barque, a brig and another schooner were all ashore. In the late afternoon Mary left the Office and joined the crowd of men and anxious dry-eyed women who from the pier were watching the wreck of a Danesacre schooner. The sea ran with bared teeth against the pier, and in the dusk sky and hills shrank into the space of a hand. The lifeboat was pulling out again and as the watchers strained into the thundering darkness a green wall of water rose up against it and tipped it over into the pit of the sea. A shiver and a cry ran through the crowd on the pier as a head here and another there, heads of husbands, sons, fathers, thrust up from the waves. There was a rush for useless lifeboats, and Mary saw a cork-jacketed man working towards the shore. She shouted and an instant later was waist deep in the screaming icy water, one in a stumbling gasping human line groping for the battered wretch. She drew breath in agony, blind with spray of broken waves, the current sucking at her feet, and fear, debasing and inhuman, rose and invaded her whole being. It was only for a moment and then she was filled with joy. The hollow booming of oncoming waves gave her a sense of pleasure sharper than any pleasure she had ever conceived. She drove her teeth into her lip in an ecstasy. The man was touched, caught, held, and with his rescuers was back in safety, and Mary, her throat torn with shouts she did not know she had uttered, and blood dripping on to her hand from an unnoticed wound, staggered into shelter.

While she changed her clothes and swallowed brandy in gulps, the crew of the schooner was got ashore on a line thrown over the ship, two more brigs were on the sands, and the old out-dated lifeboat, manned by a volunteer crew, was struggling round to them. In the evening the gale abated. Half a mile of strand was strewn with wrecks, and Mary Roxby found herself accepted as part of the town. She had been a stranger and was now at home. She was pleased and a little puzzled. "I've worked here for three years," she said to herself, "and I'm half a Garton, but they never trusted me or liked me until I went mad and enjoyed myself. It's very strange."

The memory of the pleasure she had felt remained with her long after the cut on her lip was healed. There had been first the fear and then the consuming ecstasy. She could recapture a faint reminiscent thrill by shutting her eyes and imagining herself in the sucking water. When the thrill ceased to revisit her, she forgot to think about it, and the moment took its place in the recesses of her mind, with another day and another moment now very dim indeed and almost lost. What did remain with her was the knowledge that life could blossom into an unimaginable loveliness. These rare moments could not be sought; they came, and went, and only while they lasted was she wholly, burningly and consciously alive. . . .

A year later Mark Henry Garton had to be operated on for stone. His heart, under its layers of fat, was considered to be so weak that the doctors would not risk an anaesthetic. They cut him without one, and

Mark Henry held his watch in his hand and rallied them on their slow
progress. He was still joking, with his ghastly face, when Mary was let
in to see him.

"Old Bridges was damned nervous, Mary. I said: 'It's all very fine
the way you fellows cut us up when we're not watching but I've my eye
on you, and if you as much as nick a piece——' Well, never mind what
I said, Mary. It wouldn't be suitable for me to tell you, but old Bridges
said: 'Hold your tongue, you old sinner, you're past it,' and cut into me
like a good 'un. You're a pretty piece, Mary, but you'll never be the
woman your mother was. Where is Lottie?''

Charlotte had refused to see him, but Mary did not tell him that. Her
anger was hot against the doctors. She thought that they had murdered
Mark Henry for a silly notion, and she hated Tom Bridges with his long
nose and butcher's hands for the rest of her life. Mark Henry began to
talk to himself. He laughed a little and then lay quiet. He lay all night
and most of the next day with compressed mouth and quiet eyes. The
sky darkened for storm and his eyes darkened: it cleared and they
mirrored the placid clouds. What was he thinking as he lay there with
his gaze on the gleaming walnut tall-boy between the windows? Of a
young Mark Henry pacing the smooth gleaming deck of his first
command, of a ship taking the wind and a lad looking over the side at
the curling foam running on the dark sea past the bows. Of a merry face
and warm lips tantalising his, of long days in a garden, of kind hands, of
a voice, a whisper of long grass, a rustle of silk, warmth, quiet, at last
nothing but quiet.

He died just when the old women in the town had said he would die,
as the tide turned, his gaze searching the room for Charlotte or some
other. . . .

He had left every penny he owned, the Line, the Yard, and the
Tees-side Works to Mary Roxby. The Lings were not mentioned.

Rupert Ling laughed. He came to see Mary in the house above the
Yard and laughed again. He refused to stay on with the firm. "I never
believed you'd win, cousin," said he. "I didn't think Mark Henry was
fool enough to ruin Garton's to spite the Lings. I thought he might
divide things and then I was going to marry you to consolidate it. We're

both spared something. You a husband you'd soon have hated, and
I——''

''What are you spared?'' Mary asked. She came across the room and
rested both hands on the table to support her while she looked up at him.
In some curious way, Rupert's mockery had cut the last tie that bound
her to her childish past. Not even motherhood and a husband's death
had done what a boy's insolence did in that moment. She was not timid,
or nervous, or afraid of Rupert Ling any longer. She smiled, and her
eyes, full on his face, were wide and mischievous. Rupert blinked.

''Upon my word,'' he commented, ''I've lost a pretty wife, as well
as a fortune. You're too thin, of course, but the fortune would have
been fat enough to smother the sound of my heart breaking.''

''You're throwing the fortune away,'' Mary pointed out. ''We'd
prefer to keep you.''

Rupert shook his head. ''Stay here? Stay in Danesacre, with a whole
world outside, and a woman at the head of the family? Not I, Mary.
Lord save us, to be dependent on a woman for my orders. Promise me a
ship, as soon as I've got my master's ticket—and I'll start in now. It'll
take me seven years, but at least I'll be getting a look at the world. Do
you realise, Mary, that I've seen nothing but Shrewsbury and
Danesacre in my twenty-four years? School and office. What a life.
The world's full of streets I haven't walked on, and rooms where
women are wondering why I don't come. The door opens and there
stands Mr. Ling. 'Your servant, madam. Your lips are sweet and
warm: below there are you sweet and warm? Don't struggle, pretty
bird. There and there and there.' The best part of rooms, Mary, is that
the door that lets you in lets you out again. To streets and quays and
fresh ports and foreign towns and warm spiced nights. Think of a tropic
night, Mary. Doesn't it make your cool northern blood run hotter?''
Rupert threw back his head and laughed again. ''Have I shocked you?
No, by George, I haven't. Why aren't you shocked, sweet Mary? You
ought to be.''

Mary stood there, liking him better than she had done since brief
friendly hours in their childhood. ''Stay with us, Rupert. We'll make it
worth your while.''

Rupert was retreating from her in mock alarm. "There speaks Mark Henry Garton, and there but for the grace of God. . . . I wouldn't stay with the firm for half your fortune, Mary. If it had been my fortune, I'd never have had the nerve to cut myself loose. I'd have been caught, tamed, done for. I'd have stayed on here and got as fat as Mark Henry, and quarrelled with George, damn his dull eyes—*he'll* stay—and married a wife. Now all the world's my wife, Mary, and I can put a quarrel on life will amuse me to the end of my days. Give me a kiss and I'll go."

"Certainly I'll kiss you," said Mary demurely. She drew away as he started forward. "When you've passed for master and I've given you your first command." He looked like disregarding the delay and she withdrew so coolly that he hesitated. She had gone before he realised it. He laughed and took himself off. . . .

He had been right about George. The elder Ling was a heavy young man, with a squinting eye, long limbs and a thatch of wild hair. He came to Danesacre, accepted without visible gratitude Mary's offer to raise his salary, and agreed, Thomas Prendergast having been entrusted with a commercial mission by the Board of Trade, to carry on as deputy-manager until Prendergast returned. Then he went back to Middlesborough and Mary put off a visit to the Garton Iron Works for six months. She was curious regarding Thomas Prendergast, who was her own age and had been a puddler in the Iron Works and become Mark Henry's manager the year Mary joined the firm.

Her hands were full enough. She had summoned John Mempes within a few hours of Mark Henry's funeral when the will was made public. He came and stood just within the doorway of her room until she invited him to sit near her. In the brief silence that followed he studied her. She was pale and sad, that much was evident, but he thought she was composed. She had added a white fichu to her black gown since the funeral, which surprised him a little. Her hair, coiled at the back of her head, dragged the slender neck backwards, and she rested her head wearily against her chair. She had acquired dignity, and the manager found himself wondering ironically whether it were fortune or a new gown.

"John Mempes," Mary said anxiously, "are you going to stay with me?"

"Do you want me to stay?"

She said: "Of course I want you. I couldn't——" she bit back the dismay that she felt, "I should not like to do without you."

Mempes smiled. "I'll be glad to stay."

Mary said: "Thank you. I thought"—she paused and eyed him, blushing faintly, but quite resolute,—"I thought I would consult with you on everything and what you approve we'll go on with. Ought I to speak to the men at the Yard?"

"It would be a good thing for you to do," Mempes answered gravely. . . .

She summoned up her courage and addressed the men from the slope of the Yard that afternoon. They liked her plain speaking and few words. One man told her so, but another said afterwards that her way of speaking was neither Garton nor Hansyke, and would change when the wind did. She told them that their orders would come through Mempes as before and that she would always hear anything they had to say to her personally, "up at the house, as my uncle did."

"Mark Henry swore oftener than he listened," a man said slyly.

"I'll listen oftener than I swear," Mary promised. They cheered her a little and she went away unelated, a girlish figure, conscious of an immense task obscurely begun. Later in the afternoon, she sent for Mempes, and discussed with him the future policy of the firm. When he was going she said shyly:

"Are we friends, Mr Mempes?"

The manager looked at her with a whimsical surprise on his arrogant face. "I hope so."

"Then will you use my Christian name and let me use yours?"

"In this room I will," Mempes said. "Thank you, Mary." He lingered, smiled at her, and went. . . .

During the first few months of her rule, her popularity increased. She was rarely seen. The work went on as before and there was plenty of work, with trade and prosperity increasing. There was no lack of money in Danesacre and the fact of a young girl at the head of Garton's

from a nine days' wonder became a thing of little interest. The fiercely
individual people of Danesacre disliked showing surprise. It began to
be an understood thing that Garton's niece owned the Yard and the
Middlesborough Works, but that John Mempes ruled, and there were
people who remembered Rupert Ling's malicious gossip. But it was not
open talk and the tendency was to leave Mary Roxby alone. She kept
herself quiet, she harmed no one, and she was half Garton. Let her be.
Garton's Yard was satisfied, and feeling on the whole friendly towards
its girl owner.

It would be difficult to say just when the tone of the Yard began to
change. There was to begin with a rumour that Mempes was opposing
the complete change-over to steam begun by Mark Henry and carried
forward by Mary. People said he thought she was going too quickly.
Danesacre opinion was for him and against her. The iron-framed,
teak-planked clippers building in other yards for the wool and tea trades
were superior in speed and strength to their American rivals and would
never, so far as Danesacre and the Yard could see, be supplanted by
clumsy boats relying on borrowed wind. They were a glory to behold,
and they were the natural build for a ship. No good could come of the
tea-kettle business. Iron clippers were all very well, but iron steamers
were an unnatural invention. What, in any event, the Yard asked, did a
girl and the crazier niece of crazy Mark Henry Garton know about
ships? She should stick to her feminine last and let John Mempes have
his way. She had critics in plenty outside the Yard, among her fellow
shipowners and builders. There was a widespread disbelief in the
possibility of building marine engines capable of doing the long
voyages at a profitable rate. The Yard, which knew all about the failure
of Prendergast's water-tube boilers without understanding its causes,
had its supporters in shipbuilding circles, and not in Danesacre only.
The world's sailing ships were even yet not on the crest of their form.
Seven years after Mark Henry's death Rupert Ling wrote from
Melbourne that Port Philip Bay was full of the finest sailing ships ever
launched. Decks of polished teak and mahogany shone in the sun, and
gleaming brass-work stabbed the air with long glittering lances of light.
Mark Henry's lifelong rival, called Old Smithson from his thirtieth
year, might be excused for refusing to believe in the possibility of a

steam-driven hulk ousting these radiant exquisite creations. Even when the same year saw the door of Suez swinging open, Old Smithson would not believe. . . .

The Yard talked, but since so long as there was work to be done, shipwrights and carpenters and boilermakers would do it and draw their wages, what did it matter whether the Garton Line, as the Yard's ships now designated themselves, sailed under steam or canvas, or both? The work went on and the talk went on with it.

The truth behind the talk was nearer like it than truth and rumour commonly are. Mempes had found Mary obstinate on the question of steam. Too busy to leave Danesacre, she wrote to Thomas Prendergast, and received from him twice a week long replies in a fine clerkly hand, setting out every detail of his progress in the building of marine engines, with specifications and diagrams of boilers and compound engines, and the arrangement of ships' machinery over which Mary pored until she did begin to add a measure of technical equipment to her stubborn belief in the future of the steamship. Prendergast's letters had a crude clarity in odd contrast to his lawyer-like hand. Later it was discovered that he could not write, but dictated his reports. As Mary read and re-read them belief grew into an act of faith. She laid an ultimatum before Mempes. There would be no more sailing ships built in the Yard. The Line was to become a line of steamships. The orders in hand for steamships on account of other firms when Mark Henry died would occupy the Yard for the next two years and no order for sail would be taken. The girl argued with him on the question, while he beat her down with figures from Smithson's Yard and facts about the wool and tea trade, until argument reached a stalemate and she silenced him with a definite order. Mempes was a little angry and when he found that she had been keeping back the correspondence with a Liverpool line for the building of a liner for the Chinese route, he was very angry. There was no reason why Mary should have kept the letters from him. He challenged her and she said frankly that she so disliked his attitude to steam that she intended to handle all such correspondence herself until it came to actual terms.

Her mixture of candour and secrecy baffled him. So too did her gaiety, that occasionally broke all bounds in their interviews, with the result that Mr. John Sacheverell Mempes, whose youthful grace had stiffened with the years into a rather stately courtesy, sometimes found himself rallied and railed upon with much thin sweet laughter at the very climax of one of his careful speeches. Then he became more formal than ever. Mary repented when she saw that he was mortified, and was gentle and deferential on the instant. He found himself halting on a phrase that rang pompous in his own ears even before he caught the twitching of her delicious young mouth, and began to make himself simple, not so that she should understand him but so that she should not laugh.

Her obstinacy was beginning to alarm him. The docility she had shown him at their first interview melted like dew in the hot sun. On the question of steam neither persuasion nor reason moved her an inch. He faced her across the old tulip-wood table that had been Mark Henry's working-table, an expert in the handling of women and a polished subtle gentleman with years of experience ripening in the brain behind his wide forehead, and was outfaced by a young girl with at best four years' knowledge and an unreasoning adherence to the policy she had taken over from an inspired buffoon, more buffoon than inspired here. She had the most headstrong and insensate belief in her luck. Mempes despaired when he saw orders that should have come to Garton's going to their rivals. He knew with absolute certainty that the numbers and tonnage of Danesacre's sailing ships were climbing and bound to climb. He had, and told her that he had, the liveliest interest in steam. Ultimately, he believed in it, but he did not believe that the compound marine engine would be improved on for another half century. Thus the demand for steamers would be naturally limited. It might even drop, and Garton's Yard would have lost trade and way, would be ruined before progress caught up with Mary Roxby's inherited infatuation. John Mempes was a clear-sighted man—to the end of his elegant nose. His nose was an eighteenth century nose at that. It achieved the middle of the nineteenth with tolerable ease. After that it began to block John Mempes's vision.

One day he said:

"Mary, I don't know what will become of you. You're the most ingenuous creature I ever knew and capable of the most disingenuous actions. You don't tell lies, but you conceal truths. You're as pig-headed as Mark Henry and twice as arrogant. In short, you're an intolerable woman and I don't know why I work for you."

Mary was leaning back in her shiny straight-backed arm-chair. The folds of her black frock melted into the black horse-hair of the chair back. She was looking past Mempes at the harbour, and the branch of a tree waving outside the window made warm dusky patterns on her face and neck. Mempes lifted an involuntary hand to brush them away, and as he checked the absurd gesture he knew why he stayed on with Garton's. He was lazy, hating change, and he was in love. Love was no new experience for Mempes. At thirty-nine he had sufficient experience of women to be as much amused as alarmed to find himself in love with the young owner of Garton's. It was inevitable, at his age, that he should fall under the spell of youth. He might almost have been expecting it. It was a delicious sensation and Mary was delicious and in the silence that followed his words, he gave himself up to a delicate savouring of his emotions before her beauty. It surprised him to discover that desire, the easily satisfied longing for possession, was not among them.

He wanted her to stay forever unpossessed. Forever young and faintly smiling, to recline in her chair looking at the harbour through the gracious eighteenth-century window of Mark Henry's office, with sun and shadow playing on her face and life suspended in a morning air. Forever the faint sounds of the shipyard to linger in the warm room, forever a ship, her slender masts raping the motionless air, to lie over against the house, forever peace, and life on top of expectation.

Mary stirred. She turned a clouded gaze on her manager.

"You don't see what I see," she said. "You see so much in the past and I so little, being young and inexperienced, that I must look ahead to fill my eyes. You think of steam as at best an expensive toy. You think steamers ugly, too, and though that ought not to weigh with Garton's manager it does. You think I'm rushing into a long, immensely long and narrow corridor, that may, years after I have dropped by the way, open on to a new expanse. I think you're wrong. For me the end of the corridor is so near that I can feel the new wind on my face. Call me a fool—you've often thought Mark Henry a fool, but he was Garton's and you're his manager. It's in my bones that we're on the immediate edge of change. This liner for Liverpool. You think a gross tonnage of 2347 tons too great for the Chinese route. I think it will do and do well for now, but that five, ten years, will see us smiling at the thought of building so small a ship for the Eastern trade." Mary paused and fell back on her book to supplement her avowal of faith. "Thomas Prendergast's figures convince me that we can keep the coal consumption down to twenty tons a day for every purpose. We shall improve the Garton compound engine and build a bigger. Why stick at compound! Why shouldn't there be triple expansion? I'm putting it badly because I'm ignorant, but what I dream about, Prendergast can make."

"Slowly, Mary, slowly."

"No. Not slowly. Quickly. Soon. Because the world can't wait. Can't you feel it? Can't you feel the pressure of change? It beats on my brain sometimes so that I can hardly bear it. Iron ships. Prendergast says there'll be steel ships. The *Mary Gray*, bless her, took over three months from Foochow. The new Liverpool liner ought to do it in sixty-five days, counting stoppages at ports. Do you think the world will wait the extra thirty days for the *Mary Gray* to come in like a cloud of grace, ravishing all our hearts? You know it won't. Think of all the people working in the Garton Iron Works. They weren't there thirty years ago. They were only born because the iron wanted them. They've all got to be fed. There'll have to be more ships and quicker ships, to bring them food, and iron, and to take way what they've made. Think of all the people born just to weave wool and spin cotton for my iron workers. There must be ships for them and more and more and faster and faster. Can't you see? Really can't you see? Can't you hear it coming? Or are you just shutting your eyes and ears because you hate it?"

"Ah, stay like that, Mary."

"Like what?"

"So young—and interested." Mempes smiled at himself, and began all over again to fasten a drag of argument and wise counsel on Mary's dangerous energy. . . .

The first hint of trouble in the Yard came over the Port Union. Mary
had a dislike of the seamen's and shipwrights' unions, partly the fruit of
furious warnings and denunciations dropped by Mark Henry in her ears
before she knew what he was talking about, and partly a native dislike
of interference. She was far from the courage to oppose them in
Danesacre, but when a troublesome or unsatisfactory man was also a
prominent member of the Union he soon found himself looking for
work outside Garton's. Two such dismissals coming in rapid succession resulted in a deputation to Mary.

She received it in her office, sitting stiffly upright in Mark Henry's
chair, and listened with grave courtesy while the spokesman addressed
her. His speech threatened to become a dissertation on Unionism in
general and she fidgeted a little with a paper-cutter on her desk. When
he ended she said civilly:

"I'm at a loss to understand why you came, Mr. Burrows. These
men were not dismissed as Union members, but for carelessness, and in
the case of Gill, for constant absence due to a cause you know as well as
I do."

"Gill drinks no more than the rest of us," one man observed.

"Then he has a weaker head," Mary retorted. "I don't see the rest of
you absent every Monday morning and your wives with black eyes.
I've no objection to Union men who behave themselves. I've every
objection to drunkards and careless workers. That's all."

Her position was unassailable and the deputation withdrew, to
accuse itself of moral weakness.

"You can't talk to a girl," Burrows said, twitching his brows over
blue eyes embedded in their wrinkled pits.

"Her'll be talked to before long," another retorted. "Her may have
yon Mempes under her thumb. Her haven't us."

The observation laid Mary open to a jest that came pat on his
words. . . .

The following morning Mempes saw the jest scrawled on the stone
gate-post of the house as he came through the Yard. He sent a lad to
remove it and walked about the Yard all day in the likeness of a
devouring angel, his eyes darting to detect the briefest lapse from
industry and his tongue curling round offenders with scarifying effect.

He was not surprised but he was a little alarmed. He told Mary that Gill was popular with the men and a good worker when not laid off by his unfortunate tastes, and suggested that she would be doing a politic thing if she took both men back. He had a very little hope that she would listen to him and his apprehension was justified. Mary refused shortly to hear any argument about it. Mempes went out to take the temperature of the Yard. He found it rising.

Two days later Gill's companion in misfortune hanged himself after two attempts to get work at other yards where his reputation for carelessness had preceded him. In an outburst of sentimental fury, Garton's Yard resolved to teach Mary a lesson. The men were in funds and the weather was propitious. They struck for the immediate reinstatement of Gill.

Mary refused. She sent for a guard of police and posted them at the Yard gates. Then she wrote out and had fixed to the wall a notice to the effect that all men not back at the Yard within forty-eight hours would be replaced by others. She sent John Mempes to the Tees to collect them. He tried to persuade her to wait at least a fortnight before taking such decisive measures.

"Give them time to cool down, and most of them will trickle back to work," he said. "They have too much money now. It's keeping them warm. Wait, Mary."

Mary refused to wait more than two days. She ordered him off on his errand, and shrugging his shoulders over her incensed obstinacy, he went. On the second day, going out to take down her notice, Mary found it scrawled over with the now familiar jest and with crude but unmistakable drawings. It was not familiar to her. With a grim mouth she took it down and retreated to the house. Mempes returned with his recruits and she made them a speech and sent them into the Yard.

There was no possibility of getting beds for them in the town and they spent their nights in the shed rolled in blankets supplied from the house. The strikers, who had let John Mempes and his new hands pass up Harbour Street assailed by nothing worse than insults and herring heads, now crowded round the high locked gates and overturned the carts bringing supplies of food to the besieged Yard. Dispersed by the police, they retired. The strike still wore the aspect of a holiday and it was not until more than a week had gone by that they began to plan serious measures against Mary Roxby. These involved the spread of the strike to the other Yards, and Mary found herself allied with Old Smithson and the other Danesacre shipbuilders on the side of privilege against lawlessness. Characteristically, she began to dislike her position more as her isolation vanished. She did not want sympathy. She sat at their conferences, and privately thought them extraordinarily stupid, while agreeing with them on the measures to be taken for their joint safety. A proposal to ask for soldiers from York roused her to violent opposition.

"Danesacre people ought to be able to settle their disputes without that sort of pompous interference," she said contemptuously, and all but Old Smithson, who went in terror of his neck, supporting her, the soldiers did not come.

During all this John Mempes remained cynically cool. The spectacle of the young girl riding the storm she might by compromise have averted pleased him. He loved her for her very folly. She was a gallant and picturesque fool. He had offered her prudent advice and she had rejected it, as Mark Henry himself would have done in the same circumstances, except that Mark Henry would never have pushed the men to such extremes. Or was it that the men reached extremes more easily nowadays? Mempes gave himself up to the epicurean pleasure of watching imperious youth in action.

The strike leader, Burrows, was an oldish man with a savage tongue that he had whetted to a rough edge of perfection in the half-savage town. He visited Mary and told her bluntly that she was the best-hated woman in Danesacre.

"The women would strip your clothes from your back and drown you in the harbour if they could," he said.

"You struck," said Mary, "to force me to take back a man whose drunkenness is a constant loss to me and a hindrance to his fellow workers. When you were at sea, before you gave up honest work and took to earning your living by these talkers' tricks——"

"I'm crippled," growled Burrows. Mary took no notice of him.

"——you'd have been sharp enough on a man whose habits made him a nuisance and a danger to the rest of the ship. Yet you ask me to keep on such a man in my Yard, and draw off your men when I refuse."

"Gill," said the strike leader, "is a good worker. You can't deny that. If he hadn't been a good Union man too he'd have been in Garton's yet."

Mary told him coolly that she had no love for the Union and no intention of allowing any interference with her authority. Her coolness discountenanced the man, and he went away, full of a resentment that deepened as he walked down Harbour Street and heard the crying of hungry children and saw women turn listlessly back into their houses after hearing from his lips that there was no change. He was gross and uneducated. Though he paid his Union dues and saw to it that the other men paid theirs, he had no vision of any kinship between himself and the men in other ports. As for any idea that he was somehow in league with French and Dutch and American seamen and shipwrights, he would have repudiated it with the foulest violence. He was, in short, a man without vision and without aim. But as he strode down Harbour Street after his fruitless interview with Mary, in the farthest, dimmest recesses of his being, woke and stirred a vague sense that this was not merely his quarrel with the owner of Garton's. It was part of an immense quarrel only just now beginning. There was some spirit in Mary Roxby, an insolence, a hard assurance, that his own spirit violently challenged. He was confused. Already he was conscious of defeat in this encounter. But this was not the end of the quarrel. God in heaven, no.

His perplexities and confused anger found vent in a bitter reflection. "Mark Henry, the ——, was drunk every night of his life, but there was no dismissing him."

The following day Mary, walking down Harbour Street after a meeting of the shipbuilders, was hissed and mobbed by a crowd of women. The news was carried to the Yard and Mempes, forcing his way through the crowd, had his own clothes torn and his face scratched before he came within sight of Mary. She had her back to the wall of a house and was facing her shrieking assailants with a calm face. Her hat was off and her hair about her shoulders. As Mempes reached her a woman cried: "Here comes her man." An obscene gibe, coming from a window above Mary's head heralded a volley of them. Standing in front of Mary, Mempes could see no change in her white face. A stone hit her on the head and impassively she wiped away the trickle of blood with a corner of her sleeve.

Mempes caught sight of one of the strikers in the crowd.

"Here," he called, "you there, can't you call your women off?"

The man made a somewhat shamefaced retort and put his hand on a woman's shoulder to drag her away. But Danesacre women were never submissive creatures and in a moment his hands were fully occupied in defending himself from the chastisement that fell on him. Other men, lounging on the steps of the houses, came to his rescue and Mempes seized the distracted moment to fight his way through the crowd, with Mary on his arm. One or two of the strikers helped him and he got her into safety behind the wall of Mark Henry's garden. He put her hair up with his own hands. It altered her appearance strangely, making her look younger and less composed. She was trembling, but when he got her into the house she merely thanked him and went away upstairs. He watched her go, pausing on the landing to look fastidiously at her torn skirt. Then she went on, her head high and her colour too, now.

He blamed himself for the indolence that had let him acquiesce in her conduct of the strike without a more determined attempt to make her see that she must compromise. She was headstrong, but she was the merest girl, and if he had persisted she would have given way to his experience in handling men. So he told himself and cursed his fatal lack of seriousness.

Later in the day he sent to ask Mary for an interview. She gave it to him in Richard's nursery, and the sight of her bent lovingly over the sleepy boy gave him an idea. He tried delicately to find out what she had suffered from that revelation of the hatred she had courted. She removed herself from his questions with a calm pride.

"The men are sick of this strike," he said. "I know it. I have my own ways of getting at their thoughts. Make a generous gesture, Mary, and they'll give way over Gill."

"What do you want me to do?"

"Offer to take them back, without conditions. I'll arrange it that Gill doesn't make trouble."

"And turn off the men we fetched here from Middlesborough? No."

"The children are hungry, Mary."

"Their fathers should have thought of that," she said, but he saw her wince.

He could not move her. He looked in despair at her sullen mouth, and his gaze, travelling upwards, rested on the angry cut made by the stone. She felt his eyes on it and pulled her hair down to cover the place.

"How vain you are," he said, and smiled. Richard had fallen asleep on her knee. Standing up with an easy movement she laid the heavy child in his bed and turned to Mempes.

"Dear John," she said, "don't think I'm not grateful to you."

Gratitude left him hungry and he went away, to think of her and forget the strike. He remembered, some cold hours later, that he was all but forty and that he had most signally failed to persuade Mary against her will. He recalled the grave short little girl who had followed him about the Yard, marvelling at him. He could have moulded that child to any form. Why was he not able to form the girl? "She was formed before I got her," he exclaimed. "Oh Mary, to have something, the least of you. . . ."

When Burrows approached Mary with an offer to end the strike if she would take back all the men but Gill, she refused. Anger whitened his face and she told him that a good many of the Middlesborough men were anxious to go home. This she had from Mempes. She offered to replace these men by strikers, and to take the remainder on when and if the Yard needed them. After a last struggle with his rising fury, the strike leader agreed.

"Let the men with families come back first," Mary stipulated. . . .

The strike was over, but Mary's unpopularity remained. She had proofs of it on the walls of the Yard and in every walk she took down Harbour Street. She shut her eyes to most of the evidence and Mempes kept the rest from her. When later she married and had another and absorbing interest in her life, she ceased to bother about the human side of Garton's at all. She lived in her schemes and in her husband, and if the Yard disliked and distrusted her she either did not notice or did not care.

She was unpopular in another quarter. When she succeeded to Garton's, the two Roxbys approached her with a request for larger allowances. She was more than civil. She treated them with every mark of deference, as if they and not she were the suppliants, but she added not a penny to their income. Even when a vein of ironstone was discovered on the borders of the Roxby land, justifying her prescience in keeping that part of it, she would not allow them an increase. She made the discovery an excuse for installing her own man to look after Richard's interests. The vein was a poor one and its distance from the railway lessened its profits. Mary soon closed it down but what she got from it was enough to put Richard's shrunken estate in better order than it had enjoyed for years.

She would not put Garton money into it, but she wanted it to pay for itself and be a fit inheritance for Richard. To that end she hardened her heart against Charles and James. She was not what they said she was, as mean as be damned. She could not forget what it was like to be poor. She dreaded poverty all her life, and was never extravagant save for Richard and her second husband. She kept her daughters short of money, and her personal spending was always accounted for to its last penny.

Her treatment of Archie's brothers was not purely calculating. It was a matter of feeling with her, too. She was not Mark Henry's niece for nothing. James and Charles Roxby were useless and because they were she would do just enough for them to keep them alive. Nothing more. They made several attempts to move her. She was then always kindness itself, and they retired from her kindness and her polite respect two completely defeated old men, to spend their last years writing malicious letters about her to their friends. A collection of Charles Roxby's letters came into her hands when she was an old woman, and surprised her by the depth of the resentment they revealed. She was always surprised and a little hurt when the nobility of her motives was called in question. . . .

6

The end of the sixties saw Mary's insistence on steam a little nearer being justified. She had given way to John Mempes so far as to build on her own account five composite-built tea clippers in the six years following the strike. They were as superb sailing ships as Garton's Yard had ever turned out, and revived in Mary all her childish adoration of beauty in a ship. They never equalled their wooden predecessors in light winds, but they could be driven into a head sea as the magnificent *Mary Gray* never could, and they were bigger, with more room for cargo. The first two were overmasted and paid for it, but Mempes learned his lesson and the rest were as perfectly sparred as any sailing ship on the seas. On these ships Mary lavished a love she never gave to any othes, and when the beautiful *Peerless* went down off Yokohama with all hands, the loss nearly broke her heart. She mourned her for months.

The compromise that led to the building of the clippers was as characteristic of her as her stubbornness. She would push obstinacy to its extreme and pay the penalty of it, and then, as if only then had the lesson been learned, she would accept correction on just those points where her judgment agreed with the correction.

She made that one compromise to the present, but she held to it even when in 1866 Smithson's Yard, sticking entirely to sail, was at its zenith of prosperity, that steam was bound to triumph. Steam tonnage, gradually overhauling sailing tonnage, crept up and up, and when Old Smithson died in the blaze of his triumph, she bought his yard and turned it over to steam. In the new yard she built the *Roxborough*, of 3300 tons, for the Atlantic service. She was fitted with paddles and did the trip from London to New York in nine days.

The rivalry of sail and steam was keener during this decade than ever. The emigration trade was in the hands of the sailing ship firms. The wool trade was theirs. Only on the China route were the steamers beginning to make themselves felt, and Garton's Yard built eight ships for this trade, two for the Line and the other six for London firms.

Mary never wavered from the course she had set herself by Mark Henry's chart. Though she built the five clippers, she built them for love as much as because she knew that the sailing ship had still a little time to go before it was crowded off the seas by the clamorous need of the new age for size and speed and economy of working. She built no more. She was for the new age. Of that she was never for a moment in doubt. And when the Suez Canal opened a door to the East for her steamers, she knew, if Mempes and the rest of Danesacre were still hesitant, that she was justified. She was building, being too young for the past to linger with her but as beauty in a dream, for the years to come. She was one of the moderns. . . .

She needed all the justification she could get, for she had strained her resources to the utmost to pay for Thomas Prendergast's experiments. During these years she drew for herself as little as might be out of the firm and though she felt the need of a second manager in the Yard itself, to supplement John Mempes' lukewarm interest in steam, she put off broaching the question. Not because she was afraid to offend Mempes but because she hated to spend the money. . . .

In telling the story of the years of doubt and achievement that followed Mark Henry's death I have got far ahead of the story of Mary's second marriage, and what she made of that. It might have been her first, so little mark had Archie Roxby made on her, and it came about in an astonishingly short space of time, following the strike, and when she had already more than half promised to marry John Mempes.

Mempes was an adroit and careful lover. He knew a little of Mary's first marriage and guessed that the girl might have a shrinking from the physical aspect of love that would need a gentle touch to bring her round. Moreover he himself, though her youth and the nearness of her fresh beauty could intoxicte him, was not the ardent lover he had been, to less desired women, when Mary was a very little girl. He was forty. He could not afford to wait but he could afford to go slowly and avoid alarming the young girl by an indelicate revelation of passion.

He began to flatter her, but not grossly, but so subtly that it was a mere warmth added to his speech. She missed him if a day passed without his appearance in the office, and when he made an excuse to remove himself for a whole week the transports of her greeting on his return made up to him for the pangs he had suffered in absence. It went to his head. He accepted her invitation to dinner and afterwards, with

Miss Flora sleeping in a dim corner of the room, he sat beside her in the harbour window.

Mary had dressed with some ceremony for this dinner and her shoulders rose in a slender curve from the confines of a tight bodice. Mempes talked and she listened to him with the delicate air of surprise that Wagener had remarked in her. It sprang from the depth and shape of her eyes and the line of the brow above them, and Mempes, seeing it as if for the first time, was overcome with love and pity. It made him humble, and he faltered over his declaration, with a diffidence so new to him in this situation that he lost his tongue altogether and could do nothing but repeat her name, over and over again, like a man appealing for help.

It touched Mary profoundly. All her childish admiration for Mark Henry's debonair manager joined with new affection to make her tremble at the sight of him asking humbly for her love.

She said:

"Do you really love me?"

"Mary, I do. I adore you."

"Don't wake Miss Flora," Mary whispered. "I like you very much."

Mempes groaned softly.

"Is that all? Is that all, Mary?"

His need of her at that moment was so great that he made a movement to take her in his arms. He wanted to feel the comfort of her breast. But when he had held her for a second he felt her stiffen in his grasp, as if the contact with his rising passion chilled her. He let her go and said:

"Forgive me. I need you so."

Mary stood up and leaned against the window. Mempes watched the breath come and go under the hand she laid on her throat. At last she turned to him with honest friendliness.

"I like you so much. I'm honoured because you love me. Will you let me have time to think? You see, I'm not very young——"

"Twenty-three, Mary, or is it twenty-four?"

"I've been married."

"You don't know what marriage is, my dear."

Mary shivered.

"Give me a little time. . . ."

He was afraid to press her. The fear of losing her by showing too much warmth remained with him through the long weeks when Mary hesitated, allowing him to talk to her of love and marriage but never saying: "I love you," or even: "I will marry you." He was too much of his century not to have been satisfied to hear the second if he could not hear the first. He was very subtle in his love-making, and never after that first avowal, did he allow himself to forget all that his experience had taught him of the way to handle women. Mary was fascinated by his sophisticated skill. He advanced in her heart. He felt it. She felt it too, and she could not have said why she hesitated, nor what in these days when the sound of Mempes' voice in the Yard could make her pulse flutter, was missing from the happiness he gave her. She was not capricious. And still she waited on the edge of surrender and did not know for what she could be waiting.

One day she told him abruptly that she was going to London with Miss Flora for a month's holiday. The dismay he checked before it reached his tongue prompted her to say:

"I can't think clearly about marriage when I see you, John. You distract me. I must go away." She knotted her brows. "I could buy some clothes, too."

He kissed her hand to hide the triumph in his eyes. He was sure of her now. He spent the two months of her absence dreaming of the delicate kindness he would show her. She should be very happy with a husband who had learned every lesson of love merely in order to present her with the finished product. That she did not write was no surprise to him. He smiled indulgently. Let her have her last dreams of freedom before she fluttered into his hands. But he seized on her letter when it did come, with a famished eagerness. It was short.

It ran:

"Dear John, Forgive me. I am married to a Mr. Hervey I have met here. I love him utterly. We are coming home next week, and I beg that you will let my housekeeper know. I am conscious that I should have written to you sooner and I am anxious to serve you always in any way I can, and remain,

Your humble servant,

Mary Hervey

My husband's name is Hugh. He is a year older than I am, and very kind."

John Mempes found every part of that youthful letter less cruel than the allusion to her husband's age. He suffered horribly, and it was not only his vanity that suffered.

When Mary came home he was sufficiently master of himself to be anxious that she should feel no awkwardness in greeting him. It was the cruellest stroke of all to realise that she was too absorbed in her happiness to feel anything outside that. . . .

Mempes pulled himself together and never failed but on one occasion to show Mary's husband a formal friendliness, to which Hugh responded by frank liking, calling him "sir" and treating him as a nice youngster might treat a Don for whom he had a respectful admiration. John Mempes stood it creditably well, except on the one occasion alluded to, when he suddenly lost his temper in the most outrageous and startling fashion over a question of port. "Port," he shouted, "port, you fool, is a wine only fit for men at Oxford and aged mumpers whose palates have been ruined by years and debauchery. A vile drink, sir. A noxious, poisonous mixture."

He caught Hugh's amazed glance, and subsided into his protective courtesy. . . .

Book Two

MARY HERVEY

CHAPTER ONE

1

MARY spent her first week in London very quietly. She visited a few shops, but for the most part she stayed in the rooms she had taken on Miss Flora's recommendation and read, or thought of John Mempes.

The rooms were in Kensington, in a small house with an apple orchard at the bottom of the tiny walled garden. They belonged to a widowed friend of Miss Flora's youth and the two old ladies talked in their thin wavering voices, while Mary dreamed over her book. It was late Spring and she could sit in the garden. The relief from the long strain of Garton's gave her a sense of irresponsible freedom that she was reluctant to lose. She thought of John Mempes less and less. He did not seem to belong to this world where youth sat under blossoming trees and dwelt deliciously on another long interrupted day.

At the end of a week she wanted action. She ordered herself a plum-coloured habit and hired a horse and a groom to ride with her in the Park. The morning of her first ride was cold with a light cold wind, that whipped her cheeks. She made the groom ride well behind her and as the riders thinned she ventured on a gallop that left him out of sight. A top-hat, scudding before the wind, rolled across the track, almost under the horse's feet. He behaved as badly as an over-conditioned horse can and she was forced to punish him severely before he quieted down. The owner of the hat came up in time to see the end of her exertions. He was profoundly shocked at his hat's conduct and overwhelmed her with apologies. Mary was so pleased to have someone to talk to that she answered him with frank friendliness. It encouraged him to make good use of his time; when the groom came up he found his morning's mistress halted by the rails and talking to a clean-shaven young man whom she apparently knew well. He reined in his horse and drew back to wait.

What Mary was saying with every mark of intimate friendship was:

"That man alarms me. I am sure he knows we've just met."

"My name," said the young man, "is Hervey. Hugh Hervey. My sister would like to call on you."

Mary laughed. "How do you know she would? She doesn't know me."

"She will when I tell her about you," he said anxiously.

A sudden shyness deepened the crimson of Mary's cheeks. She contrived to irritate her horse into plunging wildly, and left the forward young man standing hat in hand at the side of the track. He was still there when she came round again. She drew up almost unconsciously, as if she had not meant to leave him. This time he learned her name and where she stayed before she rode away and did not return.

Mary's mind was distracted by an echo that eluded her until she was sitting, languidly happy after her ride, in the tiny sitting-room facing the orchard. Then she remembered, and the memory brought her to her feet in a wild longing to hide herself from the two nodding old ladies. The young man of the Park reminded her of Gerry Hardman. As if she had seen them yesterday, the boy's form and features, that at any time in the past few years she could not have recalled but in a vague blurred image, rose in front of her. She heard his voice. She almost felt the touch of his hand, and trembled at it.

She thought of Hugh again. There were differences, not only of age. Hugh's hair, like Gerry's, was dark, parted almost in the middle, and worn shorter than the fashion. His eyes were grey under dark brows, more level than Gerry's. His face was narrower across the cheek-bones, but he had Gerry's slightly aquiline nose and Gerry's small mouth. The resemblance was disturbing enough. It disturbed Mary. She thought: "I've never dared to wonder why he didn't come back. I suppose he thought of it as a foolish impulse. I waited for him. Would it have made any difference if he had? I might have married him; Richard might have been his son. Ah! . . .we might have quarrelled. Perhaps our marriage would have ended like my mother's did. Oh, it wouldn't, it wouldn't. Why didn't you come back? I'd have loved you and helped you and we should have been happy working for each other.'' The sense of irretrievable loss drove her upstairs to her own room and she thought of Gerry and Hugh until her mind began to play her tricks and it was Hugh Hervey she had lost and found again after nine years of bitter lessons and barren toil. It occurred to her that she was still only twenty-four and looked younger. The thought cheered her greatly.

Hugh's sister called on her the next afternoon. Louise Hervey was a small dark woman, very well read, with pretences to scholarship, and a witty and malicious tongue. She thought Mary rather stupid, but she was civil to her for Hugh's sake, and made Mary free of their circle of friends. Hugh had fallen in love at first sight. In less than a week he told Mary so, standing in the Kensington orchard. The friendly dusk hid them from the windows of the little house and Mary was lying in his arms for a long time before either of them said anything more.

She stirred first:

"Is it true?" she asked softly. "Has it really happened?"

"Don't move," Hugh said urgently. "My love, my love. Don't move. I like you here."

But she sat up in his arms and kissed him, giving him her love in a surrender that made him a little dizzy. He held her to him with triumphant strength. "You are mine?" he said. "Mine, all mine? Mary, we've got to be married soon, at once."

"I didn't care for marriage before," Mary observed.

"Don't think about it," Hugh said fiercely. "I—I can't bear it. I've never touched another woman."

Mary thought grimly: "It was I who had to bear it," but she set herself to erase the unpleasant thought from her lover's mind and succeeded so well that a moment later he was teasing her with mischievous tenderness on her reluctance to marry. He teased her until they both lost their heads a little and clung together with a passion that shook them and drove them apart.

"You see—we must get married soon," Hugh stammered. "We—oh, I love you so."

Mary drew herself out of his reach.

"It will be all right, won't it?" she asked desperately.

"You're not afraid? Not of me, Mary," Hugh said sternly. His voice softened. "You adorable little girl. I wouldn't hurt you."

"Promise."

"I promise."

They were married by special licence. Louise Hervey told all her friends that Hugh had done far better for himself than his foolish ideas had led them to expect. "Of course, he has his own money," she said. "But he's been taken up with these socialists as they're called, and anything might have come of that. The girl's as stupid as an old boot, but ravishing to look at and has twice Hugh's money. I wonder how she'll take to London."

2

Long after Hugh had fallen asleep, with his head in the curve of her arm, Mary lay awake. The weight of his thin young body against hers was a joy she was reluctant to forget in sleep. When at last she slept, it was to wake very early in a quiet dawn. She raised herself on one arm to look at her husband. For long moments she studied him as if she were trying to get his features by heart, adding together flushed cheeks, curving lashes, mouth softened by sleep, and every dear attraction that he had. He stirred and she thought: "Oh, don't wake yet. You're all mine when you're asleep. Don't wake for ages yet. My love. My dearest dear."

He woke, gazed at her for a moment with a dark quiet look, and then turning, buried his face against her shoulder, and lay for a long time, his arm across her breast. Mary held him with triumphant gentleness. This then was marriage, this exquisite sense of completion and power. This was life. She was really living at last. In a passion of gratitude she pressed her lips to Hugh's smooth hair and murmured foolish phrases of tenderness and pride.

3

Her young husband was an increasing joy to Mary. Part of her joy was for his very youth. A year her senior, he seemed immensely less experienced and less mature. He had done nothing since he left Oxford but play with the idea of a book on mediaeval guilds for which he had collected a quantity of notes and made a dozen separate skeletons, each one more articulated than the last. He had indeed the makings of a scholar, as distinct from his witty sister's show of it, but a settled income and his own natural indolence combined to leave him at twenty-five pretty much where he was when he left Oxford with more ambitions than honours to his account. He had lately drifted into friendship with some eager and charming young social rebels, and while they pricked his ambition into fresh life they took up so much of his time that the book got very little further. And now here was Mary, and the days were not long enough to share with her, to take her to Oxford and watch her surrender to the bewitched city, to show her Richmond and the river, to teach her to dance and talk to her of music, and study and socialism and love, and love, and again love.

And Mary listened. Hugh talked with a freedom that shocked her, so much more startling was the language he used than the limited profanity of Mark Henry and the Yard. She liked to be shocked by Hugh. It gave her a delicious sense of having been gathered into a new intimacy. Here for the first time was someone who teased her and laughed at her, said what he pleased in the language of his generation, was familiar and tender, disregarded all the half-unconscious pruderies she had drawn round her since her first marriage, and made her feel befriended and secure. It was a happy feeling. She gave herself up to it with an almost voluptuous joy, trying, under Louise Hervey's bright cruel glances, to keep the worshipper from looking out of her eyes when she and Hugh were together in company.

Hugh talked readily and very well. He leaped from one subject to the next with a dexterity that fascinated Mary, who could never talk in public unless she were deeply moved. Hugh's trick of picturesque exaggeration was delightful to her. Everything that happened to Hugh happened with more force than to anyone else. He made the recital of a walk down Regent Street sound like an adventure among man-eating savages. Mary listened to him with a brave pretence that he was not the centre of her world. Her own failure to contribute anything to the entertainment distressed her not at all. Hugh was amusing enough for two. She watched his changing sensitive face and thought: "All these people only see him as he is now, animated and bright-eyed and deliciously self-sufficient. They don't know what he's like when they go and he turns to me and says: 'Darling, thank God that's over,' and talks only for me, quietly. They don't hold Hugh in their arms when he's tired and comfort him and love him. Dear Hugh. Do I like you best when you're unhappy and come like a little boy to be soothed or when you're madly alive and saying: 'Let's do this, and this?' I don't know. I love you all the time."

Hugh was indeed very young, and entirely undisciplined except by his delicate senses. Life had taught him no such lessons as it had taught Mary. He had almost everything to learn. He made an engaging and softly affectionate lover. His life, since his mother's death, had been rather starved of affection, and in his pleasure in Mary's love he gave her everything he had, his thoughts, his young adoration, passion in its first sweetness, everything that a sensitive youngster whose intellect and sharpened senses are dividing his energy between them, has to give to the first woman he loves. If he knew that there were dark shadows in Mary's experience that his had never compassed, he would not look at them. He made delicious protecting gestures towards her.

But there the shadows were, and one fell across their companionship when Mary spoke of going home. Hugh gave her a quick surprised look.

"But you are at home, Mary. Do you want us to live somewhere else? We will if you like, but I love this house. Does Louise bother you?"

Mary looked round the book-lined sitting-room of the house Hugh shared with his sister and shook her head.

"I don't mean that," she explained. "I mean Danesacre. I've stayed away longer than I ought to."

Hugh bounded to his feet.

"But, Mary, we can't live up there," he cried. "It's the end of the world. Darling, you're joking."

But Mary was in desperate earnest and when Hugh realised it, realising in the same moment that his young wife had another and absorbing interest beside himself, he behaved like a wilful boy. He accused Mary of having played at love-making and so bewildered the girl by his vehemence in complaint that she felt a criminal and had hard work to control tears of same. Yet she was sure that she was right and Hugh wilfully shockingly wrong. She tried argument.

"But, Hugh, I told you about Garton's. The Yard. The Works. You knew everything about it. I've been there six years, since you went to Oxford. Think, Hugh."

"Then it's had enough of you," Hugh said angrily. "You've got a manager, haven't you? Let him look after it. What is the use of paying someone to work for you and doing it all yourself?"

The point of view was so novel that Mary paused to consider it, and Hugh followed up his advantage by pleading with her in the gentlest way, coaxing, teasing, laughing, melting her to a strange weakness as she looked down at this dear husband. But still she came back to the immovable fact of Garton's. There it was. It was hers, her burden if you like, though she had never thought of it as that. But something she had to carry. She conceived of herself for a moment as having abandoned the Yard, and the picture filled her with dismay.

"Whatever should I do without it?" she demanded.

Hugh had turned pale.

"You never explained to me that it meant so much to you," he said.

"I did," Mary said humbly. "But you don't listen to me very much. . . ."

It was not a soothing remark, and Hugh walked away and left her. In his absence, Mary came through bewilderment to a cold lucidity. Hugh must give way. There was so much less for him to give up in coming to Danesacre than she would lose by staying in London. The idea of sacrificing Garton's was preposterous. She thought it out as Mark Henry's niece, and forgot that she was Hugh Hervey's wife, until he came in late at night when she was ready for bed, and she saw by his face that he had been wrestling wretchedly with his problem. Then with a superb gesture she threw everything away and ran to put her arms round his neck.

"We won't go, Hugh darling, you shall do what you want. We'll stay here and never go back. There, will that do? Dear, will it do?"

Hugh held her away from him, and read her face.

"No, it won't do," he said roughly, and strained her to him again. "We'll go there as soon as you like. To-morrow."

She leaned back in his arms and he saw the joy and relief in her eyes.

"You—you'd be unhappy here," he said queerly, and loosed his hold. Mary stood in the middle of the room in her night-gown, with her hair falling about her. She was so much the neglected little girl that he turned back and caught her in his arms.

"It's all right, my little love. I don't really mind going to live among the savages with you. You're all that matters, really. Don't you understand?"

Mary was crying in his arms.

"*You* don't understand," she said, choking. "I don't want you to give anything up for me. I only want——"

"Only want me to want the same things that you do," Hugh finished for her, mischievously.

"Why, yes, I do," Mary said, laughing through her tears.

"You little egoist," Hugh said, "you dear beloved little egoist. You absurd baby. What right have you to be the owner of a line of steamships and furnaces and engine works and Heaven knows what else? There, I love you. Is it all over? Are you happy?"

"Yes, I'm happy. I'm always happy when you are. But you were so angry."

"Well, I'm not now."

With Hugh's arms round her, Mary was in no real doubt on the point, but she sighed.

"What is it? Hugh, what's the matter?"

"Nothing," Hugh muttered. "Nothing. Except—I love you."

"Oh, my dear. . . . Yes, I know."

She thought, in her innocence, that she was going to faint, and reeled a little when he loosened his hold. "I never felt like this in my life," she confided to him.

Love and mischief competed for place in the beloved face above her own. . . .

Hugh was falling asleep, with his head on her shoulder, when the thought struck him that she had an odd strain of hardness for one so soft and loving, but he put the thought away and fell asleep, like a contented child, sure of being kept safe and warm in her protecting love. . . .

They arranged to go to Danesacre in the following week. Louise found an opportunity to condole with him on having married into a barbarian tribe. He was very short with his sister, for whom he had a real affection, and some of his irritation transferred itself to Mary. He smothered it and took her to Bloomsbury to meet his rebel friends.

A colony of young wives and husbands lived together in a house in Queen's Square. The wives wore their hair cropped in page-boy fashion, and dressed in odd delightful gowns cut after the fashion of Italian primitives. Their husbands were clean-shaven like Hugh. Mary was tongue-tied and fascinated. She sat beside a vivid young creature with red hair. The lines of her body, when she moved, revealed approaching motherhood, a circumstance of which she presently spoke with a frankness that startled Mary into lively blushes. The other young woman laughed softly.

"I'm sorry," she said. "I forgot Hugh had married a young lady. My name is Andrews, Sylvia Andrews. Do you think you could ever come to tolerate us? But I hear you're taking Hugh away to reign with you in Hell. There, you're shocked again. Do forgive me."

Mary smiled, feeling a quick liking for Sylvia Andrews.

"It's not exactly Hell," she explained. "It's only a shipyard."

"The same thing," Sylvia retorted, shaking her cropped head. "Do be kind to Hugh and don't overlook him when you're back on your throne. He's very sweet, but he easily gets discouraged."

A little vexed by this young woman's pretensions to understand Hugh, Mary turned her attention to the other people in the room. As no one took any notice of her she could examine them at her ease. The room itself was remarkable enough. It was furnished sparsely, with chairs and a table as unlike the heavy mahogany of Mark Henry's house as anything could be. They were new, but they reminded Mary of much older furniture in Roxby House. Across one wall hung a crimson

banner, embroidered in white with the words: "Workers of the World
Unite." More and more people came in, some apparently working
men, and two old gentlemen in formal dress, one of whom Mary saw
spitting vigorously into a bowl of flowers after tasting something
handed round in quaintly coloured cups. He caught Mary's eye.
"Water in it," he said darkly, and proceeded with his purging. "Very
dangerous."

With the exception of the captious old gentleman and his friend,
every one in the room was young. Most of them were very young.
There were few women, except the short-haired young hostesses in
their decorative clothes. One tall woman dressed in faded red velvet
and apparently a foreigner, entered in with two bearded men and
possessing herself of a plate of sandwiches sank down heavily beside
Mary. She examined every sandwich with long dirty fingers before
offering one to Mary.

"You eat nothing? It iss all right. No animal food. I haf searched.
My stomach revolts at the animal. One morsel and poof, he iss rushing
before me." She made signs expressive of a cascade or a volcano in
eruption. Meanwhile the sandwiches disappeared and Mary sat nervously watching for any evidence of undetected animal. But all seemed
well and the woman began to talk with bewildering rapidity about
something called the International. Mary shook her head in polite
ignorance.

"I don't know," she murmured. "What is the International?"

The other started back as if Mary had bitten her. "You know not?
Franz. Emile. A spy. Here." She broke into voluble denunciation,
standing up, beckoning, and gesticulating towards Mary, who was
angry and very uncomfortable. Hugh hurried across the room, and
Sylvia Andrews came to slip her arm in that of the excited woman and
explain that Mary was the wife of a friend, untaught indeed, but quite
harmless.

"Sheep!" ejaculated the woman. "All sheep. Here you will haf no
revolution. Sheep do not revolt. Except in the stomach." As if the word
had roused an unpleasant train of thought she looked about her doubtfully and hurried out of the room. Hugh sat down beside his wife, and
between laughter and annoyance tried to explain that the International
was a society of socialist workers founded in London a little over a year
ago.

"What will it do?" Mary said.

"For one thing, prevent little children being worked to death in mills and potteries and bakehouses. Literally to death, Mary. Poisoned, maimed, squeezed of life."

Mary gave him a look of startled horror.

"But—are they?"

"You're like all the rest," her husband said bitterly. "People don't know."

"You can tell me about it," Mary answered rapidly. "But go and talk to your friends. They're looking at us. You'll have years to talk to me."

Hugh touched her hand.

"Bless you," he whispered. He moved away and came back to breathe in her ear: "I love you." The crowd swallowed him up and Mary shut her eyes the better to keep his face before them.

After a while Sylvia Andrews drifted back to her, and from her scrappy talk and more from the chattering crowd, Mary began to gather an extraordinary impression of eager youth engaged in high and romantic adventure. How these young wives and husbands worked. There were no servants in the house. Sylvia herself, with her child heavy in her, went every day to a room where poor mothers left their babies during working hours. She sewed and scrubbed and played with them. Another of the little colony had two children whom she was educating herself and yet found time to copy out her young husband's book from his untidy manuscript and look up facts and references for him. Two of the husbands ran a printing-press for revolutionary literature, one was an experimental dyer and all, wives and husbands alike, were working and praying and looking for an event they called alternatively the Revolution or The Dawn. How the Revolution appeared to their candid eyes, Mary could not clearly see, except that there would be no blood and no horrors, and after it the cities would be clean and dignified, the children rosy and well fed and the whole land a place where vigorous men and healthy radiant women worked side by side for each other and their children and the children of all the world. It was The Dawn.

These confident young creatures expected Revolution every moment. They lay down at night on their rather hard couches and slept side by side in the happy thought that to-morrow would see it breaking

over a travailing world, and rose up to work joyously in the sure hope
that the evening would bring their dreams out of the womb of the day.

They were so joyous, so confident, so honest and kind, that Mary's
own generous youth ran to meet theirs. She was almost ready to tell
Hugh that they would give up Danesacre to join the little colony of
workers for the dawn and work with them. She spoke about it to Hugh
when they were walking home through the deserted streets.

"Lord, Mary," Hugh cried, "you couldn't live in that house; it
would drive you crazy in a week. Neither could I, for that matter.
Andrews is my best friend and Sylvia is a pet, but they use each other's
handkerchiefs and have babies all over the place. You pick them
new-born out of coal scuttles and things. My little love, you'd hate it."

"I only thought," his little love said wistfully, "that you hated the
idea of Danesacre, and these people are your friends."

"And you are my love and my wife, and all I want," Hugh said. "I
can write in Danesacre as well as here. Better. I shan't be so distracted.
Besides, you'd hate it really if I'd said: 'All right, let's stay.' Wouldn't
you?"

Mary sighed and kissed him solemnly, standing under a lamppost to
do it. Afterwards, as if he were afraid that he had betrayed his friends,
Hugh began to talk to her about the Yard and Garton's Iron Works. He
told her that these ought to be run on proper decent lines. The men
themselves should run them and decide what was to be done and how to
do it, and Hugh offered, in a burst of enthusiasm, to give up writing his
book, and help her to reorganise things.

His words chilled her. She knew that he was talking the most arrant
nonsense, but she hated to tell him so.

"The men wouldn't like it," she said slowly. "They wouldn't take
orders from John Burrows. Besides, Burrows would probably bully
everybody once he got power."

"You must have patience," Hugh declared. "They've been slaves
so long that they think and act like slaves. They must be educated to
freedom."

"But what's going to happen to my ships and the Works in the
meantime?"

Hugh laughed and called her a crystallised little Tory, and promised her a Cossack for a birthday present, to oversee her workers.

"The Yard would make short work of *him,*" Mary observed, and added suddenly: "You're a Tory, yourself, really. The other's only a dream you had. Oh, a charming dream, but a dream. . . ."

His words remained with her. She thought: "It would be dreadful if Hugh talked like that to John Mempes; I couldn't bear it. John would think he was a fool. Or to the men. It might make incalculable trouble. Hugh's a darling, but he doesn't know anything about life."

A day or two later she began to discuss with him the arrangement of a room that was to be his study. She said shyly: "You'll need to buy some more books. There are no works of reference in Danesacre. I should like to give them to you. Could we go out and order them? You must finish your mediaeval guilds. I'd hate to think I'd spoiled that."

"Keeping me out of mischief," Hugh thought acutely but he threw a glance at Mary's honest little face and kept the thought to himself. The books were ordered, and a few days later the young Herveys travelled north.

4

Mary was sitting up in bed waiting for Hugh. They had been home a month, but she had not yet got used to sleeping in the big front room that had been Mark Henry's bedroom. Up to the very day of her eventful visit to London she had slept in the smaller room on the second storey that had been hers since she came from Roxby House six years before. Nothing had so definitely marked her altered state as did her discovery, when she stood in the hall on the evening of their arrival, listening to Richard's delicious shy greeting, that on her own responsibility the housekeeper had moved her things downstairs to the unused best bedroom. Of course she ought to have thought of this, and commanded it. Shame for her own inexperience thus ruthlessly exposed, and an exciting sense of new rich aspects of life spreading in front of her sealed her lips. She never even commented on the change. And to the end of her life she never knew that the woman, distrusting her own impulse, had consulted Mr. Mempes on the change, and received ironical commendation that struck a chill to her heart.

It still surprised Mary a little to find herself lying in Mark Henry's bed. Its size and heavy magnificence robbed her of self-confidence and she was always glad when she heard Hugh open the door of his room across the landing. There would be a second's pause, and then the door in the wall to the right of the bed would open softly, and reveal Hugh wrapped in the thick silk dressing-gown she had bought him in London. Coming quickly across the room he kissed the glowing young face lifted at his approach, before slipping off the dressing-gown and climbing on to the bed, which thereupon ceased to be for Mary a vast and rather terrifying expanse of smooth sheets and became the securely secret place where she and Hugh continually surprised each other by fresh revelations of grace and exquisite kindliness.

There was a moment, with Hugh's hands clasped one on each side of her little body when she felt her life stirring and throbbing in her like a bird struggling for freedom between the hands that held it. She was half frightened and wholly thrilled, with a dizzy sense of her own powerlessness and an ache that she knew was caused by her inexpressible love for this dear Hugh and pride in his need of her.

To-night Hugh would be late. He was dining at the club, a special dinner given by Old Smithson to celebrate the roofing of his splendid new house. When the last slate was in place the men at work on it had emptied the casks of beer provided in anticipation of the moment. The rejoicings thus traditionally begun were now to be rounded off at considerably greater refinement of expense. Hugh was attending the ceremonies reluctantly, having already had experience of the chasms yawning between himself and the shipping society of the town. He went off swearing to return as soon as he decently could and by eleven o'clock Mary had already begun to expect him. He did not come, and gazing dreamily towards the canopy over her head she gave herself up to a pleasant sensation of melancholy. It seemed so long since, as a very small child, she had come into this room once a week on her way downstairs, to ask for and receive her weekly threepence, standing, divided between scorn and apprehension, beside the bed while Mark Henry went through the regular pretence of having to be convinced that

Saturday had indeed, past all decency, come round again. What a defenceless creature that stolid self-confident child now appeared to Mary Hervey, how far, how pathetically far from realising what lay before her, of grief, humiliation, agony, disappointment, of immeasurable and unutterable comfort and bliss. None but herself knew what dark shadows made her present happiness so bright. A faint reminiscent shudder in the depths of her body was all that remained of two frightful nights spent at the side of her first husband. And there was not even a line on her face, when she examined it in the glass, to recall the years of struggle and poverty that had followed Archie's death. The memory of those years was enjoyable. She was preparing to enjoy it for the hundredth time when her reflections were interrupted suddenly by a shiver of cold. The age of unbridled fresh air was not yet, but Mary had queer ideas, and a cold breeze was blowing through an open window across her bare shoulders. Slipping down between the bedclothes she gave herself up to one of her rare moments of triumphant pride. Why, she had made a success. Mark Henry himself, succeeding to his father at the mature age of thirty-three, had not managed any better. . . . A walnut tall-boy standing between the windows caught her eye. The glow of the fire played across it, like light on water; in its depth a shoal of tawny curling flames flickered and slid. It was in this tall-boy that after Mark Henry died, she had found his papers and all his personal possessions except his clothes. No Garton had ever died leaving fewer traces of himself behind. As Mary went through the meagre pile she laid Mark Henry's years aside one by one. At the top of the pile were the things he had used last, a pen, a sheet of paper covered with notes of ships' engines, his will. Underneath these, she came upon a letter or two, one from her own father, Richard Hansyke, concluding: ''My service to Mr Mempes, and I am vastly in his debt for the trouble of procuring me the cask of cognac from the French shipper. Speaking by the purse, I am the more pertinently in your debt for that same cask, but I have spoken with my purse on this question and find it so depleted by reason of my obligations to your sister and my wife that I would wish you would come and look in it yourself. You are very welcome to all you find there. Ever believe me your oblig'd faithful and affectionate brother-in-law, Richie Hansyke,'' and another that Charlotte had written him from London when she and Mary were living there and wanted money . . . a miniature of Mary herself as a very little girl . . . below that, almost nothing, not a letter from his youth (his youth had never written to him), not a single object that might be a token of love or friendship, nor more miniatures, no dead flowers pressed between the pages of a book, nothing except a locket that had been his mother's. It was empty and the hinge broken. At the very bottom of all was a boy's exercise book, and a crude drawing of a boy on horseback. "Charlotte Garton drew this of her deare brother, but hee is more handsome than she could make him." Nothing more. Young Mark Henry Garton stood for a moment beside his niece among his discarded years. The sun glinted on his thick red curls and illuminated his boy's reckless beauty. A smile touched his shapely lips. Then he was gone. Like the sun sliding off water, like the dip between waves of the wooden clippers he loved, Mark Henry Garton disappeared from men's sight. One of the acquisitive Gartons had died, leaving behind him these poor shreds of possessions.

His ships outlived him; and the will giving them to Mary was dated only the day before his operation. She shivered, lying in his bed, not at the thought that he had died there with his eyes sliding from tall-boy to window in search of life, but at the thought of the narrowness of her victory. She might have lost. The daughter of one Garton and niece of another, she might have lost Garton's to the Lings, in whom ran not a drop of Garton blood. Thank God, oh thank God. . . . She might have thanked, for her present splendour, wise counsellors and a geographical revolution coming just in time to justify her inexperience. She preferred to thank a Deity distant enough to leave the worldly glory to herself.

At this moment she would have defended even her pride. An exultant sense of power filled her as the warmth of the bedclothes gradually entered into her shivering limbs. She felt able to deal with anything that was likely to confront her. What could be too much for a young woman who in less than seven years had got herself accepted as a personage in the town, and crowned that achievement by marriage to the most charming and distinguished man who ever walked at a young wife's side through the enchanted streets of Danesacre? She liked Hugh's faintly quizzical smile for the oddities, human and topographical, of the little town. She liked his rather dandified air. John Mempes was not more elegant, and Mempes had not the advantages of youth, dark hair, and a romantic grace that invited the dashing lines of a coat cut slightly tighter above the waist and slightly longer below it than any other coat in Danesacre. She liked to walk beside Hugh's coat, and she thrilled every time another woman's eyes, after greeting her, slid round to Hugh's face. She knew that she was envied, talked about, criticised. The thought of criticism stiffened her small body and curled her beautiful lips. Nothing could touch Mary Hervey, secure in her pride of place and her husband's love. How full life was, and gay, and splendid—like a street with the flags out and bands playing. Music—ah, music. The air was music in these days. Life went to a beating of drums and a glory of fifes for the wife of Hugh Hervey.

The thought struck her suddenly that she had gone near to missing this rich existence. Suppose Hugh had utterly refused to accompany her to Danesacre. She would have had to choose between him and Garton's. Impossible to give up her ships, and yet—had she not offered to give them up? She allowed herself a brief voluptuous contemplation of the sacrifice she had been willing to make for Hugh. It was a proof of the grandeur of their love (no one had ever loved as they) that each had been ready to make tremendous sacrifices. A faint sense of relief that it was Hugh who had been called upon to make the gesture of immolation crossed her mind. She dismissed it at once. It made no difference to Hugh whether he lived in Danesacre or London. It made no difference to his work . . . . if the writing of books could be called work. Mark Henry Garton's niece had doubts to which she did not own. . . . Mark Henry had none. He strode in, with a model of the *Mary Gray* under his arm, as if he had just come from the offices of the Garton Line—he had come from the head of the church steps, and the model of the *Mary Gray* was standing on the top of the tall-boy where it had stood when he died and for many years before that—and laughed at his niece's choice of a husband. What a fool! To write books while his wife built ships. Mark Henry laughed to wake the dead. . . .

Mary turned uneasily in his monstrous bed, and wished that Hugh would come in.

She was supremely unconscious of the faint touch of arrogance in her love. Lying waiting for him, she marvelled that Hugh should have found her admirable enough to marry. She mused over the catalogue of his charms, his young sensitive face, his confident delight in her and in the resilient energy of their bodies, eager for the most gracious pleasure, his quick mind, and the violent fastidious likings and dislikes that made living with him the most exciting and amusing thing in the world.

A door banged, echoing through the silent house, and Hugh's footsteps sounded on the stairs. Mary had fallen asleep and she did not wake until her husband sat down heavily on the edge of the bed. Then she woke suddenly, blinking in the light, and put out a hand that Hugh took between his own hot fingers.

"How warm you are," she murmured. Rousing herself, she saw that his eyes were very bright and his mouth comically pursed.

"Come to bed, Hugh. It must be dreadfully late."

Hugh shook his head. He drew his dressing-gown tightly round him and sat swinging his legs and smiling mischievously.

"It's not very late, and I'm wide awake," he observed.

"Do you want to talk?" Mary asked drowsily. "I could listen."

Hugh's eyes, sliding away from her, fell on a letter propped against a box on Mary's dressing-table. It was addressed to Miss Louise Hervey, in Kensington, London, and a curious expression crossed Hugh's face as he studied it.

"You wrote to Louise, then?"

Mary was silent. Her heart had set up a furious beating. This violent behaviour of her heart frightened her. She put a hand against it, hoping that it sounded less loudly in Hugh's ears than her own. Strange that any part of her exceedingly stolid little body could be so affected by a certain tone in Hugh's voice. Strange that a heart, repository of the obstinate strength of a family whose women lived to be very old and whose men could hardly be killed with a pole-ax (as one of Cromwell's own captains had found to his cost on the person of a seventeenth-century Hansyke), should be so easily startled. It knew Hugh well enough. He had lain above it enough times.

"I wrote to her just before I got into bed. I asked her to put off her visit for another month."

"Why?"

Mary lay looking at Hugh for a full minute before she answered, taking in every detail of his bearing, from the obstinate set of his lips to the lock of hair that fell in an untidy curve above one eye. She longed to fling herself into his arms.

"I wanted to get things straight," she answered coldly.

"What things? The house is perfectly all right. How much straighter will you be at the end of a month? I don't understand, and I don't like having Louise put off when she has offered to come."

Offered! Mary swallowed her outraged retort. That it should be considered a condescension for Louise Hervey to come to Danesacre. It was too much. Mary blamed Louise. A man could not be expected to see what was going on in that London woman's mind.

Yet even in this moment, with all the Danesacre housewife (that primeval creature) in her up in arms, Mary acknowledged to herself that had it been anyone but Louise she would have suppressed her feelings and accepted the self-invited guest. She was really a remarkable young woman, in more ways than one.

Nothing of this appeared in her face as she looked at Hugh, wondering how to put an end to an intolerable dispute. Slipping from the edge of the bed, Hugh stood rocking on heels and toes, with hands on his hips. He was flushed and absurdly charming. Mary thought: "You're hurting me and I love you for it." She realised that Hugh was rather drunk. He must have been very bored at Old Smithson's dinner. Regardless of the cold, Mary sat up in bed, and stared at her young husband. She was not afraid, she was not shocked. Most of the men she had known habitually drank too much—her father, Mark Henry, her first husband, her fellow shipbuilders. It was a common, even a gentlemanly fault.

No, she was not shocked. But she was moved by no ordinary emotion. Her whole world had changed its aspect. She could not even fathom how profound the change was. An obscure sense of outrage stirred in her body. It had nothing to do with Hugh. It belonged to

another existence, almost to another woman. In fact it did not belong to
a woman at all, but to a horrified child of fifteen, plunged into the
depths of another bed, in another different room. For a moment the
friendly room round Mary was filled with malignant shadows. The
outlines of Mark Henry's bed wavered and changed, became something faintly obscene. She pulled herself together, and spoke un-
certainly.

"Hugh."

Hugh approached the bed and leaned over her with the smile she
knew so well. Alas, she thought, Hugh's smile would always be her
undoing. She felt herself weak and defenceless.

"What's the matter, Hugh? Darling."

"I'm dreadfully sorry," Hugh said softly. "To tell you the truth, I'm
not quite sober. It was so hot at that infernal dinner, and they talked, my
God, how they talked, and boasted and toasted, and praised
themselves. Do forgive me. I'll go and sleep in my own room."

Mary touched his arm with a hand that shook in spite of herself.

"You needn't. Unless you want to."

"I oughtn't to have come in at all. I didn't mean to. But I saw the
light under your door."

"Are you tired?"

Hugh nodded. "If I shut my eyes I should fall asleep on my feet."

Mary smiled, a radiant exquisite tremulous smile. She felt strangely
tranquil. Everything was all right. Hugh looked very young and beautiful as he stood there, half ashamed of himself, and half mischievously
aware that she did not care what he did so long as he came to her about
it. She lay down again on her side, her little body making a meagre
show under the clothes.

"Turn out the lamp, Hugh. And get into bed. Quickly."

Hugh did both things. Mary drew him into her arms and he went
asleep there with violent suddenness. She did not even know he was
asleep, and lay for a long time in a very uncomfortable attitude. Like
any old wife of Danesacre she believed it to be fatal to sleep to rouse a
person from the twilight consciousness that precedes it. When at last
she moved her cramped limbs, she discovered that nothing would have
roused Hugh. She lay awake a long time, revelling in the sense of her

complete possession of him. He had gone to sleep with the abandonment of extreme youth, surrendering himself to her with the sublime trustfulness of an infant towards its mother. How happy and triumphant this made her. Extraordinary to be feeling like this, considering the circumstances. Extraordinary Hugh, to be the cause of her feeling it. She smiled to herself in the darkness, and stretched an arm across the unconscious sleeper.

It was impossible that she should be aware as she lay there, so small, soft, and yielding, that she was indulging her most powerful instinct, the instinct of possession, the longing, the passionate need to possess, that she had inherited from generations of fiercely grasping Gartons, men who had torn possessions from the grudging hand of life, from that first forgotten Garton who, standing in the door of his cliff-fast cottage, had conceived the idea of owning a boat of his own, and had thereafter never rested until his new and inconceivable hunger was appeased. He died and left more possessions than his boat, less tangible than it, to his son. Garton's Yard existed in the imagination of four generations before Mark Henry's great-grandfather gave it a form and a being. The very bed on which Mary lay was a tribute to the grim intensity of desires outliving the brains that had cherished them. Mary Hervery, born half Garton, was the heir of their immortal rage. Her adoration of Hugh was rooted in the knowledge that he was hers as nothing had ever been, as her son could not be. He belonged to her and to her love. She would have him always, to live with him until they were both old, and even beyond the grave, in the dim but undoubted heaven of Miss Flora's faith and hers. Dear Hugh.

The thought of the grave and of dying struck coldly across her happiness. Heaven was all very well, but the dissolution that preceded it was a prospect on which no Garton cared to dwell. It was too complete a defeat of the faith by which they lived. Unconsciously, Mary tightened her hold on the other warm, softly breathing body close to hers, and so fell asleep, one hand clenched round Hugh's relaxed fingers.

5

Mary was very happy. Every instinct to extravagance that had been stifled in her during her years of poverty now ran wild, not for herself but for Hugh. Already, in London, she had realised that ordering meals for her new household would not be the simple affair it had been. One rule ran in every decent Danesacre house: ''It's always best to buy the best,'' and no good cook in Danesacre ever used cooking butter or lard, even for greasing her tins. But Hugh's tastes fell in that class of exquisite simplicity so difficult to achieve. Mary was proud of the strain he put upon her resources and secretly tremendously impressed by the complicated nature of his tastes. The Hansyke, no less than the Garton in her, rose exultantly to the emergency. She discovered that Hugh never ordered his own underclothes. Louise did that, and trembling, afraid of making some frightful mistake, she undertook this duty too. Once made free of the world of male elegance, she rapidly became a connoisseur of the severest kind. Nothing but the best was good enough, in shirts as in butter, and Hugh found himself the possessor of an increasing store of stockings, shirts, and more intimate wear of exquisite and superlative quality. Sometimes he protested, but not often, since Mary, pleased to be giving him something, was a sight that made him chuckle even while for no discoverable reason it wrung his heart.

When Louise at last paid her visit, she came to the conclusion, watching them together, that Mary was more in love with Hugh than he with her. She was Hugh's first love, the first love of an inexperienced young man whose quick appreciative senses are more mature than his groping mind. Bur for his wife, Hugh was a revelation for which the years since her first marriage had been unconsciously preparing her. She was a grown woman in love with a boy. Or so it seemed to the sharp eyes of Hugh's sister.

Mary was blissfully unconscious of the older woman's scrutiny. She felt so wise, and looked, even to Louise, so crudely pitifully young. She had never learned to hoard herself or to think that in loving Hugh she was conferring a boon on him. Her emotions had a simplicity that made her dangerous. There was no duplicity in her love and she could imagine none. With a nature divided between a haughty independence and an innocent youthful softness outliving all her premature initiation into the mysteries of experience, aware, for the first time, that her beauty was a power to incline men's hearts towards her, lost in love, it would have been in fact strange if she had not fumbled in dealing with these infinitely complex and sophisticated Herveys.

Hugh seemed content. He had made his own discoveries about his young wife. He would never have believed, until the first time he saw it happen, that Mary's mouth could set in an ugly sullen line and her enchanting face assume so stupid and obstinate an air that it lost all charm, even all youthfulness, in a moment. But the moment past, she was so eager to be friends, and so passionately humble in her repentance, that he could not resist her. Kissing the lips that trembled and clung to his, aware by the tension of her small body in his arms how near she was to a storm of weeping, he forgot his profound resentment in the luxury of consoling her.

He was aware that she felt herself the wiser of the two, in the strange maddening way that women have, of arrogating to themselves some secret knowledge of life, a hidden wisdom, that gives them an intermittent sense of superiority over their men. Mary had this sense. She mothered him too much. Except in the moments when he asked for it, Hugh disliked being mothered. He did not want a mother. He wanted a friend and a mistress, interest and passion. Half consciously his untried youth rebelled against Mary's indulgent tenderness.

6

Mary was dressing herself to go to a Watch-Night service. New Year's Eve was the only night in the year on which a service was held in the church on the cliff top. It required too much lighting, and the way to it, up the dizzy steep of unlighted steps, was not considered safe after dark. On a stormy night it was not in fact safe, and the closing night of 1866 was a splendid example of those grim winter nights in Victorian England when the very climate drew a rigour from the stern downright virtues of the English character. The ceremonial nature of the occasion did not allow Mary to wear the unfashionable dress she wore every day in her office, but she had chosen the most modest of crinolines and over the close-fitting bodice wound a thick silk shawl brought from China by one of Garton's captains. Over that she wore a short fur-coat, cut close to her waist, with a basque and high collar into which she tucked her veil. Thus secured, so far as possible, against the icy cold outside, she waited for Hugh. An enchanting picture she made, standing poised, like a ship taking a wave, between the massive bureau and the door open on to the hall, and so Hugh would no doubt have thought her, if he had been there to see. Mary tapped the floor impatiently with one small foot and glanced from time to time at the clock on the mantelpiece. It was an elaborate affair of mahogany and brass, representing the Court of Neptune, and a dear possession, but now she saw only the face with its hands moving ever further past the hour when she ought to have left the house, and still no Hugh.

He had gone alone to dine with the one man in Danesacre for whom he had a liking, a shipowner of the name of Benham, whose unnatural passion for Italian pictures of a type shocking to the prevalent taste of his day was considered to account for his ill-success with ships. Mary disliked everything about him, from his arched eyebrows to his slow smile when talking to her, a smile that made nothing of her position and her experience, and left her feeling positively naked. She considered that her distrust was now amply justified.

At last she set off alone. A wind from the north-east was blowing directly down Harbour Street from the sea, and at the end, when she turned to climb the church steps, flying spray from waves five hundred yards distant stung her cheeks and pricked her eyelids. Half way up the steps the gale caught her and flung her against the iron railing. Luckily she did not fall, or she would have found it almost impossible to rise again, hampered by her dress. A hasty glance at the sky revealed it awash with blown clouds, and when her long climb brought her within sight of the church she was already exhausted. She reached it at last, and entering it by an outside flight of steps leading up to a side door, sank thankfully down in the Garton pew, in the gallery above the altar.

From this place she could look down into the shadowy pool of the church. Immense chandeliers, suspended from the whitewashed beams of the roof, bore a panoply of candles. The three-decker pulpit had its share, and a smaller company winked and glimmered round the musicians in the opposite gallery. The rest of the church was dark, full of shadows that strangled the few shrinking lamps placed at intervals along the walls. Peering down, Mary saw the bowed figures of Danesacre people kneeling in the square high-walled pews. Impossible to distinguish a face, but she knew where each family sat. At the far side of the church was the old Roxby pew, into which she never went. It was empty. To the left of it, below one of the low windows, like the windows of fishermen's cottages, that pierced the thick walls, was the banker's pew. The thin crouching figures of the banker's wife and daughters seemed stricken and bowed down with fear. It was said that they never raised their voices above a whisper when the husband and father was in the house. Probably they thought of God as a Being at least as ruthless.

The majority of the worshippers was in the body of the church, and all round Mary the big pews, like rooms without roofs, were empty, save for one man in the narrow white-painted pew inserted between Garton's and the next. She sat stiffly upright. Her cheeks had been stung by the wind to a vivid richness of colour that glowed even in the dusk of the gallery. Her eyes, when John Mempes caught a gleam from them under her lowered lashes, were unusually dark and bright. He wondered why she had come alone, and whether she had noticed his attendance, a phenomenon startling enough in his life to have attracted attention even at this solemn moment. To be quite truthful, Mary had noticed him, but her mind was in such a tumult of anger, disappointment and perplexity that she gave him no second thought. She had looked forward all the week to appearing with Hugh at this service and pictured herself standing for a few moments afterwards, in the wide stone-floored vestibule with the flickering candles set round its panelled walls, receiving the handshakes of her friends and exchanging New Year's wishes with the wives of inferior men. And now she was here alone, and nothing, nothing, would ever efface the memory of that humiliation. She knew that she could be observed from almost every corner of the church, sitting alone. The Garton pew was too prominent, even in this gloom. She bit her lip, and the blood, rushing to her cheeks, stayed there and made her look what she was, a beautiful angry girl, placed in a situation that called up all her dignity, and mocked it at the same time.

The service went on. As the hour of midnight approached, the voice of God's minister on the topmost deck—the bridge as it were—of his high place fell silent, and the congregation waited on its knees for a year to die and another to be born. In the silence the wind beat down on the old walls, without rattling a single window. Few of them were made to open, and those on the sea side were shuttered. One would have thought that in eight centuries the wind would have learned the folly of trying to impress the squat grey building, but it continued to bluster without the least effect, even on the hearts of the kneeling worshippers, though most of them had had reason at some time or another to listen with anguish to the terror abroad between sea and sky. Perhaps the tranquil place, in which not a breath disturbed the slender flames of the candles, persuaded them that ultimately they were safe. Perhaps a certain grim arrogance, born of their incontestable superiority over all other people in all other towns of a county that was as supreme among the rest of English counties as England among the countries of the world, held them rigid and unmoved, in their attitudes of assumed humility, every time a blast like the rending of a world broke over the church. No doubt they were not altogether unmoved. Some had ships, or husbands, sons and lovers abroad at sea. And no doubt their humility was not entirely a matter of posture. But much more than any humble yielding it was an immemorial gesture made by sound upright men to Another like themselves. They depended on God, and He depended on them. Between them, they and He sustained the splendid fabric of Victorian civilisation, in all its harshness, its grandeur, its superb complacence, its monstrous self-discipline, and its touching belief in human permanence. If they had not believed in God they would not so magnificently have believed in themselves, and the world would not have seen a social spectacle the like of which had never before existed and will not exist again. To the men and women kneeling in the shadows of their church on that wild night it seemed as invulnerable as the walls between which they knelt. The wind beat on it, the sea thundered, and it stood unmoved, a rock in a high place. The forces at work to destroy it made no sound.

The minutes passed. Mary Hervey's face was pressed convulsively into her hands. The mysterious influences of the church, that had seen so many generations of Danesacre people come to it to be christened, married and buried, and of the Garton pew—which when she was a child had so impressed her by its size, high walls, and rich carpet, that she had wondered whether the towering pulpit itself could be more sacredly important—were beginning to assume their accustomed sway over her mind. The tumult in her heart died down, and she forgot Hugh's defection in the overwhelming thought that she should be kneeling here, not as she had knelt on past Eves, but as Mary Hervey. She was a different creature from that earlier Mary, with a body that had been made new between her lover's hands, and a mind so altered, so full of new vistas of experience and unimaginable dreams and tendernesses and hopes that when, as now, she was left alone with it, she hardly knew it for her own.

She knew that she should be thinking of spiritual things and not of Hugh, but she found herself repeating words that came into her head from the quiet solemn air. "Let me make him happy, dear God. Let me keep him always and make me worthy." She repeated her prayer over and over again, until the clock fixed in the outer wall of the Garton pew gave one deep stroke, and the benediction, dropping from the pulpit into the deep shadows at its foot, was followed by peals of bells with the deep tolling of the Town Hall bell sounding below all the rest.

As she paused to arrange her crinoline for passage down the narrow corridor between the wall and the back of the pews Mary found John Mempes beside her.

"Let me take you home, Mary."

She smiled at him, a dazzling smile. It was the palest reflection of the ecstasy she had experienced in her brief prostration before the Throne. Outside she took his arm and they descended the steps, with a darkness tenanted by the North Sea on one hand and the dark roofs of houses clinging to the cliff side on the other. Mary held to the railing with her free hand, and almost in Mempes' arms, managed to reach the comparative quiet of Harbour Street. There she released her hold of him, and breathless, her dress swaying about her legs, picked her way down the cobbled street. Mempes did not ask her why she was alone, and though she would not have known what to reply she was annoyed with him for not saying: "Where is Hervey?" It was the natural thing to have said.

They reached Mark Henry's house, and Mempes, in the character of First Foot, preceded her into the hall. Mary suffered a fresh pang. It should have been Hugh who did that. He was already in, and greeted John Mempes with civil indifference. Glasses of Mark Henry's 1820 port were poured out, and they drank to the New Year, Hugh with pleasure, the older man with barely concealed disdain. Mary sipped hers and put it down, thinking that nothing would make her really enjoy wine. Something of the anger that her emotion in church had swept away, returned, as she caught Hugh's air of delicate irony at a mention of the Watch-Night service. Why had he not come home to take her to it as he promised? She was thankful that he offered no incriminating apology in front of John Mempes, but when the manager had gone she turned swiftly on her husband.

"Why didn't you come? I waited for you."

"It was later than I knew," he murmured. "And I had to take Mrs. Welham home. I knew you'd be all right. Mempes told me this morning he should be there."

Mary blushed crimson, ashamed to have discovered that Hugh was willing to leave her to the chance escort of John Mempes. On Watch-Night, too. Her simple mind could not conceive the unimportance to a Kensington bred Hugh, of Watch-Night service in the "Old Church," and she was struck to the heart by his mention of Mrs. Welham. Hugh had thrown his wife over for that woman. It was the end of the world.

Mrs. Welham, known to the profane as the Town Widow, was the wife of an explorer whose absences left his wife with nothing to do but employ the talents Heaven had given her, a magnificent pair of eyes, a roguish smile, and a fine opulent figure. Long practice had brought her in the use of them a dazzling assurance, and few sons and husbands in Danesacre society had not at one time or another pierced the heart of a mother or a wife by playing the second (and minor) rôle in her drama of the Deserted Wife.

Pride sustained Hugh Hervey's wife now, stifling on her lips the comment that rose to them. But even her monstrous pride could not prevent those lips from curling nor keep the disdain out of her face. Hugh wore the air of a mischievous boy bent on seeing how far in mischief he can go. Indeed at this moment he was a boy, and Mary a woman, hurt to the roots of her being. She was the very image of outraged womanhood as she stood in front of Hugh, her veil thrown back and her head up. He could see the rapid breath come and go under the silk of her bodice. He knew that he had made a frightful blunder, and if Mary had shown any softness he would have been down on his knees apologising for it. There was nothing in her face but the most malignant dislike, and he steeled his heart against the mute appeal of her slender trembling body. Where now was Mary's adoring passion? Where the girl who had prayed to be made worthy of this careless creature with raised brows and mocking smile, this philanderer? Gone. Dead and buried in a forgotten past. Mary's lips quivered and the thought crossed her mind: "What a way to begin the New Year."

"I never meant to stay with her," Hugh said carelessly. "I don't like her," which was true, "but you know how it is. She just wanted someone to condole with her on her lonely life. Her mother was there of course—asleep. I thought I'd stayed five minutes and I stayed fifty."

To tell the truth, Mary did know how it was, being unique among women in that respect, but nothing would have persuaded her to admit it. She saw Mrs. Welham in the likeness of an angel with a flaming sword standing at the door of every drawing-room in Danesacre telling the occupants where Hugh Hervey was when his wife was at Watch-Night service alone. She said cruelly:

"I suppose if she had wanted someone to condole with her all night, you'd have stayed on to do it?"

Absurd Mary! Every word cut into her own shrinking flesh, and all the effect it had on Hugh was to produce on his face a meditative smile.

"I don't suppose I should. But it would be very natural. It might happen to any man who was rash enough to put himself into the position I did, sitting practically alone at night with an attractive woman while she tells you her husband neglects her."

Then indeed Mary was beaten. The vision she herself had conjured up of Hugh in another woman's arms was too much for her. Tears rushed into her eyes, and she turned and fled from the room, with a sudden relapse into girlishness that at another time would have amused her husband. Now it merely made him angry. He hated scenes. A strain of cruelty, hiding in an obscure corner of a subtly fastidious nature, made him in anger more than a match for Mary's quick temper. He was angry and cold.

He was not vindictive and he was in love with his wife. A few minutes' thought sufficed to fill him with remorse. He thought of her lying in that great bed upstairs, probably crying, and the wish to comfort her, to feel a sob stifled against his body and a quivering mouth pressed to his, drove him upstairs. Hurrying over his undressing, he went softly into her room. The light was out, but in the glow of the dying fire he could see Mary lying on the edge of the bed.

A queer excitement seized him.

"Mary," he said gently.

There was no answer. Could she be already asleep? He came nearer, and saw Mary's eyes fixed on him in cold scrutiny. Instantly his excitement fled, and left him standing foolish and unwanted in the middle of the room. What should he do? He could not bring himself to an inglorious return to his own room. Wistfully, he glanced again at his young wife but she made no sign. He did not want to get into bed beside this enemy, and he found himself doing it. Estranged and miserable, with the width of the bed between them, the two ridiculous young creatures, their minds filled with one and the same desire, lay silent and awake. Neither would make the first move, and after a while, such is the power of youth, they fell almost in the same instant into an untroubled sleep. For the first time they had gone to sleep in unkindness. It was the most momentous thing that had ever happened to either of them.

7

One evening—it was less than a month after an inauspicious Watch-Night—Mary and Hugh were discussing the bankruptcy of Hugh's friend, Benham, the shipowner. They discussed it cautiously, aware of unplumbed depths in each other's mind on this subject of Benham's failure to survive in his world. That world was sitting in judgment on

him with justified severity. It knew precisely why he had failed, and
how culpable he was. Freights were high, and shipping booming.
There was no reason, except his criminal neglect of it, why his firm
should have chosen this moment of prosperity to fail and throw some
hundreds of men out of employment, not to mention unpaid creditors
and a mysterious scene with the Town Widow on the evening before his
public downfall. Mary was only voicing Danesacre's considered opinion when she observed that if Benham had thought more of his ships
and less of paintings and dissipation he would never have made such a
mess of things.

Hugh's face underwent a change with which she was becoming
familiar. The eyebrows shot up, lending it a peculiarly merciless air of
mockery, and his delicate mouth was pressed into an edge of pallid lip.
A haughty expression appeared on her own face.

"You think of nothing but what you can get," Hugh observed.
"You're quite incapable of appreciating the point of view of a
gentleman."

"I don't see," Mary said curtly, "what being or not being a
gentleman has to do with it. Mark Henry Garton wasn't what you would
call a gentleman but he never let his men and his shareholders down by
going bankrupt."

Hugh was struck by this observation, and inclined, having secret
personal reasons of his own for doing so, to agree with it, but some
mute unseizable obstinacy drove him to oppose her. He would not be
overborne by the force, leaping from her small thin person to demolish
him in an argument, that always astonished and usually silenced him.

"You and I," he said disdainfully, "cannot possibly have the same
notion of what constitutes a gentleman. It's not a question of class. It's
a sort of *politesse du coeur.*"

Mary confronted him with blanched face. She was in fact appalled.
A moment ago they had been walking side by side, warily it was true,
but with perfect amiability, and in a moment this frightful pit had
opened between their feet. The wilfulness of Hugh's criticism stung
her. Profoundly mortified, she told herself that at last she was seeing
him clearly. He was utterly incapable of sympathising with the
difficulties of her life. What on earth had she been about to suppose that

he would? An amateur of the arts, an indolent delightful creature, and no use to any one. . . .

Who would have believed that judging him so mercilessly, she burned with shameful longing for his approval.

"Gentlemen," she said at last, "should keep out of the shipping world. It wasn't Mr. Benham's gentlemanliness but his incompetence that ruined him. I dare say that is why you sympathise with him."

They were both perfectly calm and civil, two charming young people conducting a polite discussion. A short while ago they had been lovers, Now they were completely indifferent. The revelation of each other's real natures had killed in the space of a few moments all the mistaken tenderness they had been cherishing. Still, one must be civil. A devil was raging behind each smooth face. Hugh rapped his on its knuckles and it laughed. The sound was more than the other devil could bear.

"How dare you laugh at me?"

"I'm sorry. I apologise."

"You needn't." Mary controlled her face. Surely he could see that she was bleeding to death? The devil had gone out of her with that last defiance. She was hurt, she was dying of grief. She looked quickly at Hugh and an emotion that was not quite pain and not quite joy filled her. She was suffering but she was thrillingly alive. This was real, and without Hugh she would never have felt this fury of living, this exquisite unhappiness. Her body trembled.

Suddenly Hugh rushed across the room and dropped beside her on the floor with his arms round her waist.

"Darling, darling. Forgive me, I'm a fool. I'm a brute. You're a thousand times better than I am, and a thousand times cleverer——"

"I'm not. You're much cleverer than I am." It was true.

Hugh's face was transformed with emotion. His eyes beseeched her. "The truth is I'm jealous, Mary."

Delicious moment. Mary bent over him to hide the triumph in her eyes, and her voice was the immemorial voice of women flattering the folly of their lovers. "Why are you jealous, my heart?"

"You spend your days with John Mempes. It's to him you talk of the things nearest your heart. You live your real life with him. Ships are your life. I'm an addition. It's—it's monstrous."

"Oh my dear, my dear." Mary was carried away by her passionate eagerness. "You know that's not true. I would have given it all up if you had insisted. You know I love you more than anything in the world." She was overwhelmed by remorse and gratitude. Thank heaven everything was all right, and she had said none of the unforgiveable things that had risen to her lips. She bent to press them, quivering from the narrowness of their escape, on Hugh's head. He jumped to his feet and pulled her up against him. Exhausted, they rested quietly in each other's arms. The thought crossed Hugh's mind that he and Mary were never really at one except in their moments of passion and passionate surrender. He dismissed it impatiently and set himself to stroke her smooth hair. He was by no means tall, but her head came below the level of his chin, and as she hung from him, managing to cling to him and look up at him at the same time, he had to stoop lower still to kiss the vivacious young face. That pleased him. A pleasant sense of his power over her deepened his love.

"Are you sure you love me, Mary?"

Mary looked at him soberly. She thought that it would be a very queer woman who would not love this adorable creature. Generous, kind, sweet-natured—he was everything she was not, and undeniably attractive. She was quite simply convinced that no man had ever been more charming to look at than Hugh. She loved him for it, as well as for his more serious qualities. Tightening the arm round her shoulders, Hugh brought his face close to hers and as she yielded herself to his embrace she knew that what she loved in him was neither his magnanimity, his sweet soul, nor any other of his admirable qualities, nor even his charm. What she loved in him was a kind of youthful extravagance he had. His capacity for complete abandon made the most powerful appeal to her. Never could she so surrender herself as Hugh, in such moments as this, could and did. If she had once been capable of it, she was not now. The reckless fury with which Hugh flung himself into an emotion was forever impossible to Mary Hervey, who had been Mary Hansyke and Mary Roxby before reaching her present haven of refuge. She felt very wise and sad and profoundly happy. How pale Hugh was. The dark hair above his temples was wet. She resolved that there should be no more such scenes. In future she would manage Hugh much better.

Her eyes were those of a young girl, shining with the wise innocence of extreme youth, and the shy droop of her head might have ravished even a less interested onlooker. Impossible to believe that this was the same woman whose rancour and miserable pride had just expressed itself with such frightful bitterness. She smiled enchantingly.

"Dear Hugh. Please smile at me. You have no idea how delightful you look when you smile."

"Thank you," Hugh said.

CHAPTER TWO

A FEW weeks later, Mary realised, from a casual question put to her by Old Smithson's wife, that she was carrying Hugh's child. It was characteristic of her that just as she had failed to observe any of the early signs of it, so she put off telling Hugh. She put it off until she began to be afraid someone else would tell him. Then she blurted the news out, coming purposely from the Yard to Hugh's study in the middle of the afternoon, to tell him.

She was nervous and apologetic. Hugh's sudden smile bewildered her.

"You don't mind, Hugh?" A blinding memory of Mrs Maggs's kitchen hung between her eyes and Hugh's face. It confused her, filling her with an extraordinary emotion in which shame, a queer shame that she should have remembered Archie at all, predominated. She would have liked to erase Archie from her life, As she stood there, leaning against Hugh's desk, nothing was real to her but Hugh, neither Richard, nor the life unstirring and relentless within her.

It was absurd to think of Hugh as a father.

He sprang forward and taking her in his arms sat down with her in an arm-chair.

"Mind? Did you think I would? I like it."

Mary looked at him doubtfully. He was laughing. His smooth young voice was soft and reassuring. He bent his face to hers.

"Tell me all about it, Mary." Now she caught the familiar mischief in his voice. Her heart leapt.

"There's nothing to tell you."

Hugh's face altered. His brows drew together in an anxious frown. "You'll be all right, won't you? Promise me it's all right, Mary." He had turned pale.

"Oh, my love," Mary said. She raised herself, so that she could nurse his head between her arms. Her small face was transfigured with happiness.

"Of course it will be all right."

"I couldn't live without you, Mary."

"You won't have to." Slipping out of his arms, Mary sat down on the floor at his feet and embraced his knees. She did not look at him.

"I promise, Hugh." He had to bend down to hear. "You're the only person who matters to me. Even this," she laid her hand against her body in a strange delicate gesture, "doesn't matter, beside you. I—there isn't anything I wouldn't do for you."

In the recesses of her mind a voice repeated: "Richard matters, Richard matters," but she ignored it.

She felt Hugh's body shaking between her arms. He said nothing, but presently lifted her up. They subsided into the depths of the chair again and were consolingly silent and aware of each other only as of another beloved family face, very close in the homely dusk. . . .

Autumn, that year, was reluctant to leave Danesacre. In innumerable gardens flowers that should have been gathered up with the harvest lingered on. The breath of the earth was warm, even in the early morning, and up the valley the trees turned gold, then scarlet, then tawny, and remained so, like great somnolent beasts, secure in their strength. They were not like dying trees. They were like young trees of a new strange species.

Hugh rode alone between them. Last year's leaves deadened the sound of his horse's feet, but no single leaf had been stripped from the branches above him. When he emerged from the wood on to the bridle path that led up to the moors and the high road to Danesacre, he rode under an immense ball of blue sky, where the superb white clouds seemed as changeless and permanent as the autumn trees. The little town at the lip of the river seemed the impermanent changing thing, pathetic in its smallness. As Hugh clattered down Harbour Street, the narrow ghauts and valleys on either side of him were filled with a rumour of life, like the murmurs of children in Pompeii, the evening before its submergence.

He was always, when he got so far as this on his homeward journey, consumed with anxiety for the short remaining distance. He went in search of Mary at once. The sound of her voice from any part of the house was enough. Satisfied, without seeing her, he went up to his room to change.

The advance copies of his first book had arrived on an afternoon post. He found Mary frowning over her copy. She was reading it with avid care, like a child learning a lesson, and every now and then she turned back to re-read a page before going on with what she evidently found a difficult task. She sighed heavily, and Hugh ran across the room to snatch the book out of her hand and offer himself as an alternative occupation.

"What were you doing with my book, baby? You can't understand it. Any more than I can understand freight sheets and diagrams of engines. Why do you bother your adorable head with it? It bores you. Confess it does."

"I don't understand it very well," Mary acknowledged. "But I did want to read it, Hugh darling. Because you wrote it and because it's a splendid book. If it had not been, Mr. Murray would not have paid you the money to let him publish it. Don't you want me to read it?"

"No," Hugh lied. "Kiss me, Mary." Her judgment of his book's value left a wry flavour in his mouth.

Mary kissed him, and began to discuss the subject that lay near her heart at the moment, which was the new bathroom. No bathroom approaching it in completeness and beauty existed in the town, though that, as Hugh pointed out, was no great triumph, since the bathrooms in Danesacre could be counted on the fingers of both hands.

To celebrate the publication of his book Hugh opened a bottle of the '57 *Perrier Jouet,* a majestical wine, just as its perfection, absolutely right, and Mary had ordered and supervised a dinner as nearly flawless as so important a meal should be. Hugh was too excited by the arrival of his books to notice her extreme pallor, and it was not until dinner was over that she turned to him with something between a gasp and a cry.

"Hugh," she said weakly.

"What is it? What is it, Mary?"

His alarm steadied her at once. She sent him off to find her woman, and went tranquilly upstairs. Charlotte had been ill, and was in bed. Mary turned over in her mind precautions against rousing her. She did not want her mother's presence. A forgotten sense, welling up from her childhood, of Charlotte's unreliability, flooded through her. She wanted no added worries. In her heart of hearts she was terrified, as she had never been when Richard was born. Then she did not know what it would be like, and proceeded from terror to terror by imperceptible stages. Now she saw the whole thing in front of her.

She wished it had not happened on the very day when Hugh's book had come. Louise Hervey, who had been in the house for a week past, thought contemptuously that it was just like Mary to have miscalculated the affair by a month. Neither of them knew that the child so near birth was to evince during her life an almost incredible capacity for mistiming her effects. This was nothing but the first instance of her habitual clumsiness.

Later, Mary asked Hugh to go away. Her suffering was becoming so intense that she did not know how much longer she could endure it. Hugh's face receded before her on a dizzying wave of pain, coming close again in the brief intervals of peace. He was holding both her hands.

She felt his grasp less as a consolation than as an appeal. He was appealing to her, in this room full of grown-up strangers, like one child appealing to another for comfort. She pressed his fingers.

"It's all right," she whispered. "Go now. Love."

Hugh stood up. The thought crossed his mind: "She's been through all this before." Thoughts of that other man who had been before him with Mary tortured him. He turned to go. Suddenly, swinging round again, he dropped on his knees, pressing his forehead against the bed. Mary's hands quieted at once. She laid them one on each side of his dark head.

Her being was suspended in an instant of calm. She was reluctant to let Hugh go. In this instant she felt, deep in some untortured part of her body, that he would never again be so much hers. It was as if Hugh were leaving her, with his child. Pain engulfed the instant forever. She relaxed her hold. Hugh went away, and she forgot him.

She had another instant, of overwhelming satisfaction, that at last she was correcting the blunder that had made Archie Roxby the father of her son.

"Give him to me," she said.

The briefest pause. Then Louise Harvey's voice, unsubdued, the voice of the childless woman.

"You have a daughter, Mary."

CHAPTER THREE

1

FOR some time there had existed in Mary's mind a strange new conviction. It was so strange that at first she had done no more than glance at it and pass it by. But it had made itself felt again and again appearing at inconvenient moments, a perpetual accompaniment to her waking thoughts. Occasionally it got into her dreams and she woke up profoundly troubled.

It was no other, to put it as briefly as possible, than the feeling that she had done wrong to keep Hugh out of Garton's. Once admitted, it grew and grew, and assumed the monstrous proportions of a fixed idea. She had not admitted it willingly, or at once. She had been married four years when it became with her a recognised article of belief, and during these years she had learned a good many things about Hugh.

Part of what she had learned was not, one would have thought, such as to strengthen her belief. There was, for instance, Hugh's carelessness about money. He had backed Benham's bill for five thousand—a sum he could never hope to pay if the bill were not met. Of course it was not met, and for a long time Hugh said nothing to anyone about it and was on the brink of disaster when he told Mary. There was enough Hansyke in her to find Hugh's conduct not inconceivable, but Mark Henry Garton's niece was shocked and upset. To have thrown away all that money! She cleared the bill, and Hugh never repaid her. Moreover, he seemed quite incapable of seeing that he had done a

158

foolish thing. He told Mary blandly that she did not understand the obligations of a gentleman. Mary swallowed the obvious retort that this gentleman's obligation had obliged her to find five thousand pounds at an inconvenient moment, and took the precaution of going through Hugh's bills. She found several outstanding for large sums. Hugh had lately taken to keeping a stable, and this, together with his extravagant need for books and documents, ate up all and more than his income. Mary approved of the stable. It was the right thing for a gentleman of leisure, and appealed to her Hansyke training and instincts. She preferred ships, but there was no doubt that horses were more genteel. She paid Hugh's debts and continued to pay them.

But all evidence to his unfitness notwithstanding, her wish to have Hugh in the firm grew steadily. She said nothing to anyone about it, not even to Mempes. An obscure jealousy was at work in her. She was jealous of Hugh's writing. She could neither understand nor enjoy it, and at the back of her mind was a curious sense that she was not getting the full use of her property. She would not have admitted this feeling but it was there. Her love for him seemed to double itself in an effort to regain lost ground. She tried to take an interest in his work and cut a rather pathetic figure, sitting for hours over books on mediaeval history. She came to various conclusions about the Middle Ages, at which Hugh laughed. Sometimes she had a queer flash of emotion, in which it came to her with the force of a blow that at a given moment in time, on some familiar village green, men and women had stood and gossiped in living voices about the world round them. They had been alive. They had laughed, and cried, and suffered, and lain down to sleep. At these moments she had a sense that she was about to make an astounding discovery about life. She was on the brink of plunging into a profound and unparalleled experience, and then the tide of light receded and left her where she was, unchanged. These strange fleeting moments she could not share with Hugh.

He was in the middle of a new book. He had a acquired a secretary, a friend of his sister, who came from London, took rooms in Danesacre, and worked with him for six hours every day. Sometimes they worked in the evening, and then Mary sat with them, poring over her own papers, or idly watching Hugh's head close to Miss Jardine's as they bent over her notes. Miss Jardine was tall, taller than Hugh, with a complexion of extraordinary fairness, and hair of uncounterfeited gold contrasting with her dark brows. She had a small pouting mouth, an ugly nose, and a rather affected carriage of her body and poise of the head. She was very conscious of her position as an independent woman. At times, she bore herself more like a portent than a woman. She was an admirable secretary, and with her help Hugh was achieving something like research.

For a long time he remained entirely oblivious of Mary's attempts to draw him into Garton's.

She proceeded with them in her secretive fashion, the slow tenacious fashion of a mind that will wait years to accomplish a desired end.

Their second child, born a year after the first, was another girl. Mary named her Sylvia—the first had been called Clara after Hugh's mother—and was pleased because she was like Hugh. The older child, by some freak of the selective imagination, bore a striking and ludicrous resemblance to old George Roxby. Charlotte noticed it first, and thereafter Mary could never look at the fat solemn child without seeing George Roxby in his steel frame, groaning and rolling about his house. She had been fond of George, but his reappearance in her family annoyed her, and before she was four years old Clara knew better than to approach her mother on any errand that Sylvia could be made to do. Neither child saw very much of their mother. They spent most of their time in a cottage on the moors with Miss Flora and the most admirable of nurses, whose polite hostility to Miss Flora embittered the old Scotswoman's last years on earth.

Hugh was perfectly well aware that her daughters bored Mary. . . .

They had one unmistakable effect on her. Their coming made her curiously subservient to Hugh. She ceased to quarrel at all with him, giving way with a new gentleness on points that a year earlier she would have disputed to the last word. A quality of submissive tenderness entered her love, some faint hint of appeal. . . . The swift radiant confident-speaking Mary was still there. She laughed still like a boy over the irresistible absurdities of life and people. But there was something a little wistful in her adoration of Hugh, a new softness . . . Hugh hardly noticed it.

If her girls disappointed Mary her son did not. Richard was eleven years old when Sylvia was born, a tall handsome boy, with dreaming eyes behind long lashes. He had a tutor, with whom he was very friendly, but he contrived, plotting it out in his own mind, to secure at least an hour of Mary's time every working day, and for her ears he saved up his more interesting adventures and his secret dreams. He was a mixture of innocence and self-possession that baffled his tutor and his stepfather, and continually surprised his mother.

She had a model made for him of a steam-engine. It had a boiler which was heated by oil, and a funnel with a safety-valve. During its making Richard was in a state of tremendous excitement. He hung round the workshop and could hardly bear to wait until the red paint on it was dry before he carried it off to show Mary. But Mary was shut up in conference with John Mempes and did not emerge until Richard was in bed, with the engine on a chair by his side, where his eyes would fall on it first thing in the morning.

"Does it go?" Mary asked.

"I don't know," he said gravely. "I shan't try it until you can be there."

Mary had to hurry away to Middlesborough first thing the next morning and it was three days before she got back. And then she was busy all day until the late afternoon. So that it was after tea, on the fifth day of possessing it, that Richard started up his engine. He filled the boiler with hot water, lit the tiny old lamp and waited, his hand clutching Mary's. The water began to bubble. Steam rushed in a thin white jet out of the safety-valve. The piston worked. For five minutes the engine was a centre of hissing, throbbing life. Then it all died down, the piston, after a final convulsive jerk, ceased functioning, the jet of steam wavered and disappeared. It was all over.

Richard stood looking at the dead silent thing. To the unbearable excitement of the last few days succeeded a dreadful blank. His very body felt empty. "Is that all?" he thought. He looked up and caught his mother's eyes fixed on him with an expression he could not fathom. For one moment he thought she was laughing at him, and then that she was sorry for him. Suddenly she knelt down and hugged him closely. After an infinitesimal moment of rebellion, he yielded to it and laid his flushed cheek on her neck. She was wonderfully comforting and soft. He loved her enormously.

"I'm not kissing you because I love you," he said suddenly, "but because you feel so soft. Let's go for a walk."

They walked rather silently along the top of the east cliff. After a time Mary said:

"You could drive a crane off that piston."

Richard brightened.

"I could," he said, and slipped his hand into hers.

"I should like to be an engineer," he observed.

Mary was aware of a sharp pleasure.

"What sort of an engineer?" she asked. "An engineer who makes engines for ships?"

"No, not ships," Richard said thoughtfully. "Something that gets you about. But not ships. I don't care much for ships."

His mother was a little disappointed, but she began an account of the various branches of engineering, to which he listened in silence. Abruptly his mind made one of its bewildering leaps.

"Would my grandmother be interested in engines?"

"I don't know," Mary said. "I don't think so. She doesn't know much about that sort of thing. You'd better talk to me about it."

Richard gave her a clear look.

"We must be careful what we do," he observed. "A woman's heart soon breaks."

Mary stifled a gasp of laughter.

"Do you think so?" she murmured. "I dare say it does. Yes, I've sometimes felt as if my heart was breaking."

"Oh, your heart's all right," Richard said callously. "I meant my grandmother's."

Mary could think of nothing to say. She supposed Charlotte must have been talking to the boy about her ruined life. Probably she had told him that every one despised her. Mary felt a spurt of anger. How dare Charlotte confuse her boy's mind with all that nonsense. She glanced at her son, and felt intuitively that Richard was not at all confused. He had accepted the odd fragility of a woman's heart and added it to the store of incomprehensible facts existing at large in a world which interested him very slightly. He was far more interested in his dreams, whatever they were. Mary felt a pang of the grief that visits mothers, when they remember that the clear-eyed trusting son of their body will go out into that world and discover that men and women are mean, unkind, cruel to each other, treacherous, cowardly. She wanted to snatch him up and guard him from the intolerable unkindness of men—and other women. She waited for him to scramble over a stile after her, and kissed him when he reached the ground. . . .

A month later Charlotte Hansyke died. Her husband had died suddenly a few months before. He had grown queer-tempered in the last years, and turned away all his servants except one fierce old man, as queer as himself, who refused Mary admittance when she went to visit her father in his illness and could hardly be persuaded to let Richard Hansyke be prepared for decent burial.

An old will left everything to Charlotte. With unusual decision she ordered Mary to sell the whole place. Mary sold it, and for the first time in seven hundred years, no Hansyke held land in Roxborough. The severing of those ancient roots seemed to affect Mary very little. She told Hugh that she had driven her own roots too deep into Danesacre. She felt more affection for an orchard in Kensington than for the bleak stretch of upland field and moor that had become so much Hansyke that no new ownership could persuade Roxborough people to call it anything but "Hansyke's." Up at Hansyke's," they said, when the new housekeeper ordered her purchases to be sent to the house. The new housekeeper ground her teeth and the new master was displeased, but that had no effect on Roxborough.

Mary said she did not care, but she avoided Roxborough after the sale. The new owner invited her to come and see the alterations. She was very civil, but she steadfastly refused to go. . . .

Charlotte's death was a sharper sorrow. Mary's vitality rebelled wildly against the thought that Charlotte would never see Danesacre again, nor the crowded lively harbour, nor the old church with its immemorial peace, nor any of the steep narrow streets that she had known as a child and as a young proud girl, and a woman heavy with life. The ships would sail out of the harbour, the little streets would echo with the feet of Danesacre people, the sun would glitter on the

multitude of small dancing waves, but Charlotte Hansyke would no
see it. Everything would go on without her as if she had never been
Mary choked with grief and pity. It was as if she wept less for Charlotte
than for Charlotte's bitter loss of living.

2

After this, she made up her mind quite firmly that Hugh must and
should become part of the life of Garton's as he was part of hers. A
feeling that she would thus be securing him against nameless dangers
supported her. About Garton's there was something permanent and
solid, which in the midst of an impermanent world consoled her with its
assurance of immovable foundations. Confronted at every turn by
shocking evidences of the truth that in the midst of life we are in death
she sought persistently, foolishly—blasphemously, Miss Flora would
have said—for something deathless on this side of the grave. And as the
Yard had outlived already several generations of Gartons she began to
see in it a power that conferred a kind of immortality on its servants.
Nothing in England was safer than Garton's, not even that sacrosanct
pattern of all property and institutions, the Bank of England. Once
attach Hugh firmly to this tremendous institution, and she felt she could
sleep without fear of the dreams that haunted her, dreams in which,
with her mother dead and Richard away from her in some far country,
she had lost Hugh, and was seeking for him in an anguish that gradually
woke her. Then she would sit up and bend over him, touching him to
make sure of the reality of his presence at her side. She listened to his
regular breathing, and sometimes, incomprehensible creature,
remained awake until dawn, to have the pleasure of seeing the outline
of his face, softened in sleep, emerge from the obscurity of the room. It
gave her the same sharp stab of pleasure that she felt on seeing the
lovely line of a ship emerging from its cloud of scaffolding.

She might have proposed to Hugh quite simply that he should join
her in directing the Line and the Yard. But it never occurred to her to go
straight to her goal. She approached it down every conceivable by-way.
She brought him problems of Yard and Line. She tried to enlist him on
her side against Mempes in the great question of steam versus sail. She

showed him Prendergast's accounts of his experiments with condensers and pressure, supplementing her gifts of silk shirts and costly books with these more romantic tokens. Hugh was very civil, even mildly interested.

Outwardly he had changed little during four years. His manner was still that of a very young man. In spite of debts, horses, the writing and publishing of two books, the fathering of two daughters, and election—due to the position of Garton's in the town—to the committee of the shipping club, he had still at times an air of inexperience and boyish naïvete which caused some of the older men to regard him as a fool. It deepened Mary's passion for him. He was, for her, the young husband of the first weeks of their marriage, and the way he confided in her, no less than his periods of almost sullen withdrawal, filled her with an increasing gentleness and anxiety to please him. She coaxed him as one of her captains would have coaxed an awkward ship, feeling his life taut and quivering under her hands, feeling her heart quicken with joy when he responded and she could see a clean run before her.

She felt that she had no one but herself to blame for his moods of sullenness. It was she who by her arrogance had shut him out of part of her life, and she whose stupidity made it difficult for her to enter properly into his. There had been a moment in the first month of their marriage when Hugh was eager to help her and she had made him understand that Garton's did not want him. She was bitterly ashamed of that spiritual discourtesy.

She persevered with her excursions into the Middle Ages. And now she found herself confronted by an unexpected obstacle. Hugh did not want her to be interested. He made that devastatingly clear. An incident that occurred one day towards the end of 1869 made it clearer. Mary and Richard had been discussing their Christmas plans and when the little boy left, Hugh said abruptly:

"Count me out of it. I shall be in London."

Mary swung round, startled by this blow.

"At Christmas, Hugh?" To withdraw from one's family at the season of orgiastic reunion was a project that had never occurred before to the head of any household in Danesacre. Mary could not credit her ears. She would not have been more struck if Hugh, in the same casual tones, had announced to her the end of the world approaching down Harbour Street.

Hugh's eyebrows shot up. "Why not? What is the difference between Christmas and any other holiday? You and Richard always manage to amuse each other, and I'll send the babies something special from town."

Mary rallied her wits. Of course, Hugh was right. There *was* no difference between Christmas and any other time. Seizing on his words, she proceeded to make a platitude out of what was no less than a denial of one of her most cherished beliefs, one of the sacred beliefs of all decent people, as sacred as the institution of property itself, and derived from a source at least equally divine.

"Why, of course. You'll enjoy a Christmas in town, Hugh." No one looking at her would have guessed that a moment before she had been confronted by a vision of her hearth deserted, England in ruins, the whole solar system toppling about her ears. She wanted every one, herself and Hugh included, to realise that this revolutionary departure from custom was no revolution at all, but the most likely and sensible thing in the world. In the depths of her mind a voice kept repeating over and over again that it was in fact a revolution. That something was wrong. Something was happening of which she had no knowledge and over which she could exercise no control.

Her mind, proceeding from revolution to revolution with amazing facility, put forward another suggestion to diminish Hugh's.

"Suppose I were to come with you, Hugh darling?" Visions of Richard's piteous disappointment passed through her mind, to be ruthlessly dismissed. At this moment no one existed for her but Hugh. She waited confidently for his answer.

It came at once.

"Oh I shouldn't do that if I were you," Hugh said quickly. "Richie would break his heart."

He left the room at once, before she could reply.

It is doubtful whether she would ever have replied. She was stunned. Tears of shame burned in her eyes.

All the time her mind was composing phrases of the explanation she would give Richard, her servants, and the incredulous rest of Danesacre. Poor Mary.

Fuller knowledge broke on her one evening some weeks later, with the startling swiftness of the earlier blow. Hugh was in love with Miss Jardine. They were already lovers. He was planning to go away with her, not for ever, only for a month. One month of perfect happiness, and then back to work. Mary stared at the proof, placed by most unlikely chance in her hands, and tried to realise what had happened to her.

She could not. These things happened to other women, but not to her.

Minutes passed. She held the betraying letter in her hand. Thought stirring in her benumbed brain suggested to her that she had better burn it. There was a candle on the table beside her. She held the letter in it while it caught fire, and shrivelled to a black wafer. She went on holding the fragment in the flame. Then she dropped it and wandered across the room. After a time she became conscious of pain in her hand.

One finger was horribly burnt, almost to the bone.

The dressing of it took some time, and when that was finished Mary began to cry. Slowly at first, and then with sobs that shook her body, a deep-down visceral grief. It tore and shattered. . . .

When Hugh came in she was standing by the fire in his room, still in the frock she had worn at dinner, with a lace bodice cut down between her breasts and full rucked sleeves that would have looked absurd on less slender arms than his wife's. He thought that she looked tired and came to press his mouth lightly on the back of her neck. Surprisingly, she turned round and taking him in her arms covered his face with kisses. They had a quality that set the blood throbbing in his temples, but when he would have returned them, she put him gently away.

"Dear," she said and paused and began again. "This Miss Jardine. Do you love her very much?"

"What have you done to your finger?" Hugh asked, after a pause.

Mary glanced down at her hand. The consciousness of pain had left her again.

"I burned it," she said indifferently.

She was studying his face with a passionate intentness, as if for the second time in her life she had to get it by heart, before it was lost to her. Hugh was pale, and his mouth was compressed out of all softness or kindness. He looked very young and a little cruel.

"Do you love her so much?"

"I love her," Hugh said, and left it at that.

They seemed then to be launched upon an interminable discussion, in which Mary asked the most frightful questions, and was determined to strip herself and Hugh of every decent pretence that might have been wrapped round the affair. She hurt herself so dreadfully, running blindly against walls and swords, that in very pity for her, Hugh would have gone away. He did not know what to say to comfort this shaken desolate Mary, who cried to him for comfort and repudiated it and him in the same breath. He was shaken himself, and wretched. He had never meant his new love to touch Mary or hurt her. He was almost ready to throw Miss Jardine away, to do anything that would save his wife from the agony of self-abasement and grief she was enduring under his very eyes. Almost—not quite. Fanny Jardine's surrender was too present with him. It was too warm and living and passionate an experience. He wanted her. He wanted her, he thought, more than he had ever wanted anything in his life. Mary's tears came between him and his new love and hurt something in him of which he had forgotten the very existence. Absurdly he ached to comfort her. She had been a dear and generous lover. He felt a quick throb of some feeling that was almost resentment against Fanny Jardine. He wanted to take Mary in his arms and say: "There, there, my little love, it's all right. Don't mind. Everything's all right." But he stood in front of her and stared at the sullen bitter woman, whose face, distorted with weeping, was like a gross caricature of that young girl he had loved, and married, and irremediably hurt and failed.

"Hugh," his wife said, "didn't you feel that you owed me some loyalty? I don't mean that you did. I'd hate"—her voice faltered—"to keep you against your will. But didn't *you* feel that?"

"I might have felt it," Hugh said slowly, "if you had ever been wholly mine."

"Oh Hugh, I was. I was."

"At least half of you belonged to Garton's," Hugh said.

Mary said something incoherent and apparently rather stupid about another lesson and went away, groping a little with her hands like a blind woman. . . .

Nothing in Mary Hervey's life had prepared her to learn this lesson, and every obstinate quality in her fought against accepting it. She thrust it away from her, would not believe it had happened to her, but in the end, and because she always did learn her lessons in the end, she began trying to see what could be got out of it. The Garton in her kept on insisting that something could be solved. What?

She thought of Miss Jardine almost impersonally. But jealousy can exist as an impersonal emotion, and the image, recurring again and again, an irrational torment that came and went and came again in moments of fatigue, forcing itself on her out of unimagined depths of shame and self-loathing, of Hugh in the girl's arms, being caressed, caressing her, drove her through days of torturing madness and nights of frightful crazy grief.

She did not show it. After the first open rout she pulled her forces together again. Though Hugh saw her every day, he did not tell her what he going to do, and she supposed from the fact that "the Jardine woman" never now came to the house, that she had been told to keep away. Mary became very tired, and she bore her little body about with an air of resentment, as if she were always asking it: "What have I done that you should turn on me like this?" She tried to despise Hugh. She ought to have known that no good could come of a hasty London marriage into a family she knew nothing about. This was what she had been brought to by her precipitant folly. To this dreadful humiliation of knowing herself put away for an inferior woman. Mary knew that Miss Jardine was inferior. "Only a mean woman," she thought fiercely, "would have done such a thing to me. I've been kind to her." But she believed that Hugh was irresistible, and she could not despise him. Hugh was not a fool. She acknowledged it. He was young, incredibly young and dreamy, but, incongruous and shocking as it seemed to his wife, the Jardine affair had roused and hardened him. Mary revolted at the means. But she had to admit to herself that she was confronted by a new Hugh. Not a quick-tongued soft-hearted boy, but a stubborn intractable man to whom she no longer meant everything. Pride urged her to drive this man out of her life. "Away, take this woman you prefer to me, and go out of my sight." Pride sustained her through each day of silent refusal to question Hugh or to admit the questions she could read in his eyes. And pride again, urged to it by her native prudence, led her to make cautious inquiries about her position if Hugh left her with Miss Jardine.

She found that with incredible difficulty and at an expense that horrified her she could divorce him. At any other time the publicity involved would have revolted her father's daughter, but now she was as determined as ever Mark Henry Garton might have been to assert herself, at no matter what loss of personal dignity. She was beyond troubling about dignity. She was actually making the calmly monstrous assumption that nothing she chose to do would be improper. Let Danesacre make what comment it liked—there would, she knew, be comment enough on her equivocal position as a woman with a divorced husband—she was still the owner of Garton's Yard and Garton's Line, not to speak of blast furnaces and an engine works on the Tees.

Stiff with dignity, she sat alone in her room, raging against Danesacre and Miss Jardine. It always ended in the same fashion, with tears and a girl rocking herself to and fro on the edge of her bed, her hands clasped over the little beating of her heart.

But if her treacherous pride could not save her, youth and the tenacious spirit in her were already at work. And when the thought came into her mind that Hugh could be defeated if she were to submit herself completely to him, if she went to him and said (in effect): "I am your slave, trample on me if you like, but give up this woman," she had the wit to reject it. She was not too proud to bow her haughty young neck under Hugh's feet. She was learning to respect the new Hugh for qualities her young husband had never shown. But she was too decent. What a way to get a man back! Better let him go than that. With trembling lips she faced the prospect squarely. If she could not force and might not coax him to give up his way what was she to do? Resign him? Could she resign what she had already lost? "Oh I loved him, I loved him so," she cried. She almost perceived that love was not all that went to the making of a decent marriage. There was something more, that she had missed.

And here it suddenly occurred to her that Hugh would get tired of Miss Jardine. The girl was stupid. Mary realised this with a little shock of certainty. Hugh would weary of her, and then, because he could never abandon her after dragging her through the disgrace of divorce, he would have to stick to her. He would look for consolation elsewhere. He would find it, and grow weary and look again. She saw Hugh drifting through all the casual intimacies, the shabby back-room adulteries of an anchorless man. He would creep furtively with his love of the moment to some rendezvous for such smirched meetings, a little bored with it, a little revolted, afterwards hating it, and inevitably going again, and hating it again. Her Hugh, that boy whose kisses in the dusk of a Kensington orchard had opened to her a world of beauty, of amazing tendernesses, of confident adventure and excitement, and the quiet happiness of friendly intimate experiences shared. It was unbearable. It must not be like that.

She was in the office when this thought came to her, and with a sudden vigour, whirled out of the room and ran to Hugh's study. Miss Jardine was there, standing by the window, facing Hugh with a perturbed and flustered urgency. Evidently Mary had interrupted a conversation of some importance. She swept it aside. She swept Miss Jardine aside with an imperious gesture.

"Go away," she said impatiently, and when the girl did not move— "Oh, do *go*."

The secretary hesitated. She looked to Hugh for guidance and getting none, went reluctantly away, shutting the door behind her with a resentful click.

"Hugh," Mary said breathlessly. "Hugh, what did you mean to do at the end of your month with that woman?"

Hugh gave her a queer look.

"Come back."

"Here? Come back here and live with me again?"

"Sounds fairly revolting, doesn't it?" Hugh said bitterly. "But you see, there are the children. There's even Richard. And there's you. Damn it all, Mary, I haven't stopped loving you just because I've fallen in love with Fanny Jardine. I don't expect you to believe that, but it's quite true. I never meant this to come near you or hurt you at all. It's a totally different sort of thing. And I *loathe* scenes." He was white-lipped and Mary suddenly perceived that underneath his reserve he was strung inordinately tight, as if the strain were becoming more than he could stand.

"Could you give her up for me?" Mary demanded.

"No," said Hugh, and after a pause, again: "No."

He contemplated Mary, gone a little white under this thrust, and said:

"You see, she's utterly and absolutely mine. As you've never been, Mary. Don't, my dear."

Mary rallied. She thought: "I won't worry you more than I can help, you poor boy." She spoke hurriedly but managed to give an effect of choosing her words with some care.

"Hugh. Why shouldn't you do just that?"

"Do what?" Hugh asked wearily.

"Go away with"—Mary faltered and recovered herself sternly—"this girl. Very quietly, without any fuss, or anyone knowing. Have your month, two months, as long as you like. Then come back again."

Hugh was looking at her with something like horror, as men do look at their women when those immature creatures have said one of the Impossible Things, things that are not said. But she was so set upon her purpose that she was entirely self-forgetful. There was something in the erectness of her slim body as she stood facing him in the dusk that stirred him to a sudden warmth of grief.

"Come back here, Mary? To you?"

"Is that so dreadful a prospect?" Mary's smile was a rather pitiful affair. "I didn't mean it quite like that, Hugh darling. I meant, come back and live in the house. It's big enough for both of us. I won't interfere with you. Or ask questions. We can be friends," she said, her spirit torn with unimaginable memories. "It's not impossible. Think, Hugh. How is it different from what you meant to do when you thought I wouldn't know?"

In her excitement she came close to him and held him with both hands, pleading with him to help her to save the boy Hugh from that dreadful fate which she alone saw. And if the thought crossed the depths of her mind that this was one way of keeping a hold on him, it in no way lessened the resolute pressure of her desires. These were all for Hugh, full of fierce pity and a fierce inarticulate hunger to have him at least within sight and hearing for some of the time. And in the end, shaken by her soft urgency, by the very loveliness of her face as she lifted it to his, with its sweet air of surprise still shining through her woe, he gave in. He promised every thing she asked. Only then, with a half frightened glance at him and beyond him, she ran away, ran away and left him wondering what in life is more bitter than achieved desire. . . .

It was not until the day of his going that Mary seemed to realise that this was the end. Then all her courage left her and she hung about in his room, watching him pack. She fetched him things to lay in the open box, trotting here and there like an obedient little girl, jeering at his incompetent packing. Only when all was over, and the box stood between them, strapped and locked, she broke down.

"Hugh," she said, "Hugh, you're not going? Don't go. Don't, don't go."

For the first time it seemed to strike Hugh that he was hurting himself as well as Mary, hurting them both, dreadfully and irrevocably. Mary clung to him and they kissed and he tore himself away and held her off at arm's length.

"Don't you see it's no use," he cried. "Mary, don't you see it's just no use. You didn't love me. Yes, you did. You did. Brute that I am. You did love me, but only half of you. You kept me out. You pushed me away. . . . You can look after yourself . . . you've always made that quite plain. . . . *She* can't. . . . I don't know why I'm saying all these things to you. They're none of them true. You've been the dearest sweetest wife. . . . I've hurt you. I've made you ashamed."

"No, no. I've been happy. Hugh, Hugh darling, stay with me."

Hugh was shaking with fatigue and the strain of the last week. He shook his head and then rested it on Mary's shoulder. She stroked his smooth hair and listened to him with a familiar constriction of her chest. It threatened to choke her, but she had to keep herself quiet, very quiet, for Hugh.

"I can't. Mary dear, I can't. There isn't any going back. There'd be all this between us. You think, now, that it would be all right. It wouldn't. How many times a day would you look at me and see—*this?* I couldn't bear it . . . and neither could you. We couldn't make anything of it. Could we?''

"You want to go to her, don't you?'' Mary said softly, still stroking the dark head near her own. Hugh straightened himself wearily.

"I don't know,'' he said. "Mary, I don't know. At this moment, I'd like to lie down and be smothered in my sleep. What a state of mind for an elopement.''

Mary achieved a little joke.

"Wives don't usually see their husbands off on these occasions. . . . All right, Hugh, I won't worry you any more. Good-bye and bless you.''

Still Hugh did not go. Mary could not guess what he was thinking. Of Fanny Jardine, probably, waiting for him somewhere. Of the mess he and Mary had made of their marriage. Of the impossibility of bridging the gulf that in a few weeks had opened between them. Her mind played her an old trick, and she had the odd fancy that she had married the boy of the long-ago morning at Roxborough. It had all ended in this dreadful failure and now Gerry was leaving her. But it was Hugh who was going and leaving her alone and with him was going all warmth, all the sweetness of shared joys, all that made life other than an empty weariness. She remembered odd things about him . . . the way he could make himself seem small and defenceless when he was tired and wanted to lie in her arms and be comforted . . . a trick he had of smiling at her through his eyelashes . . . small, absurd things, a note in his voice, a gesture when he turned to her . . . Hugh waking in the morning, with untidy hair and very bright eyes. . . . He was leaving her and taking her youth with him. A terror of loneliness, a sense of infinite loss seized Mary and she stumbled towards him, with tears pouring down her face, to cry in his arms.

"I'm not trying to keep you. Only just this . . . I love you. I've had you. I'm grateful for that. Don't ever think I'm not. I want you to promise me one thing. If ever you want me again . . . if she isn't kind to you . . . if you want me, you'll come and tell me, won't you? Don't think anything of me but this. That I'll be glad for you to come back. Promise. Promise, Hugh.''

He promised.

Mary drew herself out of his arms, and stood dabbing at her tears.

"It seems to me," Hugh said unsteadily, "that I love you more now than I ever did in my life.''

Mary was too exhausted to answer this by anything more coherent than a feeble crow. . . . There was a knock at the door, and the housemaid announced that the cab was waiting, and should the man fetch the master's box?

The box was dragged out, while Mary stood impassively by the window. Even now, perhaps, it was not too late, if she made another appeal. But she could not appeal any more. Things had gone too far. They were being driven on by the pressure of their own decisions. Hugh was probably right. It wouldn't work . . . she would be galled by the memory of Miss Jardine . . . Hugh would regret, feel cheated, tied down. . . . The cabman was hoisting the box up beside him, to the accompaniment of shrill objurgations from the servant. Everything was ready. It was all over. Hugh and she kissed for the last time, holding each other closely, and then he hurried away. Mary heard him go. The front door banged. The wheels of the cab crunched on the gravel of the drive.

"Hugh," Mary said softly.

With enormous force the thought struck her that Hugh had never meant to marry Miss Jardine unless his wife forced him to it by divorcing him. Surely a man who loved a woman wanted to marry her? This was an extraordinarily complicated affair. What on earth was Hugh after? Romance? Mary gave a little shriek of laughter, thinking of Fanny Jardine's ugly nose. . . . The room was full of Miss Jardine's nose . . . Mary clapped her hand to her mouth, frightened by the sound of her laughter. . . .

She got through the night somehow, and in the morning there was still her work to be done. And that day passed. And another night. And the next day.

CHAPTER FOUR

1

AS if time had stood still for Mary Hervey while she watched her husband tearing their life across with a wilful gesture, it leapt into activity as soon as he had gone, and sprang, spinning and whirling, into the upward curve of a great arc across the world. It would not have been surprising if she had lost her head, so did life and time hurry on her. The sixties were just not in when young Mary Roxby came to Danesacre, and just not out when Mary Hervey's husband left her for *le pays bleu* with romance in the shapely person of Fanny Jardine in his arms.

After that, while she was still in hours of sleeplessness or fatigue fighting the recurring agony of her loss, time took hold of her and catapulted her into the tremendous seventies. The year Hugh went was the year when the Suez Canal, swinging open, delivered the trade of the East over to her steamships. Another three years, and the people who had jeered at steam were falling silent. The beautiful sisters and successors of the *Mary Gray* were still proud upon the seas, but more and more frequently they met in their splendid passage funnelled boats past which they swept in all their disdainful glory of sail, mocking the clumsy interloper. The interloper wallowed after them, and the dun shadow of a smoke-stack fell across their radiant wake.

One fine Spring morning in the early seventies Mary was in the Yard, standing close to the ship on the stocks. The hammers of the men at work on her sounded clear and bright, like bells ringing in the sunshine.

Up the valley the trees were covered with a fine feathery green; in the light air their branches swayed up and down, sharp and distinct under an intense blue sky. White clouds, soft and thick, tumbling from the zenith, dazzled Mary's eyes. She looked away from them and was dazzled again by the multitudinous waves in the harbour, ruffled up by a fresh breeze. A man on a boat broke into singing; his voice floated away and was lost in the middle air. Mary took a step nearer the ship. Her glance ran lovingly over the lines of her hull. Sweet lines she showed, sound and graceful, very different from the hull line of Mark Henry's first steamer. She would take the water almost like a clipper. A delicate glow of satisfaction spread through Mary's body. On such a morning it was delicious to be alive, to see the ship that had been first an idea in her head, then a design on the architect's drawing sheets and a model that would later be carried up to her house, shaping, springing into life above the keel laid down four months ago. Nothing thrilled her as the upward curve of a ship from keel to bows thrilled her, nor gave her the same exquisite sense of rightness and contentment. Her imagination—she was a slow-thinking and conscientious young woman for the most part—was released in ships, it went fluttering down to the sea in full-rigged ships and plodded to East and West in the wake of her steamers.

Freights were high and going higher. The Yard was full of work, building iron-screw steamers for Plymouth and London firms, and sending them round to the Tees to take in their engines. Garton's was lifting and riding on such a swelling tide as Mark Henry had never seen.

Mary recalled abruptly an unanswered letter from the John Roxby who had gone into trade in the forties and dropped out of the family's cognisance. He had written, signing himself her Humble and Obedient, to ask whether she thought it possible that Roxby House would come into the market, James Roxby having died of age and port, and Charles reputed to be dying. Her Humble and Obedient sounded cocksure. Mary made a wry face. She would write him a formal letter. "For the attention of your good-self. There is not the *very slightest chance* that My Son Richard Roxby will sell his inheritance." The man must be making money. Every one who had the luck to have anything to sell could not help making money now. An army of sellers was invading all the corners of the earth. They sold to the people at home until these had no more money to spend. Then they sold to the heathen Chinee, the Red Indian, the ordinary Indian and the black man. In top-hats and morning-coats they penetrated the ports of northern China, and presented themselves bearing gifts before mandarins, negro kings, and Persian satraps. It was called, indifferently, stimulating desire and opening new markets. Sometimes nations came into collision in the new markets and then there was talk at home of wetting the event with blood. But the world, for all it was being so rapidly foreshortened and stimulated and opened up (like an oyster attacked by a galvanic battery) was still so large, and the whole adventure so new and splendid and progressive that no one could imagine its coming to an end, and the Hervey's of the shipbuilding world were put to it to build fast enough to cope with the running to and fro across a changing world.

Still thinking resentfully of the Roxby brother-in-law she had never seen, Mary turned her back on the harbour, and saw John Mempes coming towards her from the direction of the sail loft. He walked slowly, holding himself erect, his grey top-hat, the only grey topper in Danesacre, balanced over one eyebrow. A half smile played round Mary's lips. She had a deep affection for the manager, partly, so to speak, her own, and partly a legacy from the serious stolid child who had followed at the heels of dandified young John Mempes in Mark Henry's shipyard.

Mempes must be nearly fifty, she thought. He looked older, for all his stiff back. He had broadened, and his face had settled into grim lines. He shaved, exposing a menacing chin, but his hair grew down his cheek-bones and curled a little over his ears. It struck Mary, watching his slow progress, that he was oddly bigger and sterner than the men of her own generation; she could not imagine Hugh at fifty having that majesty of being.

She checked a sigh. John was a splendid man. He steadied her. He was a faithful second self, a cautious temporising voice in the back of her mind, the most loyal of advisers and friends, but an unsatisfactory companion for the young owner of Garton's. He agreed that the Canal, now three years old, had altered the face of things, that the orders placed at the Yard were perhaps bringing nearer a move to the Tees from the confined shipyards on the Danesbeck. He had agreed to the building of two more steamships for the Line. But beyond that he was a sealed fountain. He contributed nothing to Mary's glowing vision of the future. He was a tired man in these days and a man in whom the springs of life were definitely running backward. He said that the vision of modernity sickened him, a queer enough thing to say, if it meant anything at all.

"Good morning, John."

Mempes smiled at her, standing with the grey top-hat held negligently in one hand. The sight of her gave him a sharp definite pleasure. Such a vivid glowing young woman she seemed, standing there, hatless, in a grey frock, with lace at her throat. She was often hatless, and in the house or out of it never wore a cap, a flouting of convention much canvassed by Danesacre's matrons, old and young, and bitterly resented by Mrs. George Ling, who was three years Mary's junior and bore herself as befitted the wife of the under-manager of Garton's Steel and Iron Works and the mother of four fine growing Lings. John Mempes liked it. His eyes rested with secret satisfaction on her small uncovered head with its crown of lustrous dark hair.

"You'll get a sunstroke," he grumbled.

Mary laughed. "My hair is too thick."

Vain of it, Mempes thought. Well, let her be. There was not a head of hair like it in Danesacre. From under his brows he examined the small round face offered to his gaze, narrow squared chin, and eyes like rock pools under a blue sky, as deep and secret. The long lashes rested on her cheeks for a moment, and then lifted, with that familiar effect of surprise and pleasure.

"I'm going over to Middlesborough, John."

Mempes twitched an eyebrow at the disconcerting young woman. What was she after? He distrusted the Cornish manager of the Works. The fellow was undoubtedly crazy. He wasted money.

"What are you going there for?"

"To see Thomas Prendergast about the new German contracts for steel rails."

Mempes growled something unintelligible.

"They're good contracts," Mary said defensively.

"The man's not sound."

"He has ideas."

"He may have the plague for all I care," Mempes said. "It'ud de him and us less harm in the end. His ideas cost us money. More money than we have any right to be spending."

"Garton's can afford to spend," Mary observed. "We must experiment to advance."

"Oh, experiment," Mempes said. "Build another *City of Truro* perhaps?"

Mary blushed. The *City of Truro* had been a dreadful and humiliating blunder. Would John never stop talking about it? She looked at him with anger. It glanced harmlessly off the manager's heavily debonair face. She could do nothing with him when he looked like that, the deep-lidded embodiment of everything Garton's had been and nothing it was. She might as well stare at the back of his head.

Her sense of humour, a rare possession and lurking very far down in her feminine soul, came unexpectedly to her help. The *City of Truro* had a funny side. Two funny sides. A smile came and went on Mary's red mouth.

"Garton's hasn't got where it is by being afraid of mistakes," she said mildly.

"Another mistake like that, and you won't be in a position to make 'em," Mempes observed. His heart had leapt in sympathy with that fugitive smile, but he would not show it. He liked her courage, and her youth, indomitable at an age when the run of Danesacre's wives and mothers were passing maturity. Why, he thought, she must be thirty and over; she had the skin of a young woman and the figure and poise of a girl. Her small body radiated health and abounding life. He liked the way she had balanced between her belief in her luck and her apprehension of yawnings in the ground under her feet. What he did not like was the element of recklessness and insecurity in all her enterprises since the Suez Canal had opened for her like a door opening on a new world. She had rushed into her world. Danesacre had had more than one occasion to recall the fact that she was Mark Henry Garton's niece. They said she was turning out such another adventurous fool, and hopefully prophesied the crash.

Mary could not conceive the possibility of a crash. Mempes could and he was often afraid for her. When she would not listen to him he was angry, and when her disobedience was justified he trembled because success gave a fillip to her wilfulness. What could you expect with a chin like hers? It was the spit of Mark Henry's.

He could not make her see that the present flood of orders was bound to slacken. She behaved as if the Yard would go on for ever working at full pressure, turning out ships for firms who could not get them fast enough; as if freights would go higher and higher beyond their present dizzy altitude. They *would* go higher, but they would drop again. Mempes did not share the prevailing complacency about the splendid times he lived in. The seventies, ay and the forties and fifties and sixties, were too splendid for his fastidious stomach. He knew how the thing worked. There were good years, when wealth added into vast towering fortunes, and threw up fabulously ugly buildings and great factories and workshops; in their shadow grew and spread congested areas of meanly conceived towns and houses filled with men and women who sometimes had enough to eat and sometimes had not, and then they grumbled or starved to death or rioted and in any event lived or died disregarded by the master brains who were riding in on the swelling tide of the nineteenth century progress. The process caught up women and little children and squeezed the blood out of them, and a few misguided people, mistaking progress for murder, kept trying to stop it and were dubbed Radicals and traitors for their pains. Mempes had no sympathy for Radicals and little for oppressed men and women. The sight of misery angered him. But he knew what happened at the climax of every period of expanding trade. The expansion went just too far, until the warehouses and wharves were glutted. Then the factories closed down and the shipyards fell idle and silent, and the people in the dark quarters of towns and cities, and in the squalid cottages of picturesque little villages, were brought face to face with such elemental things as hunger and disease and death, and faced them as best they could, as their forefathers faced pestilence and Black Death coming on them by an act of God, until the hard times passed and good times began again. And if John Mempes cared nothing how many men and women starved to death during the hard times, he cared agonisingly for the safety of Garton's, because Garton's was Mary Hervey, and he loved her, with a tight-lipped craving to possess not her body only, but her mind and soul, that never left him. He had lost her, and he ached over her courage, and her wilful venturing and her warm beauty. The world might choke to death with its overreaching greed for all he cared. But not Mary.

His doubts made him a very solitary man in Danesacre. The shipping people told that his eyes were set backwards in his head, which explained why he saw nothing good later than the last century. It was only partly true. He walked about Danesacre, his hands clasped behind his back, his grey top-hat well forward, a grim figure of a dandy, and made uncomfortable remarks in the club about upstarts. There was more than one shipping fortune made in Danesacre during the early seventies, and the upcomers did not like the slighting air of Garton's manager. His beaked nose, thick twitching eyebrows, and jutting chin intimidated the younger men. They left him alone. He sat for hours every evening in the club window, looking out to sea across the tumbling roofs of the old houses on the cliff below. What visions rose at him from the swirling grey bosom of the water? He saw the ships passing north and south, the spreading canvas of clippers, crowned and caressed by the envious sun, the smoke-smudged track of steamers, the small coasters, sail and steam, wallowing along with less grace than persistence. The light faded and sunk in night, sea and sky lay in a soft profound obscurity. The lights of the passing ships, like stars fallen from the thickly scattered sky, pierced the over-arching darkness. Sea and sky, ships' lights and stars, were one, as if the little town were perched on the verge of space.

Then he turned his back on the window and gave himself up to other thoughts. He thought of the Yard and the Works and of the owner of yard and works, of a slender neck and a head heavy with dark hair, of a rebellious young mouth and eyes glowing with wilful fire, of a soft voice saying: "I like you." How long ago. Eight years, and then she had married the London fellow, who had left her. The fellow had come back again, but no tale of an Italian holiday had taken in John Mempes. He knew better. Besides, he had seen the yellow-haired piece who had been the fellow's secretary standing in the garden of a cottage in a

sequestered village up the valley. Keeping her there, was he? The fool.
Mempes growled aloud, and stalking across the room, went home,
troubled by the world, by Mary, and by the frightful vision of Mary
broken on the world's inexorable wheel, alternating fat years with lean
ones, and by her own refusal to look beyond present fat to coming lean.

He did not like the news that she was going over to the Tees. Quite
apart from his distrust of Thomas Prendergast's ideas, he viewed
Mary's friendly attitude to the fellow with jealous dislike. Damn it, the
man was nothing, a common dog of a puddler picked up between Mark
Henry's thumb and finger, no companion for a lady. He called Mary a
lady because she was half Hansyke; the Garton strain was middle-class,
a coarse strain in fine stuff.

"You don't need to go to the Tees to overlook Prendergast's contracts," he said. "Let him write over."

"I prefer to go."

"You'll get into mischief."

Mary gave him a clear look, and he turned away angrily. He heard
her voice in his ear. "Don't be silly, John. I hear there's trouble on the
Tees. It doesn't affect us, but I'd like to look at it. I want to look at a
number of things. We shall move there some day, after all."

Mempes' gaze took in the Yard and the old harbour. An unreasoning
regret possessed him.

"You're like the *City of Truro*. You've grown too big for decent
handling. You'll presently go down in a storm with others like yourself,
and a lot of poor wretches clinging to you."

Mary laughed at him and in a flight of misguided imagery he told her
that she resembled a hankering cow, overfed and under the impression
that the whole world was one lush meadow. That was more than enough
for Mary. She went away at once, with her head up. His face relaxed
into a grim smile, reminded by her retreating back of an offended little
girl who had left him standing in the identical spot. . . .

Mary drove over the moors to Roxby House and found Charles
Roxby ill in bed. He had been dying so long that no one believed in the
imminence of his end, though he had wasted until he was more like a
catgut than a man, a mere whispering spite in a lawn night-shirt, with

long fingers that sorted silks and plucked at the sheets. His face
wavered at Mary and he said:

"I hear Hervey's on with a golden girl. You have to pay for youth.
Archie gave you no such pangs."

"Be quiet," Mary said grimly.

"I'll be quiet," Charles chuckled. "I'll be as quiet as death. But
can't you hear them whispering together in the night? *Come close, my
darling, and closer and warmer.* Eh, Mary?"

It hurt her quite horribly for a moment, but she recovered at once.
Her air of self-sufficiency, the armour she had begun to clasp round her
as a little girl and had laid aside for Hugh, was not proof against this sort
of thing even now. Her face expressed nothing. "Hard little devil,"
Charles commented to himself. He had never been able to touch or
understand her, but he was very old and so near death that he had given
up trying to explain things to himself. There were several things he
wanted to explain to other people before he died, but it hardly seemed
worth the trouble. It was easier to go on making malicious remarks. Die
as you've lived was his rule of decent conduct. He lifted his thin old
eyelids suddenly and saw Mary looking past him with an expression of
unfathomable doubt in her eyes. They reminded him that he had seen
the same expression in the eyes of a young deer in Roxby Park when he
crept to within a foot of it before betraying his nearness. He was
startled, almost shocked, and recoiled among his pillows. No young
woman had the right to expose herself in such fashion. What could have
made her afraid? He considered for a moment telling her that nothing
that could happen to her mattered so dearly as she might think it did, but
the effort was too much trouble. He closed his eyes and pretended to be
asleep.

Mary's wistful face before old Charles Roxby was no accident. Even
to herself, she was awkward and uncertain. She felt less certain than
young Mary Roxby with her baby and her injudicious dreams. That girl
had not had Hugh. She did not know how easy it is to make the most
frightful mistakes—by chance, in a chance moment of distrust. She
knew nothing, and was not dishonourably afraid. Mary Hervey was
afraid of several things. She had been taught distrust of herself by

Hugh. Because he had turned from her she believed herself to be an unlovable woman.

No one knew what she felt. This gives her comedy its faintly tragic air. She was so strong that there was nothing she could not endure in silence. Her small, apparently fragile body was the guardian of a spiritual vitality handed down through generations of landfast Hansykes and resolute acquisitive Gartons. She had sometimes thought of death, during months when she worked until a fatigued body could be trusted to fall into sudden sleep and roused to work again, but a strange ironical sense of her own powers of endurance had carried her through it all. She knew that she would live down her loss. And after all she had lived it down.

She left Roxby House and continued to drive over the moors northwards, sitting stiffly in her carriage, with hands folded in her lap and eyes staring blindly. The moor was wild with Spring, every peaty stream bubbling madly down, every larch tree offering its shy enchanting flowers, the bogs starred with asphodel and sundew. The carriage jolted down into a small valley and passed a cottage standing in an orchard. The half-opened buds of apple blossom, spraying up against the blue sky, filled Mary with an ecstatic sense of happiness. At the same time she was surprised to feel tears forming in her eyes. She accused herself of becoming shamefully sentimental, and strove successfully to get rid of them without having recourse to lifting her veil.

She had recovered completely from the shock of Hugh's unfaithfulness. Nothing lasted, not even so sharp and biting a sorrow. Time dulled it and in the end took it away. It did not hurt her now. Nothing remained of it but her ironical enduring belief that she was an unlovable woman. Nothing would ever hurt her so deeply again.

Memories came about her like a cloud. There had been another orchard and another Hugh, young, confident, softly affectionate and dear. He had been sure of himself then, and sure of her. Mary stirred uneasily. Would nothing free her from the last light finger touch of memory? Perhaps it was true that marriage had bound her to Hugh in an intimacy from which nothing, no disillusion, could wholly free her, as if the first moment of unequivocal surrender had given into his keeping a Mary who could never again escape him. And then, after that, the living Mary had blundered cruelly away from him. She had lost him to Miss Jardine. She thought of her life as spoiled and of her devotion to the Yard as a blunder, but in her heart of hearts she did not believe that she could have behaved differently. She might have stayed in London and made Hugh her whole life—and perhaps kept him. Yes, she could have done that, but only by denying reality. Her desire of ships was real, and had sustained her when Archie frightened a child out of her senses, when George Roxby died and left her and Richard with nothing but an unencumbered estate. It was as real as her marriage, as real as her love for Hugh.

All this was true, but the thought that in cleaving to the Yard she was in some way betraying the boy Hugh stabbed her through the memory of his cruder betrayal. Even now it shook and hurt her beyond speech or tears. She tried never to think of it. She could bear to think of Hugh's passion for Miss Jardine, but she could not bear to think that perhaps she herself had not loved him enough. And yet she would—quite simply—have given her life for his.

Another orchard, far below her in the valley, like a pink and white carpet flung down at the foot of the hills. Now she recalled Hugh's unexpected return at the end of six months. He had made no announcement. He came, in the middle of the afternoon, when she and John Mempes were at work in her office. There were the sounds of his arrival on the gravel outside . . . and John Mempes going out into the hall ostensibly to greet him, really, as Mary knew well, to avoid the meeting between husband and wife . . . Hugh's voice in the hall: "Good afternoon, sir. Where is my wife?" And at the faint proprietary echo in the words Mary had buried her face in her hands. "I *am* your wife," she thought. "I've been yours. You've had me. I'm glad." . . . She saw herself standing up to greet Hugh with a friendly clasp of the hand.

The weeks slid past after his return. Mary ceased to spend sleepless nights, tortured by exasperating images of Hugh in Fanny Jardine's arms. Hugh and she became tremendously more friendly and gay together, and the gulf between them widened and widened, until the figures of those young lovers who had once found nothing more dear, nothing more worth while in the world than their reflection in each other, dwindled into specks, always receding, infinitely pitifully remote. . . . She could smile at them now and at herself, but at the time it had been torture. No one, she thought, would ever understand the crisis through which, without assistance from any living soul, she had passed, nor the greatness of her abnegation. To have let him go—as she had done. Simply to have loosed her hold on what had belonged to her in the highest and deepest sense of possession. To have set him completely free. Never once by look, word or gesture after he returned, to have reminded him that he had once been hers, that he had betrayed her. Oh, it had taken all her strength. It had nearly killed her.

She wondered where Miss Jardine was living. Somewhere in one of the villages up the valley, she thought, from the direction of Hugh's periodic disappearances. She had been replaced, as secretary, by a dark-haired gnome-like creature, who irritated Hugh very much by her inability to punctuate. Her manuscript resembled a battlefield at the end of a day's fighting, strewn with dismembered phrases, trunkless heads, and commas like abandoned weapons dropped in furious disorder. Poor Hugh!

Mary roused herself with a strange smile. There was nothing left but memories as shy and delicate as larch flowers and an elusive pain that came and went, hurt less and remained a shorter time in her thoughts than the common disappointments of the day. Mary sighed. And smiled again at a baby rabbit that shot across the road under the very wheels of the carriage. The coachman stood up and waved his whip, shouting loudly. "They be a greät nuisance," he said apologetically, "and shamefully merry. Light feet and a light heart mun lead straight to sin. 'Tes the law." He brooded over the shocking levity of rabbits for the rest of the journey.

They came down into the ironmasters' district on the south bank of the Tees as night turned it into a palace of dusky courtyards and dark columns, lit and crowned with flames and quivering with sinister clangour. Beyond the furnaces lay the river, blackened with docks and shipping, and on its farther side the hidden disorder of the town, a slut in a torn bodice showing starry rents of light.

Mary's carriage left the ironworks and blast furnaces on the right and set her down, still outside the town, at George Ling's house. Mrs.

George Ling sat on a sofa, yawning at George. The jet beads on her bodice rang like the crystals of the chandelier, punctuating her boredom. There Mary learned, what had been rumoured the day before in Danesacre, that there was trouble in the shipyards, spreading among the iron works and threatening a complete stoppage on Tees-side.

"It began among the brassfounders," George told her. "They objected to the ironmoulders making the large brass castings that the brassworkers couldn't undertake until they had learned how to make them. The engineers joined in, with a quarrel they fixed on the boilermakers, who keep a tight hold of jobs to do with angle-iron that the engineers think they ought to do. Work on a ship in one of the yards fell dead. Every one on her was quarrelling. Other ships and yards joined in. Lord knows where it will stop. It's among the ironworkers already. This *Sillery* should have been frapped, though I can't say I like it. I prefer something with a kick; give me a sparkling wine and you can have all the still stuff that ever dropped dead on a man's palate."

"But—madness," Mary said. "Can't they settle their quarrels without stopping work on the ships?"

Dinner with the Lings was a portentous feast, enlivened by Mrs. George's references to the state of George's digestion and George's involuntary testimony to the same. When it came to an end at last Mary refused coffee and escaped into the garden. The house stood alone on the gentle hill that stretched up from the iron district into the fields and lanes of the country-side. It occupied the outposts of an advancing change of taste that was pushing the houses of ironmasters and managers out of the town on to the surrounding slopes. Mary leaned against the low wall dividing the garden from the lane. The night was dark, with a moonless sky pressing down on the sinister flaming labyrinth of furnaces and shafts. Every few minutes a column of flame-riven smoke shot up into the sky, illuminating the ironworkers' quarter and the docks beyond. A blade edge of river flashed in the short-lived glow, and the sky was flushed with a tawny bloom like the bloom on dusk-red berries.

Mary was stirred to a strange excitement. The darkness throbbed with a steady beat as if some monster were alive and moving in the night near her. The threat of trouble, blowing up down there among the narrow streets clustered round the works, sharpened her senses. With a half turn of her head she saw Mrs. George's figure silhouetted on the blind of the drawing-room window. She would choke if she had to sit in that overheated room, with all this shut out. George talking comfortably of a stoppage vexed her intolerably. A few weeks of "trouble," and the monstrous heart would cease to beat. The power would fail, the fires slacken and die down. And all through the greed and folly of a few insubordinate workers.

A man approached out of the darkness, coming down the lane from the fields behind the house. As he reached the wall of George Ling's garden a curtain drawn back in an upper room of the house let out a flood of light, revealing him as a squat hulk of a man, an ironworker by every sign. He eyed Mary curiously in the dim yellow light. She shrank back into the shadow from that primeval stare. He passed, and was followed at a distance by a shawled weary woman. The light fell on her colourless face and the thin hand grasping her shawl. Thus must be his wife, and the tired crying children dragging at her skirts his. "Come on you," the woman said, in a harsh exhausted voice. "It's the last time I'll take *you* out for a picnic, misery." One of the children clutched a bunch of flowers. He was dropping them as he walked. They gleamed faintly on the dark path.

The little procession was swallowed up in the night; a faint sound of crying came up to Mary for a moment before that too was lost and smothered. The picnic party was going home, to sleep, down among *that*, in the unlit odorous blackness lying like a pool round the feet of the red-tipped chimneys. Mary turned and hurried up the path to the house. She had had a fleeting glimpse of something that disturbed her and on which she did not care to dwell. The front door was opened by George's wife, in a strange quilted garment covering a calico nightgown fretted with tucks and frills. "I've put you an apple preserved in cloves in your room," Mrs. George said kindly. "It is so good for all disorders. Do you often go out at night? George is displeased with you, but I told him to remember that we are living in the seventies after all."

She leaned forward with her long jet ear-rings swaying on either side of her face like funeral plumes. Mary submitted mechanically to her embrace and escaped to bed.

2

Thomas Prendergast had been the manager of the Garton Iron Works, raised to that eminence by one of Mark Henry's more farsighted whims, from the year of Mary's arrival in Danesacre with Richard in her arms and her small studded trunk bumping about on the box of the Roxby barouche. During that time Mary Henry's whim had justified itself and him over and over again. Prendergast had an inventive genius. He was a Cornishman, the son of a Cornish tin miner and a north country mother who when her husband died brought her son back to her own people in Middlesborough. Young Prendergast had the naturally gentle manners of his father's people. He had, too, their mercurial temperament and their divine instability of mind. Women loved him for his looks and his gentle sing-song voice, and disliked him because of his incurable catholicity. They had no hold over him, since he forgot what they had looked like to him when he was pursuing them. He lost an excellent job in the railway superintendent's office because he could not resist the temptation to drama that presented itself in an election. He forgot, the day after it was over, that he had been a chartist and an inciter to riot, but his employers did not. Their dismissal of him gave his Radical leanings an unusual permanency in his mind, but at the moment he thought less of the poor man's wrongs than of his own needs. He applied for the job of puddler at Garton's Iron Works and spent his days stirring at the mouth of hell. That was what it looked like. It was in reality an operation requiring the nicest precision of hand, strength and brain, and he was the best puddler in the mill. An idea he worked out for the mechanical rolling of the malleable iron bars brought him to Mark Henry Garton's notice. The idea was impracticable, Mark Henry said, because it would have meant reorganising the whole place. A short time later the whole place was reorganised, and Prendergast's invention, improved and credited to half a dozen other men, was in use in every iron mill in the country. Long before then Mark Henry had quarrelled with his manager and dismissed him, and obeying one of his freakish impulses, had sent for Prendergast.

"Could you run these works?" he asked.

Prendergast pondered. His head was bent and his dark meditative glance was hidden from Mark Henry.

"Yes," he said finally.

It took him a day to prove that he could. In that short space he dealt with the only immediate trouble centre, a giant of a foreman, by the simple process of plucking him up and throwing him out. In a week he had the place running with a smoothness it had never achieved before. The men worked for him because they liked him. There was a curious sympathy between him and them, a current of secret energy flowing from Prendergast to the ironworkers. It passed into the iron and became one with the human elements that belong to all inanimate stuff that is worked over and tamed by man's brute intelligence.

When the Garton Iron Works became the Garton Iron and Steel Works, making steel by the new process that converted ore into steel without the intermediate iron process, Prendergast reorganised the works until they were a miracle of efficient running. This was no easy task, for Garton's Works, growing out of the original huddled sheds separated by a stretch of blackened earth from the two furnaces where the pig-iron was melted down to become wrought-iron rails, had spread out in the haphazard way of the times, proliferating like the undergrowth of a jungle. There were now six furnaces and the steel smelting plant. There was also what was called indifferently the Foundry or the Works. This was in reality an entirely separate organisation, and had begun making ships' engines only a year before Mark Henry's impulsive purchase. But there was one manager for the double enterprise, and he needed to possess not only more than the usual equipment of technical knowledge but double springs of vitality. It is significant of the spirit of the age that Prendergast's predecessor was the first man to fail under the duplicated demands on him. Prendergast proved himself to be a born superintendent. He was more than that. The effortless ease of strength, the seeing hand, the intuitive eye that had made him the best puddler in Garton's Iron Works served him as well when he was turned loose in a position where his tormenting ideas could be eased out in material expressions of power and use.

His mother was a dark tiny creature with a suspicious turn of mind and an unnatural aptitude in voicing it. She took a fond secret pride in her son because he was successful and had the manners of a gentleman. She strutted about like a little peahen, despising the mothers of the clumsy louts who had been her son's fellow-workers. At the same time she would not leave the ironworker's cottage where she and Thomas had come to live when he became a puddler. It stood in a row of similar cottages and backed on to another row. This double street had a common ashbin and a common latrine. Prendergast's fastidious soul loathed its squalor, but his mother would not move, and he would not leave her. "Get me into a big house," she said fiercely, "and the first thing you'll do is to marry one of those large-size women you're always running to, and turn your mother out to be the laughing-stock of every other woman in the place."

"I shan't marry," Prendergast said calmly. "You're the only clever woman I ever knew and I'm not allowed to marry you. I hate stupid women, except in bed." His mother scolded him, but she was pleased. They loved each other with a grudging passion that could not express itself in words. Everything Thomas did was for her, even his experiments with boiler tubes and condensers. When she heard him moving in the first chill of dawn, getting ready to go over to his experimenting shed, she slipped out of bed and made him tea and cut bread and butter. He ate and drank in silence, tugging at his boots, which he never allowed her to clean, as the other women cleaned their men's boots. Then she gave him his lunch, bread-and-dripping sandwiches in a tin, and a can of tea, with an apple or a small pasty, and Thomas Prendergast went off, laden like the ironworkers who passed him on their way to relieve the night-shift coming off work. These emerged with bowed bodies and white faces, stumbling along in the half light, weary and bent like very old men. They failed to recognise the manager as he pushed through them, a tall heroic figure in a frieze of defeated effort and fatigue.

During Mark Henry's lifetime, Prendergast's experiments were hampered by that erratic shipbuilder's habit of cutting off supplies in a fit of pique. After the failure of the water tube boilers that Prendergast made for the *Mary Roxby*, he could get no money for his research for many months. Mark Henry descended on him and threatened to dismiss him if he wasted any more time and money on fantastic nonsense.

"I'll leave," said Prendergast.

"You'll stay," Mark Henry roared at him. "You'll stay and do as I tell you, or I'll have you pushed into the new furnace and we'll see what sort of iron you make." His voice changed. "You wouldn't ruin me now, would you?" he wheedled. "Here am I a poor weak old man depending on you as a father on his son. Bless me, shall I marry you to my only sister? She's got a husband already, but I understand that's no barrier to your exploits in that field."

The young Cornishman looked at the wicked buffoon prancing round him, and laughed loudly. He stayed on.

When Mary inherited she told him that he could have all the money she could spare for his experiments on ships' engines. She kept her promise and in the intoxication of freedom, Prendergast ran wild and had built, to his design, by a Tees-side firm of shipbuilders, the *City of Truro*, that monstrous portent of the seventies. She cost Mary a hundred thousand pounds before she was finally sold at a heavy loss to a London firm of cattle shippers and went down off the coast of Schleswig-Holstein on the first voyage she made for them.

The *City of Truro* was enormously long, 692 feet. She was fitted with a triple-expansion engine, and was the first ship to make a trial of this system, not adopted for many years after Prendergast's expensive throw-out. Her boilers were a modified form of the water-tube boiler on which Prendergast had been working for so long and she was propelled by a single screw. From the very beginning she was a disastrous and unhandy creature. The first attempt at launching her was a failure. Her enormous weight rested on two gigantic cradles which were supposed to slide down an incline to the water. They slid a foot and stopped. Five months later a hydraulic arrangement persuaded her sideways into the water. A man was killed during the operation and that, for old sailors, sealed the ship's fate. She was a killer. She did not live long enough to kill more than three people, a man who got fouled in the anchor chain and jerked overboard, a boy whom she mysteriously did away with at sea, at night, and her first captain, who burst a blood-vessel in a rage at her shocking conduct during a storm. As a matter of fact, there was nothing malignant about the unhappy *City of Truro*. She was merely clumsy. The running of her engines was less a matter of propulsion than a continuous revelation of complicated problems of stress and pressure that might have been worked out in a forty-four ton boat with more ease and at a fraction of the cost. The running costs of the *City of Truro* were incredible. She was uncertain and heavy to handle in quiet weather, and in a storm became frankly panic-stricken. She behaved like an immensely obese and agitated old lady who has been pushed into a large pond from which she is making frantic efforts to escape. In more than a spoonful of wind she blundered and staggered and halted and retreated and swallowed vast quantities of water and generally behaved in a manner calculated to break any crew's heart. When she went down, inadvertently drowning the last boatload of men to leave her, the rest heaved a sigh of relief.

In spite of her losses, Mary did the same. As for Thomas Prendergast, he had come to hate the ship. He loathed the thought of her. If a man wanted dismissal or damnation he had only to mention the *City of Truro* in Prendergast's hearing. She represented a lifelong humiliation. He called her "the —— cow," and likened her to the apocalyptic beast.

At the same time, she taught him and other experimenters a vast number of facts about stresses and pressure. And she proved conclusively that the triple-expansion engine was a practicable thing. Prendergast set to work again with a mind enormously enriched.

The same could not be said for Mary's pocket. She showed him a flash of Mark Henry's spirit, and refused her permission to carry out his next scheme, the building of an entire vessel, bottom plates and all, of steel.

Her refusal disappointed him bitterly. He was convinced that if steel of a trustworthy quality were used, containing only a small percentage of carbon, it would prove the perfect material for a ship, far above iron. Mary wrote him tartly to get some other dog than Garton's to try his milk teeth on. The remark set a coldness between them that lasted for months. Mary took to writing orders through John Mempes, and for a time Prendergast confined himself to finding new markets for his steel and iron, and arranged American contracts that paid big profits and repaired the hole made in Garton's finances by the *City of Truro*.

He made his peace with Mary over the contracts, after a strained interview during which he was desperately civil and Mary tried to remember what she had written to him in the fury of their late quarrel.

As did Mark Henry, she liked the man the better for having quarrelled with him. She began to take Prendergast into her counsel. She discovered him distracted by moods, a passionate childlike creature one day sweeping her aside while he told her what could be done by adopting the principle of a twin screw for ships, and the next dejectedly explaining that there was not a reliable maker of good steel castings in England and that his own experiments in that line had proved him a bungling fool. He impressed her as largely irresponsible, a casual god playing with the stuff of creation. He blundered about among the terrific forces latent in molten iron and captured heat, and sometimes failed to make any use of them, and sometimes brought off, with a delicate and miraculous precision, the most astounding success. . . .

The days that followed Mary's arrival at the Tees were filled with a growing sense of trouble and uneasiness in all the docks and mills. The strikers held meetings at the dock gates, and the ironworkers leaving the mill stopped to listen and were adjured to join in the dispute, which every day grew more complicated and less likely to be concluded except by the exhaustion of both sides. At last there was a meeting in Garton's mill, and the men voted to strike at the end of the week. Prendergast took the news to Mary.

"Very well," she said, her anger flaring out at this dragging of Garton's into a dispute that was none of her making, "we won't wait for the end of the week. Put up lockout notices to take effect to-morrow, if the men don't withdraw."

"You're sure that's what you want?" Prendergast said. "The men are in a fighting humour."

"Let them fight," Mark Henry's niece said, before Mary could have stopped her even if she had wanted to. She did not want to.

The lockout notices were posted and Garton's was idle, except for the non-union men who fed the fires. The strikers did not interfere. They seemed glad that the fires were being tended. They stood about

helpfully when the men came off work and offered advice on the
eccentricities of each furnace. When Mary appeared, they were silent
but entirely respectful. The end of a fortnight brought a change in their
attitude, so far as it concerned her. A rumour concerning Prendergast
and Mary got about, and was received with due credit. The men's liking
for him swung round to violent contempt, and they attributed the
lockout notices to his influence. He was buying favour with the wanton
woman by a show of implacable rage against his own kind. A crudely
insulting ballad was made about them, and sung to the tune of a popular
song when Mary paid her daily visit to the works. Odd copies of this
curious production still occasionally turn up among the rubbish in the
little Tees-side shops. Strictly speaking, only the first verse was
printable, but the whole was printed and provided an outlet for the
strikers' feelings, so near the surface of the incomprehensible English
character are the gross springs of laughter. The English are the only
race who make good-tempered fun of their enemies. The angry
hammermen and puddlers almost liked Mary again when they had sung
a few dozen times the song that begins:

> "See Mary spring up in her elegant shift
> Prepared for a jacket to run, lads
> The Cornishman runs to oblige her with his,
> And our Mary is quickly undone, lads,
> May angels attend on her bonny brown head,
> They'll find she's not left them much room in her bed."

The trouble might have stopped here and the strike ended in the
exhaustion of the strikers' funds but for Prendergast's fit of rage. A
verse of the ballad floated across the wharf as Prendergast strode down
it on his way to the Works. John Mempes would have condoled with the
singer on his bad rhymes, but Prendergast was in a vile temper. He hurt
the man severely and threw him into an empty dock, whence he was
rescued fuller of water than song by a passing body of strikers. After
this episode, the strike as it affected Garton's Iron Works became
unpleasant. Some of the strikers' rage against Prendergast got itself
transferred to the non-union workers, and the very men who a few days

earlier had been most profuse in friendly advice were now ripe for outrage. A shift of non-union men was attacked leaving the mill and brutally handled. The next day, a stone flying over the gate stunned a man working at the open door of a furnace. He reeled forward and was horribly burned before he slid to the ground in a grotesque attitude of surprise and horror. After this the soldiers were called in. A small red-coated group stood compactly inside the high iron fence to the left of the gate, in charge of a very young and excited little officer, who kissed Mary's hand when she came, and expressed a wish to teach the world some lesson or other.

Mary and Prendergast walked over to the office. Prendergast was very pale and listened to Mary with a remote air of expecting some other sound. Once he roused himself to answer.

"The men are right," he said dreamily. "No, not in fact. In the abstract. They ought to fight each other's battles. It's their only chance of emerging from *tha* ." He nodded towards the ironworkers' cottages.

"How can you talk of abstract rights in face of this idiocy?" Mary said angrily.

He smiled with unexpected sweetness.

"Nothing is abstract for you, is it? It's all hard and bright and definite. Ships and more ships, a husband and children. That's your life. For me all images are blurred and unreal, except the feel of things in my hands. Iron is a glowing mass that can be moulded and bent as I choose. Wrought-iron, and steel, can be coaxed into machines that will drive heavy ships through the water. Think of iron floating. Perhaps it can be coaxed to fly in the air. Why not? My fingers tell me that nothing is impossible to the human will. They tell me that women are warm and soft and will yield in my grasp. Everything I can touch yields up its secret and is real. But the rest? What do I know of your spirit, that never speaks to me? What do I know of the spirit in iron and steel and released gas? We go on playing with these things and making ships and guns and machines, more and more, and bigger and bigger, and to what end? So that you can gratify your ambitions? So that the men who work for you can live meanly and feed coarsely and think confused, angry, gross thoughts? What is real? It would be something real if all these men said: 'We are servants and brothers and we stand together.' But they don't."

Their attention was drawn by an increasing clamour outside. Standing side by side at the dusty little window of the office, Mary and Prendergast saw a ragged procession pouring itself into the works, having lifted the padlocked gate off its hinges. It was a straggling and undisciplined procession that seemed to have no more definite purpose than that of holding a meeting on the disputed ground. A man stood up on a barrel rolled in at the tail of the crowd and addressed the meeting. He was an odd figure, thin and undersized, with a large head sunk between his shoulder-blades and a white ravaged face. His trousers flapped against bony structures that tolerated rather than supported his misshaped body.

"That's none of the men," Prendergast murmured. "It's a district delegate from one of the unions. I know the type."

The gesticulating figure on the barrel had ceased talking, distracted by the irruption into the crowd of the little officer. The strikers handed him through from man to man with a jeering friendliness, that presently landed him, in a state of pink and agitated disorder, with his jacket unbuttoned and his head bare, at the delegate's feet. There he delivered a brief speech, the purport of which was inaudible to Mary and Prendergast, and departed, waving his tiny fists. The crowd opened to let him through.

Mary strained her ears to follow the resumed address. A sharp movement of Prendergast's arm directed her attention to the far side of the works, where the soldiers were busy in some operation that she could not understand.

"What is it?"

"They are going to fire," Prendergast said.

His words were swept away by the volley. The crowd scattered wildly, the little man on the barrel doubling up and running with astonishing swiftness. A staccato rattling on the tin roof of the office startled Mary into a cry.

"The soldiers fired over their heads," Prendergast explained.

"Oh," Mary said, relieved. The painful excitement that had enclosed her throat when she realised the soldiers' purpose receded. Her eyes sought the little officer. He was out of sight behind his men.

The strikers were drifting back into the open again, reassured by the silence.

Mary clutched Prendergast's arm.

"They're going to fire again."

A ragged flight of shots followed. One man fell forward and with no more than a brief shuddering of his body lay still. Another had the air of pressing something red and strange to the side of his jaw. A third man lay in a pool of blood that widened round him. There was a distorted fragmentary look about him, as if some part of him were missing. The other men stood for a moment frozen into attitudes of amazement and arrested flight. Then a man ran away and another dropped to his knees beside the man in the widening pool. With a certain hesitation his fellows ran to help the man holding his jaw, and a dozen more of the strikers emerged into the open.

At this point, the little officer suddenly discovered that it is much easier to start firing than to stop it. His screaming order went disregarded in the mechanical activity of reloading and firing the third round. More men dropped and the space between the office and the soldiers was cleared except for certain figures, some moving oddly and some quite still.

"But this is murder," Mary said suddenly, on a note of surprise.

She started for the door, with a confused intention of stopping any more of it by some energetic gesture. Prendergast snatched her back. He looked round thoughtfully and sighed.

"Stay here," he said absently. "You'll be in the way," and vanished through the door. From the window Mary saw him stride across the littered ground, with an arm outstretched. He avoided the bodies and walked steadily toward the small active company in the far corner. It became sporadically active again when he was half-way across. There was a rattling noise in the air. Prendergast stopped, as if a sudden thought had halted him. He spun round, his hand still stretched out, and collapsed on the ground. After a paralysing moment of fear, Mary ran out. She was half-way to him, heedless of stray balls that struck the ground near her feet, when another crowd, composed this time of women, rushed through the dismantled gates. Foremost among

them was Thomas Prendergast's mother, bonnetless, with her black
hair about her face. She flung herself beside the motionless figure of
her son, bent to his heart, thrust a hand in his jacket and brought it
away, wet. Her shriek rang above the growing confusion.

"Murderer," she said, and shook her fist at the little officer, now
prancing wildly in front of his men, as a last means of stopping their
misdirected efficiency. Mary knelt beside her. "You too," said
Thomas Prendergast's mother. "You killed him. You got him into this.
My son, oh my son. Why did you do it?" She began to scold him
angrily.

"Is he dead?" Mary asked. She touched the screaming woman's
hands and got some of his blood on to her own. Then she lifted his head,
lolling off his mother's knee. At that she knew he was dead. His face
was white and unamazed, his eyes wide open, and his mouth parted
over his clenched teeth. . . . A second ball had shattered the fingers of
his right hand. It seemed an unnecessary and wanton piece of cruelty.

Mary staggered to her feet. The gyrations of the little officer caught
her eye. She ran across to him and, catching him by the arm, wheeled
him round.

"Are you firing any more to-day?" she demanded.

He stammered: "It was a mistake. There was only to have been one
volley into the crowd."

"Very stupid of you," she said tonelessly. "Send your men for
doctors and bandages. Some of your mistakes are only wounded."

She took charge of the crowd, driving the frenzied women back with
a white-faced fury. The uninjured strikers gave her rough help. She sent
for water and began to bandage the boy whose jaw had been shot,
tearing the flounce off her underskirt and talking to him in a low quick
voice. His moans ceased and he submitted to her touch with a rigid
courage. . . .

She sent a message to John Mempes that night, and before he arrived
she went herself in search of the little district delegate who had run with
such agility at the beginning of the firing. He fixed on her eyes that were
hot and raw-rimmed from the fires that consumed him inwardly. Mary
asked him his name.

"Robert Estill."

An echo that was neither memory nor instinct vibrated in Mary's mind, a vague troubling of her spirit, like a shadow passing across water.

"Your starting that meeting yesterday brought about the death of three men. What are you going to do to help me clear things up?"

The haggard creature sawed at the air with his face. He poured out a spume of words, a tale of resentment and squalor and misery among the workers with which some strain of personal resentment and tale of wrong done himself was inextricably mixed. Mary listened and could make nothing of it. It was like listening to a swell of angry water.

"I can't understand you," she said helplessly. "I'd like to, but I don't seem even to hear you. Never mind that. You're a boilermakers' delegate. You had no right among my men. If you won't help me, at least keep away. . . ."

Whether he would have refrained from meddling she never knew, for the next day he was summoned to headquarters, and deprived of his fiery breath, the strike collapsed like a deflated balloon. Nothing remained for Mary to do before she went back to Danesacre, leaving Mempes to find Prendergast's successor, but to call on Thomas Prendergast's mother.

Mrs Prendergast cowered over her fireplace, rubbing her thin hands.

"It's the custom of Garton's to pay a pension," Mary said wearily.

"Then you may pay it to the young woman who was here yesterday saying Thomas was her son's father, and so he may have been. She was that sort. A fine world it is for men, doing what they like and getting themselves killed for a show at the end of it. Why do men have wars? For vanity, and Thomas died for vanity. He thought he had only to show himself to the soldiers and they would stop firing."

Mary's tears dropped on to her hands.

"What are you crying for?" Mrs Prendergast said sharply. "You were not one of Thomas' women, so far as I know, and the world's full of finer men. You may stop to tea if you like, and I'll let you drink out of our Thomas's Exhibition mug. He was always at me to take him up to the Exhibition, but I didn't care to go and he wouldn't go with his aunt. He won the mug in a race, and he was as pleased as a king to give it to

me. 'Here, mother,' he says, laughing, 'see what I've brought you.' It
was a pity they smashed up his hand, but as he was dead I suppose it
didn't matter. He was clever with his hands. I always said he'd come to
something, if he didn't make a fool of himself with his laughing and
joking. Many's the time I've lost patience with him. You can't deny he
was more of a clown than a man.''

Mary drank her tea to a recital of Thomas Prendergast's faults. He
seemed to have been the least worthy Prendergast ever born. She stood
up, pulling down her veil to hide her face, and said good-bye to his
mother. She was taller than the bent little creature by a head, but she felt
a child and her private causes for grief a child's sorrows. ''My mother
died four years ago,'' she said. ''She sent me an Exhibition mug when I
was a little girl.''

Mrs Prendergast overlooked this irrelevance.

''Good-bye,'' she said relentlessly. ''Don't cry for Thomas. I dare
say you'll miss him, but he's not worth any woman's crying over. No
man is. . . .''

Thomas Prendergast's death hurt Mary more than she cared to own,
though less than she thought. Several people called, after her return to
Danesacre, to ask her about the riot, and she found herself, among her
fellow shipbuilders, the object of a not unsympathetic curiosity. It was
felt that she had shown commendable firmness in her handling of her
strikers. The Yard, with memories of its own strike, was offhand with
her when she went through.

She was surprised to discover how little she had to tell her callers.
She knew that it had been a critical business, but it had seemed at the
time, like every other crisis in her life, a mere question of getting
through with it. Until the moment when it had ended with that stretch of
blackened ground, the sprawling bodies in the sunshine, and the poor
dripping bloody indignity in the widening pool, and Prendergast crumpled across his mother's knee. All she had done until then was to stand
in the dusty office of the Works and watch men dropping between her
and a row of red-coated automata. And afterwards she had walked out,
too intent on getting to Prendergast to give more than a passing thought
to the danger.

The thing that haunted her imagination was Mrs Prendergast's tragic rage. Beside that, beside that worn bent old woman, accusing her son, everything else was unimportant. Even the dead man. His blood, soaking quickly into the black friable ground, vanished from the earth, except such tiny part of it as still ran in his mother's veins. But her bitterness lived on. It seemed a bitterness of all women, an anger born afresh with every man child tearing himself from his mother to begin a separate life.

One day, Old Smithson, meeting her in Harbour Street, said broadly:

"Eh, missus, ye taught un a lesson on't Tees."

"I did nothing of the sort," Mary retorted. "You can't teach men. They're fools and always will be."

"Hoity-toity," the old man cried. "Seems ye've getten a bit above yourself, Mary Hansyke." Maliciously, he reduced her to childhood.

Mary smiled unexpectedly. The astonishing thought crossed Old Smithson's mind that her eyebrows were like the narrow wings of a bird spread for flight. He was shocked, and went home to clear his brain with turkey rhubarb.

But Mary had discovered what she most resented about the riot and Prendergast's death. It was its sheer wastefulness, offending some instinct rooted deeply in her nature. She thought of the inconclusive strike, and the confusion, and the idle works and silent docks. There was no sense in it anywhere, in the futile quarrel, in the soldiers' fatal automatism, in the silent huddled bodies that a moment before had been centres of throbbing nerves and tense muscles, alive with hopes and anxieties and needs. Men were shamelessly wasteful. They wasted with an extravagance for which there was no excuse, and when they had nothing else to waste, wasted the only thing they could not replace, life. A sudden inexplicable anguish seized her at the thought of Richard. What could she do to instil in him a loathing equal to her own, of the incalculable spendthrift folly of men? He would grow away from her, as far as Mrs Prendergast's little boy had grown from that eager running child; there would be another riot or a war and he would rush into it, emptying his bright blood on the greedy ground that must surely have had enough of blood since the world began. She saw him flinging himself towards death as Thomas Prendergast did, and she said to herself that she would never recover from it, never.

At the thought that he might hold himself back, she was uneasy. Torn in two, her heart bled invisibly, drops like Mrs Prendergast's few bitter tears.

She forgot what she had come out to do, and stood still on the bridge, looking up the harbour. The tide was coming in, and the water ran up into the folding hills, shaking the moored ships and sucking past the wooden piers of the bridge. The curve of the hills closing in the upper harbour was very comforting. It had been given so many men's dreams and thoughts to hold that it had the air of stooping to the water with wide gentle arms.

Mary had lately given Richard a young horse for his birthday. She saw again the boy's darkly blazing eyes and crimson cheeks, and heard his voice, stammering with pleasure. She felt the thrill it gave her to watch Richard happy because of something she was doing for him. At these moments her little body ached with an exquisite sense of lightness and excitement. But she watched him with a calm face, as who should say: "Don't think I'm giving you anything out of the ordinary, or that you're anything but an ordinary boy." In an everyday voice she said: "You must mind his knees on the upper road. He's not like one of your rough little ponies."

Richard glanced at her. As if she did not know that he would die rather than graze that satiny skin. As if she were not excited herself. He slipped an arm round her neck, squeezing it hard. The nearness of his smooth glowing face, a boyish replica of her own, gave her a strange dizzy sensation. "Thank you, thank you," he whispered.

"Don't choke me," Mary said. She kissed him. . . .

Suddenly afraid that something might have happened to Richard, she turned round and hurried back to her house.

CHAPTER FIVE

1

NOTHING warned Mary of Gerry Hardman's reappearance. Her thumbs did not prick, and she had not been thinking of him the day before. Even the signature: "G. Hardman," at the end of a letter laid by Mempes on her desk woke no throb of memory. So little do the gestures of our bodies conform to the naïvely romantic impulses of our minds that when she saw him she neither turned pale nor felt that her life to this moment had been a dream. She could not have written down her stock of experience to so low a figure.

Our journey through this world is marked by gravestones, under which we bury the things we find it necessary to discard, our eighteenth year, a dance, a treacherous ambition, a book of verse, our youth, our first love, our dreams of freedom. In the last grave of all we bury ourselves and every coffin contains a bankrupt. No memories that Gerry Hardman might have had of Danesacre had prepared him to find there a ghost from one such grave. If they had he would have turned tail and fled for his life. He had seen and left Mary when she was a girl of fourteen, shy and untried, when neither men nor life had laid hands on her dreaming mind. When he found her again she was a woman of thirty-three. Her slender body had lost the angularity of extreme youth. Her eyes were shadowed with the shadows of things suffered and things feared, and the smoothness of her skin—he remembered it as incredibly smooth and flawless—was blemished and faintly marked. Even at that

she was lovelier than he remembered, though there was about her
loveliness an indefinable suggestion of arrested development, as if her
youth had been halted on the verge of maturity and she were destined to
grow old, to fade, without having come to perfection. She faced him
across a wide flat-topped desk in her office in the house above the Yard,
and her face, for a fraction of time, was the face of young Mary
Hansyke, deliciously surprised. . . .

She said in a voice of amazed gladness:

"I should have known you anywhere," and immediately became
very practical, concentrating on the business that had brought him. He
was a candidate for the position of manager to the Yard, John Mempes
having announced himself, to Mary's secret relief, unable to manage
both Yard and Line any longer. Mary asked him every question
Mempes had prepared for the candidates. She went through all his
papers. Once or twice she made as though he had answered her, while
he was still manifestly hesitating over phrases.

"It's absurd that I should be asking you these things," she
murmured. "You know everything and I almost nothing. Mr. Mempes
would have been here to help me, but he's away ill."

In the end, sighing, she sent her apologies to two other engineers
whose persons and abilities were at the disposal of Garton's, and
cleared a space on her desk with a sweeping gesture. Propping her face
on her hands, she looked wistfully at the man in front of her, studying
his face with unselfconscious care, noting how fine-worn it was and
nervously lined, remembering things she had forgotten about the boy,
his small mouth and arched narrow nostrils. She remembered then that
she had once thought Hugh like him, and marvelled that they were no
more alike than a blurred sketch is like a cameo. She was looking for the
boy in the man, and finding him in the demure friendliness of Gerry
Hardman's smile.

"Why didn't you come?" she asked simply.

Gerry leaned forward on the desk.

"I started," he answered, with an equal simplicity. "My horse fell
with me. He was a wretched hack, the best I could get. My leg was hurt
and my head. I was out all night. I caught some sort of fever and was ill
for months. Afterwards I tried to get back to you, but they couldn't

understand why I wanted to go back to *that place*. Did you remember that I didn't even know your name? My family took me south for a rest. It's maddening to be a boy and have to go where you're taken. We're kept children so long. I was crazy with anxiety half the time and half the time enjoying things. Do you know that feeling? I was a year late going up to Oxford, and in my first long vac I rushed up to Roxborough. I found your house. They told me you were married, and your name and where you lived. I suppose they thought I was mad when I began to laugh. I went away to that lane where I saw you first, and I *cried, Mary.*" Gerry paused, and it was still in the room. The room was adopting a respectful attitude before these human ghosts. "I'm telling you about a boy who died a long time ago," he said apologetically. . . .

"That boy," he began again, and hesitated. "People would say it was absurd. They'd say that a boy of sixteen and a girl of fourteen can't be in love. I was in love. . . . I went back to Oxford and stayed another year. Then I threw it up. I couldn't stand it any longer. It was all childish and futile, playing about there, talking. Pretending to study. And heart-sick. Mary, I was. Do you mind my calling you Mary? I couldn't be the careless young idler you've got to be to enjoy Oxford properly. I couldn't even tolerate it. I left. I took up marine engineering instead of the other thing. . . ."

A man's pleasant voice was raised in the garden below the window. "Richard," it called. "Ritchie."

"My husband," Mary murmured.

"Roxby?"

"You remembered? No. I married again." She thought: "There's everything to tell, and I shall tell him nothing and ask him nothing." All that mattered had been told in the explanation of his failure to come back. An enormous relief filled her mind. She did not wonder why she, a grown woman of thirty-three, with three children and two husbands to her account, should be feeling this ridiculous happiness and lightness of heart at the clearing up of an incident that had happened years ago to a very young girl. She glanced up at him with a disturbing mixture of shyness and pride. "My friend . . . you are my friend, aren't you?"

All her distrust of herself was in her voice; a glance at his face encouraged her.

"I waited for you that night at Roxborough. For hours."

"Not for hours, Mary? Oh, poor girl. Poor Mary."

"I'd have waited years for you if I'd known," Mary said. . . .

Again there was silence in the room, while these two who had touched hands before life seized and twisted them, looked at each other across nineteen years of separate experience, and tried to remember those confident unspoiled moments. Memories came out of the years, stood at their side for a little space and went away.

"I don't even know what you're doing here," Gerry said at last. He smiled at her, and again his smile filled her with an exultant happiness. "I haven't done any of the things I meant to do when I left Oxford. I've muddled about in odd corners of the world. I've wanted to know things, more, much more, than I've wanted to do them, with the result that at thirty-five I have no settled plan in life, almost no settled ambition. I fought in a revolution. I've seen a few things. The hills of North India, Singapore. I spent six years in Singapore. I married. I've drifted through the world."

"With your wife?" Mary asked in a flattened voice. It could have no special significance for her that Gerry had a wife waiting somewhere for the result of this interview. No. It merely destroyed all her pleasure in it. That was all.

"No. Alone. I don't live with my wife. I've been alone for a long time. One sees more. . . . I don't think I'm a very sociable sort of beast."

Mary looked at him carefully. He had quite evidently suffered severely—over his missing wife, or something else. It was written ineffaceably on the sensitive face over against hers. A strange emotion seized her, composed of regret, pity, and a shameful curiosity. She knew it was shameful and in the effort of subduing it, her cheeks grew scarlet and remained so.

"I'm glad you've come back," she said hurriedly, with an air of having just escaped saying something less proper to the occasion. "I thought of you sometimes, and wondered what you were doing. It's more like a miracle than chance—your coming here."

Gerry said nothing, and smiled. He was not nearly so deeply stirred by this meeting as was Mary. If she had been more experienced, she would have read, in that attractive half mischievous smile, that she was talking to a man who had long ceased to believe in miracles. There were very few things in which Gerry Hardman believed, least of all in a divine intervention in his life. Why should any God trouble about him? Why should Mary Hervey? He did not know that Mary had already, with her astonishing capacity for seeing only what she wanted to see, begun to regard him as different from other men. That she was already measuring other men by him and finding them less attractive, clumsier in mind and body, less sensitive, less appealing. Her mind exulted in the prospect of seeing him every day. She tried to subdue the delight his mere presence gave her, but Mary Hansyke had taken possession of Mary Hervey's body, and the woman was only able to resist faintly the young girl's intense pleasure in the moment. Useless now to have told her that this was not the confident dreaming boy of that far-off day, but a tired man, a man weary beyond any weariness she had ever endured. Life presented itself to her as a vista of intoxicating possibilities. Visions of endless, delicious conversations on the subject nearest her heart—ships—floated through her mind. They might ride, and talk as they jogged along, their horses amiably consenting. Did he ride? Of course he did. He fell off. The terrific consequences of that fall of his rushed upon her. But for that, there would have been no Roxby House, no Hugh, perhaps, for her, no Yard. She was awed by the mysterious workings of life. Impulsively she put a hand fairly on his as it rested on the table.

"Isn't it odd," she said solemnly, "that we should be sitting here like this after all those years, both grown staid and sensible? With years and years to be friends in. Are you pleased? I'm so pleased I don't know whether to laugh or cry at you."

"You're very like Mary Hansyke," Gerry said irrelevantly. "You have the same faintly surprised little face. You are little, you know, Mary."

"You're not very tall yourself," Mary said, and her face flushed with sudden joy as she looked at him.

Gerry Hardman was a slight compact creature, apparently all nerve and muscle; the strength of his body was in his long narrow back, the strength of his face lay all above his eyes and its beauty lay in them and

in the delicately arched nose and small mouth. He was fined down to a
mind. The mind was balanced and had once been impudently gay. But
though the gaiety in him was not done for, it had all the air, when it did
appear, of having been perverted to cynical uses.

"I like you," Mary said, and suddenly shy, got up and held out her
hand.

Just before Gerry went it occurred to him to ask whether he had been
selected fairly for the Yard or not. He put the question harshly, with an
expression of haughtiness on his face that suggested at least one reason
why he had found it difficult to remain long in any job.

"If you knew me better you wouldn't ask that," Mary said quickly.
"I have a single mind about Garton's."

Gerry was satisfied, but the question threw her into an extraordinary
confusion. "I couldn't possible have let him go," she thought.
"Suppose he hadn't been good enough. I'd have chosen him just the
same." She pressed the palms of her hands to her cheeks, appalled at
this discovery of treacherous depths in her mind. The lines of her face
softened into laughter. "I don't care," she said in a light joyous voice.
"I don't care. I'm glad."

2

John Mempes was sitting in his room in the pier-side offices of
Garton's Line. His back was to the low partition that divided his room
from the big room where the clerks sat. When these stood up they could
see his broad shoulders and the back of his head. There was an
expression about them that hushed every tongue. Young Russell,
whose brother sailed as second mate in Garton's newest steamship,
took a piece of paper and wrote on it: "Manager in a rare taking about
something, we think." The recipient nodded and tore the paper up. He
pushed the pieces back to young Russell who, standing up to drop them
in the waste-paper basket, knocked a ruler off the table. He turned
horribly white, and held his breath, waiting for the explosion from the
next room. It did not come. Young Russell subsided into his chair, a
faint colour stealing back into his cheeks.

Mempes had heard nothing. He was thinking with concentrated

precision about the position of Garton's. Freights stood at a height that would probably have killed Mark Henry. If old Bridges had not finished him off before the middle of the sixties he would have died ten years later of the millennium.

Millenniums were all very well, but Mempes had seen them before, and knew what the aftermath of a millennium was like. He could remember nothing in the way of millenniums like this of the seventies, climbing from its glorious beginning with the gates of Suez opening, to a dazzling noon in this summer of 1874. And he knew that this was the turning point of the curve. Freights had gone to their limit. Every damned thing in the country had gone to its limit. What else could you expect with that Jew at the head of it? Ugh! Mempes twitched the muscles of his shoulders. If he had been a dog the hair would have bristled along his back. He had the same sense of danger that a dog might have.

And Mary refused to listen. A touch of something suspiciously like Radical rascality was creeping into her attitude. She had started a system of bonuses at Garton's Yard, and with some hesitation extended it to the Iron Works, where it was more successful. Mempes' ears reddened with indignation when he thought of it. The fantastic idea occurred to him that it was to propitiate Prendergast's spirit, so violently thrust out of life, that she was offering him this small concession to his beliefs. The colossal silliness of the thought brought him up at a sharp turn. The fact was that Mary was developing convictions. Mempes had seen as many people ruined by convictions as by falling freights, and Mary's were already embroiling her with her fellow shipbuilders in Danesacre. She had met and talked to that infernal agitator Plimsoll, and had thereafter made a voluntary offer to the Board of Trade to accept their ruling in the matter of the loadline for her ships. Mempes groaned in spirit. He faced her about it. She sighed. She disliked offending her own class, but she was too obstinate to withdraw.

That, of course, was the whole trouble, her damnable obstinacy. She was no fool. She was doing at Garton's only what every shipbuilder and shipowner in the country was doing, over-building, over-spending, over-chartering. She was spending far too much money on trials and research. Garton's profits were large, of course, since both Yard and

Works had been making more money than either made in Mark Henry's day. But the firm's reserves were smaller in proportion to the turnover than ever before. How much smaller, Mempes had only just discovered. The discovery was written all over the back of his head for the awed clerks to read. If they had seen his face, they would have found it written there even more plainly, in deep lines running from nose to chin and brows drawn into one unbroken thicket of grey hair jutting over restless eyes.

But no one dared to look at his face, as he stalked through the outer office on his way home. He shouldered his way down the pier, seeing no one, and paused for a moment on the bridge to look up the harbour. An old sea captain stood at his shoulder. Suddenly he spoke to Mempes.

"See yon ship," he said, pointing to a small barque that lay moored in mid-stream, with a broom tied to her masthead, a signal that she was for sale. "That was my ship."

The regret in his voice reached Mempes through the thick cloud of his own troubles.

"A good little boat," he said gently.

"Shoo's a bonny ship," the other murmured. "A bonny bonny ship. Suddn't ha' been shogged off yet."

"One of Burdon's boats, isn't she?"

"Too small now, they say. Shoo wasn't too small for th' old man. Young Burdon doesn't know a good ship when ah sees un. Why, fellow's never handled a rope in ah's life. They'll tek her for coaling." He addressed his lost ship again in a voice of indescribable longing. "Eh, thoo suddn't carry coal, thoo bonny thing."

Mempes left him standing on the bridge with his hands clasped firmly round the rail, and his weathered face turned stiffly to the harbour, a queer figure of an idealist. Walking down Harbour Street towards the Yard he thought bitterly of the day when Garton's would move to the Tees. Vast sums of money were being expended on building new yards there. Money poured in and poured out again, leaving nothing behind for the lean years Mempes saw coming. And Mary was talking of selling the Line. Well, if she was going to sell, now was the time, before freights began to drop. Mempes could not bring himself to urge it on her. Something would have to go; Garton's was far too big and covered too many interests. But to sell the Line. Mempes drew his lips back from his teeth in a kind of snarl. The thought was unbearable. It would reduce him to the position of that poor devil on the bridge.

He quickened his steps. In the Yard the first person he saw was the new Yard manager, talking to Mary. Mempes halted, and retracing his steps went up into the sail loft, from which, through a low dusty window, he could watch Mary and Gerry Hardman walking slowly, absorbed in their conversation, across the Yard. He sat down grimly, sideways to the window, and continued to watch them. His attitude was that of a spy. He knew it and did not care.

Hardman's head was too close to Mary's and her face, upturned to his, wore an expression Mempes did not like to see. She admired the fellow. The very turn of her head as she walked, her eyes searching the fastidious animated face near her own, gave her admiration away to the jealous eyes watching her from the sail loft. Mempes pulled himself together. He had nothing to say against Gerry Hardman, who was a good enough manager and an excellent engineer, the best Garton's had ever had. Danesacre said he had a tile loose about the need for better ships' engines, and Mempes had heard that he gave up half his days and almost his nights to it. Like enough. There was a look about him as if he slept on a hard bed and got up when he fell out. Mempes rather relished the idea. The "beggar" knew how to work, though, which was something in these days. He was reorganizing the Tees-side works, moving the boiler and engine works away from the blast furnaces to the site near the docks that that old fox Mark Henry had bought before he died. It cost money of course, but do the fellow justice, he was not wasteful, like that fool who had got himself killed. He knew where he was going when he made experiments. A queer elusive fellow. Rather to his surprise, Mempes found himself thinking that if Hardman had not been so much his junior he might have been on friendly terms with him. But—friendship. No. His friends were all dead, the men he had drunk with, who knew how to drink, play for decent stakes, and conduct a quarrel like gentlemen. The breed was dead. . . . Though Hardman was not a puppy. That was a good stroke of his, getting the order for engines for the new warships. He had raised a laugh against himself in the club by declaring that the triple expansion system was perfectly practicable and that he was only waiting for chance and a far-sighted customer to try it out. He would wait a long time when freights began falling, Mempes thought grimly.

The two of them were almost under the window now. Their voices came up clearly to the invisible listener. Gerry Hardman's voice, low-pitched and pleasant.

"I wish you'd remove George Ling from me, Mary." Called her Mary, did he, damn him. Mary was laughing at him, with her eyebrows arched in amused surprise.

"He's so clumsy and unpleasant an object that I can't stand him, especially in the morning. He's hairy, too. I dislike the George Lings of this world, Mary. They're such comfortable decent settled people. They think what they're told, being entirely inaccessible to ideas; they eat to repletion and take pills. They tell you about it, too. Heavens, how I dislike them."

"I can't dismiss George," Mary said thoughtfully, "I did him out of a fortune."

"All the more reason for getting rid of him," Gerry said sincerely.

Mempes twisted his neck round to get a better view. He missed Mary's low-voiced answer. Talking of George Ling, were they. Well, there was nothing in that. A moment later, they moved into the direct line of his vision. They had ceased talking, of George Ling or anything else, and were looking across the Yard, with an identical expression on their faces, as if both saw the same thing. Mempes followed the direction of their glance, but there was nothing to be seen, only the sunlit harbour clearly visible through the bare ribs of the new boat, and the blue distant line of moor. He brought his gaze back to the unconscious pair. Now they were looking at each other. That fellow's face was very still and his eyes rested on Mary's with an expression in them that brought Mempes to his feet, the blood surging in his ears. He had no right . . . Mary's hand trembled upward and dropped again to her side. A faint smile touched her mouth to a lovely softness. Mempes strugged to control himself. Talking innocently of George Ling and looking like that. It was damnable. It was a vile and intolerable flouting

of all decency. With some vague idea of putting a stop to it he started for
the stairs. Half-way down he stood still. There was nothing he could
do. Mary was her own mistress. If she liked to become Gerry
Hardman's who was to stop her? She had no husband. And he,
Mempes, had no rights over her, not so much as the right to criticise
her. By God, hadn't he? Every one had the right to criticise a thing like
that, when it happened among decent people. Had it happened?

When he returned, mastering with difficulty the trembling of his
limbs, to the window, those two were out of sight.

3

Mary had thought that there was no need to tell Gerry anything about
herself, but in the end she found herself turning over the years of her life
for things to interest him and make him laugh. She brought him
experiences, flashes of wit, and laughter, as she had once brought Hugh
costly shirts and diagrams of engines. A profound humility filled her
when she thought of him and she was afraid she had nothing that would
keep him at her side, nothing to satisfy so fastidious and restless a mind.
Entirely unconscious of duplicity, she had fairly entered on the dangerously engrossing business of adapting herself to Gerry Hardman's
moods. A powerful instinct was at work in her, forcing her to throw off
the reserve and timidity under which her youth was gradually being
submerged. If Gerry had come a little later he might have found a
woman as tired and distrustful as himself, in whom there was nothing to
rouse. The woman his coming recalled to life was a complex creature,
with the shy and violent emotions of the younger Mary existing beside a
strange new tenderness and sympathy, irresistibly soothing and
attractive to this man. He was so eager for it that he was afraid. He led
Mary a pretty dance. One day thinking that she was progressing in
knowledge of him, she found him on the next so aloof, so withdrawn
into himself that she despaired. Yet she never gave him up. She seemed
where he was concerned to be without pride. Never would she have
stooped like this to conquer a mood of Hugh's. She did not know
herself. By every subtle device that suggested itself to her she coaxed
him back to warmth and life. There was to her something profoundly

wistful and appealing in the way he retired into himself, like a child who has forgotten how to play. She rejoiced in her ability to bring him alive.

She shared his thoughts about the Yard, she liked looking with him at the smooth virgin flank of the ship on the stocks; she discovered trivial things about him, that he liked Indian sauces and walking in the rain, that he smoked too much and hated himself for it and made fretful attempts to give it up and failed. And she hoarded these scraps of knowledge as if they were some sort of charm against misfortune, the misfortune of losing her friend.

She carried out one of her plans, and she and Richard and Gerry rode in the early morning, clattering up the hill behind the house to the country lanes and the moor. One morning Richard's horse fell with him. Gerry was the first to reach the slender body crumpled up on the heather. He looked up as Mary, white and despairingly composed, dropped from her horse beside him.

"He's all right, my dear. Your boy's all right."

Richard was dazed and lay for a long time with his head on his mother's knee. She forgot Gerry and everything else in the world except the thought of her inalienable bond with Richard. She had got him when she was too young to know the value of the gift, but not too young to value it even then, and every year made him dearer to her. She was a little ashamed of her pride in him, his good looks, his aristocratic manners—the languid Roxby manner to the life—his manifest quickness of brain, so unlike her own plodding methodical mind. And she tried to pretend that she was just the mother of an ordinary son. The pretence deceived no one, not even Richard, who knew quite well that however much his mother seemed engrossed in the cares of her extraordinary life, he had only to address her in a certain tone of flattering softness to have her all ears and anxious longing to understand and please him. She would say: "Ah, you can't get around me like that, my son," and all the time she was being got round and rejoicing in her shameful weakness and in the innocent smiles of the deceiver.

The thought that he might have been killed turned her faint. She had never envisaged so atrocious a possibility. If she had not had to sit quietly to support Richard she would have sunk down on the moor, unable to sustain her own trembling body.

Gerry Hardman sat quietly a few feet away, patiently waiting for the other two to remember him. When Richard's colour came back and he stood up, Mary looked anxiously at her friend.

"We'd better ride home," Gerry said.

"I'll contrive a leading rein for Richard," Mary suggested.

"No." Gerry was decisive. "Richard must ride home properly. Do you want to make a fool of the boy?"

Richard was up on his horse already and smiling down at his mother. His brown face and seventeen-year-old length of limb made him suddenly a different person from the child he had been. Mary looked helplessly from boy to man. The years that made Richard dearer to her would remove her farther and farther from him, until when he was a man she would be only an old woman to him and he would never cease to be a little boy to her, her little boy.

The thought did not cross her mind—it would have crossed, in real or ironic consolation, almost any other woman's mind at such a moment—"I have my daughters." The truth was that Mary neglected her daughters. Not physically, of course. She saw that they had the best nurses, directed by the failing but still admirable and incorruptibly devoted Miss Flora. She sometimes thought thankfully of the moment when Wagener had prevented her from casting Miss Flora off. What should she have done without her? Miss Flora did everything for the two little girls, ordered their frocks, supervised their meals, their daily walks, their prayers. Banished, except for special occasions, from the house above the Yard—which was in fact not large enough to have accommodated them and their attendants in any comfort—they lived in their roomy cottage on the edge of the moors a life not unlike that of an early Christian colony. It was altogether too Christian for their excellent nurse, but for whose softening presence Clara and Sylvia would have run some risk of being crushed by simplicity and good example.

Mary descended on this colony at frequent and always unpredictable moments, with a fierce energy that covered her impatience to be gone.

"Well, my babies," she would say, "how are you? Good? Happy?" She kissed them both, with an impartial affection, examined their samplers, frowned on Sylvia's bitten nails, and accepted the shyly-offered gift on which Clara had been working since her last visit. Then she was gone, oblivious of the child's heavy eyes and trembling lip. She did not mean to be unkind. She thought she was a wise and sensible mother. Unconsciously, her mind had persuaded her that these mites were Hugh's rather than hers—his property, with which she ought not too intimately to interfere. She saw to their bodily and mental welfare and left all inquiry into their spiritual state severely alone. It was not devotion, but it was at least less wicked than present-day habits of poking at a child's mind with a treatise on psychological workings. Clara and Sylvia Hervey had the good fortune to belong to an age that knew nothing of complexes. Consequently they had none that Miss Flora, with her cup of Senna Tea, could not cure.

Having visited them, Mary forgot them for days, until a sudden twinge of memory sent her hurrying off to see them, often when she was already very tired. If she had no devotion she had a profound sense of duty.

It was different with her son. She never felt that she owed him a duty. He was hers. He belonged to a part of her life so much simpler than the present that sometimes she had a dim feeling that she and Richard were of the same generation. And then came moments of dreadful knowledge, like this, when she knew that they were divided by impassable gulfs. Never would she be able to look at Richard and think: "I am all in all to him. In him I have a sure refuge." She was not and could not be all to him, and the older she grew the less she was to him. She seemed to be facing a future of unendurable loneliness.

Her strong common sense rallied against this mood of despair. She glanced from Gerry to Richard. "You two understand each other, don't you?" she murmured ironically.

Richard said with grave mischief: "Men have to understand each other. I understand Mr. Hardman, but you will let me ride home properly, won't you, mother? Let us go round by the low road. There is a new bridge over the beck, so fine it is a pity you should not see it at once."

Gerry lent her a hand for her mount and smiled at her. But the moor had become an empty place for Mary. She searched it with her eyes. There was nothing anywhere for the old woman waiting in young Mary Hervey's heart.

"You came too late," she said to Gerry. "I can't count on you, can I? Why didn't you come before?"

Gerry understood her at once.

"I forgot you were the only thing that mattered," he said in a low voice. "It's so easy to forget. Now that I've remembered it, you're unattainable. Do I want you to be attainable by so ordinary a man as I am? Probably not. I like to think of you as a little aloof and sure of yourself. Shall we ride home? . . ."

On another occasion, she told Gerry about Prendergast, very much ashamed of the story of the strike when she came to tell it. "If I had not been so selfish, thinking only about myself, it wouldn't have happened," she said humbly. "You see how really worthless I am." At this moment she really did feel herself worthless, a hasty reckless fool, too inexperienced to do anything properly, and too conceited to learn better.

"I see how honest and brave you are," said Gerry.

"Oh, no, I'm not. I'm not at all brave." She added thoughtfully: "Once I stood on the edge of the cliff and thought of throwing myself over because I was unhappy."

"A blind man could see that you and Hervey aren't married," Gerry commented. "I never ask you any questions. I haven't the right to ask questions, but I wish you'd tell me why."

Mary answered with perfect simplicity.

"Hugh got tired of me. At least, he wanted another woman as well." It seemed to her that she was clearing up a whole stretch of her life in those few words. She was amazed at the ease with which she could talk about it. "I'm not clever enough to feel that I could ever share my husband. I couldn't. I couldn't even pretend. I was dreadfully unhappy and disappointed. I never imagined anything could hurt as that did." She paused and looked at him in a way that startled him. It was like seeing down into the water on a clear day at sea. He lost the sense of the ground under his feet and hung over her, waiting for her to speak. "If I had known that you were coming, I shouldn't have cried over Hugh and Miss Jardine," Mary said simply.

"Hush," said Gerry. "Do you know what you're saying?"

"I know that you're here and I'm happier than I've ever been in my life. Shall we go? Don't go. Are you tired of Danesacre already and wanting something else to happen to you?"

"Nothing like you will ever happen to me again," Gerry said. He was quite sure of this, but he avoided Mary's eyes. He preferred not to know how far this avowal had carried him. This pleasant companionship, this sense that one other human being was profoundly interested in him, was moved by his presence, was fond of him, filled him with surprise and pleasure. It was already so valuable to him that he dreaded to lose it by talking about it. He thought ironically: "I may be terribly and completely this woman's slave. I don't know. It can only be a bad business for me and perhaps for both of us." With a deeper irony he reflected that had he been ten years younger no such considerations would have entered his head. The enjoyments desired by a young man were much hastier and easier of fulfilment than the slow rich savouring of happiness he desired now.

He would have been startled if he had known how many of Mary's waking thoughts were directed on him. When she was not thinking of Garton's or occupied with Richard she was thinking of Gerry Hardman. Into her thoughts of him were compressed all those inward forces that, in the hands of saints and prophets, have worked miracles, and all her inherited craving for possession. She had admitted to herself, soon after he came, that she loved him, but the word was so inadequate to describe her engrossing interest that none of the consequences of being in love with her Yard manager occurred to her mind. She longed to be sure of him, but only because of the immense tenderness in her thoughts of him, and because she could not pour it out on a man who, however much he needed it and unconsciously asked her for it, might turn out to be only coolly interested in her. It did not matter to her otherwise.

She was conscious of immense reserves in his mind. He had asked her about Hugh and he had told her nothing of his wife. It never struck her as odd that she, who had so violently resented the differences between herself and her young husband found it impossible to resent anything this man chose to do or leave undone. But though she acquiesced in his right to be silent where he pleased, she was still a woman in love, and she wanted to know the other woman who had loved Gerry and been loved by him. Besides, he had been hurt, and Mary wanted, as she had forgotten she could want anything, to comfort him. The powerful instinct that had forced her to try and dominate Hugh was forcing her now to break down Gerry's reserves. Her instinct warned her that she could not dominate this man, but she could conceive no reason why she should not so possess herself of all his thoughts and secrets that she and she alone was his friend and intimately acquainted with him. Surely he needed her?

She had empty moments when she reminded herself that Hugh had found it quite possible to do without her. After a time, she became sure that Gerry would have liked to talk about his wife, and was held back by an incomprehensible reluctance. It was nothing more subtle than a man's reluctance to give his wife away to anyone, even an intimate friend. Mary was an unusual woman but she would not have understood that.

They contrived, by an impulse that was mutual but always sprang from Mary, to see a good deal of each other outside the Yard. Then intimate conversation became possible, and Gerry talked. He never talked to her about himself, only about things he had seen. He seemed to want her company, and feeling that, Mary could not keep away from him. It became—she was too arrogant to practise any subtlety—so obvious that Hugh noticed it, and one day asked her:

"How long have you known this fellow Hardman, Mary?"

Glancing at him, Mary saw that he was white, and pinched about the nostrils. It was like the old Hugh to ask a simple question as if his life depended on the answer.

"We've known each other since we were fourteen."

"Are you in love with him?"

With a quickness that startled her, she answered: "I'm fond of him. It means nothing."

"I hardly thought it did," Hugh said. "In that case need he come to dinner so often? He's finished the *Lafitte* and started on the best of that Spanish wine. He's what you might call an experienced drinker."

Mary had not the least idea whether he had believed her or not. His lips were pressed together and he was looking at her with an intense scrutiny. The intolerable idea came into her head that Hugh had grown tired of Miss Jardine—who indeed would have expected that to last so long?—and wanted to be reconciled to his wife, and she shivered. There was no place for Hugh in her present world and he had no right to stand forlornly on the edge, reminding her of something she had forgotten and did not now care to remember. She put him out of her thoughts and forgot the lie as quickly as possible. Hugh was not even real. Nothing was real but the happiness she held in her hands with agonising care. It possessed her to the exclusion of everything else. She was proud of the submissiveness of her love and thankful that it never left her. She had been half afraid that one morning she would wake up and find that there was nothing different about Gerry at all, that he was just an ordinary man with no power to change the whole colour of life for her. And every day that this did not happen her gratitude to him deepened. The very Yard, which had always been to her the most exciting place in the world, became more so when there was a chance that as she crossed it on her way from her own office to the offices of the Line on the pier she would catch a glimpse of Gerry, or meet him hurrying down Harbour Street, or standing outside the architect's office, engrossed in talk with that portly man. There were several points on her journey where she might see him if the nearer ones drew blank.

So few were the people with whom she had anything approaching intimacy that no one said to her: "How is all this going to end?" Of all the tumult of warning, hatred, and longing that occasionally appeared on John Mempes' heavy sardonic face when she sat opposite him and Gerry at her own dinner table with Hugh affable and elegant on her right, she saw nothing at all. She had the illusion that she was impenetrable. Absurd creature. She was as impenetrable at these times as a moor stream with the sun on it. Her thoughts darted to and fro in the clear water for all who looked to see. Every glance she threw at the man facing her gave her away to Mempes' fierce grey eyes, and she threw a good many. Gerry drew her like a magnet. The longer Mempes watched the more convinced he grew that Mary was the fellow's mistress. He was quite wrong. Gerry Hardman had not thought of asking her to become his mistress, but she was none the less possessed of him more completely than by any physical possession. Small wonder that Mempes, incapable of metaphysical conceits, raged inwardly and indulged himself in an abysmal contempt for her husband's blindness. Until one day he caught Hugh scrutinising his wife with an air of painful perplexity, and after that despised him not for blindness but for a shameful modern squeamishness. Not for Mempes were any vulgar notions of delicacy between husband and wife on the subject of the wife's affection for another man. Have it out with her. Make her behave herself. More than once he had an impulse to chastise Mary himself.

4

One evening, after dinner in his rooms, Gerry Hardman walked to the house above the Yard, preparing as he went an excuse for calling there. He needed an excuse to cover his nakedness. He was afraid of the surrender Mary unconsciously demanded. She would strip him of everything, his thoughts, his gestures, all that covered the reality of him from other eyes, if once he submitted himself to her. He was afraid to give any person so much power over him, and afraid not to give it to Mary. The thought of surrender was infinitely attractive. During the six months he had been in Danesacre she had invaded his mind in a way he would not have believed possible. He had ceased to wonder how far he was possessed by her. He craved the sensation of throwing up his hands and abandoning himself to her to do with what she liked, but in nineteen years Gerry Hardman had learned caution. He found himself ridiculously engaged in repeating her name aloud in the emptiness of his room, and the only way he could rid himself of the sense of her presence was to plunge into work. He worked long into every night and went to bed exhausted, to remember her as his eyes opened. He did not know whether he loved her or not, but he knew that he did not desire her, which he found strange until he thought about it, and saw that to him she was still Mary Hansyke and his young innocent love.

His state would have been incomprehensible to John Sacheverell Mempes. So for the matter of that would Mary's—to Mempes and to all other right-thinking people who have ceased to believe in the visitation among men of love as an irresistible destroying spirit. Mempes had another word for it. He was not charitable enough to call it a madness.

As he hesitated outside the gate of Mark Henry's house, Gerry saw Mary at the foot of the short slope running down to the Yard. It was almost dark. He knew her by the slope of her thin shoulders. She was coming up to him, walking with her head tilted back, and he waited for her. Her face swam up towards him through the layers of dusk, a pale drowned face floating up to the surface of dark water. He felt her approach as if it had been going on for a long time, for nearly twenty years. At last he moved to meet her and they met half-way up the slope.

"Were you coming to see me?" Mary said.

"I wanted you."

They turned down again towards the Yard and walked across it. The skeleton of a ship saw them coming. It lay between them and the harbour, until they passed the other end of it and reached a broad grassy path following the walled edge of the harbour to a small house on the edge of the hill. They stood still. The water lay still at their feet.

"If there was anything I could say to you," Gerry began, "that could explain to you what you are. Have I the right to talk to you?"

"All rights," Mary said, and clasped her hands, drawing her shawl closer across the thin silk of her dress. A fleeting regret crossed her mind that its rich deep crimson had blackened to invisibility in the dark. She shivered, less from cold than a nervous tension.

"I want to tell you this much. My wife left me ten years ago, when we had been married two years. She left me at Marseilles, on the voyage out. I had no warning of it, of her desire to go. She told me one evening that I was"—Gerry moved his head stiffly—"an unsatisfactory husband. She left me in no doubt of it, and the same night she went ashore. I gave her all the money I had with me and told her that she would always find money, what I could spare, to her account with my solicitor; he would give it to her on her signature. So far as I know, she has never called upon him: she writes for money when she needs it, from Marseilles, and Paris, and once from Lisbon. She—I didn't try to stop her. That's not true. I implored her not to leave me, but I took no measures to prevent her going. Should I have done? She was a very resolute person, eight or nine years' my elder, very dark and beautiful. I think I was still something of a boy. She dominated me. I loved her. For five years, the years of my marriage and three after she went, I loved her entirely. I thought of her, I wanted to absorb her as she had absorbed me. I pursued her with my love." A spasm of bitterness crossed his face. "I got so low as writing letters for my solicitor to forward with the money." He thought over that for a moment. As if just remembering the woman beside him, he spoke in a softened voice. "Am I hurting you, Mary?"

"Give me a moment. You don't hurt me, only what you say hurts."

Gerry let her lean for comfort against his shoulder.

"Go on," Mary said. "Did I stop you? I'm sorry. Go on now."

"Your face stopped me, and there's nothing more to tell you."

"But now?" It cost Mary a violent sacrifice of the pride she had thought subdued, to ask the question. She would not have asked it if she had not felt that she could not go on living without the truth.

"Do I love her now? No, I don't. I stopped loving her seven years ago. I don't hate her. I couldn't hate anyone to whom I had given so much. She lost her meaning for me, that's all. I don't want to see her again."

"Shall I lose meaning for you?" Mary asked in a low voice.

"You are my meaning," said Gerry, surprised by his own words, and repeating them with a sudden overwhelming delight: "You're the meaning of everything. Nothing else is of the least importance. Do you understand? Dear Mary, do you understand me?"

"I won't pretend I don't," Mary said. "What do you want me to do for you, Gerry?"

"Nothing. Only exist."

Mary sighed. "Well, I don't want anything of you, except to remember that I give you everything, and ask for nothing in return. There's no price on me, Gerry." She looked up at him with a smile full of a delicious humility. She was a little afraid of all she meant by that smile. "I won't be a burden to you, or expect that you should do things for me because of this, or give up anything for me or in the least way be obliged to me."

"I shall never ask you for anything, Mary."

"Yes, you will, my dear."

"Shall I?"

"How sweetly you smile at me. You will ask—all men do—and whatever you ask I'll do for you."

"You're too good," Gerry said simply. He was unbelievably happy. He was going to say: "I've been looking for you ever since I forgot you," but he kept quiet, trying to steady himself in the rush of emotion that threatened to sweep him off his feet. It was so many years since he had felt like this about a woman; he had thought he was safe from it for the rest of his life and he was startled at discovering in himself depths of which he had never suspected the existence. The promise of a danger-ous ecstasy beckoned and warned him in the same moment. This was something outside his experience; he was no longer a young fool. He might come out of it badly. "I'm mad to-night," he thought. "In the morning I shall be no better than Gerry Hardman again, engineer of no reputation except in a few places not really on the map, confused with dreams, restless." He revolted at his hesitation. "I'm spoiled, Mary," he said suddenly, "and rather meanly cautious. Are you sure you care to have me back?"

"More than anything in my life."

"Then take me. I haven't any secrets from you." His body, support-ing Mary's, trembled. "I give up all my secrets. Let me be your friend for the rest of my life. Let me be kind to you, and worship you. Let me be so close to you that I can't fail you or lose you." He paused and looked at her with longing. "I'll always remember you as you are now, your pale cheeks, and your eyes. I like your eyes. How kind you've been to me. You're so close to me now that I can hardly see you." He thought that if he put his hands on her, they would not feel her; so completely did she seem to have passed into him that there was no space between them.

"Are you happy, Mary?"

"Yes, happy."

Mary was trembling with happiness, but she felt quiet and com-posed. Her soul folded its hands and rested on the surface of the darkness.

"Do you hear anything?" she asked.

"No. There are no sounds, only your voice, your dear voice."

Mary listened again and heard a wind a long way off up the valley, the sigh of a tree in the darkness near them, the water moving at their feet. The movement came from the beating of a pulse in the sea, the heart of the sea sending a faint infinitesimal tremor to its farthest shore.

"Oh, how glad I am to have learned a little before you came," she said. "I should have made so many mistakes."

"I'd rather have had you and the mistakes."

Mary was cold. In the last half-hour she seemed to have spent all her strength. She touched Gerry's hand.

"Do you mind if I go in?" she asked timidly. Wonderful to feel for a moment that she could ask him this, as if he were master of her comings and goings and she submitting to him.

They walked back, past the spectre of a ship, up the slope to the gate of the garden. The house invited Mary in, but she turned her back on it to look at Gerry. They leaned towards each other, their lips touched in a fugitive kiss, the lightest breath of love. Neither of them had spoken of love or used the word in their thoughts. Mary drew back.

"Good night," Gerry whispered.

"Good night."

5

One morning—it was some weeks after the meeting in the ship-yard—Mary woke very early. The dawn mists were floating off the surface of the harbour. Like the black and silver scales of a fish the water glittered in the sun, slipping, sliding, shivering. The masts of a schooner lying at Garton's wharf made the most delicate and inviting gestures to the trembling air, and above it all, above wharf, water, ships, stretched a sky of limpid purity.

Mary felt about this familiar scene very like a man married to a beautiful woman. Sometimes when she looked at it, a poignant emotion of surprise shot across her habitual complacence. She thought: "Why, it's beautiful," and with a warmer thrill: "It's mine."

During the past month she had changed a good deal. The change was apparent as she stood in the bright light at the open window. Her mouth curved more richly, and her beauty had glowed and softened into sudden maturity. John Mempes set down the process to the account of her sinful connection with "that fellow." Grimly untouched as he was by the moral fervour of an age in which he had the air of a survival, he could yet find no words harsh enough for Mary's conduct. He groaned over her in secret.

Nothing could have been more innocent, and from his point of view more incredibly silly, than the relations between the two concerned. They were so much in accord that they felt no impulse to talk about it. There were no more meetings at night. Their glances were as satisfying as kisses would have been. They looked at each other, in the Yard, across Mark Henry's tulip-wood table, under John Mempes' formidable nose, with smiles of understanding. It was so innocent, so full of an idyllic contentment, that Mary would have been shocked to discover that Mempes disapproved of her. She thought of herself as a very experienced woman, because she had had two husbands, one unfaithful. The idea was dangerously misleading. She was one of those women whose simplicity of mind and purpose protects them from all the assaults of life. No young girl—the young girl she had been and still seemed to a grimly ageing Mempes—would have been more unsophisticated in her attitude before her lover. She felt (and forgot she had ever felt it before) that at last she was learning what life is, and the ultimate mystery of marriage. Yes, that was how she thought of Gerry Hardman—as the man to whom she had been married for a long time, long enough to discover that a woman's sharpest joy in life is to help in the making of a man and her privilege to stand back and admire her handiwork. In no other way could she have reconciled her frank passion for him with the code of morals in which she had been trained and to which she still held fast.

Nothing warned her that she was at the beginning of an entirely new experience, the discovery and knowledge of spiritual love. Nothing warned her that spirits are united by pain as bodies by pleasure. Knowledge of past griefs endured apart, and prescience of a future darkened by the dread and sorrow of separation sharpened her love to a point where it was a knife in her heart, and gave her the most exquisite pain. She pitied Gerry from the bottom of her heart. And the more she pitied him the more she loved.

In these first days she felt nothing but an overflowing happiness. Her life went gaily—with the flags out again—a scarlet one flown in either cheek.

Astounding as it seems, she never reflected that the passion and the code of morals could not for long continue to lie down like the lion and the lamb. That day at Roxborough, half a lifetime away, seemed a complete justification of her present madness. She was quite convinced of the guileless nature of her love. And it was in fact guileless, and simple, as guileless and simple as any love ever was.

But so insidious is the process by which in the fallible heart of man an innocent weakness becomes a roaring fury that she was already, on this bright morning, planning a means of seeing Gerry with more ease and secrecy. She did not think of it like that. She had no definite end in view, except the satisfaction of her longing to prove how kind and understanding a companion she could be. The thought of Gerry's need of comfort and her fitness to give it turned the knife in her heart. It was a terrifying and unique sensation.

Her imagination was so ready with ways and means that she might have been surprised at the extent and ease of her duplicity. Calmly, she selected one of several plans that occurred to her for getting him to herself.

The *Mark Henry,* one of the composite-built clippers she had built for the Chinese route, was being used now in the French wine trade. She was due to leave for Tonnay-Charente for a cargo of cognac, and Mary proposed that Gerry should sail on her. The French shipper had been giving considerable trouble which correspondence, between two people imperfectly understanding each other, was complicating to a point where the *Mark Henry's* captain had difficulty in dealing with the Frenchman at all.

It was not Gerry's job to clear up the inward freight people's troubles, but he could do it. And there was ample precedent in Danesacre custom for his doing it, since managers and owners in need of a holiday took it more often than not in the form of a business voyage in one of their own ships. Her heart, that clever pander, assured her that Gerry needed a rest, and had needed it since he came to Danesacre and for a long time before that. Mary decided to send him to Tonnay-Charente in the *Mark Henry* and at the last minute, when all was settled, to announce her intention of making the voyage herself, with Richard. The excuse, a change of air for Richard.

When she came to tell Gerry, she felt a new diffidence, caused by the fact that she was wishing he had seen the need to arrange something like this himself. His answer devastated her.

"It doesn't seem the most politic thing we could do." He flung her a quizzical glance.

"I don't think it matters what people say about my sailing in the same ship as my manager," Mary said at last. "For every man in the town who talks there'll be another to tell him to hold his tongue. Danesacre is like that, a little of the decent sea blows into our streets; think of the old walls covered with flowers. Besides, we'll have the captain's wife as duenna. But if you'd rather not——"

She tried to speak indifferently but her face gave away her pathetic mortification. Gerry pondered for a moment the impossibility of explaining himself. Her single-mindedness terrified him. It was ferocious. Really, women were the most amazingly reckless creatures.

He gave himself up to the luxury of being overruled. "I hate myself when I've made you look like that," he said. "I can't think what possessed me. Well, I can. But I don't want anything except to be alone with you."

"Is it true?" Mary asked wistfully.

She looked at him shyly and he smiled at her. Gerry's smile was as destructive of her strength of will as her simplicity was of his. She saw in it something childish, something delightfully appealing and ingenuous, the same quality, in fact, that she had once found in Hugh. She was one of these women for whom men rediscover the trustful, softly appealing smiles of their first years. Oddly enough, though Gerry's smile soothed her it destroyed her self-assurance as much as Hugh's had always done. She felt weak and foolish as she gave him an answering glance.

The *Mark Henry* left Danesacre a week later, and had brisk following winds. She was a beautifully-modelled ship, heavily sparred, and carried a main skysail yard. She never needed driving, would not have stood it, and in light airs passed easily ahead of anything sighted. Mary rejoiced in her with a child's delight (this voyage was many years overdue), and Richard was allowed, by an agreeable and private arrangement between himself and Captain James to sign on as supernumerary apprentice for the voyage. He was idiotically happy. If there had been an ounce of superfluous flesh on his slender bones it would have been thinned off by his ceaseless activity. He turned the colour of the teakwood fittings and moved about like a flame walking. Just after the Needles were left astern the wind freshened, and the *Mark Henry* lay over like a swooping bird to the foaming water, Richard went up to the fo'c'sle head and stood there with legs wide apart, bracing his body against the wind. It swept past him as the sea swept past the ship, parting on either side of her with a sliding hissing noise. Richard was thrilled in every part of his body, and when he caught at the weather rail to steady himself an answering thrill rushed through him from the plunging ship. For the first time in his life he felt that he was really living and not merely sharing the life around him, his mother's, his stepfather's, his tutor's, and Mr. Hardman's. He was Richard Roxby. He was acutely aware of his strong slender body and in this moment he promised himself to use it to the utmost limit of its strength, to stretch his strength until it rang like thin spun steel. He meant his body to obey him in finding out everything there was to find out about the vaguely intoxicating wonders of the world. He meant to see queer places and bury his face in the aching sweetness of a life he had not thought very much about until this moment of life outside the world, with the *Mark Henry* plunging and rushing between sea and sky like a live creature, like a creature with a heart beating up through the deck to the ropes that sang about his ears. His own heart plunged and rushed on with her and when her bowsprit came up against a cold white sky his heart leaped up and he pressed his lips together to keep back the shout that would, past all decency, have broken from them.

When he went back to the cabin and sat in that warm room watching the firelight wink on the stout brass rail round the cupboard where Captain James kept the Madeira he only drank in port, he had nothing to say. He sat quietly with shining eyes, hugging to himself his glorious certainty of life. His thoughts sang in his head like the wind through the rigging of the *Mark Henry*. When his mother and Mr. Hardman came in he pretended, to keep them from guessing his secret, to be reading the copy of the *Poems and Ballads* he carried romantically in his pocket. After a time, he thought that they were not taking much notice of him or of anyone else. What did older people think about? Why were their glances equivocal and troubled? He had only just realised that this was so. Even Captain James had the air sometimes of looking for a thing that he knew was not there but could not yet quite give up hope of finding. Richard gave it up. He knew that he knew more than these other people, more even than his mother and Captain James, the two people who in his eyes were in their differing ways more knowledgeable than anyone else in the world. And seeing that neither of his companions had eyes for him he gave up his pretence of reading and stared out through the closed port on to a black sea made visible by streaks of foam, like the diamond-bright edges of knives. He at least was going to find something in life. And when he had got it he was never going to let it go. Never.

The captain's wife spent the days in her cabin, writing up her Household Book. She loved ports, and disliked the sea that divided them from each other; in every port she managed to acquire some new recipe or piece of household wisdom, which was added forthwith to her bulky manuscript book. She wrote a very gentle hand and committed atrocities of spelling.

So the two who had come to the flattering conclusion that they were the only perfect friends in an imperfect world had the starboard side of the poop to themselves. They were screened from the helmsman, and neither captain nor officer on watch thought it part of his duty to trouble passengers with more than Good-day. The isolation of a ship, a speck swinging in a waste of waters, favoured the illusion that they were alone, a company of two against the world. Mary felt an enormous relief in escaping from the pressure of Garton's; she laughed, told Gerry stories to amuse him, remembered scraps of verse, and coaxed him to talk to her. The first night out was warm and starless, the sky an immense hoop with black whalebone of cloud. Mary had her chair placed on the poop to leeward of the skylight, and Gerry sat on the skylight seat, bending over her. He began abruptly to talk of marriage.

"We can't marry, Mary. You couldn't endure the scandal, could you? I couldn't endure it with you, I'd rather have you as my mistress. I'd like you to come away with me for a long time." He owned to himself that he was behaving badly. Yet he had never had the least intention of saying this when the voyage started. It had leapt at him quite suddenly and now he was completely possessed by it. He must have this woman to himself. He must have her soon, almost at once, as soon as she could bring herself to it. He felt like a very young man again, and like any youngster of sensitive mind and senses he had until now thought of nothing but his astonishing good fortune in being capable of feeling and rousing such a pure exquisite passion as burned within himself and Mary. Alas for the impatient minds of men. That first delicate ecstasy was already past. It had been left somewhere on the wharf when the *Mark Henry* slipped away. He must be further convinced of his luck, make further, less equivocal advances in experience. Gerry Hardman trembled like a boy before the little body of his mistress. The least sensual-minded of men, he craved for her because in no other way could he find relief for his frightful loneliness. "Forgive me, won't you?" he said rather desperately. "I don't want you to come yet, but the time is coming when I shall. Will you contrive to come away then?"

"I'll come," Mary said. In one part of her she was terrified by this acquiescence. But she could not help it. "You asked me once before to come to a gate in a lane. Do you remember?"

"You came and I failed you. Pray Heaven I shan't fail you again." She looked very frail, rolled in her rugs—a child with clear eyes. That she was no child but a woman of great if narrow intelligence and a spirit that occasionally daunted his, he well knew. But the most independent and spirited of women will often seem a child to the man who loves her. Gerry was divided between desire and shame. Yet he felt that whatever he said contented her. He tried stumbingly to explain.

"I don't just want your nights, Mary. You understand that, don't you, and that I'm not asking you to slip out of your house in Danesacre and meet me in some obscure room? I couldn't stand that. I want you to come right away to live with me for a long time, as long as we can. We must go away often. Do you think you can manage it?''

"For us both to leave Garton's together," Mary began doubtfully. "It's not easy. John Mempes could take charge, of course." He was startled by the smile she gave him, with its revelation of complete surrender. "You must have what you want. Tell me when you want me, Gerry, and I'll think of the way."

"You think of everything," Gerry said, stooping over her until her hair blew against his face. "My dear. Am I making things too difficult for you? It's not just what I want that matters to you, is it. You want it, too? Mary?''

Mary's upturned face was under his, and they kissed long and tranquilly, her hands holding tightly to his wrists.

"You know I want it," Mary said under her breath.

"I know. My dearest, I know. Poor Mary. You love me too much.''

"You never speak of that," Mary said. "Have I more love for you than you for me? Tell me the truth. I don't mind.''

Gerry was silent for so long with his arm protectively round her shoulders that Mary grew very afraid.

"All there is of me," he said slowly, "is yours and for you, but there isn't much left of the boy you knew. I gave my wife so much, everything. Ah, you're hurt. Forgive me, I'd rather die than hurt you, you're everything to me now, all I have." He had not wanted to say this to her. He said it in spite of himself, forced to it by the strain of cruelty that lies dormant in every sensitive nature. It was as if he must hurt her to make sure that she was wholly his. And he was telling her the truth. He was tired. He was almost finished, *un huomo finito*, infinitely far from the overweening confidence of early love.

Mary did not answer him. She was hurt, but she rejoiced in it. "Most women of my age," she thought quaintly, "would be pleased to feel as I am feeling now. My life is very strange. After all these years, so crowded with events, I am learning how full and rich life can be." Compared with her, Gerry was a child, a hurt child afraid of the fire. She was surprised to find her lips trembling.

"Are you sorry you had to tell me that?" she said wisely. "Never mind, my dear." Part of her mind was telling her that he ought to have kept it to himself. She was glad that he had not. Not for worlds would she have foregone the bliss of this moment, and the delight of feeling herself completely necessary to him. Why, without her, he would have nothing.

Gerry seated himself on the deck and pressed his forehead against her wrist. With the unreasonableness of a man, he would have preferred her to show a little less composure. He caught sight of her lips and was shaken himself.

"Don't you want me?" he asked. "I couldn't bear to lose you, but I have to tell you the truth."

"Of course."

"I told you that for five years I was completely in love with my wife. When she left me I thought that side of life was finished for me. I crushed it out in myself, I'm only part of a man. Oh God, I need you so. I'm all yours, what there is of me. Do you believe that?" He paused, unable because of the wretched inadequacy of words, to explain to her that finding her again had been like finding God, the peace, the love of God. He recalled the many occasions on which he had quarrelled with his wife; he had always had a sense of her as a person separate from himself, sometimes hostile to him. Mysteriously, he had no feeling of separation from Mary, she was part of him. "If this voyage could only go on forever," he exclaimed. "I'd like to stay like this with you for the rest of my life. I'm so happy with you."

"That," said Mary, "is all that matters." She sat perfectly still, thinking that Gerry had given his wife the finest flame of his devotion and young selfless desire, so that he could give her everything but that, admiration, tenderness, but not the protective passion that asks nothing except to be allowed to serve and worship. It did not seem to her to matter very much. A good deal too much fuss was made about these things. She wanted nothing except to comfort Gerry. For herself, she asked nothing, not even comfort. Vaguely she knew that she had not always been capable of this devotion, and an obscure voice—it was a Garton voice—warned her that it was extravagant. "I can't help it," she thought. "I feel like that. What a detestable woman his wife must have been. It's very queer that a woman whose name I don't know, should be making so much difference to me."

"What is your wife's name, Gerry?"

"Mercy. She wasn't very merciful."

Conceive, if you can, the simplicity with which Mary Hervey faced a course of action for which nothing in her experience or training had prepared her. She was quite assured that what Gerry demanded was nothing less than a sin against God. Miss Flora's pupil had no escape from the conviction of sin. She never wavered from the simplest straightest belief in the punishment of sinners in Hell, she who could override every tradition in her shipbuilding remained all her life the slave of the narrowest traditions of her religion. She thought: "You are a wicked woman. There is no excuse for you. None." It made no difference. This really virtuous woman accepted the certainty of private damnation without a quiver of her eyelashes or a tremor of her thin little body. What Gerry wanted he must have; she gave him her eternity without turning a hair.

It is doubtful whether Gerry ever understood the profound nature of the revolution silently accomplished in Mary's mind. When he asked her to come away with him he was thinking at least as much of days spent in her company as of nights in her arms; he wanted both now, but he did not want the nights without the days.

He wanted her more every day, but he was still, on board the *Mark Henry*, persuaded that he could be content with snatched months. He had had nothing for so many years that a little assuagement seemed a very great deal to him. As for Mary, she did not think about it; she never wondered what it would be like to come back to Danesacre, to a house that held Hugh and Richard and sometimes Hugh's daughters, after life with Gerry; she had so little imagination about herself. The *Mark Henry* rushed on, under an immensity of sky, the captain's wife wrote in her recipe book, Captain James pondered in his slow way over a number of problems, such as the French shipper's queer ways, and his wife's inability to spell; the life of the ship, a self-contained state, followed its regulated way; and its passengers lived in their peculiar world as if the world that contained it had no other reason for existence.

At the ancient little port of Tonnay-Charente, Mary and Gerry went together to present their compliments to M. Duvelleroy and to ask, in the most delicate and friendly manner, why it was impossible for Garton's captains to extract a full cargo from his warehouse. Every voyage now there were a few casks short, and though on one occasion the captain had seen with his own eyes the missing half-dozen casks, he had not been allowed to take them, and no explanation, or none that he could understand, was ever forthcoming.

M. Duvelleroy was a small rosy man, with the face of a peasant, and dressed as became the most prosperous shipper in the *Petite Champagne*. He threw himself violently on their mercy. "Imagine," he cried, " 'ow pleased I am to deal at last with people of sensibility and refinement. You will understand, madame and monsieur, the delicacy of the 'eart and how impossible it was to explain to your excellent stout-'earted captain—oh, that stout English 'eart, 'ow nobly it beats and 'ow stupid it is—what I desired to be done with the casks he saw in my warehouse, marked all with a red cross, the symbol of passion. Such passion, madame! Now that I am old and fat and my wife is fat, admirable creature, I cherish the memory of it, I say to myself: 'Pierre, my boy, you are a foolish stout little man but you 'ave been a fine fellow, you 'ave been in 'eaven, you 'ave known sublime love, devotion, passion, ecstasy. Warm your old bones, you 'ave been young.' Thus, madame and monsieur, the red crosses on those casks."

"Forgive me," Mary murmured, "if my heart beats as stupidly as my captain's, but do I understand that the casks were being kept for madame your wife? Because I cannot see——"

M. Duvelleroy interrupted her with a strangled cry.

"For my wife! Give my wife the noblest *fine* in the district! You mock me. Madame, you mock Pierre Duvelleroy, you refuse to believe that a great passion once dwelt in this withered breast. My wife! My dear good Christine, who has not the palate of a cow, 'eaven forgive 'er. I, Pierre Duvelleroy, 'ave not become what I am by wasting money. No. I design those casks for that kind lady who was my adored, my ravished one, in the days of my youth and 'ers. Ah, London, London, most romantic of all cities, 'ave you ever sheltered more romantic lovers than I and my little white bird with the soft breast! Forgive me, madame, and monsieur who understands, it is so long ago and my wife is so fat. Now she 'as written to me. 'My poor Pierre, I am old and white-haired, and the body you have kissed is bent with rheumatism. Think of it, Pierre, the pains we shared, and the pains I have now. Does it not make you laugh?' I do not laugh. Not I. I think of 'er poor pains and I weep, and then I consider what I can do for 'er, for my little old rheumatic one. Why, madame, the thing answers itself! Cognac! The best, the finest, the noblest in the world. I 'ave it 'ere, under my 'and, what will protect 'er from the murderous English climate, and I choose out six casks, six special casks and mark them with my love, and I say to your splendid captain: 'You shall deliver your cargo on the wharf for your customer, but you shall keep back these casks and them you shall forward at my charge to this lady what I shall tell you the name.' But did he understand me? Did he say, as a man of refined soul would 'ave said at once: 'Monsieur, I understand you, and in this matter my 'eart beats with yours.' No, 'e did not. 'E said: 'I was chartered to fetch a full cargo of brandy for our London customer, and I'll fetch it, but I don't know anything about carrying stuff that's not on the bill of lading.' I 'ave spoken with 'im like a reasonable man, I said: 'You can imagine to yourself, my good fellow, 'ow impossible it is for me to write that lovely lady's name in your miserable papers. What will my clerks say when I tell them: "Enter six casks for Lady Constance Polchester." They will smile to themselves and wink and talk, and my wife, my blessed saint with the long ears, will come to 'ear of it. You are a man of the world like myself,' I say to 'im. 'You understand the delicacy required in these things, is it not so?' Ah, the splendid fellow. 'E 'ave understood not one word, and for now it is five voyages 'e 'as made out 'ere for my brandy and still my special casks are in the ware'ouse and one day Christine will go in and see them and I am a sacked city. She will ask 'What are those casks?' and she will perceive my emotion, she 'as such a quick instinct, my Christine. What a sack, what a sack! Ruin and desolation. Madame, monsieur, I appeal to you. Every year you carry all my brandy and my life is devastated if I must make a change, but she dies, my little dove, she wrings 'er poor 'ands and dies of 'er rheumatic pains. The casks must go. It is absolutely beyond question that they shall go.''

M. Duvelleroy wiped his brow and breathed as if his heart were beating too quickly for him. The appalling insensibility of the English was more than he could bear. If these two people, looking at him silently, their eyes round with wonder, did not speak, he would scream, he would roll on the ground and spit at them, and very likely they would go home and declare war on his country to avenge the insult.

Mary thought the poor little man looked strained, and assured him gravely that she would arrange for the marked casks to be delivered as he desired. M. Duvelleróy wept and invited her and Gerry, the captain, and the captain's wife to dinner, which enabled good Mrs. James to add half a page to her book. "An exselent strong clear soope, served in small pankins with handels, an omlet very good, two (2) yonge chickens with middling sizd oisters, and at the side a little Pye, made, as well as I could see, of swetbreads seasoned and forst meat, and larks or other littel birds strowd in with spinage and sparrowgrass. At the ends a Caramell and four littel Puddings. A very good Dinner, all very well served and nice. Shal try the little Pye, with rookes, at home."

Admirable Mrs James, let us pray that the captain liked your Pye, but I am very much afraid that he preferred a good roast joint to any of the refinements you collected so carefully in every port where you landed with your recipe book and your bright observant eyes, watching for any new thing. He was not an Athenian.

The next day, while the cognac was being taken on board, Mary and Gerry journeyed to Bordeaux, with Mrs James. They put up at a hotel near the Quai des Chartrors, and the captain's wife promised herself a ripe harvest in the restaurants of the town. But the journey had given her a sick headache and after struggling heroically to control the spasms that defied her active mind, she gave way and retired to bed, leaving Mary to dine alone with Gerry. In the early dusk they walked through the elegant city that owes everything to that eighteenth century Marquis de Tourny whose imagination worked over it with the sensitive ardour of a lover. From the Allées de Tourny they entered a narrow street leading to a quay. The superb arc of the Garonne swept away to right and left like the points of a crescent moon. Mary uttered a cry of delight.

"I've seen so little of the world," she said apologetically. "I wish I'd been with you on your wanderings."

"I wish to God you had, my dear," said Gerry. "The world would have been a different place and I a different man with you."

They turned their backs on the river and entered a small café in the

Place Richelieu. The place was bigger than it looked from the street, a long room, lit with chandeliers of wax candles and decorated with panels of plump nymphs placidly watching the destruction of a massive youth clad like a good French burgher; a singularly respectable and prosperous Actaeon he was, and the hounds of Diana must have relished him. Gerry ordered dinner, and when he had consulted with the sommelier leaned back and gave himself up to the pleasure of watching Mary. She was sitting forward, her hands clasped on the table; her gaze took in the room with ravished satisfaction.

"Do you like this, Mary?"

"I like it, I like being here with you." She smiled at him dreamily. It was so long since she had been in a restaurant, not since the early days of her marriage, when she and Hugh occasionally took a meal in public, with what had been for her a delicious sense of almost immoral luxury. She looked round her with an air of calm assurance. How much more she knew than the proud diffident girl of those days, and how happy she was, happier than she had ever expected to be when Hugh left her. She felt for Gerry's hand under the table-cloth.

"What a lot of queer people," she whispered to him.

"They're nearly all the most repectable of middle-class Frenchmen," he said teasingly. "You absurd insular child."

Mary blushed. "You're laughing at me, but I don't care. I suppose they're all right, but they dress queerly and I don't know enough French to understand what they're saying. They may be saying *anything*. But I am very happy." She looked over his shoulder and frowned. "A woman in a yellow dress has been staring at us ever since we came in. She's at a table against the wall, directly behind you, Gerry. Do you suppose she's English?"

Gerry threw a quick glance behind him, and his face, when he turned it back to Mary, was old and blanched.

"That is my wife," he stated.

Mary stared at him in consternation.

"Oh my dear," she said. "I am so sorry. What shall we do? Would you like to go away? Does it hurt you to see her, would you like me to go away?" She made a movement to rise from the table.

"Don't," Gerry said under his breath. "Please don't go." He

glanced at her face. "It's all right, my dear, I never felt less liking for anyone, I'm just startled. I can't quite think what I ought to do. It's rather awkward, don't you think? Do I just bow to her on our way out, or ought I to speak to her? . . . Ten years. . . . She's changed."

"She's coming over here," Mary said quietly.

She watched the aloof civility with which Gerry greeted the woman in the yellow dress, and in her turn murmured a conventional word. Mercy Hardman looked from one to the other with a smile.

"You might ask me to join you," she said pleasantly.

"Please," Mary said. Her lips moved stiffly to produce the single word. She found it difficult to speak, because Gerry was not speaking. His numbness affected her. She looked at the woman sitting between them and could not imagine her Gerry's wife.

She saw that Mercy was handsome in a rather battered way, had been beautiful, with a skin of the whiteness that suggests depths on depths of whiteness beneath it, and dark eyes, not set straight in her face, but tilted at the outer corners. She saw that Mercy had a long mouth, red and shapely; she was tall, taller than Gerry and much taller than Mary, who sat collected within her small body, not at all afraid, and ready to spring at the tall handsome woman. She turned her head to look at Gerry, and her face quivered in spite of her. He looked into her eyes and his lips moved. What he said was of no importance. She smiled at him and nodded, and watched the tension of his slight body relax. He leaned forward against the table and spoke to Mercy. He asked her formally if she were well.

"You don't ask me if I'm happy," said Mercy Hardman. Her smile held Mary's attention. It was less a smile than a lingering emanation of the smiler's thought; it was unkind and shockingly unreal, almost meaningless, and what meaning escaped from it revealed Mercy as old and tired and dreadfully knowledgeable. "You know everything," Mary thought, and her horrified eyes sought Gerry to discover how much he knew about his wife. Gerry sat bent, looking down at his folded hands on the checked cloth, and Mary realised that he was not thinking of Mercy at all; he was thinking of a past that had nothing to do with either of the women who were watching him, a lost past of simplicity and hope. He did not look up, and in the silence a frightful consideration rose to the surface of her thoughts, and she knew, as clearly as if the words had already been spoken, that Mercy Hardman was going to ask her husband to take her back. Mary felt herself caught in a whirlpool made up of her own thoughts and the other woman's; she was dragged round and round and down until she was almost at the bottom of the whirling dark water. ''I'm fainting,'' she said to herself, and made a great effort that flung her up and out into consciousness of the lighted café. The constellations of the candles danced across the ceiling.

''Are you all right, Mary?''

She nodded. Already, she knew quite well what was going to happen. When Gerry's wife asked him to take her back, he would not be able to refuse. He was a fool. Her thoughts yearned over him as never before. The wilfulness of his folly silenced her, as women are silenced when their men choose war. It shocked, outraged, and thrilled her unspeakably. She wanted to cry, to snatch him back, to plead with him. Did he know that he was giving her up, leaving her? She sat silently with her hands in her lap. In the attitude she had adopted to watch Mark Henry's ships leave the wharf, to wait for Charlotte in Mrs Maggs's kitchen, to sit beside Richard's cradle in Roxby House, to listen to Hugh in the early days of her marriage, she now waited for Gerry to take, under her eyes, the step that would separate them forever. ''I am not like that,'' she thought. ''Never would I admit such a woman into my house. It's not strength, it is madness.'' She accepted the fact of Gerry's madness on this point, as she accepted everything else about him, but her heart sank.

What was going to happen to her? She reflected with merciless scorn that her own indiscreet scheming had brought Gerry here—to meet his wife. It was what might have been expected of such a folly. Grimly she assured herself that she had always known it could come to nothing, her mad passion for Gerry and his for her. The first touch of reality had thrown down the poor structure they had erected between themselves and the truth. How could it ever have been managed that they should go away and come back again to Danesacre, as Gerry had suggested and she agreed? It was not merely wicked. It was something far more deadly to her pride. It was foolish, the sort of unregulated behaviour of which she had always believed herself incapable. It never occurred to her to despise Gerry for making the suggestion. His situation was different from hers. It was herself she despised. Her eyes were opened and she saw that she was capable of the worst and vulgarest follies.

There was worse to come. With her eyes on Gerry's face, she knew that there was no folly she would not have committed to make him happy. Her pride compelled her to acknowledge the final consequences of her infatuation. What was the use of pretending? She would have taken him on any terms. That was the extent of her madness, as far past the comprehension of sane people as his. She looked at him and her glance said: "Whatever you do I love you."

Gerry shut his eyes because of the love in his Mary's face. When he opened them again Mary was leaning back between two folds of the dark curtain behind her. She was very pale and composed. The waiter was carrying away untouched dishes and placing others. Gerry poured himself out a glass of the *Latour* recommended by that excellent fellow, the sommelier, the friend of all the world. "To your good health and bless you," he apostrophised the sommelier. The *Latour* was all that dear friend had promised, a rich splendid inspiring wine; it warmed Gerry and eased the tightened nerves behind his eyes.

"Well, are you happy?" he asked Mercy wearily.

"Not at all," she said promptly. "I am unhappy. I want you to let me come back to you, Gerry. I should have come to look for you if we had not met here. You haven't forgotten that when I left you—how many years ago, my poor friend—you said: 'If you ever want me I am ready to help you; I'll always want you and you can always come back. Will you remember?' I have remembered, you see. You have remembered, too. You could never forget a promise like that."

Gerry straightened his back.

"On the contrary," he said civilly. "I have forgotten it entirely. I don't doubt your memory, Mercy. It is precisely what I should say under the circumstances. I was very distressed." He looked across at Mary and felt that she understood him; she understood that he had been in agony when he made that promise. He looked from her small colourless face to the face of his wife and his spirit rebelled within him.

Why should he admit this stranger into his life, this smilingly unpleasant woman, whom already he disliked and feared? She disgusted
him. She was old, her face was old under its skilful cosmetic, her mind
was ruined and unkind.

He said bluntly:

"I don't want you back, Mercy." He thought Mercy winced and
then that she was laughing at him.

"You promised."

"Would you try to keep me to a promise made at such a moment?"
he asked ironically, knowing the answer. Not from the woman who had
injured him could he expect generosity. At this moment, he
remembered with vivid accuracy the details of his last interview with
her, and heard himself making that despairing promise. Good God,
how he had suffered. He could almost feel the salt taste in his mouth as
he pleaded with her to stay. He had meant every word he had said, and
what a fool he had been. "Fool I was and fool I am," he thought, "but a
man who has neither the wits nor the moral force to keep his wife has no
right to complain if she goes off." With a grim humour he reflected that
now, when it no longer mattered, he was more than able to cope with
her. She would behave herself if he allowed her to pass the remainder of
her life under his roof.

"Of course I keep you to it," Mercy Hardman said. "You made the
promise freely of your own will. If you refuse, if you push me back into
the life I'm living here, you will not be happy as long as you live. You'll
remember that I came to you and asked to be taken back and
that you refused me. Wherever you are and whatever this Mary Hervey
of yours does for you and is to you, you'll never get rid of me
again."

Gerry leaned across the table and spoke to Mary.

"I think she's wrong," he said clearly. "I think I should forget her
again as soon as we got away from this place. She flatters herself
grossly in supposing that she'd haunt me. But she is my wife, and I did
promise to take her back. I don't suppose that anything she has done or
any number of years could make her the less my wife. I married her and
I've got to look after her as long as she wants me to. Do you see that, my
dear? I think I hardly need have said all this aloud, except that this is

something you cannot care to see. If you don't see it I shan't be surprised, or mind.''

Mary stirred and smiled with a faint childish hauteur, because Mercy was looking at her. ''I am behaving worse than a fool,'' Gerry thought quietly, ''to take the woman back, but I must do it.'' He looked at Mary again to assure himself that she was still what he knew her to be. She put out her hands in a gesture meant to express complete acquiescence in whatever he chose to do, but suddenly he felt that he was losing her. He looked at her with helpless anguish as if she were dying, as if he were standing beside the bed where Mary lay dead.

''Mary,'' he cried.

Mary's fingers touched the stem of her glass; she lifted it, and swayed, falling forward across the table. The wine was spilled from the broken glass and ran out in a thin stream, but when Gerry got her out of the café and into a cab, what he had thought was wine on his hand turned out to be blood, from a cut on Mary's wrist. He tied it up, and held her in his arms while the cab lurched slowly across the quays. The lights of a wide square fell across Mary's face and she struggled to sit up.

''Gerry,'' Mary said, ''did we do right?''

''Hush,'' he said under his breath. ''Please hush.'' It had just occurred to him that he had only given her two kisses since he first saw her, and he covered her face with kisses. His whole life up to this point drew itself into a blinding ray of light that poured into him as he sat in the jolting cab, with the smell of musk and old leather in his nostrils and his love in his arms. His body was blazing with light, like a house of lit windows.

''My dear,'' he said, stammering, ''my perfect love, my life.''

Mary lay still in his arms.

''We can never go away together now,'' she said dreamily, ''because we could never come back. Mercy would find us out wherever we went. Oh my dear, my dear, why did you do it, why did I let you do it? Love. I should like to die, now, before I have to let you go.''

''The Garonne is running out with a full tide,'' Gerry said wildly. ''Shall I stop the cab?''

Mary smiled and took her arms away from him. Her smile said: "How absurd you are and how I love you."

"We're not like that," she told him, "and Richard is waiting on the *Mark Henry* for us. You dear Gerry. Every time I see you coming unexpectedly from the Yard into my room I am so happy I could dance on the tulipwood table, like Mark Henry Garton when he launched the *Mary Gray* of which he was so proud. A long time ago, when I was a little girl, I used to think there would be sure to be a shipyard in Heaven with the sound of hammers and blocks and men singing *O away you rolling river;* until Miss Flora told me that they didn't need ships because of their wings. I was disappointed and then I saw that it wouldn't have been at all exciting since nothing could go wrong." She stopped, unable to explain to him that though everything had gone wrong for them she was happy because nothing could take from them the past evening. "Sitting in that café," she said, "I felt your body on mine, do you understand me, as if we were married and shared one soul between us. Nothing better than that will ever happen to me. I shall remember it all my life. There are tears in your eyes. Put your head here and let me hold you. I never thought I should make you cry, Gerry."

"I'm not crying because of you," Gerry said, "but for both of us and for what I'm losing, for what I lost that day at Roxborough."

The word filled Mary with longing for her home. On the hills was peace. She wished that Charlotte had not sold Hansyke Manor, because she would have liked to go back there and comfort herself with something that was hers. She would like to lay herself in the life of her family as in a cool narrow grave, a child returning to the body of its mother. Gerry's head was heavy against her shoulder; she could not take Gerry with her there, he had no part in the life of old dead Hansykes. "He is part of my life," Mary said to herself, "but he did not come out of my past and when I am dead I shall go back to Roxborough and Danesacre, the moors and the sea; my feet will remember old streets and I shall not remember Gerry, but I shall remember the shipyard and the old old church on the cliff and the old road across the moor."

The cab lurched aside into the street where their hotel was. At the door of her room Gerry took Mary into his arms. She leaned against him.

"Are you all right?" he asked her.

"Tired," Mary said. "Deathly tired."

He watched her walk unsteadily into the depths of her room. The room swallowed her up, and he was left leaning against the wall in the dim corridor.

6

On the first night of the return voyage Mary shared her cabin with Mercy Hardman. Mercy came aboard in the yellow gown she had worn in the café, with a small box, so small that Mary thought she must be wearing her only frock, and remembering the days when one frock was all she had to wear in Mark Henry's house, felt a moment of sympathy for Gerry's wife. She stayed on deck when Mercy retired, talking to the captain's wife, until she thought that Mercy had had time to get into her improvised bed on the couch. Then she went down to her cabin, knocking on the door. Mercy was seated on the edge of the couch, her face smothered in a white grease, which she was wiping off, using one of Mary's fine damask towels. The process revealed her face moulded into hollows and wrinkled like an old yellow candle. She was in her chemise, an intolerable garment that clasped her flattened body too closely.

"I'm getting old," she said dispassionately. "I'm nearer fifty than forty and my life has made me older. If I had not such a thick skin it would be in worse state than it is. You have one of those delicate northern skins, they don't exist in the south. I don't like you. I don't think you're beautiful, but I envy you your health; I never had as much. I suppose Gerry has resigned you; he's not the sort of man to go gay with a wife in his house. That's of no importance to me, but I don't like you any the better for it. Your eyes offend me and so does the way you look at me."

"Forgive me," Mary said. "I did not intend to offend you."

Mary Hervey had a great dignity for so small a woman; it stiffened her back as she stood in the centre of her desecrated cabin. Mercy Hardman moved uncomfortably on her couch, but she was too hardy to be quelled. A wish to assail Mary's innocence seized her and pushed her past caution. She began to talk to Mary of her life, forcing on the

younger woman knowledge that sickened her, and all the time Mary
brushed her long hair with a steady motion, neither answering nor
checking the flow of Mercy's malice. Mercy talked herself out and laid
down between the blankets, her face turned despitefully towards the
room. She knew that Mary loathed the thought of undressing in front of
another woman, and kept her dark eyes widely open.

Mary finished brushing her hair. With a great effort she gathered
herself together in the quiet of her mind, shutting out the cabin and the
curious and intolerable woman who was Gerry's wife, until she seemed
to be standing alone on the rocking floor of the boat. The port above her
bed was open, and the sea tilted past her eyes and sank again below the
level of the port as the *Mark Henry* slipped along in a gentle westerly
breeze. Mary undressed, turned out the lamp and got into bed. There
she lay for a long time, tossing in the immensity of the safe decent sea.
Every now and then her eye sought the vague shape against the door
which was the other woman's yellow frock, hanging there and swaying
in a foolish jig like an unhouseled ghost. At last she fell asleep.

In the morning she could not face the prospect of sharing her cabin
with Mercy Hardman for the rest of the short voyage. She rose early and
went up on deck. Gerry was leaning against the taffrail, watching the
water pouring past the side of the boat as the *Mark Henry* slid and
swung over enchanted green hollows lucent in the sunshine. Mary went
up to him and said directly:

"I'll let you and your wife have my cabin "

"That wouldn't do at all," Gerry said simply. "I couldn't share a
room with her."

"I had to share mine," Mary said, and then understanding him
turned away, blushing deep red all over her face. She saw their life
Gerry's life with his wife, as it would be, Gerry living in a house with
this woman whose room he could not share, seeing her across his table
talking to her, sharing in her life in spite of himself. "It's too much,"
she exclaimed. "You can't endure it, Gerry." But Gerry stared out
over the sea as if he did not care to look at her, or as if he saw something
that he preferred not to let her see.

Later in the day Mary sought out the captain and explained to him her difficulty about Mrs Hardman. Captain James made no bones about understanding her.

"I appreciate your feeling, ma'am," he said. "I wouldn't have that woman in my cabin for half Garton's. No, ma'am. I'd rather sleep with a serpent, in a manner of speaking, and Mrs James feels the same thing. I am happy to say that we are in accord on this point, as on every other except her refusal to learn to spell. As I say to her, 'Suppose we had children, you couldn't teach them, could you?' And she says, 'If I only had a child, Mr James, I'd teach myself anything.' So there we are, and in a manner of speaking I take you. I will see to it that Mrs Hardman has another cabin. She can have the second mate's, he being a young man and this his first voyage on his ticket has no right to complain where he sleeps. Leave it to me."

Thankfully, Mary left it, and for the rest of the voyage had peace, so far as the *Mark Henry's* return trip could be called peaceful. Not that the ship herself was unquiet, there never was a boat steadier at sea than the *Mark Henry*. But an atmosphere of morose unrest and impatience hung over her from the officers' mess to the fo'c'sle. It was distinctly felt that there were too many women aboard. Any feeling about a particular person will run through a whole ship with lightning quickness, and before noon on the first day out Gerry Hardman's yellow-gowned wife was taking the blame for every misfortune that occurred, from a dropped coil of rope to the cook scalding himself in his galley. In the Channel they narrowly escaped being cut in half by an American schooner; the danger averted, Captain James addressed the Yankee in a mournful voice: "Damned stop-for-nothing fool," he said gently. "Doesn't care a curse for God, the devil, or the other fellow. May he rot to-night in hell." But Mary overheard the bos'un laying direct responsibility for the affair on "that yellow——," a sentiment which the second mate, probably suffering under a sense of personal injury, received with a certain disregard for discipline.

So the *Mark Henry* came home with one more passenger than she took out, and Mary offered Gerry the house above the Yard to live in with his wife.

"It has grown too small for me," she said, "now that Clara and

Sylvia ought to have a proper governess and live at home. I shall move into St Mary's Terrace, which is a long way from the Yard and the office but on the right side of the town. Harbour Street is not a very nice street, after all. I shall buy Old Smithson's big house there; they say his widow will take less than it cost him to build it to get it off her hands. This house shall be yours."

"I couldn't afford the fair rent of your house, Mary," said Gerry.

"Ah, my dear," Mary said, "may I do nothing for you? The house is an addition to your salary. You will need more money now."

"Thank you," Gerry said grimly. "You are very good."

Tears came into Mary's eyes in spite of herself.

"I love you," she whispered to him.

"Yes, I know."

CHAPTER SIX

1

THE drawing-room of Mary's new house in St Mary's Terrace was in her opinion its most satisfactory room. The rest of the house was full of furniture from Hansyke Manor, most of it very old and of a marvellous quiet austerity, but this one room she had furnished herself and to please herself. It contained all the best of Mark Henry's mahogany furniture, large chairs and carved heavy tables polished to such perfection that when Mary looked at them she seemed to be gazing down into depth on depth of tawny golden flame. Against one wall stood a great sideboard of exquisitely marked wood, made to her order by John Calverly, the old furniture maker of Harbour Street, who lived alone, and among the pots and pans of his meagre breakfast made furniture for every Danesacre bride who could afford it; he had been six months making Mary's sideboard, with mouldings and heavy beadings round the doors and the lovely curved door in the front. Hansyke silver covered it, and on the walls, hanging strangely between the monstrous birds and pomegranates of the wall-paper, were the fruits of Charlotte's childish toil, the landing of Prince Charlie and Flora Macdonald in woodwork, the colours a little dimmed and yellow, and a Holy Family in many coloured silks, fading almost visibly in the sun that poured through the long glass doors opened to the garden.

Issuing slowly on to the lawn through one of those same glass doors, Mary paused for a moment to admire the square front with its twenty tall windows glittering in the slant rays of the sun. Old Smithson had built himself a good house out of the profits of his yard. A cautious old fox, he got out at the top of his fortune, when freights were high and sailing ships approaching the pinnacle of their glory. He had sunk a large sum in this house, building it of stone from the Roxborough quarries. Every inch of wood in it was solid oak; from roof to cellar not a splinter of soft wood. It had been three years building and he enjoyed it barely one, delaying to occupy it until he thought it fit to live in. No Danesacre man ever rushed headlong into the perils of an imperfectly humanised house. "Let your new house to a stranger the first year, a friend the second, and live in it yourself the third." Old Smithson could not endure the thought of anyone else occupying his house, but he kept it empty and fires burning in every room for six months before he went in. After so much forethought he deserved a better enjoyment of it than he got, cut short at the end of ten months by a stumble at the top of his cellar stairs. Breaking his leg at the bottom he died of chagrin two days later. His widow was a poor stick of an ex-governess, whose anxiety to rid herself of the house Mary recalled with contemptuous kindliness. The poor woman was willing to take any price, and would undoubtedly have lost money had not Mary scrupulously insisted on paying her a fair price, not a penny below or over.

Turning her back on her house, Mary walked diagonally across the lawn to a green door in the wall. It was not a very large garden, but where the other big houses of this elegant terrace had gardens running steeply down to the road, Old Smithson had had the ground banked up in front of his house to make a level stretch of lawn from his drawing-room windows. It stood thirty feet above the road, a smooth green plateau, set about with lilacs and laburnum; against one wall a small rose garden carpeted with black pansies, and on the other pear trees, a tracery of black boughs and fragile blossom on the rough stone.

Mary lingered, her hand on the latch of the door. She was reluctant to go away. The solidity of her house was a refuge in these days when she was discovering how far Garton's had built out on what were at best perilous foundations and in places no foundation at all. Freights had been dropping for three years. There was no sign that they had touched bottom. Half her ships were laid up. One of her yards, Smithson's

Yard, was not building, and the orders in hand at Garton's Yard were not enough to see the year out.

She was not, thank God, alone in her peril. In this bitter close of the great seventies shipbuilding firms were in trouble all over the country, and for one that was riding the storm, ten were shipping heavy seas. Garton's, because of its overloaded commitments, was in worse case than many. There was an overdraft at the bank. The money had been spent in building the new Tees-side yards, begun in the swell of the good years, and persisted in during three bad ones. She ought to have suspended the work when the first strain wiped out her reserves. That had been Mempes' advice, strongly supported by Gerry. . . . Mary threw back her head in unconscious imitation of Mark Henry. The older she grew the more of his gestures she used, entirely without knowing it, as if the years were uncovering in her young body a buried resemblance to that grim old rascal. . . . The work on the Tees would have to be suspended now, and hating the necessity, she put off from month to month giving the order. John Mempes' triumph was a pill. He had been right all the time, Garton's was going too fast. It had become like an over-sparred ship and the storm was punishing it. . . . She would let the work at the Tees go on a little longer, six months longer. Things might look better in six months.

The millennium was very bitter now in the bellies of the shipping people. . . .

She shut the garden door behind her at last, and doubly reluctant, because of her anxiety about Garton's and her destination, walked slowly away. She was going to call on Gerry's wife, for the first time since the *Mark Henry* brought her home. She had not been able to bring herself to call sooner, in spite of an odd pity she felt for Mercy Hardman's isolation in the town. If Danesacre people did not take to the stranger coming to live among them the wretch might as well have been dead. Danesacre did not take to Gerry Hardman's wife, and left her entirely alone. She walked through its streets ungreeted by man, woman or child, smiling in a curious inward fashion, as if her face and her long mouth had some jest they were enjoying together. Her yellow frock and monstrous swinging earrings made of her an exotic figure in the little town where only the gardens and the old walls were allowed to dress gaily. She always wore yellow, a procession of yellow gowns, far more, said Danesacre, than Garton's manager could afford. Yellow silk, with flounces from waist to hem, primrose, lemon, pale daffodil, mustard, or deep chrome yellow, attended her walks abroad, and the men leaving the Yard glanced up at the windows of Mark Henry's house and caught a movement of yellow behind the panes, like the slow swaying of a tropical flower on the dark glassy waters of a lake.

Mary looked round Mercy Hardman's sitting-room and wondered at its inexpressive air. Mercy's manner suggested that she was pausing in the house on her way elsewhere. She smiled at her visitor.

"Would you like to see your house?"

"No, I thank you," Mary tried not to speak stiffly.

"See, at least, Mr. Hardman's room," said Gerry's wife, and led Mary to what had been Mark Henry's office and her own. In this room was nothing but the tulipwood desk she had left him, a chair, a bookcase painted white, and over one wall a curtain of an exquisite and enchanting beauty, embroidered with birds and old flowers in deep rich colours on a ground of royal purple. Mary examined it in growing wonder.

"I'd give anything to possess that," she said. "I never knew Mr. Hardman had such a curtain."

"There are a few things you do not know about my husband," Mercy observed. "He produced it out of one of his boxes when we came here. I think he said he found it in Norway. Perhaps a Dovrefjeld witch gave it to him, he looks sometimes like a man who has had to do with fairies."

"Do you like your house?"

Mercy looked amused. "Why, I don't know. It's a house like any other. When I was a little girl I thought I should like to live in a forest high up on the side of a mountain and hang a waterfall from my doorstep to the valley below."

Mary turned her small surprised face to the face of Gerry's wife. Mercy Hardman repelled her with a suggestion of evil lurking in the back of her mind, like a witch's broomstick behind the door; but she had an air of freedom that drew Mary against her will. She thought: "How hard and old you look, you've seen life as men see it and suffered from men because you're a woman. I believe I could talk to you, and understand what you said."

"Why did you marry Mr. Hardman?" she asked.

"Because he was enchantingly innocent and impudent, and deep in love. He will never love you like that."

"How you could bear to leave him, having had him," Mary said slowly, "I don't know." She spoke against her better judgment, urged by a shameful curiosity to find out something about Gerry's marriage.

"I'll tell you why if you like. I left to better myself, as I thought, but I wasn't so experienced as I had supposed I was. I hate and despise men, but they're stronger than we are and the world belongs to them. I had an idea that I was stronger than the world, that it would have to let me alone, but it broke me as easily as if I'd been any sort of female fool. I daresay you think you're strong, but step outside your world and see how much of your strength and courage is left after a year of drifting from one foreign place to another. I'm old and I'm dirty to my bones. That's what it's done to me. I'm hard, I wasn't defeated when I came on you in Bordeaux but I was getting tired of a losing fight. I've no respect for the world because it's beaten me, I don't respect anything but cleverness. I'm clever but not clever enough. I'm tough, I shall outlive Gerry, but I shan't live long enough to see the day when a woman can afford to be as greedy as a man."

"I wish I liked you," Mary said abruptly.

Mercy smiled. "I don't like you. You're young, young enough, and although I've beaten you by coming here, this is a fight where the loser wins. Bah, I'm old. So will you be, and tired and disappointed."

Mary rose to go.

"You're right," she said steadily. "We could not be friends. I don't think I shall come here again. Good-bye."

At the door she glanced back. Mercy Hardman was standing in the middle of the shadowed room, her long white face thrust forward above the yellow stem of her gown. . . .

At the gate of the Yard she met Gerry. He gave her a queer look, half grateful, half surprised, at seeing her come out of his house in her formal silk gown with her hands clasped over the fine carved handle of her sunshade. Looking at him, Mary saw that he was very tired; his eyes were bloodshot and strained, and his face fined to the edge of vital tension. He carried his body like a man in constant danger. She left him and hurrying home wept fiercely, angrily. . . .

2

The end of six months found the situation of Yard and Line not better but worse, and Mary face to face with what the shipping journals called Difficulties and John Mempes more simply and annoyingly a Judgment. In Danesacre only one new ship had been launched in the past year. It was out of Garton's Yard: the firm which had ordered it went bankrupt a month later, and Mary had to sell at a loss to another firm. Freights were so low that she could do nothing else, except lay it up. She could not afford that.

She had changed a good deal in the past year. The bones of her beauty were still intact, but she looked worn and tired.

She thought about the Difficulties one night, standing in the window of her bedroom, watching a big moon climb slowly across the sky. Leaning far out, she could see over the roofs of the houses built far below hers, to a thin streak of harbour and a few masts and wharves, remote and strange in the white light, like the ships and quays of elfland. The upper harbour was very full, with the tide just on the turn, and the moon running where water should, under the bridge. Stained with light, the hills folded in the little town, letting the brown Danesacre slide between them to the sea.

A wry smile crossed Mary's mouth. She was recalling Mempes' face as it had confronted her from the other side of her desk during the afternoon, one minute after another dropping heavily away while he waited for her consent to stop the work at the Tees. She had given it in one word, feeling like Mark Henry under old Bridges' knife. Could freights go any lower? Falling, falling, beating down on her brain; she heard their monotonous rhythm even while she slept. Things were very bad in the country, but no one would have guessed it. What Mark Henry called ''goings-on'' were in full blast. They had made the Queen an Empress, and Disraeli a peer. The last was a going-on would have hit Mark Henry hard. But what hadn't the man done! The Suez Canal purchase was certain. The Transvaal had been annexed: young Smithson was going out, they said, and breaking his mother's heart. A poor thing. . . . The Jew had been in Berlin, talking. He was the father and mother of all "goings-on." Peace with Honour, and the depression that had been falling on industry and commerce like a gentle rain from hell—Mempes out of Shakespeare—at the darkest wettest moment of all. What a peace! What a country! Could freights go lower?

Looking back over the foundering seventies she observed curiously that for all her prosperity, now vanished, and all the money she had spent on research, she would have had little at all comparable with the startling sixties to show a Mark Henry miraculously restored to her from some incongruous beatitude. The great swing-over from wood to iron and sail to steam had been accomplished in her Yard before the seventies began. During them she had spent enormous sums of money on experimental work: her files were choked with Gerry Hardman's notes and reports, over which she pored with a good deal more intelligence than she ever brought to Hugh's slow output of scholarly books. But the steamer she had built a year ago, carrying one propeller and fitted with one tandem compound engine, was an advance in details only on her seven years older sisters. Sensible shipbuilders in Danesacre said that progress had been crystallised for another half century, but Mark Henry Garton's niece—at the very moment when her mind should have been too crushed under the imminence of Garton's peril to entertain visiting angels—was suddenly convinced that they were wrong. The more she thought about it, when she ought to have been thinking about her overdraft, the more her spirit was troubled by the shadow and thunder of approaching change. As once before in her life, when Mempes argued with a young girl about steam and sail, Mary stood consciously between the past and the future and heard both roaring in her ears like great seas. Sail and steam, wood and iron. *Steel.* She had forgotten how many years it was since she had refused Thomas Prendergast permission to build a steel ship. Her imagination fastened on the thought of steel ships. They would have to be built on the Tees where the steel was. Danesacre would never build them nor the old bridge open to let a steel ship through. Her fleeting resemblance to Mark Henry passed across her face like a shadow passing over water.

She longed to comfort him with a steel ship to match the iron ones he
had left her. Match them! Why, steel was stronger and lighter than
anything Mark Henry had ever imagined. "That's something I'll teach
you," she told him, nodding her head, as if Mark Henry were lurking in
a corner of Old Smithson's garden. (Impossible to believe that the spirit
of Mark Henry Garton lived on anywhere outside Danesacre.)

She discovered in her memory a hoard of detailed knowledge on the
possibility and advantages of mild steel, acquired at various times from
Gerry, and suddenly become alive in her mind. "Two years from now I
shall build a steel ship," she said, without remembering that work on
the Tees-side yards had been suspended. When she remembered it she
smiled rather grimly and brought herself back to the present. But safe in
a harbour of her mind lay the steel ship; its sound graceful lines
ravished her eyes. It left the harbour and sweetly took the sea; it had the
clean movement of a clipper and twice the strength of iron. It was right
and perfect with the exquisite rightness and perfection of good ships,
the finest things men make. . . .

A young wind had got up with the moon. It stole upon Mary
unawares and blew a strand of hair across her eyes. Her room was filled
with scent from the ghostly lilacs below the windows, and the toll of
falling freights ceased clanging in her brain. She felt unreasonably
happy and peaceful. Time, like a captured flame, hung motionless in
one of those moments when the spirit discovers what it is to be *quick,*
aware, in every particle, that it lives. Her fear of time, snatching away
day by day the warm beauty of the world, left her, and the exquisite
sense of an unending tide of life flowed into her body. She no longer felt
alone, since nothing in Danesacre could be wholly alone or unfriended.
Not an old boat, too old for sea, lay abandoned on the muddy reaches of
the upper harbour but was companioned by a ghostly company of proud
and lovely ships. Mary thought that if she could see clearly enough she
might see the glorious *Peerless,* sunk years ago off Yokohama, fluttering home to Garton's wharf. "*I* built the *Peerless,*" she said aloud, and
felt herself thronged about by many friends, the men who had built
themselves small boats when Danesacre was a cluster of Saxon huts
below a church, and with them the builders of little ships who went out
to board and capture French frigates, and the men who launched the

wooden whalers, generation pressing on the feet of generation of shipbuilders who had seen their thoughts become ships on the stocks in old yards. And there were others, less shadowy, at her side, Mark Henry Garton, that boisterous dreamer, and a stolid little girl, watching the *Mary Gray* stand out to sea. . . .

She felt suddenly tired, and discovered that she was chilled to the bone. Shutting the window down, she turned her back on the inhuman magic of a moon-ridden world. She roused the fire to a blaze, and sat down at the end of the bed, her hands folded on its heavy carved foot, and her chin resting on them. She sat erect, never having learned to loll. She looked younger, staring out at the flames from under the canopy of the great bed she had brought from Hansyke Manor. The kindly light obliterated the marks which life and her endurance of it had set upon her.

Without any warning she found herself facing the knowledge—it might have sprung at her out of the heart of the fire—that she was waiting for Gerry to ask her to go away with him. When he did that, she would give up everything else and go. After all, nothing else mattered. Garton's, all the careful elaborate structure of her life, did not matter at all. She pulled herself up. That was not true, and rather silly. They did matter—she did not know how much—but Gerry mattered far more. Burying her face in her hands, she saw the years of her life pass behind her eyes: a grey panelled room at Roxby House and Archie's sour Hanoverian face, the naked body of her baby son, Wagener's death, kind good Wagener, Mark Henry Garton and the long apprentice years, a London orchard, and her young beloved husband. The thought of Richard wrung a moan out of her, forcing its way between her lips like the cry of some small animal, caught and mortally hurt in a trap.

Recovering herself at once, she began to prepare for bed by taking down her hair. It was as thick as ever and had lost none of its gloss and colour. When it hung loose, she folded her hands in her lap and sat quietly for a long time, thinking, resolutely excluding all extravagance from her thoughts. Why had not Gerry asked her to leave everything and go? Why did he continue, day after day, working for Garton's as no one had ever worked but a Garton, sitting up half the night at work—so Mempes said—in the room that had been Mark Henry's office and then hers? He talked to her every day in the Yard, but he never looked at her. It was hardly credible that he had confessed his dreadful need of her on board the *Mark Henry*. . . . Mary pressed her lips together. John Mempes had once said to her: "Women have no sense of decency, at least none that I can understand." What was this masculine sentiment that allowed Gerry to ask her on the *Mark Henry* to steal months for him and restrained him now—though he must have known she was waiting to be asked—from requiring her life? She told herself that she was losing everything because of his incomprehensible silence.

And this was the woman who, in order to keep her ships and her Yard, had withstood the wishes of an adored husband. She had ceased to wonder why she was ready now to behave in an entirely different fashion. It was not that she—a Garton—desired any less to build ships in the old Garton yard. If she could have kept Yard and Gerry she would have thought herself the happiest woman on earth, but she had long since come to believe that happiness was not the important thing, not even the normal thing in life, in her life at any rate. What she wanted was important, whether it brought her happiness or not.

Ever since the scene in the Bordeaux café she had known that she could not, this time, have both man and ships. And if on that evening she had doubted which she wanted the more, she had no doubts now. Her ultimate instincts were involved in this, the intense narrow pertinacity that had moulded her character from its earliest days, and the reckless almost scornful generosity that accompanied it. Gerry belonged to her and he was eluding her. He was overworking too. He was killing himself, destroying what was hers. All other things she possessed, however dear and hardly got, were less to her than the undisputed possession of this one human being. She had ceased even to have illusions about him. She knew that he was abnormally sensitive, that it was a weakness in him. She knew him to be less tenacious than she was herself, that he had courage but not endurance. She loved him the more for these weaknesses, as if she were the only person who knew of them. Probably she was, and yet she could not impress her will on him. He had a fineness that she had not, a curious gentle haughtiness of spirit that she respected without understanding it more than a little.

Mary sighed. Gerry's face, as she had seen it a few hours earlier in the Yard, nervously alert, a little grim about the eyes, and smiling, floated up to her from the pool of black and silver shadow under the window.

She sat huddled up in the dusky circle of the firelight, crouching on the bed, her back arched protectively in the attitude of a woman holding an exhausted child in her arms. The shadow between her breasts might have been Gerry's dark head, and as though it had been, her head drooped forward and her mouth wore a brooding delicate smile. He was her child, her hurt tired child. Her outstretched arms ached, her breast ached for the pressure of his slight body, her body trembled. It was because he had been hurt and set on edge that she wanted him so much, because he had belonged to another woman, because he was tired, distrustful, spoiled. Strange and dreadful mystery, that she should want anything so much as she wanted the rejected lover of another woman.

What she felt for him was not young love, the ghost of her love for Hugh—if any ghosts walk at noon? Her pains were real, a fire that burned her past assuagement, a hunger of mind and soul. She discovered how much of love lay beyond desire, a world of tranquillity and tenderness. She would make up to him for everything, if he would ask her.

An hour passed, two hours. Mary lay face downward across her bed. Her dark hair spread out on either side of her like the hair of a drowned woman. There was nothing ostentatious about her grief. Her face being hidden, only the long-drawn quiver of her body showed that she was crying. It ceased at last and she lay still. . . .

The next day Mempes brought her word that the bank was unable to renew her overdraft. She went down to see the banker. He had been Mark Henry's friend and school comrade and she could not believe that he would refuse to help her out.

William Adam Todd, called Sweet William in the town, was a lean man with legs so widely bowed that anatomically he was more of a monkey than a man. His face was in majestic contrast. The portrait that hangs to this day in the bank at Danesacre, showing discreetly only a head and shoulders, is that of a Victorian gentleman of the sternest period, powerfully browed, large-nosed and firmly jawed, a massive creature of massive emotions savagely repressed. He had a spiteful

tongue, and kept a wife and a large family of daughters in adject terror.
At meals he was served alone at the head of an immense table; round its
foot clung his female dependents eating the meagre scraps of Sweet
William's meal of yesterday. Once he tied his eldest daughter to a thin
rope and led her down to the pleasure-gardens on the west cliff. He
scandalised the frequenters of that respectable family resort, strangely
called the Saloon, by hobbling her to the leg of his chair and sending her
to sit a dozen feet away: he said she had been insolent. This action of his
was considered by most people to have overstepped the bounds of
justifiable severity. No one, of course, disputed his right to rule his
household in any way he chose, but it was distinctly felt that he should
not have risked distressing the less Spartan instincts of other people.
And there was something distressing about the posture of that lean, still
youngish woman, with the faint flush on her thin cheeks and the hands
folded in her lap twitching every time they came in contact with the
rope. . . . Sometimes he whipped his daughters, though they were all of
mature years.

He greeted Mary with an overpowering courtesy, scampering round
his room to fetch a footstool on which he disposed her feet, standing
back to admire his effect.

"Exquisite," he said. "What a foot for a dance. You may not
believe it, my dear, but I have a passion for the waltz. I don't dance,
because my legs are capable of moving off in two different directions to
spite me, but *Ehren on the Rhine* ravishes me; my body squats on its
hoop on the ground and my soul flies through the sky like an archangel.
I have only danced once and that was with my wife before I married her.
If she had not been a poor-spirited wretch she would have refused to
stand up with me. Can you wonder I despise her?"

Mary explained her errand. Sweet William heard her out and then
began to build a rampart of books on his desk. When he could no longer
see over the top, he addressed her at length, poking his head now and
then round the barrier to see how she was taking it.

"These are modern times," he said. "Very modern. Shockingly
modern. A woman in shipbuilding, it's an awful thing. Nothing in the
Bible to suggest that female labour would have been acceptable to build
the Ark. How I ever came to advance you fifty thousand pounds I can't

think. And now that the Joint Stock company are taking me over my sin has found me out. Here they were, in this room, poking round: 'What loans are out, Mr Todd? What security, Mr Todd? For what period, Mr. Todd? Fifty thousand pounds to Garton's. 'Aha,' I said, 'come and look out of my window. There, across the other side of the harbour, there's Garton's. See that beautiful ship building there now.' I rubbed my eyes, I stared, they stared. There was no ship. The Yard was idle. Idle! Empty! I blinked, I slunk from the window, I said: 'The ship must have finished and taken away in the night.' But they didn't believe me, and the end of it all was that they refused to take over the bank unless Garton's fifty thousand pounds is repaid at the end of the term. What could I do? There were no ships to show them. Oh, poor Mark Henry, God bless his soul, he was a dissolute ruffian, but he did use the Yard for building ships.''

''Mr Todd.'' Mary struggled between laughter and rage. ''You knew quite well there was no ship on the stocks at Garton's. There's not a ship being built in the town. And equally well you know that Garton's security is as good as any in England. You advanced that money on the Line, the Works, and the Yard; they're still there, and freights will go up again.'' She put her head round the books and William Adam Todd screamed.

''Don't you look at me. I can't do anything for you. There weren't any ships when I took those Joint Stock pelicans to look. Shipping is no security nowadays. No security, no security.'' He waved his arms. The topmost books of the pile fell down, and he glared at Mary, defying her to approach him over the ruin.

Mary sat still; the wide panelled room, its windows opened to the harbour, receded before her eyes. She was very angry, and exceedingly puzzled. William Todd was a mountebank. He was also the shrewdest and hardest business man in the county. His refusal of credit to Garton's was a deadly stroke. What puzzled her was his motive in mis-leading—no other word for it—the purchasing Company about Garton's. He knew that the security was good enough, for all the present pinch. Something more than the disobliging nature of Joint Stock ''pelicans'' was at the bottom of things, and whatever it was, it was no whim of the bank manager's. Sweet William was full of whims;

he was whim-ridden and the town's familiar buffoon, but he never let whims into his business. He was the sanest lunatic in Danesacre, which was full of lunatics, sane and insane.

Sweet William watched her. His eyes gleamed through a fine growth of reddish hair. Suddenly he leaned forward and said quite calmly:

"I regret I couldn't persuade the Joint Stock people. I regret we're putting you to inconvenience. I know it can only be temporary, since your resources are large and I have confidence in you. You're not a woman, you're a sensible creature. I have confidence in Garton's. I would risk a good deal on the future of Garton's."

The quietness of his manner was terrifying after his late performance. Mary was startled. She recovered herself quickly.

"But not," she observed mildly, "your assurance to the Joint Stock people that Garton's is a safe debtor."

William Todd shot out of his chair and toddled across to the window. Mary thought he had retired again behind his clown's make-up, and half expected him to go down on all fours and roll about the room like an animated croquet hoop. But he turned round with a placid face and his hands in his pockets.

"You misjudge me," he said. "You do indeed. The most sensible of creatures and you misjudge me. Is it my legs you don't like? I don't like them myself but I have a head as well as legs. Haven't I just said I would risk a great deal on Garton's?"

Mary sighed and rose. She attempted no further argument, but all the way back to her house was puzzled by an elusive sense that she had missed some significance in the bank manager's antics. Impatiently dismissing everything but the reality of defeat, she felt her heart beating with a sudden emotion. Things might be bad, but their badness was exciting.

In the hall, she met her husband, dressed for riding. He had just returned from his ride and he invited himself to take tea with her. Mary was too absorbed to notice the wistful air with which Hugh looked round her sitting-room before dropping into a chair.

"I don't believe I've been in your room a dozen times since we came to this house," he observed. "Either you're not in it or it's full of

Richard. I'm very fond of Richard but, upon my soul, Mary, I never get you to myself for a moment."

"Do you want me to yourself?" Mary asked idly.

"Why not?" Hugh smiled at his wife. "You're better company than the rest of Danesacre."

"Hugh," Mary said, stirred out of her preoccupation, "do you regret very much coming to Danesacre and marrying me?"

"I regret a good many things, but not marrying you, and my regrets matter to no one but me. They matter least of all to you, my dear. Why did you tell me you weren't in love with Hardman? You treated me decently enough nine years ago; I hope you'll allow me the chance of helping you—not to Gerry Hardman. I couldn't quite do that. But if you stay here you'll be unhappy, and if you run away with him you'll be just as unhappy. Tell me how I can serve you, and I'll do what I can."

"Thank you, Hugh," Mary said. "I'll tell you what I intend to do, before I do it. I'm sorry I lied to you about Gerry. I knew my own mind then but not his." She tried not to speak stiffly.

She was trembling. This surprised her.

"Do you know it still? Have you made it up to running away? I suppose not, or you wouldn't be worrying about Garton's. You would, of course. I can imagine that you would prepare for an elopement with all the neatness in the world."

"I can't help it," Mary said under her breath.

"Such a queer girl you were when I married you, a mixture of stolidity and romance. Earth and air, the elements are all wrong." Hugh laughed. His mouth was compressed with pain. As if seeing him for the first time since she had schooled herself to look at him without a tightening of the nerves across her chest, Mary noticed fine lines round his eyes, and a deep one dug straight across his forehead. The hair above his ears was grey. She was shocked, and filled with an absurd sense of tenderness and anger, as if she could not help resenting the years that had taken away her young fastidious lover.

"Do you remember?" Hugh began, and paused. "Don't remember anything," he said fiercely. "Don't remember anything that ever happened to you before, my dear. You'll be hurt if you do. No doubt you ought to have married Gerry Hardman, but it happens that you didn't; you married me." Jumping to his feet he turned his back on her. When he faced round again he was the self-contained Hugh of everyday, the man who had taken the place of Mary Hervey's young husband. He asked what the banker had said to her. A frown appeared between Mary's eyebrows. It had made a line there as deep as any of Hugh's, but she never noticed it.

"I failed," she said grimly. "I shall have to meet the overdraft. I must sell the Line, if I can find anyone to buy at such a time. I intended to get rid of it before we moved to the Tees, but not now. I shall have to close down the furnaces next week, by the way."

"I've thought a good deal about Garton's lately," Hugh said. "I've come to one or two conclusions. Do you care to hear them? Don't look so surprised, my dear. It's not flattering."

She was deeply touched by his evidence of interest in her, and spoke eagerly. "Please go on, Hugh. It would be kind."

"This thing"—Hugh waved a hand to encircle Yard and Line and Works—"is too big for you. It's too big for any one person. You should have help; I don't mean more managers, I mean financial help, a board, a company. I don't know the jargon. You've got it under your hand in the town. The banker——"

"I told you the bank won't help, Hugh."

"Not the bank. The banker. Todd. William Adam Todd, knight of the legs. I suppose he's the richest man in the county: he must be worth a million since old Todd died, and he'd give his lovely legs for a share in Garton's. I know. He almost told me so the other day at the meet, and stopped because I wasn't looking such as a fool as I usually do when bankers address me. A gleam of intelligence must have escaped; he shut his mantrap of a jaw and irritated his horse into trying to buck him off. A hopeless attempt, for Sweet William's legs were locked together under the animal's belly. But I couldn't have mistaken him."

"That's what he meant this afternoon."

"I'll talk to the foxy old devil for you if you like," Hugh offered. "You needn't be afraid I shall compromise you. Let me try. I'd like to. He won't approach you. He'll let Garton's smash while he waits to be approached. William is the most sensitive creature, as well as the most ruthless, in Danesacre.''

"How do you know that?''

"Oh I know. This town is as full of enchantments as the White Cat's palace.''

"Try him, then.''

"If you want me to.''

Mary was silent and Hugh looked at her curiously. What did she want? She was the strangest mixture of fragility and strength. narrow-minded, and obstinate as the devil. He had never understood her and he was damned if he did now. Perhaps that other poor devil did. He wondered whether, when all was said and done, anything mattered more to her than her ships. Gerry Hardman? The looks she had given him across her own dinner-table ought to prove something, but you couldn't tell with a woman. Her eyes, very clear under their fine arched brows, gave nothing away. Queer that he had never noticed before—or had he forgotten—what a funny little walk she had, like a shy bird. He drove his hands into his pockets, startled by a sudden impulse to seize her and shake the truth out of her slender body. The room darkened round him. He was losing his head. With an effort he drew his hands out of his pockets and strolled to the door. Safe outside, he leaned against it, mopping his brow. Phew! That was a close shave. He had been as near as possible to shouting at her. What a fool he had made of himself over Fanny Jardine. Suddenly every thought dropped away from him but the thought of Mary as she was in the first year of their marriage. He recalled her face, the face of an eager girl, the yielded sweetness of her body in his arms, and her kindness. She had spoiled him, and he had hated it even while he loved her. Love! He had not known the meaning of the word. He was not sure that he knew it now, when all he wanted was to turn back into the room he had just left, and dropping on his knees beside her, look up to see her looking down, with the remembered gladness in her eyes.

The moralists were having the laugh of him after all. If only, instead of talking fatuously about sin, they had warned him that he would wake up in the daylight, and feeling with sudden hands for his beloved, find nothing there. . . . Nothing? Mary was still his wife, and he had rights. All decent people would be on his side. . . . With his fingers already on the handle of the door, he laughed. His hand dropped to his side. Heaven mend his wits and save him from joining the sorry company of husbands who invoked their rights. . . .

A few days later, with suppressed ambassadorial pride, he reported that the "foxy old devil" was certainly hoping to be approached. Mary thanked him and took his conclusions to John Mempes. Mempes received them with an odd expression on his face. What he said was odd enough.

"Upon my soul, I thought your husband was a fool. It shows how careful we should be not to write a man's epitaph until he is dead. I had an admirable marble ready for him. 'Here lies Hugh Hervey, a fool who drank port for pleasure and wrote very civil books.' I shall have to throw it away, along with yours, on which I had written: 'Here lies an honest woman.' "

Mary was disconcerted but contrived not to show it.

3

William Todd was obsessed by the idea that Mark Henry Garton had returned in the slender body of his niece to plague his old friend. Either that or she was reciting what the sour beggar at the other end of the table had taught her. No woman so inconceivably shrewd and unwomanly as Mary Hervey was showing herself existed. Todd was revolted. She was talking with John Mempes' tongue in her cheek. It was against nature. The only female quality she possessed was her damnable obstinacy. Trust a woman to pursue what she wanted through a cataclysm. The "sour beggar" was taking very little interest in the proceedings. His face was hidden behind his hand, while young Hardman did all the talking, except when the owner of Garton's put in a word. They had it all nicely drawn out between them. Garton's yards to be moved to the Tees and combined with the reorganised engine works to form the *Garton Shipbuilding and Marine Engineering Works*. It was a mouthful. Willing to form a private company, was she? Kind of her. A suggestion—put forward to annoy his visitors—that the name of Todd might be included in the mouthful was stared at by the body of the enemy. Todd controlled his irritation, with an expression on his face that boded ill for the wretched women in his house. . . . The Line and the furnaces to be sold when freights rose again, but that had nothing to do with him. *The Shipbuilding and Marine Engineering* was what he was being invited to join, and on the whole they were all three suspiciously offhand about it.

"Freights will go on falling," he snapped.

"Freights will rise next year," Mary said coolly. "They've touched bottom."

He glared at her.

"Garton's is in bad case, ships laid up, no orders coming in to the Yard. And your overdraft."

"Quite true," Mary said. "If you don't like the prospect, why are we wasting time discussing it?"

Unnatural was not the word for her. It was a devil and not Mark Henry that possessed her. Mark Henry would have been flustered and roaring where she sat quietly, with pale cheeks, and great eyes following him about the room, almost as if he amused her. She was right about one thing. Freights would go up. He could see the faint signs of recovery better than she could. In spite of the overdraft Garton's might contrive to hold on without any help from him until reviving trade brought relief. Had she any other resources? He could almost believe she had. They had been too frank with him by half. That young Hardman, an arrogant looking fellow, had told him everything he already knew about the Yard's situation and made him free of ten years' figures. There was nothing they had not told him except what he wanted to know and could not find out, since to ask her whether she had had any other offers would give too much away. He recalled having been told, some years ago, that Hervey had money, and common sense suggested that she would not take in a stranger if she could keep it in the family. But you never knew with women, and it was common talk in the town that she and Hervey were not on terms.

The sour beggar had removed his hand from his face at last. Thinking it possible that Mempes had something to say worth listening to, he eyed him with an expression that said plainly: "I don't believe a word you're going to say."

What Mempes, settling his stock, said, was: "This is the third meeting, and we're not getting anywhere. I propose that we adjourn indefinitely, until our excellent friend here has had a chance to examine the costs of the proposed reconstruction and the prospects of success if reconstruction is carried out."

"I agree."

"I agree."

Todd rose. "Very well," he said spitefully. "I'll send for you when I want you."

Holding the door of his room open for his visitors, he watched them file through the bank on their way out, Mary and that young Hardman in front, she smiling at something he was saying with his mouth close to her ear. John Mempes was following behind. It struck Sweet William that the look on the older man's face was strange, very strange. Shutting the door, he considered it for some time, until light broke on him, and he chuckled. He chuckled again at the thought of how he would annoy his wife that evening, with tantalising morsels of the splendid scandal he had just glimpsed. She was a poor stick. What a fool he had been to marry and fill his house with pious women. He thought regretfully of days when he drove his own coach up to London for a month in the middle of the season. There had been himself, Mark Henry Garton, old Ritchie Hansyke, who afterwards married Mark Henry's flash sister, and Archie Roxby, a solumn devil, and dead now like the rest. They always had a box at the Opera, to please Hansyke. There was no singing nowadays worth hearing, and no acting. The actors had lost fire, and the women! Sticks, without legs or bosoms. He chuckled, with real pleasure this time, at the memory of a fairy Mark Henry had driven down to Richmond. Addy was her name. On the return journey she tied up the horses and Mark Henry's moustaches with yellow ribbons off her petticoats, and hardly waited for the horses to draw up before she was jumping down into Mark Henry's arms crying: "Catch me, Harry, I love you so much I don't know what to do with myself." He had envied his friend that day. . . .

More than a month went by before William Todd sent a note up to the house in St Mary's Terrace requesting a private interview. Reading it, Mary wondered what trap he had laid for her. She had reached in the protracted struggle a stage of weariness when she felt that she could see Garton's smash without a tear if it were not that her bankruptcy would throw Richard, with nothing at his back but an unprofitable estate, on his own resources or on Hugh. Neither alternative struck her as desirable. She had in good measure her generation's kindly contempt for the succeeding one.

She went down to the bank and sat looking through the window at the dappled harbour, with the feeling that neither success nor failure would mean much after the agonising effort that had preceded it.

Sweet William wore his most formidable face.

"Hey," he said in a loud harsh voice when she came in, "what do you want? Money? Mark Henry Garton never had to beg." He glared at her with contemptuous blue eyes.

"Neither have I," Mary said. "I came here at your invitation. If you don't want to talk to me, I can go away again. I've nothing more to say. You've had all the details of the reconstruction I intended to carry out alone."

"Found you couldn't do it," Sweet William jeered. "Very like a woman."

"Garton's has sprawled," Mary said placidly. "Blast furnaces, our own line of boats, building for ourselves and other people, a marine engineering works, an experimental department. We've spread too far: it's unwieldy. To recover, we shall have to concentrate. D'you see? Given time, Garton's can become, outside the Government, the most complete building yards in the country. It's all there, ground on the Tees, the men, the reputation, experience, equipment. It wants steadying, that's all. I don't intend ever to be caught out like this again. Next time there's a drop in shipping, Garton's reserves are going to see me through it."

William Adam Todd got up and rolled about the room a little; he came to a pause in front of Mary, his powerful head on a level with hers. Mary endured his scrutiny without change of colour. She felt perfectly able to hold her own with this man. A cruel pride in her youth, straight body, and strength of will sustained her.

"Any truth in this talk about you and your manager?"

"Which one?"

"Eh, you whey-faced sinner, the young one, the young one. The old one, too, I dare say. I've heard it, I've heard it. Do you know what they say about you in the town? You don't look it, but nothing goes by looks. I look like that old sinner Palmerston to the waist; below it I'm not a man, I'm a hoop. But I hope to roll after old P. into my grave without rolling to the divorce court after him, and I warn you now against trying any tricks on me. I'm not to be humbugged that way."

"We're talking about my Yard, not about my morals," Mary observed scornfully.

"Who tells you how to build your ships, if some man doesn't?"

"I'll tell you something," Mary retorted. "No one gives me directions in my own firm, and no one ever will. Garton's sails under my orders, no matter who comes aboard."

"Eh, Mark Henry, is that you?" Todd exclaimed. He went back to his desk and sat down, relapsing into gravity with the alarming suddenness that never failed to startle Mary.

"I've examined your estimated costings for the reconstruction," he said. "And the sum at which you want to capitalise the new firm. It's not high enough. I'll put up four times the cost of reconstruction and take it out in a half-share."

Mary said nothing for a moment. The swiftness of the move confused her; she was a slow thinker. For once, however, thinking fairly quickly, she turned to Sweet William with a smile. Mempes and Gerry had both warned her of this danger.

"No," she said flatly, "I won't."

"You won't what?" Todd raised himself in his seat, with his elbows pressed into the arms of his chair.

"I won't agree to capitalise at any such sum. I prefer my own figure. What we were going to suggest, to meet the expense of reconstruction, is a loan to the company by you, partly repayable over a term of years and the remainder taken out in a quarter share in the company." She glanced at Sweet William's face; the rising tide of purple alarmed her. "You have every fact and figure before you," she said hurriedly, "on which to make up your mind about the security of the investment. If you don't like it, you won't touch it on any terms. If you do like it—we've waited a long time for you to say as much—those are my terms.''

She judged it wise to leave him before he got the better of his tongue, and as she passed his house on her way to her own, put up a silent prayer for forgiveness to Sweet William's wife and daughters. They needed prayers, though they could grant none. Sweet William came home in the likeness of an avenging demon. He threw his wife's new hat and frock out of the window and when an astonished woman carried them back to the house, presented them to her with a gentleness that froze her blood; he ordered one daughter to practise her music for three hours and another to wash the timid ringlets out of her hair, standing over her while she mingled her tears with the cold water and brushed her flattened locks until her arm ached. He had the fire raked out and the gas turned off at the main, making it impossible for anyone to prepare as much as a cup of tea. Then he went off to the club for the evening, threatening them with a frightful retribution if a light was turned on or a fire lit in his absence; as he walked down the garden path the thin strains of a Couperin *Bourrée,* played with melancholy clearness, came on his ears like the sound of sacrificial cries. He was satisfied.

He had already resolved to accept the offer. It was a good offer, more generous than fair. Garton's, in spite of having outrun the constable on this occasion, was a property any man would be glad to get a finger on. And the best part about it was that the other party to the bargain did not know their offer was generous, a satisfactory morsel to roll under his tongue. But she should wait. He would keep her waiting a month or two for his acceptance. That would teach her a few things. He was to sail under her orders, was he? She should wait for her wind, and see how she liked that.

4

Two days after Mary's private interview with the banker, an apprentice at the Yard received from the manager a bulky parcel, with instructions to carry it up to Mrs Hervey's house. Opening it, Mary found the curtain from Gerry's room, with a note. "I only heard to-day that you admired this. You can conceive with what pleasure I send it to you. G. H."

Gathering it up in her arms, she buried her face in the lustrous old silk. . . .

She walked along Harbour Street to the Yard. Dusk poured down into the old cobbled street from every ghaut and alley opening off its narrow length. On her right the flagged passages between the houses ran down to the harbour, and she caught glimpses of dark water and slippery steps in the light falling into the harbour from the windows of small rooms. On her left the hillside rose sharply to the height of the cliffs, and here the houses climbed crazily up and down and across the steep face. Flights of stone steps mounted dizzily into the purple shadows, and narrow yards and alleys rushed away on either side of the street and were lost in gaping mouths of the night. Doors stood open in every alley, letting out thin streams of candle-light, with the sound of women's voices. Out of one, two young sailors came, with lights in their hands. Mary passed the old walls of Garton's sail loft, and the sturdy house built for himself by Old Smithson's father when the far end of Harbour Street was considered a suitable residence for a ship-owner. Mark Henry's house stood farther out of the town, where the road began to climb steeply away from the harbour-side, and as she paused before toiling up to it Mary realised that Harbour Street was very quiet. The children that played noisily on its cobblestones until far into the night were nowhere to be seen, there were few lights and no women standing talking on doorsteps and in the entries of the yards. It was so long since she had been down this way that she had forgotten how heavy the hand of Hard Times was on Harbour Street, and that the children were too hungry to play and the women too listless for much gossip.

Climbing the hill to Mark Henry's gate she stood for a moment looking down into the silent yard, wondering whether Gerry had understood her brief message and was expecting her. She was before her time.

The Yard was empty and silent now; in a very short time, in a year perhaps, there would be a ship building down there beside the water. But if all went well and Sweet William rose to the baited hook, it would not be Garton's ship. The Yard would have been sold; another firm would be building below Mark Henry's house, and their boats would be launched in the wake of the *Mary Gray* and her lovely sisters. Sharpened by regret, Mary's mind leaped forward half a lifetime and saw the Yard empty again, deserted, grown with grass, forgotten by the years. Shipbuilding would leave the beautiful Danesbeck, even as Garton's was leaving it now, because every year the world had less need of the wooden ships that Danesacre had built with loving perfection and every year it would be less profitable to tow small iron steamers from the ancient yards to be engined in new yards on Tyne and Tees. Already how far and half-forgotten was the time when the shipwrights of Danesacre built their ship from her laying-down to the last touch that made her ready for sea. Now ships were built in sections by gangs of specialised workers. Everything was changed. Mark Henry's wooden ships stood out to sea with a crew of skilled sailors and a captain prepared to find a cargo for the return voyage and render faithful account of it, sometimes without a single written figure. There were no sailors on the steamships, only deck hands; her master sailed under orders, her accounts were kept in the office, and her owner knew his banker better than he knew his captains. He needed to.

The glory of Garton's Yard was going: already it had passed from Mary's keeping, as far and as far beyond recall as had passed her old simple desire for ships. . . .

Night, like a great cat with its haunches in the east, was licking at the fields behind them, when they stood on the cliff-top in the shelter of a loose stone wall. Neither Gerry nor Mary had the least recollection of the way they had come there. They had in fact followed blindly the *via dolorosa* of all Danesacre lovers who lived on the east side, down the narrow odorous cobbled gully of Harbour Street, to the flight of steps the street exuded like a sigh against the face of the cliff, up, up, treading the way of mourners and worshippers, until they reached the gravestones rooted among long grass, among which Danesacre lovers, breathless from their long climb, took measures to assure themselves they were alive, along the flagged path between Church and graves, and so out upon the cliff edge.

It was the hour of miracles, the hour when St Mary appeared to affrighted couples, the hour when Richard Garton, master mariner, died in 1700 of a broken skull, shifted his coffin a little nearer the crumbling edge of the cliff, in preparation for the day when he would tumble, coffin, bones, and broken skull, down the cliff side into the yards of tiny houses at the foot.

Mary and Gerry saw no miracles. Yet they were depending on one. This wall, in the lee of which they were hiding from the night wind off the sea, was an authentic miracle, a miracle of ingenuity. There was not a fragment of binding material in it, and yet the irregular stones of which it was composed withstood the fury of a North Sea gale, and the assaults of rain and time, as no more civilised and comely wall could have done. It was older than Mark Henry's grandfather, and it had supported innumerable lovers against its accommodating surface, accommodating because of its very irregularity. He was a captious lover who could not find a rounded edge that fitted the curve of his back when he leaned against it. The fields behind it and probably some of its own stones remembered the feet of Northmen carrying fire and slaughter to the town, to the Danes' Acre. In short, this wall, on which Gerry and Mary were leaning, was an epitome of romance, of human will power outliving the brief span of men's lives, of cunning northern adaptability, the very soul of dead Hansykes and Gartons. If it could have been translated into music it would have made a loud and triumphant noise like violins ascending in rapid chords. Even then it is doubtful whether Gerry and his Mary would have heard it, so absorbed were they in their own transitory passion, a romance of fugitive embraces and sighs carried away by the wind.

"What do you want us to do, Gerry?" Mary looked up into her lover's face to smile at him, and saw that he was white and intolerably perplexed. She drew herself out of the circle of his arms. "What is it?" she cried. "Oh, my love, what is it? You frighten me when you look like that."

Gerry bent her head back with a gentle hand and while he kissed her she could not see him. "I don't know," he said under his breath. "I don't know. I can't tell you what I want to do, Mary."

Mary drew away to look at him. A foreboding sense of loss chilled her and drove her back into his arms.

"Don't think of anything but yourself," she said, and sighed.

"Think of yourself and tell me what you think."

"I can't think of myself, Mary, without thinking of you. I can only think of us together. I've been trying for a year to imagine you away from here, and away from Richard, living with me in some place abroad where I could scratch up a job. It would have to be abroad, I'd get nothing in England after the scandal, and only I know what those foreign jobs are like and what it's like to live out there. I couldn't tell you. The discomfort and disappointment and the intrigue and the jobbing. And having to hide ourselves because the decent English people wouldn't know you and we couldn't stand the others. Forgive me, I'm putting it at its worst, but I know what I'm talking about. Could you stand it, living like that? Think of it, Mary. Imagine long days beset with heat and flies and foreign servants, waiting for me to come home, with nothing to keep you company but thoughts of Danesacre and Garton's and what you'd lost. I daren't remind you of Richard. Could you stand that, or would you soon hate me? Think, think. My dear, to take you out there and see you grow tired and indifferent to me, good God, I couldn't stand it. Besides, it might kill you. Most of those places are damned unhealthy."

Mary brushed aside material objections to fasten on the subtler and more dangerous stumbling-blocks she perceived in her lover's temperament. "I could bear anything that you could. You're all I want."

"Hush," Gerry said quietly. "When you talk like that I lose my head. I want you so much. Why didn't I find you in time, Mary? You're so dear, so very kind and sweet."

"I can't go on offering myself to you," Mary said sadly. "You must take me or let me go."

"I can't let you go." Gerry looked at her sternly, more like a judge than a lover. It was, after all, a stern business for both of them. "I need you too badly. But, my dear, you don't know what I'm asking you to do. I know and I'm afraid. I'm horribly afraid, Mary."

Mary felt strangely weak. She pressed her feet firmly against the short wet grass under them to assure herself of its reality. What had she been about to get herself into this quandary? The niece of Mark Henry Garton, who had successfully evaded all personal entanglements through his long and stormy life, found it hard to sympathise with the perplexities of Mary Hervey and Gerry Hardman. She thought shrewdly that if she allowed herself to dwell on the thought of Richard one half as much as Gerry was dwelling on the discomforts of foreign stations she would never harden her heart to leaving him. She could not do it except by reminding herself that young as Richard was for his twenty years and horribly as he would miss her and hate the way she had gone, he did not need her even now so much as Gerry did, and in a very few years would need her hardly at all. She knew Richard. Outwardly the most yielding and affectionate creature, he was yet almost entirely self-absorbed. She had made too few demands on him. His need of her was what she chose to imagine it, no more. She knew all this, but the thought of leaving him, of cutting herself off from the warmth of his ingenuous affection, from the exquisite thrill it gave her to think that this tall graceful young man going up to his father's college at Oxford was the tiny child she had made before she made a single one of her ships—this almost killed her.

There was the Yard too. She had had it almost as long as she had had Richard, and she actually did not know how badly, when it was lost to her, she would regret it.

Standing beside Gerry on the cliff path, between the sea and the church that contained the Garton pew and a good many of her private memories, she wondered what forces in her being—forces of which the Mary Hervey of a suddenly-remembered Watch-Night Service was blessedly unaware—had driven her to this situation and this hour, when she was calmly considering the necessity of running away with her lover. Without passion, she wondered at herself.

In this moment she knew that, for her, it would be easier to stay than to run. If she stayed she would be yielding to the mother in her and to her fears and to the hunger in her blood that had fought and schemed to get the Yard from George and Rupert Ling. Yet if she went, it would be said that she had yielded to her passions. Her mouth straightened itself contemptuously. Passion! There was none in her. She had got to the bottom of all that.

She was going with Gerry because of his overpowering need of her and because of her spiritual need of him. In him her life fulfilled itself.

With a calm pride she laid under his feet her love of her ships, her attachment to her Yard, her ambitions, her youth and the son of Mary Roxby. The sacrifice was enormous. No one knew how enormous it was. And just as she would have died rather than let Gerry guess the extent and the anguish of her renunciation, so, lest it should seem to lessen him in her eyes, she would not pretend to herself that she was not, as indeed she was, stripping herself for his sake. Mary Hervey had been a stolid wilful girl and was a proud woman. It is strange to reflect how much her pride cost her and how unconscious she was of it and how many times in her life she abased herself at the bidding of a tenderness and a generosity for which few people gave her credit. She had no vanity.

The pressure of Gerry's arm against her shoulder roused her from her solitary thoughts. He did not seem to realise that he was leaning against her. With an adroit movement she drew him round so that her head rested against his cheek. He stirred and she insinuated herself into his arms, looking up at him with an enchanting smile.

"After all," she murmured, "you have been talking as if I were the only one giving up something to come away with you, but you are giving up a very great deal. Why did you come back to England? Not because of me, you didn't know I was waiting for you at Garton's. But because you were tired and wanted peace and a decent life and England. That's true, isn't it? You don't mind my knowing the truth, you don't mind anything I know about you."

"It is true," Gerry said, with the smile that never failed to touch her. "I was tired. I am tired, and I've learned to distrust myself. I could stand anything with you. But the thought that you might come to hate it is—frightful. I can't face it yet. . . . Forgive me for not taking you away now, at once. If I took you and you couldn't stand it——"

"Love," Mary said, and kissed him, with both hands laid lightly on his breast.

Gerry shut his eyes: in a world empty of everything but sky and sea he and Mary seemed unreal, shadows talking. The light pressure of her hands on his and her body in his arms was real enough. She was quite right. He would either have to take her or let her go, go away himself. He could not see her every day and not want her. Would she be

offended if he told her that? Probably not, Mary was unlike other
women, who could tolerate any action but not the words that described
it. . . . He held her close to assure himself of her reality in his arms.
God, how tired he was. He thought confusedly of the English club at
Singapore and the handful of English women who had drifted out there
in the wake of their husbands; gallant burnt-up chattering decent
creatures, most of them. They would cut Mary, damn them, and the
husbands would eye her. It was in Singapore he had heard himself
described to a newcomer as "a damned fine engineer and can't stick at
anything." The speaker was doubtless right. He was restless, a disease
he believed to be growing on the world. . . . His thoughts turned to his
wife and he felt a sudden pity for her. If he went off with Mary she
would be turned adrift again with what miserable provision he could
make for her. He clenched his teeth over the thought. A pretty frame of
mind for an eloping lover. . . . He was hungry for Mary. His whole
body cried out for the peace she gave it. His soul loved her. Soul? He
touched her cheek and found it wet.

"I was wishing," Mary said fiercely, "that I was a little girl at home
again. . . . If you don't want me."

If he didn't want her? He suppressed a fit of perverse and spontane-
ous laughter. Couldn't she see what he felt like, helping her to ruin
herself for his sake, for the sake of living the rest of her life in Singapore
or a worse place? There were far worse places—places where a man
watched his wife die daily. The sheer cold bravery of women made him
shudder. He knew that if he once took her out there he'd never hear
from her a wish to be at home or anywhere else but where she was. And
he wanted her intolerably. The curve of her cheek in the dusk was a
temptation. Recovering himself, he kissed her hands, and they began to
walk slowly back towards the old church and the steps twisting down
between the red-roofed houses to Harbour Street and the life of the
town.

"We've only talked about Richard," Mary said suddenly. "There's
Hugh . . . and the others. They're more Hugh's daughters than mine;
they'd miss me very little, less than many daughters. Less than I missed
my mother. Danesacre would look queerly at them because their
mother had behaved badly; but Hugh wouldn't keep them here, he'd go
back to London. And as for that, I owe Hugh a debt I haven't finished

paying. One can't pay all one's debts in this life, and part of mine to Hugh must remain unpaid, if you want me."

"I shall finish paying it in hell," she thought gravely, but the face she turned up to her lover's in the light of the lamp half-way down the steps was serene, and her hand on his arm did not vary its gentle pressure. Whatever one thinks of Mary Hervey and her loving, one need not deny her courage. She descended the church steps with Gerry as placidly as if she did not know full well that she was walking straight to the unquenchable fire. As she went she noticed, as if for the first time, the shallowness of the worn stone steps and the huddled grimness of the houses tumbling down the cliff-side on her left. She glanced into the tiny fenced yard belonging to one of them. A thread of light lit up its uneven flagging and the straggling truculence of a row of plants under the fence. A fisherman's wicker-basket stood beside them. Mary felt a sudden rush of love for the worn old houses. "The man who lives in that is an artist," she said abruptly. "His pictures—water-colours of ships they are—have been praised by some London paper. He's starving, of course. No one in Danesacre will buy his pictures." She thought guiltily of the two or three she had bought herself, impelled by the painter's haggard eyes and hungry face. She hid them in an attic, ashamed of her sentimental weakness in wasting good money on such dim and trifling productions. She was proud of Danesacre's indifference to an artist in its midst. Danesacre people were like that.

"Dear," she said, when she and Gerry were in Harbour Street again, and smiled at him; and leaving him there to go back to his house and Mercy, sped across the bridge and climbed the steep hill to her own. . . .

Less than a week later, chance, which had played on them already so many tricks and merry jests, interferes in their lives again. This time chance squints, has a long clumsy body, thatched hair growing lamentably thin, and answers to the name of George Ling.

Mrs George wrote that she needed sea air and would come to stay with her dear cousin Mary in Danesacre until the nearer approach of her fifth child made a return to her own home imperative. George would bring her over and stay the night. On hearing the news, Hugh decided that it was time his sister saw her nieces and departed incontinently for London with two excited little girls. Mary was left in her big new house alone to welcome the George Lings. She did it with what grace she could muster, having a whimsical liking for George's wife that almost, not quite, balanced her dislike of George.

The Lings reached Danesacre in the afternoon and Mrs George went immediately to bed, for the benefit, she explained, of unborn Lings. Faced by the prospect of entertaining cousin George alone, Mary lost heart for the task and wrote a letter begging Gerry to invite him to his house for the evening. She sent it by messenger to the Yard. Sighing outwardly and inwardly cursing all women, even his Mary, and all Lings, Gerry returned a note asking for the pleasure of Mr Ling's company at dinner and made a journey up to his house. He told his wife, with a formal apology for short notice, that she would have to entertain a guest.

"You are not such cheerful company," Mercy remarked, "that you need apologise for adding a third."

"I am sorry," Gerry retorted politely, "that I am dull, and glad to offer you even a George Ling to amuse you."

Mercy looked at him. "I wonder," she said, "whether any woman, even such a woman as I am, would have the heart to punish another human being as you punish me for having done me the kindness of taking me back into your house."

Gerry turned on his heel and left her without a glance.

George accepted the invitation, being politely urged thereto, and Mary enjoyed the emptiness of her house, wth Mrs George sleeping upstairs for the good of posterity, for five hours. She sent her servants to bed and sat up alone to admit George, wondering a little why he was so late. Near midnight she heard his knock and went out into the hall. Clasping both hands round the monstrous key, she unlocked the door. It swung heavily back and on broad shallow steps Gerry Hardman confronted her, supporting the sagging body of her cousin.

Mary stood aside, lifting the lamp in her hand so that its light fell full on both men. Gerry's face was colourless and he was sweating in the effort of supporting the other man's weight; he breathed painfully and laid a hand on the door to steady himself.

"What is it?" Mary asked quietly.

Gerry looked at her without interest and said unemotionally: "We fought. I hurt him more than I intended. You'll have to help me upstairs with him unless you can call a servant."

"I won't call the servants," Mary said. She shut the door noiselessly, and Gerry lowered his burden to a chair, where it lay heaped upon
itself without moving.

"Brandy," Mary suggested.

"Probably make him sick. You'd better give it to me."

Mary went away, and came back with a glass. Gerry took it from her
with a word of thanks. After that, he approached the semi-conscious
George and poked him dispassionately in the back.

"Are you going to walk or be carried?"

"Be carried," George muttered.

Gerry knelt down and hoisted the limp hulk across his left shoulder;
his slight body staggered under the strain, and sweat broke out again on
his forehead. Mary went in front with the lamp and opened the door of
an empty bedroom on the first floor. Dropped on to the bed, George lay
still, groaning. Gerry eyed him distastefully.

"I can't undress it," he declared.

"Leave it dressed," Mary said and drew him out of the room,
closing the door softly behind them. On the landing Gerry swerved
away from her as if her touch offended him, and they went down the
stairs in silence.

"You're not going," Mary said. "You must rest first."

"I'd rather go," Gerry muttered, but he submitted to being led into
the drawing-room, where he dropped into a chair, abandoning himself
to an exasperated weariness. Mary knelt down beside him and he
shrugged her away.

"Don't touch me," he said briefly. "I'm not clean. I can't bear to
touch you, or be touched. I've got George Ling's blood on me somewhere, too, damn him."

Controlling herself, Mary waited until he could bear to talk to her.
After a time, she got out of him an account of his dinner party. In the
first place Mercy had made a direct attack on the admiration of their
guest, whose response, growing more and more ardent as the wine he
drank warmed him, reached a stage where Gerry could endure it no
longer. Getting up to leave the other two to their devices, he was almost
out of the room when Mercy said softly, "There he goes, to dream of
his Mary."

"Mary," George exclaimed, "does he dream of Mary? I'll teach him better. She's not his, the slut."

Whereupon Gerry's pent-up emotions—he owned to a passion of hatred for George Ling—broke bounds. Returning to the table, he knocked George down. They fought in Mark Henry's sitting-room, and Mercy watched them silently, her ear-rings quivering with the invisible tremors of her body.

"He is twice my weight and has nearly twice my reach," Gerry said, "but he's disgustingly soft and hadn't a chance. I was going to kill him. We upset some candles and the warm grease ran over my hand, it reminded me of my senses and I stopped battering him. He was a horrid sight, swollen and bloody, and I dragged him down through the Yard to the edge of the harbour to wash him. Then I dragged his vile fat body up here. I'm broken with weariness. I'm dirty and smelling of sweat and George Ling, and I loathe it and myself. Don't touch me, Mary, I can't stand it. I can't come near you like this." He moved his shoulder to shake off her hand. "Forgive me, I suppose it's something in the nerves of my body. I couldn't tolerate the spectacle of myself touching you in this state. I'm drunk, too, with fatigue, not with your brandy, my dear. Why don't you scold me for behaving like a cad and smashing up your damned cousin, and for talking to you like this?" He gave her a furious glance.

"You're not," Mary said slowly, "the first man I've seen beside himself with anger."

Gerry looked at her with dislike of the other men in his eyes. Mary knew what he was thinking and her face puckered like the face of a grieved child; she turned away.

"Forgive me," Gerry said again, coming up behind her. Couldn't she realise that although his brain was sober, his body was tired past control and his tongue likely to say things it would not say if he were in charge of it? He rested both hands on her shoulders and stood swaying in front of her. Fatigue had drawn his face into an ashen mask, and looking at him Mary felt in her body an exquisite sensation of tenderness and love.

"You miserable little Gerry," she whispered. "You poor unhappy child. Lie down on my couch for an hour, I won't touch you or worry you. Please, please do what I say."

Gerry smiled at her and she watched him walk unsteadily across the room. He flung himself down on her couch. His body relaxed and he fell almost instantly asleep, not stirring when Mary made him more comfortable and slipped an arm under his head. For an hour she knelt beside the couch, supporting his head on her arm. Careless of the promise she had made not to touch him, she dropped light kisses on his face and on as much of his body as she could reach without moving her arm. After a time she laid her head down beside his and fell asleep.

When Gerry woke it was still dark and the fire on the hearth had sunk to a handful of glowing cinders. The lamp alight in the middle of the room kept back a host of shadows; they stood like trees on the edge of the pool of light. The couch where he lay was in shadow and Mary's face, turned towards the cushions, was completely hidden from him. He felt light and rested, and stepped gently from the couch. Mary slept on. She looked uncomfortable and Gerry stooped to lift her on to the couch. Changing his mind, he knelt on the floor, circling her with his arms in an attitude of unendurable longing, while he listened to her gentle breathing. If he lifted her up she would rouse and he meant to leave her sleeping and get out of the house by way of the window and the side door of the garden. He took his arms from her and stood up. He was perfectly calm, and released from the bitterness that had raged in him after his humiliating struggle with George Ling. "Good-bye," he whispered, and turned to go.

On the very edge of the pool of light as he entered it, his foot touched Mary's abandoned slippers, which she had kicked off before carrying the lamp upstairs to light his painful ascent. Gerry picked one up and held it by the strap that clasped her ankle. He had the strongest impulse to slip it on to her foot, smoothing it to the narrow instep. He would rest her foot on his hand and kiss it when he had buttoned the strap. He felt his body trembling with love and desire, and all at once, laying down the innocent shoe, he went back to the couch and woke Mary gently. He lifted her to her feet and she leaned in his arms with a sigh of contentment.

"I was going without waking you."

Mary kissed him reproachfully. They smiled at each other very kindly, like old married people.

Gerry felt extraordinarily happy. He wanted to tell her that he loved her as if he had never loved any woman before. She was his only love, his dear girl, his true lover, his heart. Instead of talking he held her with an exultant carefulness.

"You're not afraid of me, Mary?"

Was it for her own sake as well as his that she was staying here, in this room, in his arms? Had she any unmanageable desires? He felt her lips near his and kissed her to hide his emotion. She knew sufficiently what he was feeling to yield to the pressure of his arms. He felt that she yielded. Profoundly touched, he gave himself up to the moment. He felt humble because she was so convinced of his superiority over other men. Remembering that he had once told her he would never ask her for anything he laughed under his breath at the absurdity of it. Half unconsciously, he withdrew his arms from her small yielded body.

"I couldn't love you and not want this," he told her. "My dear, tell me I'm staying here because you want me to stay." With a sudden humorous surprise, he thought: "I'm here because I fell over a slipper."

Mary smiled and trembled. Pursuing an unconscious purpose, she chose this moment to remind him that he had not yet promised to take her away.

"I must take you. Oh, your heart on mine. Mary. Love."

He would get himself a job in some not too uninhabitable part of the world. There was America. But decent Americans were even more strait-laced than English men and women of the same class, and the others—barbarians, the scourings of England. He wanted no one and nothing but her. Would she be content to have only him for the rest of her life?

"I love you, I love you," he whispered and felt the slight swaying of her body towards his as an unimaginable ecstasy. He heard her voice in his ears, strangely childish and humble. "Then nothing else matters."

"I'm not to leave you now? Let me look at you."

Her face, with its adorably surprised air, was offered to his scrutiny. He took her in his arms again and felt her deep breath like a sob against his lips.

CHAPTER SEVEN

I

OPENING the door of his room, Gerry Hardman found his wife in the hall, lighting one of the candles that stood there on the old chest that held her scanty store of house linen. He lit it for her. Holding it in front of her face, so that two tiny candles flickered in the recesses of her eyes, like lamps burning in an empty room, she looked at him for a moment before running towards the stairs. He could make nothing of the look. Mercy was an adept at these dark glances, that had once stirred in him a lover's longing to penetrate the mystery of her hidden life.

She called Good night from the bend of the staircase. Answering her absently, he waited until the door of her bedroom shut behind her. The sense of walls round him had become intolerable, and opening the front door softly, he walked down into the Yard, to the place where he had stood with Mary on such another summer night. The sky was a milky crystal now, and the faint stars swung across it, rank on dim rank, like the waves of the sea, murmuring and shifting. Strange to look from the water in the harbour to the luminous sky, like looking from sea to sea. It gave the human watcher an illusion of complete solitude, as if he were the last unregarded living speck clinging to the lip of space. He grew tired of his position at last, and rolling over so that he could press his face against his folded arms, he gave himself up to the thoughts that had driven him out of his house.

There had been a boy who had loved Mary Hansyke the moment he

287

saw her. Suppose one had told that boy, as he put his foot into the stirrup to begin the ride from Danesacre to Roxborough, how many years in the future the end of that short ride lay! For a moment Gerry was staggered by a troubling sense of the incalculable forces moulding a human life. He heard a girl's thin voice: "It's nearly twenty miles as the crow flies." What was twenty miles to a boy riding through the night with a ghost of honeysuckle all about him in the darkness and his heart dancing between his thin ribs like the beating of a drum at the thought that she might kiss him on his mouth: he imagined that her kiss would be like the light passage of one of the large white moths brushing against him as he rode. Well, the crow had flown round the world and taken twenty years to do it. And the boy had become a man and the girl a woman, and the kiss when it came was not the sharp fiery mystery of his boyish imagination. The kisses he took from Mary Hervey were charged with pity, anguish, and all knowledge as well as all bliss. It was better so. Now, at last, he had touched reality. After all the fever and troubling of dreams, and searching the world for something that would not fail him, he was finally content. Whatever happened, he had had that, the moment when his body forgot him and left him released and trembling with happiness in Mary's arms. Strange that such an experience, the most exquisite sense of freedom he had ever known, pure joy, should come to him through the body. All that his spirit had sought in strange countries, in danger, in loneliness and dreams, it had not found until the moment when its lifelong enemy triumphed over it and pinned it down to a quivering instant of fulfilment. There would never be anything like that for him again. Ironically, he realised that he was already thinking of it as in the past. Well, that was life. The strangeness, the shared imperious delight would go, and leave him with what?

Everything that makes life bearable. he cried, a friend for his mind and soul and body, relief from loneliness, hands touching in the night when spirit and flesh are farthest asunder, dear kindness, and a little warmth for days when they would both be so old that life had almost forgotten them. *Quand vous serez bien vieille, le soir, à la chandelle.* His hands clung to every moment as it passed, but nothing stayed in them. No desire but died of its fulfilment, no miracle, not even the miracle of being loved, that did not grow familiar and same. There would come a day when he would recall Mary whispering to him in the night, with no stir of the blood. That day he would be dead, however much longer he contrived to look a little like life, and he hoped he would have the decency not to insult his lost self with a kindly smile. "Youth will have its way." Damn it, he was not young, he was thirty-eight, and Mary was only a year or two years younger. It was damnable that it was so. He lacked the complacence, or the courage, that allowed a man to contemplate the old age of a beloved woman with a fatuous smile. To his fastidious senses the prospect of old age was sheerly vile, and it shocked him to think of Mary old. The dark hair he had held when he kissed her face to hide it from the inquisitive moon, would be white, and her smooth skin fallen into lines and hollows. The indecency of life! Yet lovers and sentimentalists made a song about growing old together, as if two deaths were better than one. . . .

What did it matter? In Heaven's name, why think, when all his tale of life had narrowed down to the reflection of himself in Mary's eyes, a shadow trembling between delight and pity. There had never been another woman like Mary, so honest and lovable, with the added grace of intelligence, and so kind—how absurdly protective she was towards him—nor would ever be, whatever more articulate men might say or write of their mistresses. She said so many delightful things to him that he was filled with pride and ashamed in the same moment. And he was going to reward her kindness with scandal, a huddled flight, and lifelong exile in some damnable foreign city, where only to remember an English June was to ache for death.

Good god, to think that they could get at each other only by smashing everything in their lives and hurting other people, that decent son of hers, and Mercy turned out again. It struck him suddenly that there was something pathetic about Mercy as she went upstairs with her candle.

The thought chilled him, but a moment later he was recalling, with a rush of tenderness, Mary's last words to him. "You need me so, Gerry. I shall be proud to be your wife." Such love to have come too late. Such pride to be another whip across her back in the years ahead.

He knew that he could not take her away.

He had known it, refusing to know that he knew it, all through the

past two months since the night in her house—he knew that now—yet
he felt it as if he had been shot in the stomach. He sat huddled together,
his small mouth tightly compressed. Because he needed her, to exile
and torture her for life? He couldn't face it. He had not her courage. Oh,
God help them both. . . .

Light, and the paling of the stars surprised him. For some time he had
been lying face downwards, pressing the palms of his outstretched
hands against the earth, as he might have laid them against Mary's
breast. It had not seemed a moment since the night began, but as he
thought that, it seemed an eternity, and dawn an unexpected miracle,
like water in hell. Getting stiffly to his feet, he walked through the
Yard, making plans as he went. He would get away at once, leaving
Mercy to follow him. He could do it, since the Yard was not working
and work on the Tees-side yards had been stopped. Before Garton's
needed another manager they had plenty of time to find one. What he
himself would do he hardly knew, at the moment. It was no time to be
looking for a new post. He supposed he would find something, enough
for him and Mercy. Put it that he knew he would. Engineers of his
capacity were as rare as new jobs. No need to make a fuss or scare up a
revolting self-pity. Keep his pity for Mary, left in Danesacre.

She understood everything, would she understand this, understand
that he could not face hell with her? Probably no woman could. No, she
would not understand. She would be horribly hurt, and cry at night. He
groaned aloud. She would think of him only that he had not wanted her
enough to face things for her, and never see what had made a coward of
him. And perhaps she would be right. Did any man know the depths of
his own meanness? Women were perhaps different, or merely lacking
in imagination. Well, he thought unemotionally, he would gladly have
died for her, and that was no empty form of words, and poor enough
comfort to a woman for whom he was refusing to live. She would be
hurt, and she would forget. The selfishness of him, that cried out to her
not to forget, to keep him in her heart! What nonsense he had been
thinking. As if he could forget, as if the mere return of June would not
be enough to remind him and bring back the tightened ache across his
chest that only Mary could ease away. As if he did not know to what he
was condemning himself, to a perpetual pain that time would dull but

only dying would assuage, to a life without savour and a loneliness more terrifying than death.

An upper window of his house was lighted, and looking at it with a faint surprise, he caught a glimpse of his wife's yellow dress between the curtains. He shivered, and leaning his arms against the wall, hid his eyes on them for a moment. The sense of Mary's presence in the Yard became so vivid that he fancied he saw her move quickly through the half light to the gate, and there pause with a slight gesture of her hand towards him. He closed his eyes again. When he opened them he looked all round him and down towards the shadows at the foot of the slope. There was nothing anywhere.

He turned, a slight figure, head flung up, and went in to his house.

2

Knocking at the door of Mary's room in the Line office, Mempes entered, and discovered Mary at the window. She turned round as he came in, and said: "Good morning, John," with a smile that offered her, standing there in the morning sunlight, to his intent gaze. He advanced into the room, looking at her with a meditative eye that took in every detail of her appearance, from the shawl on her arm to her glowing cheeks. Glowing was the only word to describe her. An aroma of happiness rose from her, like the fragrance from the lime in flower in the tiny courtyard outside his room. He saw the breath come and go under the lace below her throat, with a kind of quick impatience, as if she wanted to be out in the windy sunshine breathing that in. As he drew near her, a strange sensation entangled his senses, the outermost ripple of her emotion. He felt dizzy and put out a hand to steady himself; she caught it between both hers.

"Are you well, John?"

The firm warm pressure lingered on his palm, like a tangible proof of what he had long suspected and now knew. Hardman was her lover. Her whole attitude confessed it. She was marked with it, set apart, the tones of her voice and the gestures of her body said as clearly as if she had proclaimed it aloud: "I am loved, I am happy." His eyes were darkened and he felt a dreadful longing to hurt her in some physical way. She ought to be punished. She was shameless. The caressing movement of her body as she walked across the room was utterly and abominably shameless. Why, the whole town could see what she was about, what offence against common decency she was flinging in its face. They must be blind, or they would stone her for it.

His mind cleared suddenly, and looking at her, he caught an appealing glance that impressed him as strange and rather pitiful, since she was not given to asking help. The ridiculous thought struck him that she was too small to be altogether shameless. He said: "What is it, Mary?"

"I'm going away."

The tide of his anger rolled back, blotting out her face, and the clear honest eyes that so monstrously retained their honesty through all this.

"With Hardman."

"With my lover," she corrected him, and all at once his fury left him, for good, he thought, at the spectacle of her sacrificial folly. Why, she was mad, possessed. The fellow had bewitched her. She didn't know what she was doing, offering herself to insult, obloquy, disgrace never to be washed out. She had better jump into the harbour than do this, and how often, before many months were out, would she wish she had. He looked at her calm face and an exclamation of despair broke from him.

Mary was smiling at him. "Don't worry about me, John."

"You're mad."

"I'm sane. Look at me. Do I seem mad?"

Grudgingly, he admitted that she did not, and at the same moment his heart ached to think how soon that air of profound untroubled happiness would vanish, her mouth harden, and her eyes, her lovely honest eyes, learn to look past leering glances as if they had not struck on a spirit raw and quivering with insult.

"D'you know what you're going to, Mary?"

Her small face was sober enough now. "Yes, I know. I'm not a fool, even though I'm in love, too deep to get out. I know I shall regret—this." She nodded at the model of the *Peerless,* high up on the yellow-grained wall. "Don't think I shan't. I've given it more of myself than I can easily take back. I shall long for England, and Danesacre. But I'd rather be unhappy with Gerry—" Her voice, lingering over the fellow's name! "—than happy without. That's what it comes to. Forgive me for talking what must seem nonsense to you."

He hesitated over Richard's name. She must have read his face, for she turned her own away and looked across the harbour.

"Should I leave Richard if I were not—sure?"

The few words, uttered with her accustomed restraint, convinced him more than anything else could, of the hopelessness of dissuasion. He recalled the times he had been outfaced by her quiet obstinacy. He might talk, until his tongue swelled in his mouth, she would not be moved. Did she talk to her lover, he wondered, find words for him? Good God, what repressed creatures men and women were, like ships with hatches battened down in a storm. Here was himself, raging with jealousy and pity, stuttering his few inexpressive words, and Mary, smiling and serene in the grip of an emotion that was destroying her life, scattering it in a little whirl of angry dust. He recalled Gerry Hardman's slender face, its mask of arrogance a little awry—that poor devil was too sensitive by half. Hervey, too. Mempes had a poor opinion of Mary's husband, but he found himself suddenly willing to concede that the fellow might have his own repressions. What a world! What a supper of jests, a comedy of flesh and blood puppets, silent on the rack.

"Tell me what you want me to do for you, Mary."

"Thank you. There's everything to do. This morning William Todd wrote accepting our terms. I was waiting for that. Now I'm going to offer to sell out to him. If he had refused our offer, I'd have looked elsewhere for a purchaser. I shall make him the first offer and look elsewhere only if he won't bite."

"This is a bad time to sell out."

"I know. I don't like it, but Todd's acceptance forces my hand."

"He'll buy—at his price. At least, you'll have something."

Mary's face, sweet and surprised, confirmed his worst fears.

"I'm not selling out for that. The money's for Richard."

He argued with her, roused past discretion by this unexampled folly and furious with her when she said: "Happiness has no price, John." There was no sense in anything she said, she really was mad. His arguments had no effect, as he had known they would not, and unable to stay there any longer, contemplating the finality and completeness of her fall, he left the office and strode along the pier into the town, walking without aim. He had no relish for his ridiculous position as Chorus, punctuating a tragedy with his useless comments. Half-way along the darkest narrowest street in Danesacre, he stepped on to a strip of flagging to avoid the wheels of a carriage being driven furiously in the direction of the railway station. A glance in the window showed him Hardman himself, leaning back, with his eyes fixed straight ahead on some point in the driver's solid back. The look on his face shocked Mempes into a smothered exclamation.

The carriage rattled past, and he found himself shaking. "I'm getting old," he muttered. "But—that poor devil." Leaning heavily on his malacca stick, he stalked gloomily to the club, but he was hardly there and sitting in his favourite window, when a fresh consideration brought him to his feet. The "poor devil" had not looked like a successful lover, and the cab had been driving towards the station. Without waiting to drink the glass of sherry he had ordered, he hurried off, leaving the ancient waiter dumbfounded and disapproving in his wake. By steep alleys and steps descending to the pier, he reached the office he had quitted two hours earlier. In the other room all was as it should be, every clerk bent over his books. His room led through to Mary's, and there, at the window in her own room, he found her. Her face, drained of blood, wavered towards him through the sunlight reflected from the dazzling water of the harbour. Holding a letter between her hands, she said quietly:

"He has gone."

"Gone? Where's the fellow gone?" Mempes growled. "I'll get him back for you."

"Dear John."

She smiled at him, shivered, and fainted. He picked her up. She recovered before he could carry out his intention of laying her on the table, and clung to him with her head hanging back, her eyes wide open and crazed with fear. He told her that she was "overdone" and took her home. The effort she made to walk steadily through the outer office pulled her together, and she sat quiet and composed in the cab. Horribly afraid, he went with her into the house, intending to leave her with some woman. The opening of the drawing-room door revealed Mercy Hardman, elaborately dressed as for a very formal call, her hair looped and plaited under a wide hat. The feather that adorned it lay across the brim and curled on her shoulder between the tucks and ruffles of her silk frock. If she had seemed, in the streets of Danesacre, an exotic figure, like the green and red parrots and fuchsia plants the sailors brought home and hung in their windows or cherished in tiny shell-bordered gardens, in Mary's drawing-room she was fantastic. She was sitting on a couch of Spanish leather and mahogany in the window, and hardly rose when Mary came in, an insolence that affected Mempes unpleasantly. Outside, the lawn was drenched in sunshine; the tall sunflowers against the wall were full of clear golden light, they outshone the blue sky and dropped their bright petals across the grass. One blew in through the window and drifted over the carpet to Mercy Hardman's feet; it lay among her flounces, a fragment of living yellow, yellower than her frock. Mercy picked it up and held it between her gloved fingers, crushing it slowly as she spoke.

Standing with his back against the wall, Mempes listened to the women exchanging civilities. The yellow cat had come to use her claws, he was sure, and he restrained an impulse to run. Women were damnable to each other. His sense of justice reminded him that Gerry Hardman's wife had cause for complaint. Mary, after all, had taken her husband. Poor devil, to be married to that long white face and used-up body. The long white face was making excuses for Mr. Hardman's hurried departure. "Personal reasons. Mrs. Hervey's indulgence." The crushed petal fell to the ground and Mercy lifted her yellow-stained fingers to her hat; she adjusted it so that the feather curled round her long chin. Mempes glanced at Mary, and was stung by a memory of the small glowing creature he had left those few hours ago. He could fancy he saw the slow withdrawal of light from her eyes as her spirit shrank back into itself. Women were supposed to die of blows like this. It was all nonsense so far as Mary was concerned. She would not die. She would recover, and live on, not without happiness—she was too vital and courageous a creature to be unhappy long—but perhaps without hope, a condition that killed the weak and endowed the strong with an assurance of immortality. Mempes sighed. The sight of Mary defeated, thrown over by her lover, might inspire a moralist. It disturbed him profoundly, though it was a consummation he would have given anything to bring about. There was nothing that could have brought it about but that fellow's bolting. And what had induced him to bolt—the only decent and conclusive thing he could have done—unless it were a sudden stroke of sanity, was beyond Mempes' power to imagine. He would take an oath it had nothing to do with his old catamaran of a wife who was now, with a complete abandonment of the pretence that this was a civil farewell call, telling Mary that she was not jealous.

"Because only fools are jealous and because I don't need to be. Months ago I told you that you and I had played a game in which the loser wins. I thought you were the loser then; I see that I am and that I've won. Mr. Hardman will be very civil to a wife he doesn't like, and after a time I shall make him like me again, in a fashion. He'll even be happy. I dare say he'll dream of you, but that, in the circumstances, I won't grudge you."

Mempes felt the hair standing up on his back. Well, really, women!

Mary had risen, compelling the other to rise. She looked round her room and out into the green and golden pool of the garden. "I've never liked you," she said steadily, "but I think that in some other life I might have liked you."

Impossible, Mempes said to himself. "You're too decent, my dear." He admired Mary immensely at the moment, watching with grim amusement the effect of her serenity on that Hardman woman. The injured wife was being outmatched and elbowed from the room. It was as good a piece as he had ever seen.

"I should like to have been Mr. Hardman's wife, as you are." Mary's steady voice sank to a whisper. "Perhaps men and women after us will understand us better than we do ourselves. Perhaps they'll be more fortunate, or braver, and kinder to each other. They may not be asked to pay so high a price as we were. My poor Gerry."

Very unnecessary, Mempes thought, and watched the slow widening of Mercy Hardman's lips in a smile. For the first time he saw Mary's calm break. She lifted her hand to her eyes, but dropping it instantly, stood aside for Gerry's wife to walk unattended to the door. Mercy hesitated, glancing at Mempes, who averted his eyes. The yellow stain on her white glove caught her eye: she brushed her fingers disdainfully together, and walked towards the door. On her way, the stiff woolwork figures of Flora and the Prince arrested her attention.

"How strange," she said. The remark seemed to take in the room and all of Danesacre that could be seen beyond the garden. Then she went away, lifting her yellow dress from the gleaming floor of the hall. The front door shut behind her, and Mempes offered up a fervent prayer that he might never see her again. He never did.

There was silence after her departure, broken by Mempes.

"My dear."

The turn of her head, the raised delicate brows above the changed eyes, gave him an unpleasant sensation in the back of his neck, a swelling under the skin of the nape. He paused and lifted a finger to his stock. There was a sound of wheels in the road behind the house and a door opened and shut. The colour rushed into Mary's cheeks and her eyes opened widely, blazing with light. He knew what she hoped, and the sight was more than he could bear. Hurrying to the door, he pulled it open wide enough for them both to see Hugh crossing the hall in his riding kit. That careless devil, was it? He must have driven home from the stables. Mempes shut the door gently and leaning his back against it, watched the light die out in Mary's eyes and her hands go up to her face. It did not last long. She recovered herself and said quietly:

"I shall soon learn not to expect him. I did before."

"Why did the fellow run off?"

"Didn't you want him to?"

"Don't want you to be made unhappy, my dear Mary."

Mary smiled and stretched out her arms as a woman might to her lover. Her eyes looked straight past Mempes.

"For two months I have been perfectly happy. Do you suppose many people can honestly say that they have had as much. Can you?"

Mempes was silent. After a moment he took up his hat and stick from the chair where he had dropped them. Mary seemed to have forgotten him, and he decided to go without speaking to her. She was leaning against the window, her head flung up, and as he lingered, a faint smile crossed her mouth, like the ghost of a caress. What was she thinking of? Of her lover? He had seen her smile like that at a ship building in the

Yard. She turned her head and he saw her eyes. He wished he had not: they would haunt him that night, he thought. They said all she would not, all her thoughts of that fellow's flight. There was nothing he could do for her. Shutting the door noiselessly, he went away, leaving her alone.

As he stalked through the narrow streets of that most lovely of all towns he was thinking not of any woman but of a little girl and of a young man gazing at her short retreating back. Head held up, small shoulders squared, Mary Hansyke walked away from him, and all Danesacre shrank into the compass of Garton's Yard on a white spring day, with steel-blue ruffled water in the harbour and hawthorn breaking up the valley, and all time was caught between two sunny moments. Forever young, forever brave, forever proud, Mary Hansyke walked across the old shipyard, while the *John Garton* moved down the harbour, her keel parting a shoreless sea, her prow lifted to the air of eternity. A lovely ship.